KNIFEPOINT

BREAKERS, BOOK THREE

~

EDWARD W. ROBERTSON

Cover art by Stephanie Mooney

ISBN: 1492184365
ISBN-13: 978-1492184362

To Caitlin, for putting up with such a silly job. Hey, if the world ever ends for real, at least I've learned how to make ethanol.

Special thanks to Geoff and Chris, whose feedback made this a much better book than I could have managed on my own.

I:

FERAL

1

They found her under the pier wearing a pair of boots and the blood of the cat she'd just eaten raw. She had been watching a gecko sun itself on a rock—it was a pretty one, with a blue head and tail, and black spots down its whole body—and she was so absorbed in it that she didn't hear the people coming until the gecko looked up and ran away.

She grabbed her knife and sprinted through the pilings, weaving between clusters of barnacles that would scrape her skin down to the muscle, but the man caught her before she got to the safety of the open pipe sloping to the sea. She lunged with her knife, flaying his arm. White bone peeped beneath a sudden tide of blood.

It was her fondest memory of the first two years after the plague.

They asked her about it in a gentle, persistent way, the woman's mouth pursed, as if she just knew it would help.

Raina always said the same thing. "I don't remember."

"What about yesterday?" the woman said in a voice that was eager and somehow sad. It was the day after they found her and they'd had to tie her to the bed to keep her from running away. "Do you remember yesterday?"

"I was at the docks," she said. "I don't know."

"What about your family? Before the plague? Do you remember your mom? Her face? Her hair?"

Raina frowned at the white wall, pretending to try. "I don't know."

"Did you have a dad?"

The man leaned in and touched the woman's arm. "Kate. She's

tired."

She breathed out in a rush, like a dog lying down for a nap. "Okay. It's okay, Raina. But can you try for me? Try to remember?"

Raina nodded, glancing up beneath her ragged bangs. "I'll try."

She didn't. After a while, the woman stopped asking. A while after that, Raina stopped trying to run away. She liked the new people. The man was kind and strong and smiled whenever he saw her. The woman was jittery like one of the little fish Raina had never been able to catch at the marina, and when she got confused she looked to the man instead of herself. But she was also patient and taught Raina lots of new things like how to properly patch her clothes and gut fish. Even when Raina got frustrated and threw the needle in the grass beside the house, the woman kept trying. Raina believed she always would.

Her dad taught her to sail with him and catch fish in great big nets. They ate every piece of meat except the heads. At first, Raina collected these and arranged them in careful ziggurats beside the dock. She liked the fish's little teeth, the looming stare of their empty sockets. And when you killed something, you took possession of it. She wanted to show the other fish they shouldn't be afraid of her nets. They would join lots of other fish that had already fed her. They would be happy together. She would look out for them.

And they looked out for her, too. Most of the time, their spirits were simply there with her, silent in the way the bricks that form a building are silent, but once in a while, they spoke up. Offered her suggestions. Wisdom. Strength. She would never kill just to gain this power from them, but surviving meant killing. And she was very good at surviving.

The man came to her and told her that it wasn't healthy or respectful to pile up the skulls in this way. Raina tried to explain how it let the fish stay in a school after they'd died, but the man—her new father—told her that it would attract predators. Parasites. She had to stop.

She stopped putting her skulls by the dock and brought them into the trees up the hill instead. Her new parents never noticed.

Her father leaned into the winch, grunting in that way of his; a rising tone of respectful effort she would always associate with wind and salt and swells. Water sluiced from the rope and dimpled the sea. At the western edge of the bay, sunlight played on the peaks of ten thousand tiny waves, shimmering closely, a school of light. A pelican wobbled on the breeze and banked from the boat.

Turn by turn, he hauled up the net, a drooping teardrop weighted down with wriggling silver bodies. He swung it over the deck, water spattering the time-worn wood. He released the pawl with a metallic clink. The net thumped wetly. Fish struggled inside the ropes. The man planted his hands on his hips and arched his back, grimacing, sun-lines crinkling his mouth and eyes.

Raina crabbed forward, club in hand, and took up the net, shaking fish across the deck in a slobbery, gasping spread. She kept her eyes sharp for rockfish. The other fish respected her as their master, but the rockfish were spiny and defiant.

It was an okay catch, a single crescent-tailed bonito flapping among a mess of croakers and surfperch. They'd snagged a plastic bag and a small squid, too. She stalked among the fish, clubbing them on the head with a sharp and bony crack. Slime and blood burst from her baton.

Finished, she sat back to catch her breath. Her father grinned and wiped his brow. A thin white scar ran the length of his forearm; the skin of his exposed armpit was as pale as the bellies of the brained fish. For a moment, she was reminded that he wasn't the father she'd been born to. He was a stranger. She had a club in her hand.

She grinned back and got out her knife and started cleaning, thumbing out the guts and chumming them over the rail. She layered the bodies in the cooler. They would probably eat most of the perch tonight. Her mom would curry the croakers to be eaten over the next day or two, the spices keeping the meat pure, disguising the taste if it went foul; she'd smoke or dry the rest, including the bass, which she'd probably barter to Wendell up the hill in exchange for more bread and eggplant. If she took them to the Dunemarket instead, these little fish could wind up carted across all corners of the valley, to the islands, to Disneyland. These little fish she'd just killed, eaten by distant strangers.

But released by her, their spirits would remain hers.

Her dad clunked to the side of the boat to bring in the lines, then came back to lend her a hand. They finished up and Raina scraped the gunk from beneath her nails with a rust-spotted file. He pulled up the anchor and she trimmed the sails while he steered back toward the dock. She helped tie off, then hauled the coolers over the side. Her mother sat in the front yard watching, resting up before it was her turn to work the catch. She waved her tan, lean arm. Raina nodded, arms full, staggered toward her with the first cooler, then went back for the second.

Her mom went around back to start up the fire. At the base of the dock, Raina's dad handed her a damp towel to swab off the salt.

"I'm going to the ruins," she said.

He smiled. "The ruins."

"I'll be back by dusk."

"It's not the dark I'm worried about."

She bladed her hand against the stunning sun. "Dad. I'll be fine."

He grinned and waved inland. "Don't max out my credit card."

She switched her gutting knife for something that smelled less like fish, grabbed her pack, and headed up the hill. The afternoon had burned away the June Gloom fog and she sweated freely. Hummingbirds skipped between the thorny flowers lining the road. A crow scorned her from the roof of a skull-like mansion. At the top of the hill, she stopped and turned, both to take in the sunshine gleaming from the bay, and to make sure the alien ship hadn't moved.

Twenty miles away, it jutted at an angle from the waves off Venice Beach, a discus of impossible size, black-hulled and broken. Silent. But it was a false silence. It wasn't the silence of the dead in the ground. It wasn't the silence of the houses with their empty windows and cobwebbed halls. It wasn't the silence of the thousands of cars rusting out beneath the gentle breath of the Southern California sea.

People tried to go to that ship sometimes, their little sloops so small in the shadow of its busted shell. They went to take from it. Maybe some went to it for the same reason she went to the ruins, to claim ownership by their presence. Maybe some went just to tell their friends they had. Whatever their reasons for going, none of them came back.

Because its silence was the silence of the predator.

She muttered under her breath. A steady speck of white caught her eye between the mainland and Catalina Island far to the south. She watched the sail for a minute, then turned and went on her way. It was hotter past the hill, but she didn't slow down until she reached the wide black mall parking lot.

Most of the car windows were smashed in, their fuel doors popped open. Raina walked between the rows with the same feeling she used to get when her first parents took her to the church. The mall's windows were broken, too. The old people had been crazy to build so much from something as flimsy as glass. The few that weren't smashed were blank with the dust that appeared every time there was a mist. Raina stepped into a stripped-out department store, walked through picked-over racks of light jackets and sweaters meant for a spring that never came, and paused to let her eyes and ears adjust to the quiet gloom of indoors.

It smelled musty and dusty. A mouse rustled in the shoeboxes along the wall. Knife in hand, Raina wandered further into the dimness of the old store. She wasn't looking for anything special; her parents more or less had everything they needed to run their home, and this was far from the first time Raina had come here. She felt compelled to visit, though, picking up caked-solid canisters of makeup and setting them back down, flipping through racks of dresses so gauzy they'd tear to pieces during a single day of work.

Part of it was about remembering, about trying to reach back to the days before the sickness. Her parents—her new parents—answered her questions the best they could, but their words were sterile, distant. The only way to understand the old people was to walk with them: their houses, their churches, their stores. To stand where they'd lived and soak in their essence and learn how they'd failed.

But she wouldn't deny that it was also fun, in a very simple and deep-down way, to pick through their things and occasional take some of them home.

She walked past a rack of what her mom called sweatpants—she didn't know why you would wear clothes designed to make you sweat—and exited into the high-roofed space connecting the stores. She skipped the neighboring shoe store (the last useful pair had disappeared a year ago and there was nothing left but foolish straps and heels) and the pretzel store with its nasty little piles of rock-hard mold. Meager sunlight slid through the skylights, illuminating square pillars of tumbling dust motes. Religiously, she skirted the light and, on the off chance something there would look better than last time, headed for the sporting goods store at the other end of the mall.

On her way there, plastic rattled on tile inside the discount store. Raina dropped to a crouch. The thing rattled again. She slunk inside, walking on the balls of her feet, breathing evenly through her mouth. Shelves of pastel eggs and plastic green baskets reached into the gloom. At the back of the store, a candle flickered, all but concealed by the metal rows.

She got out her knife and edged forward. Metal scraped softly. Something tinkled to the ground. Raina approached from the left of the candlelight. A teen boy crouched in a wavering circle of light, back turned, contemplating small pieces of metal and black plastic arranged on a blanket. Raina advanced with slow, smooth steps until she could have reached out and stabbed him.

"What's that?" she said. "More magic?"

Martin shrieked and leaped forward, stumbling into the metal racks, but careful not to trample his goods. He glared at her, sucking a scrape on his finger. "It's not magic at all."

"Then what is it?"

"I'm going to wire these solar panels to the radio." He lifted a flat-topped black stake from the blanket. She'd seen others like it lining paths of front yards and flowerbeds gone to seed. "Maybe they'll provide enough of a charge to make it run."

"Yeah," she said. "Magic."

"No, it's not. Didn't you have TV when you were a little kid?"

"I don't have it now."

He gave her a look and sat down next to his project. "What are you doing here?"

"Hunting."

"What for?"

She put her knife away. "I don't know."

"You smell like fish," he said, then blushed, as if he were the one who stunk.

"So what?" She sat down across from him, candlelight wavering over her hands. "What are you going to do with a radio, anyway? Prop open a door? Does anyone else even use them?"

He pried open one of the stakes with a flathead screwdriver. "That's what I want to find out."

She nodded to herself. Martin and his mom lived down the shore;

she had been a nurse or something, and when Raina's new parents had brought her in from the wild, Martin's mom volunteered to move in and help. Martin wanted to be Raina's friend from the very start. Even after she attacked him. Twice. There were virtually no children left their age, so it's not like he had much in the way of options, but she got the idea he would have wanted to be her friend even if he had a wider choice. She was different, and different was interesting. Sometimes she thought he wanted to be different himself.

"I'm sorry I said you smell," he said.

"But I do," she said.

"I didn't mean it like that."

"Well, you smell like grease."

Laughter bubbled from his throat. "Do you even know that's rude?"

"Oops." She reached for a green board studded with little pins. Martin looked pained, but didn't protest. She turned it over in her hand. "Want to go exploring or something?"

"I want to see if this works. If it does, maybe I can make us some walkie talkies." He glanced up from under his scruffy hair. "Wouldn't that be cool?"

"Walkie talkies?"

"Personal two-way radios. Anyway, I don't think it's a good idea to be outside right now."

"Why? Do you think you saw another tiger?"

"I did see a tiger." He scowled. "But no. Because of the men on the boat."

"What men on the boat?"

"The ones who killed Mr. Horowitz." He quit fiddling with his screwdriver. "Didn't you hear?"

"No."

"They came from the island. A whole bunch of them. They asked for some of Mr. Horowitz's corn. When he said no, they killed him and took it. Then they gathered up all his neighbors and asked them for stuff, too."

The sailboat coming from Catalina. Her blood iced over. "When?"

"Two days ago?"

She stood and touched her knife and ran for the front of the store.

"Hey!" Martin called, voice echoing in the empty space. His

footfalls chased her into the middle of the mall. "Raina! Where are you going?"

She skidded and turned. "That boat's coming to my house."

He ran through a square of sunshine, lighting up the fear on his face. "I'm going with you."

"Then keep up."

She sprinted through the department store to the front doors, pack bouncing on her back. The afternoon had cooled and a sea breeze shuffled the palms. The trees were so overgrown that a falling frond could knock her down or split her skull. She swerved from the sidewalk and ran down the middle of the empty street. Martin pounded along behind her. He was short and didn't look like much, but he spent a lot of time with his hands, including rougher work with wood and stone, and after several blocks, he'd only fallen back a few feet.

She took a shortcut through one of the burnouts, temporarily immune to the unease she felt whenever she wandered into one of the blackened neighborhoods. Grass and shrubs sprouted from the charred skeletons of houses. She thought she could still smell the scorched fat absorbed by the burnt wood. The young trees were shorter than she was and she ran in the open sunlight, sweat moistening her back. Before cresting the hill, she detoured two blocks over to a neighborhood mostly untouched by the years of fires where she would have more cover.

The street ran straight down from the hills to the shore a half mile away. A long white sailboat sat at their dock. Martin ran up beside her, breathing hard.

"What's going on?"

"I saw them on my way to the mall," Raina pulled off her pack and rooted around for her binoculars. "I didn't know who they were. I didn't know they were coming."

"Are your parents okay?"

She fit the binoculars to her nose. Even at their highest power, it was impossible to make out the details of the men swarming across the dock. A man stood alone in the yard. A couple dozen others approached through the patchy grass, spread into an enveloping semicircle. Two men rushed the solitary figure, metal flashing in their hands; he fell quickly.

Another person rushed from the house. Her mom. A woman's scream floated on the damp air, carried by the wind.

Raina rose and ran as fast as she could.

2

Walt took one last look at the pyramid that had been his base of operations, if not really his home, for the last—well, he wasn't quite sure how long. He believed he was close to turning thirty, which meant he'd spent the last two-plus years in the surrounding jungle and the nearby beach, but he'd quit keeping track of days a long time ago. What did a few weeks here or there matter? He'd start paying attention again once they announced the next World Series.

He'd figured he'd be fine as long as he knew what season it was, and any dummy could tell the difference between sweating and snowing. Then he promptly moved to a jungle not far off the equator, a place where the seasons consisted of "rainy" and "not quite so rainy." Things had gotten a little hazy. By the time he thought about resuming a strict count of the days, if only to make sure someone on the planet was still doing so, the whole idea felt daft: not only would it be inaccurate, but the end of civilization really felt like the sort of thing that should prompt you to start a new calendar.

In short, it was something like 5 After Plague, and besides getting lots of exercise, killing a bunch of animals, mostly for food, and masturbating—though much less than in his teens and early twenties, and to be fair, his daily average was below one, which he felt was pretty good, considering how much spare time he had on his hands—he hadn't been up to much worth keeping track of anyway.

Which went a long way toward explaining why he was following this woman on a three-thousand mile journey to help deal with her alien problem.

The ziggurat of Chichen Itza squatted inert under the searing jungle sun, its terraced limestone oblivious to the sapping heat and humidity beating down from the sky. In a way, it was inspirational. A lesson to us all: unless you're made of stone, stay the hell out of the jungle.

He hiked his pack up his shoulder. "I hope your car has air conditioning."

"What car?" Lorna said.

"The one you really should have brought with you."

"Will that be a problem?"

Walt shrugged. "Only if you've got something against jaguar attacks, grubs for dinner, and horrendous diarrhea."

She unfurled her long black hair, combed her fingers through the sweaty tangles, and expertly swept and pinned it back atop her head. "Our boat's on the south coast of Mexico. We made it from there on foot just fine."

He tugged up his collar and wiped his forehead. "Be right back."

He turned around, waved at the pyramid, and trudged back to its base. He opened the door to the staircase leading up its guts and got out his orange plastic bucket and a length of lightweight rope. He already had his machete and his pack. That about covered it.

"What's that?" she said when he got back.

"It's known as a bucket."

"What makes you think you'll need a bucket?"

"I don't know if you've noticed, but there aren't a lot of rivers around here. Water collects in these great big pits that aren't a lot of fun to fall into."

She tilted her head. "We have water."

"All I'm saying is it would suck if we didn't." He slung the rope over his shoulders and clipped the bucket to his pack. "Ready when you are."

She started across the knee-high grass. Back in the day, the clearing around the pyramid and the ball court and all the little temples surrounding the area had been kept clear by the Mexican government. The jungle had already begun to reclaim it, saplings and shrubs creeping in from the crush of the forest. Walt didn't expect to come back—not that he meant to stay in L.A., either—but if life's strange tide carried him back to the Yucatan at age forty, he doubted he'd be able to find the site again, its ancient stone swept under by the advancing glacier of green.

Five men waited inside the treeline. Four were white; he hadn't seen such light-skinned people in years. Lorna introduced Walt to her cousin Hannigan, a ruddy-faced dude with small brown eyes, and to Ken, a quiet and compact man with a very long and very black rifle. There were three others whose names Walt didn't catch because he'd stopped paying attention. He'd never been good with names, and Lorna seemed like a much better use of his attention.

"Okay," he said, clapping his hands. "Who's got the map?"

Hannigan eyed him. "Thought you knew your way around."

"That's why I want to see what route you're taking."

The man reached into his pocket and unfolded a road map of the Yucatan/Central America region. He traced his finger along the coast of the Gulf of Mexico, then slanted down to Mexico's southern coast.

"Look good?"

"For the first couple days," Walt said. "Then we're going to have problems with the locals."

"Local who? Tribes?"

"Not like tribes tribes. They aren't running around with poison blow darts. They're people who went into the jungle when the virus hit and never came out."

The man leaned forward. His sweat smelled less than a day old, as if they'd freshened up to make a good first impression. "We made it here all right."

"Then you got lucky," Walt said.

He touched the pistol on his hip. "Or the locals knew better than to mess with us."

"The locals are a lot more scared of outsiders infecting them with the Panhandler virus than they are of a few guns. Which they have too, by the way. Mostly AKs."

"The Panhandler's gone."

"They don't know that." Walt batted at a fly on his neck. "Do we know that? Survivors are immune, but what if we're carriers?"

The man tilted his brow forward. "This isn't a discussion. We detour, we slow down. Spend more time exposed to whatever you're afraid is out here."

"Cool. Then when the locals show up, I'll head into the jungle and meet you at the boat. If you don't show up in two weeks, I'll say a prayer for your souls and go home."

Hannigan smiled with the left half of his mouth. "We'll see about that."

They started down the road. The jungle canopy shaded them from the battering sun, but the air was damp and hot, like they were trudging through a giant sauna. Or, given that there might not be any saunas left, what it was most like was a goddamn jungle.

Walt sipped warm water. Birds and monkeys yelped from the trees. Insects buzzed constantly, seeking each other in the jumble of green, flitting into the open road to bite the humans' exposed necks, hands, and faces. Hannigan walked with an assault rifle draped over his chest, gaze ticking between the monotonous lines of trees.

"How many aliens are we talking about?" Walt said.

"We don't know," Hannigan said.

"A hundred? A million?"

"More than the first, less than the second."

"Why don't you just bomb them? It's been a while since I tangled with them, but they really didn't care for being bombed."

"They're sheltering in the ship," Lorna said.

Walt swabbed his forehead. "So bomb the ship."

"We can't get to it by boat. We've tried a few airfields, but all the jets were destroyed in the war. Not that we even have a pilot. Or a nuke. Or the desire to nuke something thirty miles from our home. We have to get inside. We need you to get us there."

"Just seeing if you'd done your homework."

The road through the green went on and on. The walk was unpleasant—in the swarming, itchy heat, moving was unpleasant—but the road made for easy going, and with plenty of water in their canteens, they made good time. Four miles per hour, maybe better. He could see the argument against scaring up a car. Cars were loud. Conspicuous. Prone to breaking down at bad times. After years sitting idle, none would turn over without a lot of work. Dead batteries. Flat tires. Corroded wires. Finding gasoline was no sure thing, either, and it would probably have gone bad anyway. The roads could be clogged, or busted up by the jungle's searching roots. The trip appeared to be five, maybe six hundred miles; substantial, but not grueling. Doable.

What he couldn't understand is why they didn't bother to try to find bicycles. Those didn't guzzle any fuel. You could walk them around fallen trees or crashed cars. Minimal risk of a breakdown. Silent. Back when he and that couple—Mia, the pretty girl, and do-gooder whats-his-name—Raymond, that was it—when the three of them were trying to get away from the invaders in L.A., they'd used bikes, and it had worked like a charm. Couldn't very well drag them into the jungle, but they could always find new ones when they reemerged from the woods.

Then again, he didn't care. He was just happy to be doing something again.

At sunset, they went inside an abandoned gas station, swept up broken glass and leaves from the aisle in front of the rotted-out freezers, and unrolled their sleeping bags. Ken went for a walk around the grounds. Hannigan lit some candles and laid out their dinner, twists of dried meat and handfuls of dried blueberries. Walt ate some of the wild bananas and bell peppers and cassava and nuts he'd brought with him from the pyramid. After, Hannigan cleaned his teeth with a metal toothpick.

"What kind of military background you got, anyway?"

"Who, me?" Walt said.

"I ain't talking to the monkeys."

"None."

"None like none? No Marines? No Army? No weekend National Guard?"

"I always thought the military was for fucking jerks."

Hannigan's smile tightened. He folded his arms, exposing a tattoo on his left biceps of an eagle crouched over the globe accompanied by the initials USMC. "And you took down the mothership."

"I had help," Walt said.

"What, the USS Nimitz?"

"A Vietnam vet named Otto. We landed a hot air balloon on the top, cracked the engines with C4, infiltrated the bridge with lasers, and shot everything that— "

"Bullshit," Hannigan said. Three others laughed. Ken and Lorna just watched. In the candlelight, Hannigan grinned in disbelief. "Can you believe it? We came for a warrior, but could only find ourselves a liar."

Walt ate a nut he didn't have a name for. Not a proper one, anyway.

He thought of them as "those little round guys that are disappointingly bland considering how hard it is to crack their shells," but he was sure the locals had a snappier term.

"If you don't believe it, why did you come down here?" he said.

"Somebody took down that ship," Hannigan said. "If we found him, we could wipe out the threat once and for all. Instead, we picked up a boasting little runt."

"Dave," Lorna said sharply. "You heard the villagers. It's him."

The man prodded his teeth with the steel pick. "That's what he told them, anyway."

Walt laughed and stood, brushing his lap free of the dry, flaky bits of nutshells. "Well, good luck to you."

"Where do you think you're going?"

"Back to my friends the trees. They don't judge me."

"Please sit down," Lorna said.

Walt scratched his beard. He hadn't shaved in weeks, but if they had a proper trip ahead of them, he was going to have to do something about that. "Then make up your minds."

"We have," she said. "We need your help."

He nodded and turned to Hannigan, who removed the toothpick from his mouth and gazed at its tip.

"Well, you're already here," the man said. "May as well come back with us."

"Great," Walt said. "I'm going to sleep."

He did. He was woken a couple times by those horrid night birds, then got up for good a little before dawn, going outside to pee and have a look around. When he got back, Hannigan was sitting up in bed, a pistol in his lap, watching the jungle.

The others got up soon after. They got on their way and followed the road through the trees. Minutes after sunrise, the air was sweltering. A couple of the men grumbled and joked. They made good time again, stopping for the night in a shabby motel with a serious rat problem. In the middle of the third day, Walt stepped onto the shoulder of the road, unscrewed his canteen, and had a drink.

"Can't use the road for a while," Walt said.

"Says who?" Hannigan said.

Walt pointed to the words carved into a trunk beside the road. "Says that."

"Looks like gibberish."

"It's Mayan. Roughly translated, it says 'Stay the fuck out.'"

"You think they'll prefer us tramping through their jungle?"

"So long as we go that way," Walt pointed south, "and stay out of everything up there," he finished, pointing first to the road, then the trees beyond.

Hannigan spat. "It'll slow us down. A lot."

"True. But you know what will slow us down even more?"

"What's that?"

He pointed to a leathery tarp suspended from the upper branches of the tree. "Getting shot and skinned."

The man rubbed his stubble. "Lead on."

Walt unsheathed his machete and stepped off the gravel. The jungle was a bitch. Three bitches and a half. Especially all the way out here, which he'd only visited a few times, and knew in only the most scant way, like when he'd left lower Manhattan to go see a Mets game in Flushing—it was still the city, yeah, but not his city.

Even so, vines were vines. Trees were trees. Six-inch centipedes with venomous bites were six-inch centipedes with venomous bites. He stuck to the trails as best he could, consulting the compass in the handle of his knife every few minutes, but even when the way was relatively clear, it was a hard, muddy, grubby slog, as exhausting as it was frustrating. After just three hours, he sat to rest.

Beside the trail, a small, leafy plant sprung from the moss in the roots of a tree. Walt pulled two sprigs, plucked the leaves, and preserved the flattish stems. He passed one to Hannigan.

The man stuck it in his mouth and chewed the end like a piece of hay. "Tastes like poison."

"Oh no." Walt paused with a fluted stem halfway to his mouth. "Oh no."

Hannigan spat out a mouthful of green pulp. "Is it poison? What the fuck?"

"No, it's just funny," Walt said. He stuffed his stem into his mouth and chewed the bitter, fibrous plant, then held up another for Hannigan. "Eat up. You'll feel better in a minute."

The man fixed the plant with his round little eyes. "What's it called?"

"Hell if I know. But it will make your muscles a lot less tired."

Hannigan chewed suspiciously, gazing into the forest. Birds whooped from all sides. "We're good on food for a while yet. Water's another story."

"Still, keep your eye out for bananas, cassava shrubs, obvious stuff. Or these little fleshy red flowers. We'll try to find a cenote tomorrow. A sinkhole."

The man nodded distantly. Walt picked the rest of the plant, handed a stem to each of the others, and pocketed the rest. At least it was shady beneath the canopy. His shoes grew damp with sweat and water. Would have to build a fire within the next couple days, get dried out. He did not want foot problems.

Parrots screeched. Smaller birds peeped. Bugs chirred. He didn't see any fruit, but late afternoon he found a patch of bamboo-like caña agria, which he deleafed, peeled, and passed around. The pulp tasted refreshing and sweet. Not very filling, but it was enough to wash the taste of travel out of his mouth.

"Well," he said. "Suppose we should call it a day."

"Can't stop already," Hannigan said. "It's an hour till the light's gone."

"More," Walt said. "And I'd like to use that light to build a shelter."

"From what? Jaguar? We got guns."

He shook his head. "Ants."

"Ants?"

"Ants, man. They're the worst. I don't know why we're waging war on some dumb aliens when the whole goddamn planet is overrun by ants."

Hannigan set his hands on his hips. "Unless that pack of yours is full of Raid, I don't see what we're supposed to do about it."

Walt lifted his shirt and fanned his belly. Not that it helped. "Hammocks. I'm guessing you left yours at home."

"We got a couple tents. Some netting. We aren't gonna get eaten alive, are we?"

"No. Probably not. Look, a few nights on the ground won't kill you. Unless the wrong kind of snake crawls up your pants. You guys live in Los Angeles, right?"

Hannigan tipped back his head. "What's left of it."

"And that place was fucked up even before the plague. But this is the jungle. The whole thing blows. And it blows even worse when ants are chewing you up in your sleep, and all you've had to eat is grass, and your feet haven't been dry for three days. Little things matter."

"I got it, man. Let's string up some hammocks."

Walt picked out a few small, bendable trees, roping them together and suspending his hammock. Hannigan had enough netting for a couple more; they fashioned a fourth out of one of the tents. That left three men on the ground. Walt thought about offering one of them his hammock, then concluded they could go fuck themselves.

He woke sore. Hadn't done much trailblazing lately. Ken took up the machete in the early morning and was spelled within an hour. Despite the protests of Hannigan and another man whose goatee was getting rather overgrown, Lorna took her turn, too, whacking at the brush with loose-armed professionalism. Walt ranged to either side of their southwesterly trail, letting the jungle's pathways take him where they would. In places the canopy choked out the sun so completely that nothing more than grass grew in the shadows, allowing them to walk at something near a normal rate.

With the sun hours past apex, Walt found a cenote. He whistled the others over to the circular hole straight down the limestone into a pool of creamy blue water. It wasn't an especially large one, forty feet across, but that was good, it meant he had plenty of rope. He lowered the bucket over the rim, let it fill halfway, and hauled it back up to the surface, the tough plastic banging thinly against the stone, water dripping back to the pool below.

"Probably want to boil this," he said. "The Ancient Maya used to throw people into these things."

Lorna frowned. "Surely they haven't reverted so quickly."

"Probably not. But animals could have fallen in. Anyway, I'm not a fan of taking hour-long shits even if I've got a Stephen King book handy, so I say we boil it. Can dry our socks, too."

It hadn't rained in the last few days. He sent the others to scoop up the driest grass and fallen branches they could find while he peeled bark from the trees and shredded it into a wooly mass. He set the kindling beside the trunk of a tall, broad-leafed tree. He still had 23 Bic lighters. He used his lucky pink one to light the fire. Ken strung up a line for their socks. Walt set his pan on a rack over the fire and filled it with water, then sat on a rock, barefoot, shoes steaming.

"This," Ken said from the stump beside him. "This isn't so bad."

"I don't think I'll miss it," Walt said.

"You didn't grow up down here, did you?"

"New York. By way of Long Island."

"Crazy," Ken said. "And you wind up here and you make it."

Walt shrugged. "People have made it here for thousands of years."

One of the troops came back with two freshly killed iguanas, which they spitted and roasted. Hannigan had salt. Walt salivated at the sight of it. It had nearly disappeared from the ruins, looted long ago by other survivors. He'd tried evaporating seawater to make his own, but it was a tedious process, taking days to create enough to season a single meal of meat or roots.

It was the best day and the best meal they'd have for some time.

They walked on through the implacable jungle, feet aching, blisters popping, socks drenched. Their food dwindled. Walt sighed, considered the others, then smashed open what appeared to be a giant heap of dung. The termite grubs inside were better than nothing. They caught a bird with a broken wing and shared a quart of berries Walt was fairly sure weren't poisonous. He angled further and further west, certain he'd find the road soon, but either they were traveling slower than he thought or the map was wrong.

People got touchy. Hannigan especially. Walt handed out orders in gruff clips. He wasn't any happier than they were. He refused to admit they were lost. Not in a meaningful way. The road was to the west. Even if the jungle had already consumed the asphalt, the ocean would only be a few miles beyond it. They'd be able to fish at least. Find their way to a highway and follow it up to the boat.

For the first time on the trip, Walt went to bed with an empty stomach. Starlight sifted through the canopy. If he'd been on his own, he could keep himself fed easily enough. The problem was all these other mouths. Killing resurgent aliens no longer sounded all that fun. He ought to abandon these guys to the wilds and head back to his pyramid-throne. He resolved to give it two more days.

At noon, they stopped to eat their remaining berries and a few of the knuckle-sized flowers Walt knew were safe. They were reddish and sweet, but didn't do much to fill the stomach.

Hannigan plunked down beside him on a log. "Let me ask you something."

"Shoot."

"You know where in Christ we are?"

He gestured to the trees. "The jungle."

"How close to the road?"

"Close."

The man's ruddy face broke into a rueful grin. "Specifics, man. My belly's grumbling. I got the runs. My feet are no good. Right now, 'close' doesn't cut it."

Walt poked a stick at an ant, crushing it into the dirt. "In case you haven't noticed, this place is fucking huge. I've only been down here a couple years. We left my back yard a long time ago."

"Your brilliant plan was to cut brush through a jungle you've never set foot in?"

"I know enough to get by on my own. I've never led an expedition."

"Great. Fucking great." Hannigan stood, pacing through the weeds. "You're the one who took us offroad. I think it's time you stepped up."

He stretched out his legs. "What exactly would you like me to do?"

"Prove you're worth it! Prove to me there's a reason we sailed all the way down here and crossed six hundred miles of miserable shit just to pick up one more piece of it."

"Why?"

"Why? Because we thought we needed you." Hannigan laughed. His smile broke; he flung his canteen at a trunk. It connected with a hollow clunk. "So you killed a few aliens. That was years ago. What can you do for us now? Why don't you give me one good reason why I shouldn't punch your smirking mouth?"

"Well," Walt said, gazing into the trees. "I've got one reason after all."

"Come on. Love to hear it."

"For one thing, I know better than to go hollering on in hostile land," he said. "For another, if I try really, really hard, I may be able to talk them into not killing us."

He pointed across the jungle. In the shadow of the trees, four men stood in perfect stillness, so short you could almost mistake them for children. Their unblinking eyes looked down the barrels of AK-47s.

3

The falling sun splintered on the waves. She thundered down the hill, running so fast she knew she'd trip, skin her elbows and face across the asphalt. She kept her balance. Between the docks and the house, men shouted, waved guns. Martin called after her. She didn't slow.

Her dad struggled to his feet, staggering away from the attackers, hands raised. He gestured behind him. Her mom disappeared into the house. The men who had struck him edged forward. One held out a pistol, the other cocked a club.

Raina screamed.

They all turned. Her dad, the men closing on him, the others watching from the dock and the deck of the boat tied to the cleats. She gripped her knife, running for the man with the pistol, zigzagging in, because you can't allow them a straight shot. The man hopped back a step and leveled his gun. Her dad shouted and ran forward, shielding his head with one hand. The man with the gun planted his feet. Raina showed her teeth. Her dad bowled into her ribs, scooping her up, pinning her knife to her side.

The man with the gun glanced toward the sailboat. Raina wriggled against her dad's grip, but his hands and arms were hardened by daily fights with wind and ropes and sails.

The man with the club squinted at Raina, then nodded. "She'll do."

"You won't touch her," her dad stated.

"Are you under the illusion we're bargaining?"

Her dad groaned, a sickly sound she could feel in her ribs. He crushed Raina's head to his chest, blocking her view. She felt him jerk his head toward the house.

"Why not both?" said the man with the club.

"We don't have all day," said the other man. "Choose."

"Shit. That fruit ain't ripe yet."

Feet slooshed through the grass toward the house. Raina squirmed. Her dad crushed her harder yet, turning his body so she faced the docks. The screen door squeaked and slammed. Her mom screamed but was cut off while the note was still rising.

"Dad!" Raina choked.

He squeezed her so tight she could barely breathe. The men in the yard shouldered their rifles, sheathed their knives. Some elbowed each other. Some stared at the sky. Her father's arms quivered. His chest shook. She fought to free her arms but he clamped down. She wriggled her face into his neck and bit his skin. He yelped, drew back, then nudged his head into hers.

"What are you trying to do, Raina?" he whispered. "Fight?"

"We have to stop them!"

"And then what? Do you want them to shoot us? Do you want to die and leave your mother alone?" He hugged her to him. "This is the only way we stay together."

She bit his neck harder, tasting blood. He didn't move. She screamed and squeezed her eyes shut, mashing her face into the sweat and blood trickling from his skin. His shoulders shook. He relaxed his hold and she fell away and shuddered. Gulls cawed on the breeze. The breakers curled in one after another, hissing into the sand.

A man rose from the deck of the sailboat and leapt to the dock with a rattle of wood. He was tall, burly, bearded, and bald. He spat into the sea and strolled onto dry land.

"What the hell are we standing around for?" He gazed across his men. "Is the day that nice?"

"Trig and Holsen," one of the men said. "They're inside."

A pained look crossed the bearded man's face. He crossed the grass. The screen door banged behind him. Raina wriggled in her dad's grip to face the house. The bearded man emerged a minute later, trailed by the man with the pistol, whose face was flushed, scratched, and grinning, and the man with the club, who walked stiffly, expression as dark as the water beneath the docks.

The bearded man stopped beside her dad and gestured at the sea.

"One week. You understand?"

Her dad nodded. "One week."

The men thumped down the dock, joking, pointing north along the shore. Sailors hollered out, bringing in lines, poling the boat away from the pier. Her dad set her down. She turned to the house. In the trees at the edge of the yard, a pale face—Martin—pulled back into the leaves.

Her dad set his hand on her shoulder and looked her in the eye. "Stay here. If they come back, shout as loud as you can. Do you understand me?"

She nodded. Her knuckles were stiff around her knife. Its edge was red. So was a line on the side of her dad's gray t-shirt. He smiled. Guiltily, she put the blade away. He stood and regarded the house for a long moment. The surf seethed up the shore.

"Dad," she said.

He started, smiled again, and walked to their home, closing the screen door silently.

Raina sat in the grass and whispered the men's names. Holsen. Trig. Holsen. Trig. She closed her eyes and pictured their faces until she'd never forget them.

Flies buzzed on the kelp stranded along the tideline. She got her knife out and cleaned it. She turned to the house, then stepped closer, telling herself she just wanted to hear them speaking, to know her mother was okay. She paused after each step, but all she heard was gulls and the wind.

Twenty feet from the house, her mother's face appeared in the kitchen window. It was blank and white and drawn. Her eyes found Raina but stared right through her, glassy, without focus, the eyes of the fish on the deck of a ship.

Her father grunted and wound in the winch. Fish slid across the deck. She clubbed them and gutted them and set them in the cooler. Her dad watched her shuck the guts into the water. She reached for another croaker. He turned away and stared out to sea.

He brought the boat around and tied off at the docks. The yard was empty. Raina brought the coolers to the fire pit and rinsed off her hands. She went into the dark house. Her mom's door was closed. She changed her shirt and got her pack and walked back into the blinding sunlight and headed for the road.

"Going to the ruins?" her dad called.

She didn't turn around. She hiked up the middle of the asphalt, pushing herself, breathing hard. She didn't look back until the top of the hill. Back at the house, smoke rose from the fire pit, a small gray rope climbing up the sky. The alien ship waited in the bay. She looked at it and said the words that kept it from moving, then walked over the hill, keeping to the shade of the trees. She got to the mall, faltered, and kept walking, heading to Western, which didn't make sense, because it ran to the north. After a long, long climb, she looked down on the towers rising from the valley, high brown mountains strung out behind them. She walked until the sun set and then kept walking more.

She came home three days later. Her dad whirled from the kitchen counter, knife in hand. His eyes were baggy and wild.

"What happened to your face?"

"I had to fight a dog," she said.

He nodded as if he understood. "Well, are you ready to fish?"

"Ten minutes."

Her parents' door was still closed. Raina went to her room to change her socks and underwear and eat one of the overripe, half-sweet lemons sitting on her desk. She threw the peel in the pit outside her window and walked down to the pier.

The men came back a week later. Her dad made her stay inside while he walked down to the dock carrying two bags, one large and one small. He handed them to a sun-wizened woman and came back inside. Raina watched the crew shove off and continue up the coast.

"They'll be back every month," her dad said. "The first Sunday. I don't want you to talk to them."

"We should kill them."

He blinked at her, eyes wide in his deeply tanned face. "We can't."

"Why not? Don't they bleed?"

"Of course they do."

"Then we should make them."

His face hardened. For a moment, she thought he might agree. He shook his head. "All they want is a few fish. Some salt. Small price for peace."

Past the docks, a pelican folded its wings and plunged into the waves. Sunlight flashed from the ever-changing water. It was a beautiful day in Los Angeles.

Her mom's door opened three weeks later. Wordless, she came into the kitchen and sat at the table. Raina brought her tea from the kettle boiling on the wood stove. Finally, her mom smiled.

Days turned into weeks, weeks to months. The sailboat came every month and her dad brought the crew their bags of fish and salt. Raina watched from the window. Once, one of the sailors said something and her dad laughed. Raina went to her room and closed the door and put her face into her pillow and screamed.

She saw Martin every week or two. Just like everyone, he acted like nothing had happened. He didn't talk about it and neither did she. He had collected more of the light-stakes and tiled a board with their solar panels, but most of the time the radio didn't work, and even when it did, he heard nothing but static.

Five months after the men first landed at their dock, Raina finished scraping salt from one of the drying-tarps and went into the house for a drink. The dim kitchen smelled herbal and brackish. Her mother stood in front of the stove. Steam spouted from the kettle.

"What are you making?" Raina said.

Her mom's shoulders jumped. "Tea."

"Can I have some?"

She went still. "This is medicine. It would make you sick."

Raina frowned and made herself some Earl Gray from one of the dried old packets. They were almost out; she would have to scavenge soon. They should start growing their own. This dependence on the old homes was bad. The sailors were due to arrive that Sunday. Raina asked her dad if he wanted anything from the Home Depot, then took his list and her pack and hiked into the ruins. She found his screws and a spare ratchet set and went into the outdoor garden. Except for the cacti and some small yellow flowers, all the plants had died long ago, brown twigs sticking from the dried-out potter's soil. She searched every single rack of seed packets, but she didn't find any tea.

In case the men in the boat were still at the dock, she made her way home through the trees. A broken stick stuck from the roots of the magnolia. Raina shuffled through the crunchy carpet of broad, mustard-brown leaves. The soil around the stick was loose. She scraped it away with her knife. The flat of her blade snagged on something yielding. Too-small fingers curled in the shadow of the tree.

She pushed back the dirt and tamped it down with her shoe.

A new family moved into the house down the shore, a man and two women. At night, their voices drifted on the wind, giggling, shrieking in the surf. Raina scratched her symbol into the trunks of the trees between their house and her parents'; if they came this way at night and they meant bad things, Raina would wake up and be ready. It was the same symbol she'd carved into the pilings beneath the pier in the city, a circle bisected by a vertical line. It had kept her safe from scavengers and dogs. It hadn't warned her when her new parents came for her, but they were there to help, so it had stayed silent.

The year turned over to rain and fog and cold nights. After a few weeks, it got warm again, though she still needed a coat when she went out at night. A group of a dozen people came to the coast and settled up the hill in the big yellow house with the pillars and the reddish tile roof. Raina's dad went to see them and make sure they were good. Except for one shriveled old woman, they were all young and lean and pretty.

"They don't know what the hell they're doing," her dad chuckled, shaking his head.

He went to see them again anyway, especially on the days when her mom closed herself in her room. He said they needed help, especially with the raiders on the boat, who had begun to ask for firewood and grain as well as their big bag of dried fish and their small bag of salt.

Her dad must not have given the young people good advice. The sailors tied at her father's dock, collected their tribute, then headed up the hill to the sprawling Spanish house. Gunshots crackled from the heights. Screams. Through the kitchen window, Raina watched the men come back to the dock. Trig and Holsen were smiling. The bald man with the beard toweled blood from his hands, a brooding look weighing down his eyebrows and mouth.

After they left, her father climbed up the hill and stayed with the young people for two hours. He came back with eyes so distant they looked like they could see past the end of the ocean. He sat on the dock and watched the birds, then came inside and went into his room without knocking on the closed door. Raina went into the trees to fetch the skull of the little blue shark they'd caught last summer. He didn't smell anymore, but she still called him Reek. She climbed up on the roof and set the skull against the chimney to watch over the house.

She went fishing with her father the next afternoon. When they finished, Raina walked past him on the dock and he hooked a finger into her collar and gave her a smile.

"I'm going to start making some trips soon," he said. "I'm going to need you to watch over your mother."

"Did the pirates kill all those people?"

"A couple." He shook his head. "If anyone comes, I want you to take her into the trees and hide. You're better at that than any of us."

"What if they still come for us?"

"Then you do whatever it takes."

She went to make sure her knife was sharp, but it always was. Her dad left three days later. An hour after the screen door banged, her parents' door squeaked.

"Do you want some tea?" her mom said.

"Sure."

Her mom crumbled brittle yellow newspapers and lit the stove and went to the old laundry room for one of the jugs of fresh water. She sat at the table and waited for the water to boil.

"You never told us how you did it," the woman said.

Raina looked up from her comic book. "Did what?"

"Survived."

She turned the page. "I don't remember."

"Really? But you were out there for over a year."

"All I remember is when you came to find me."

"That's incredible." Her mom gazed at the kettle. "You don't remember how you did it? How you made it day to day? Weren't you scared?"

"At first."

"Then what?"

Raina thought. "I changed."

Her mom leaned forward. "How?"

"I watched the things that scared me. The dogs and the night and the ocean. Then I watched how the cats jumped up where the dogs couldn't get them, and how the possums used the night to hunt in safety, and how the pelicans didn't fight the tide no matter how big the waves."

She gave Raina a funny look. "I thought you didn't remember."

"Only a little," Raina said. "When it was quiet and I was alone."

"You didn't let it get to you. You watched and you learned."

The kettle whistled. After a moment, her mom got up and took it from the stove.

After she finished her tea, she told her mom she was going for a walk, then got her snares from her room and headed to the hills. Once she got high enough and inland from the coast, the houses stopped dead, replaced by wild swaths of trees. She walked in the cool shade. At the first sign of tracks, she knelt and set a snare. She didn't go home until she'd prepped each one.

She washed the clothes, scrubbing out the sea salt and the dirt in the big orange bucket they kept out back, then hung them on the lines to dry in the wind. She busied the rest of the day sweeping the garage and the porches and scraping the boat and mopping its fish-grimy decks. Night came at last. Her mom kissed her goodnight and went to bed early. Raina waited half an hour, then pulled the screen from her window and dropped outside.

With her dad gone, she needed more than her symbols scratched in the trees to keep them safe. It wasn't the best time to ask the moon—it would be the evil eye tonight, the slanted half-moon glowering down from the clouds—but she had no other choice. And if the evil eye appreciated her courage, perhaps it would be the best time of all.

She ran up the hill toward the woods. The moon watched her every step, bathing her in silver suspicion. She ignored it for now. The trees swallowed her up, hiding her from the moon's disapproval. She stopped now and then to listen and make sure she wasn't being followed. Once, she heard the slow, quiet shuffle of a possum, but that was all.

Her first three snares were empty. The fourth held a rabbit. She was afraid it was already dead, but it had just struggled itself into exhaustion; when she reached for it, it jerked limply. She untied the snare from the shrub she'd anchored it to, grabbed the rabbit around the neck, and carried it to the clearing. Offering it in this way meant the moon would get the rabbit's spirit instead of her. She didn't like that. Not because she wanted it for herself; although rabbits could teach you to be swift and alert, she already had many. But she didn't trust what that thing in the sky would do with it.

Yet she had no choice. Under the judgment of the sky's angled eye, she cut the bunny's throat and showed its blood to the moon. In the dim light, the fluid was black. The rabbit gurgled but went still very soon. Raina watched the heavens. Thin clouds streamed in from the south, blinding the moon, but quickly dispersed. When the silvery eye reopened, it was watching Raina's enemies instead.

Its protection proved true; the men from the boat made no unexpected visits. Her dad came home safe, too, gifting her with a small bag of golden raisins. He left again a couple days later. It became routine. Once he left for a week straight. Raina climbed up on the roof and sat down next to Reek.

"Where do you think he's going?" she said. "Do you think he's trying to get away from us?"

Reek's bones grinned up at her, teeth as sharp as the day they had caught him. She wanted to throw him off the roof and jump on him, but he belonged to her. That wasn't how you treated your people. Your family. You had to look out for them even when they laughed at you. They were a part of you; when you hurt them, you hurt yourself.

Besides, Reek was the only shark she had. She might need him some day.

That afternoon, her mom asked her if she knew where to find wine. She did. She brought it back and the bottles disappeared one or two per day. Her mom asked about vodka and she brought it back in big plastic bottles with red labels. These took as long as a week to empty. Raina brought as many as she could find. When you needed something, you had to take all you could get before it went away.

She tried it herself one night, but it burnt her throat and left her gasping. Then she felt warm and had another drink. It was the end of winter, but the wind blew from the south, carrying warmth with it. Only the water was cold. She swam out past the shoreline where the waves were calm and felt the moonlight on her skin. The moon had grown fat, gorging itself on clouds until it was nearly full. It would be too bloated to care for her offerings right now. That's why it was most dangerous to hunt under its full light. But when it shrank away to nothing, that's when it was hungriest, too, and would guide you to your prey in exchange for a sip of the blood.

In the morning she felt awful. She drank more tea and left the house while her mom's door was still closed. A breeze followed her up the hill. Up top, she spied down on the house of the man with the two wives, but they weren't awake yet. Bottles glinted from their back yard. Way up north, the crashed ship still hadn't moved from its place off Venice Beach. She nodded to herself and continued to the mall.

She tried every store around it—the Ralph's, the Smart & Final, the Trader Joe's, the gas stations, the Pollo Loco—but couldn't find any tea seeds. It didn't make any sense. How had they expected to get more tea when no one had any seeds? She knew there weren't any in the mall, because she knew everything there was to know in the mall, but she went to its plazas anyway, palms flapping overhead. She climbed the metal staircase to the walkway connecting the second-floor shops, scanned the parking garage for movement, then went inside the Macy's. Inside the airy hallway beyond it, she strolled between the squares of light, careful not to let it touch her, remembering how her father held her back while the men in the boat went inside the house.

She didn't hear Martin this time. He was learning. Even so, she saw his movement reflected in a store window, a thin boy who would never be tall. She crept behind the escalator, drew her knife, and waited. He turned the corner.

"Where does tea come from?" she said.

"Man!" Martin leapt back, flailing his arms in front of his face. "I thought I had you."

"Some day."

"Tea comes from China." He straightened, as if delivering a book report. "And India. Japan. All those places."

"Does it grow here?"

"This area is a Sunset Zone 23," he said. "Or 24? Whichever it is, everything grows here."

The air smelled dusty and warm. It would be hot today. "What zone is Catalina?"

"The island?" he said. "Well, all of it's coastal, and it's pretty hilly, so I'd bet it's just like here. Why?"

She stared at him until he looked away. She touched the lucky shell in her pocket. "Who are they?"

"The people from the boat?"

"Yeah."

"I'm not sure," he said slowly. "People started taking boats to Catalina as soon as the Panhandler hit. I think they thought it would be isolated. Within a couple weeks, my mom and I started to see fires." He gazed into the hollowed-out shoe store. "One time, a boat washed up down the shore. They'd tried to burn it but it had gone out. It was full of bodies."

She touched the handle of her knife. "No wonder they're so quick to hurt others. Their people were built by it."

"Well, you'd better get used to them. They annexed us."

"An necks?"

"They took us over. We're part of their land."

"No we're not," she laughed.

Martin's face went as sober as an angel's. "Raina, you can't let them hear you say that. They own us now."

"They only own the people who let them."

She wasn't about to hear more of his nonsense. She left the mall and headed west. A church stood on the next hill, a pretty thing the Spanish must have built hundreds of years ago. Most churches gave her the creeps—if she knew anything, it was that God didn't much like humans anymore—but the steeple of this church was a spike, and if God reached down to get her, He would impale His hand and leave to swat someone else instead. She jogged up the steps to the big wood front doors, then climbed the twisty staircase to the top of the tower, where she could see the whole city at once.

She had thought her new parents were strong for surviving the plague, but they were as weak as everyone else. When the water went dry, you found a new stream. When the food ran out, you walked away. That's what her year in the ruins had taught her.

But in that year, they had been the only ones who'd tried to help instead of hurt her.

She frowned at a loud crow. She didn't have to make a decision yet. That was one more thing the ruins had taught her. You don't move just because you're scared. Movement for the sake of movement exposes you to things you didn't know were there. No. You move when you know what to do.

She walked home. She let the screen slam behind her. In the shadows of the kitchen, her parents detached. Her dad was home. Her mother grinned and adjusted her shirt.

"Hi Raina," she said. "Find anything nice?"

"Yes," Raina said, "but then it broke."

While she thought about whether to run out on her parents, she filled her days with fishing, searching for tea seeds, and talking with Martin about the men from Catalina. The boat came again and she watched from the window while her dad handed over their things. She didn't like this. A stray dog will be wary at first, but if you don't chase him off, he'll get bolder. Especially when he has friends.

She was on her way back from the church a few days later when she passed a man on the road. He smiled and tipped his hat; the bill was streaked with dried white sweat. His sneakers were pasted with duct tape. A bedroll and a bulging bag projected from his back. He winked at her, comfortable on the road with the locals.

Her mom sat under the umbrella in the front yard. "Your father and I are going on a trip this afternoon."

"Where are you going?"

"We'll be gone two or three days. We've already spoken to Wendell. If you need anything, go see him."

Raina got a cup and the jug of clean water on the counter. "You're just telling me now?"

"Well, we only just decided," her mom said. "We're going to see a friend. Will you be okay?"

"I'll be fine."

Her dad emerged from their room and grinned. "Tell her?"

Her mother winked at her. "Yep."

"Then I suppose we'd better pack."

Raina went out back to scrape salt from the tarps and bring the evaporated and recondensed water inside. Her parents didn't take long to pack. They all had emergency bags waiting for them in the front closet. Besides that, all they needed to put together was more bedding, a few clothes, and whatever luxuries they thought they'd like along the way.

Her father hugged her tight. "You'll be fine."

"You've never left me alone before," Raina said.

"All things considered, I think you're plenty old enough." He laughed. "Don't you?"

"You don't have to work," her mom said. "Just stay safe. Go see Wendell if you run into any trouble."

She watched them climb up the hill. As they reached the top, panic shuddered through her, but it was replaced at once by a calm coldness. They would be back. And if they weren't, it wouldn't matter.

She hadn't had any for a while, so before it got dark, she went to the docks to cut mussels from the piling. She shucked them from their shells and boiled them with lemongrass from the garden and pepper from the cabinet. She had a bite of chocolate for dessert, then poured a small amount of vodka into her thermos, cut it with water, and sipped it as she prowled the shore toward the home of the man with two wives. The moon was fat and full again. Too drunk and logy to do anything but watch what was beneath it. The man and his two wives sometimes swam naked in the waves and the moon that night was perfect.

There were no blankets or bottles on the tideline. The house was dark. She crept through the tall grass, listened, and then, emboldened by the warmth in her veins, knocked on the door. No one answered.

That was weird enough that she tried knocking again in the morning to check on them, but they were still gone. She went up the hill to the house full of young people and asked for Chris, the woman who came to her parents' house on occasion to borrow a tool or a spice, but the blond woman who answered the door said she was out. Raina headed west across the dead lawns overlooking the ocean from their heights. Wendell stooped over his yard, hacking at weeds with a short-handled hoe.

He blinked at her, mouth half-open, then recognized her and smiled. "Fall into trouble already?"

"I got bored," Raina said.

The old man spread his hands at the hills and the sea. "With all this to explore?"

"I got bored of not finding what I'm looking for."

"What's that? A comb?"

She gave him a look. "Tea seeds."

"Why do you want tea seeds?"

"To make tea trees."

"I think they grow on bushes." Wendell wiped his hands on his overalls. "And I don't think they grew a whole lot of tea in Southern California. If they did, you might find some at the nurseries."

She considered the rich brown soil. "I saw a stranger on the road the other day. He had a hat and tape on his shoes. I didn't like how he looked."

"Everyone looks funny after they've been on the road long enough," Wendell said. "Though he had some funny questions, too."

"Like what?"

"Like what I thought of Catalina."

The little farm was just high enough up the hill to make out the black edge of the crashed ship. Raina watched it a moment. "What did you tell him?"

Wendell chuckled. "That I think whatever they tell me to think. He smiled and thanked me and went on his way."

She talked with the old man a while longer, but her mind had already moved on. Her parents' energy. The suddenness of their departure and how it had come right on the heels of the stranger's visit. The stranger's single question for Wendell. It was all connected, and Raina had a pretty good idea what it meant.

Her parents were rebels. Her parents were rebels, and she wanted to join them.

4

The men from the jungle waited in poised silence. They were short and deeply tanned and wore jeans and t-shirts for Joust and Pac-Man and celebrating the San Francisco Giants' 1989 World Series victory, which Walt was 90% certain had never taken place.

"Only four of them," Hannigan said. "We've faced worse."

"Four of them they want you to see." Walt set his hands on his knees. "The rest are behind us."

Hannigan craned around. One of his men took a step forward, speaking in Spanish. Machine guns tracked him.

"Tell your dudes to stay still," Walt said. "These people observe the Twenty Paces Rule."

"Twenty Paces Rule?" Hannigan said.

"Come within twenty paces, and they shoot."

"Seems harsh."

"It's how they kept the disease away." Walt rose slowly, hands up, and called across the tree-shadowed grass. "Hola. Somos amigos. Hooray!"

One of the men lowered his AK by an inch. He spoke in Mayan at a clip Walt could barely comprehend. "Who are you and what are you doing here?"

Walt replied in halting, poorly-accented Mayan. "Walt, and leaving."

"Why are you here?"

Hannigan leaned closer. "What's he saying?"

"He's saying the Irishman should shut up." Walt turned back toward the gunmen. "We go through."

The other man stalked forward, returning his gun to his shoulder. "Go through us?"

"Passing through!" Walt tried in Spanish, then moved back to the Mayan he'd picked up from the people around the pyramid. "We go." He gestured at Hannigan's crew. "We go away. Please."

"You bring sickness."

"No," he said. There was one word he knew well: "Survivors."

The man with the gun said a word he didn't understand. Walt shook his head dumbly. The man tried again, then hissed through his teeth and said, "You can't be here."

Leaves stirred in the shrubs behind Walt. Hannigan grabbed his arm. "What's going on?"

"We're about to be turned into fertilizer."

"We have salt. Coffee beans. It's as good as money ever was."

"Great," Walt said. "While I attempt to buy passage, you figure out how to convince them not to just kill us and take it."

He knew the Mayan word for salt, but not coffee beans, especially the green, unroasted, pea-like beans Hannigan scrabbled from his pack, an action that drew shouts from the gunmen. Walt spoke in a mix of Mayan, Spanish, and English, first calming them, then indicating he would like to offer their goods as a toll.

"Put the something on the something," said the man with the machine gun, using several words that meant nothing to Walt.

"The what on the what?"

"The gifts," the man tried. "Put the gifts on the something. On the tree."

"The log?" Walt said in English, pointing to a downed trunk covered with moss and fungus and ants.

"Yes."

"Okay, we're doing an Arab barter thing here," Walt told Hannigan. "Set the salt and the coffee on that log, then back off and let them inspect it."

"And then?" Hannigan said.

"Make your peace with Jesus, because they're going to shoot us anyway."

Hannigan glanced between his men, then at Lorna. "Things might be about to get shooty. If they do, Ken hits their leader, the rest of us drop in a scatter-and-fold."

"Not likely," Ken said.

"You got a better plan? It'll work if you let it." Carefully, maintaining eye contact with the Maya, Hannigan set both bags on the log and backed away through the thick brush. The others followed. The men with the gun stalked forward.

"It's the lack of gratitude that really gets me," Walt said. "I killed the aliens. They should be giving coffee to me." He muttered the Mayan word for the creatures, then mimed an explosion. Leaves crackled beneath his retreating feet.

The youngest of the strangers frowned, eyes flicking between Walt's. He babbled something to his leader, who scowled and stopped to argue with the young man. It was too fast for Walt to follow, but every now and then he caught a word: alien, ship, doubt.

"What's going on?" Hannigan murmured.

Walt shrugged. "The young guy thinks you'd taste better boiled, but their leader says boiled meat loses its flavor."

The leader asked Walt a question. When Walt shrugged and shook his head, the man repeated one word, pointing at the sky.

"I don't get it," Walt said.

The young man who'd recognized him rolled his eyes. "He wants to know if you're the Starbreaker."

"You speak English?"

The man waggled his hand. "Some."

"Yeah," Walt said. "That was me."

The man spoke to his captain, who said something about Chichen Itza. The man turned to Walt and translated. "He asks if you're the Starbreaker, the man from Chichen Itza, then how many steps does it have?"

"Counting the top?" Walt said.

"Counting all."

"365," he said. "Just like the year. 91 on each side, plus the one at the top."

The man grinned and spoke to his leader, who gestured in a swooping, skeptical motion. The young man turned back to Walt. "Is that all of them?"

Walt flapped his hands. "I never counted how many were on the inside. That staircase is scary as shit. Always felt like the whole pyramid was going to close on me like a fist."

The two Maya spoke at length, interrupted by a third member who shouldered his gun and gestured as if stroking an invisible beard. After a minute, the young man looked to Walt.

"Where you going?"

"Puerto Aristo," Walt said. "Far southwest."

"They're taking your gifts. I'll show you the road. If they see you in the woods again, they'll shoot you."

Hannigan pounded Walt on the back. "Nicely done."

"What's this Starbreaker business, anyway?" Walt said to the young man. "You guys think I'm a demigod or something?"

"What are we, retards?" the man laughed. "It just sounds cool."

The other Maya took the coffee and salt and said goodbye to the young man, who led Walt and the others to a winding trail. As they stepped onto the relatively dry, uncluttered path, Hannigan's men grinned at Walt. Lorna gave him a look that might or might not have been significant. Walt winked.

Birds called from the branches. The young man swore and whacked his machete into a bright green snake curling across the trail. Hannigan picked up the corpse and coiled it into a grocery bag for dinner.

"Some of my friends say you flew to the ship," the young man said to Walt.

Walt snorted and yanked a thumb at his back. "See any wings?"

The man rolled his eyes. "With a plane."

"Sorry. No, it was a balloon."

"That's what I told them. I told them the aliens shot any planes that came near. They told me a balloon is too stupid."

Walt laughed. "They're probably right."

The young man looked ready to say more, then pointed ahead. "There it is."

Abruptly, it was there, a swath of asphalt bordered by encroaching grass and saplings. The young man pointed them southwest—Walt had already known that much, at least—then handed Walt a pen and a folded piece of paper that turned out to be blank.

"What's this?" Walt said.

The man's eyebrows crunched together. "Can I have your autograph?"

"What?"

"I'm sorry." He reached for the paper.

"No, of course," Walt said. "But if I see this on eBay, I'll hunt you down like a dog."

The young man blinked. Walt scrawled his name on the crumpled paper. Back when he used to see himself as the next Bukowski—a vision that had no evidence whatsoever besides a mutual affinity for beer—he used to dream about this moment, the signing of an autograph for a grateful fan. Those dreams usually involved chesty women and not short, watchful jungle-dwellers, but even so, it felt pretty damn good.

"Here you go."

The young man grinned and pocketed it. Hannigan rolled his eyes. Lorna gave Walt a small and unreadable smile.

"Told you I'd find the road," Walt said. "Now let's get a move on."

They managed a couple hours along the highway before Ken returned from scouting to let them know he'd found a tour lodge with a working well. Walt and Lorna stoked a fire while the others hauled up buckets of water to scrub off the jungle and refill their canteens. Once the smoke was boiling up the chimney, Walt filled his plastic bucket, headed a short distance into the twilight jungle, spread his tarp beneath him to keep away the worst of the crawlies, and rinsed off himself and his clothes. He dressed in his spare pants and brought the rest to the fire to dry off.

Gunshots pealed from the trees a quarter mile off, but the rhythm was all wrong for fighting, with as much as three seconds passing between shots. None of the men seemed alarmed. A few minutes later, Ken and one of the troops returned with a clutch of rats, already gutted. They placed them over the fire. Hannigan got the green snake out of his grocery bag and peeled the skin in one long tube. He laid the meat alongside the rats.

Walt didn't blink. He'd eaten far worse. At least it was cooked, and didn't have an exoskeleton—the hard little feet of crickets always stuck in his throat. Hannigan brought in oranges from the garden out back, long gone wild. He sliced them into wedges and passed them around while the greasy, gamey smell of the meat permeated the too-warm lodge.

"You really did it, didn't you?" he said to Walt.

Walt spat a seed toward the corner. "I'm starting to wish I hadn't."

"Yeah? So they could finish the job? Wipe us out completely?"

"At least then I wouldn't have to hear anyone else accuse me of being full of shit."

Hannigan scratched his growing beard with his toothpick. "Did you have any idea what you were doing?"

"Not really, no," Walt laughed. "Still want me?"

"It's more need than want. It's complicated."

"You shoot them, they die. What's so complicated about that?"

"It's more than just us and the aliens," the man said. "There's another group, too. Gang-bangers. For all I know they've taken Long Beach by now. We need every edge we can get."

Walt wiped orange juice from his face. "Listen, that's tragic and all, but I'm not coming with you to shoot people."

"Our first concern is the aliens. You want to bow out after we get them under wraps, I'm sure the boss-man will send you on your way with a smile."

Fat sizzled from the other room. Walt nibbled the peel of his orange. It was bitter, but bitter was better than most flavors. "What's it like up there? Do you guys have government?"

Hannigan tugged his beard. "We got a president of sorts."

"How about electricity? Running water?"

"We built a wind turbine and a little solar. But without a proper grid, it's all messed up. You know what we use to grind flour?"

"What?"

The other man leaned in, smiling. "A watermill."

Walt spat out a piece of peel. "Really? Do you make the workers wear clogs? Those little square hats?"

"Square hats?"

"Wait, I'm thinking about windmills. The Dutch. Who I guess are just as dead as everyone else. Man, the next generation won't know what the hell we're talking about, will they? They'll be as alien as the aliens."

Hannigan shook his head. "We got a few young ones, but we don't got time to teach them the old ways. We got fields to farm."

"At least you're not starving. How's the rest of the country doing?"

"Not great. We get a few wanderers every now and then, but from what I hear, the whole nation's a ghost town."

"At least American went out on top," Walt said. "Am I right?"

Hannigan gave him a look, then twitched his nostrils. "The rat's ready."

"I can't believe I consider that good news."

They ate. Split seven ways, there wasn't much meat to go around, the greasy little spears flavored with salt and pepper and a pinch of dried greens. Oregano? Thyme? It had been too long since Walt had either to remember. Whatever it was, after the slog through the jungle, it was good.

In the morning, they bottled all the water they could and set on down the road. Hannigan let one man range ahead and another trail behind. They were few enough and fit enough to do some jogging, padding along for ten or twenty minutes before one of them called for a slowdown. They made remarkable time—four to six miles per hour, sometimes more than fifty miles per day. It left Walt's feet in constant soreness, but his calluses prevented any major blisters.

He kept a sharp eye out for more tree-sign. Twice more, he had to detour into the jungle to circle around claimed territory. Once, they found an abandoned village, but all the dried food had long ago been eaten by rats and birds, and even the canned goods were useless, swollen with bacteria and botulism. Some of the gardens thrived and they spent a day harvesting bell peppers and potatoes and avocados and limes.

They passed a handful of real towns and cities, and three of the men made a desultory effort to get a car going, but they were rusted through by the tropical humidity, batteries dead for years. Probably all kinds of other shit wrong with them, too. Walt didn't know. Before the plague, he'd been a New Yorker.

It didn't matter. They emerged from the cover of the canopy four days later and followed the road through farmland gone to seed. The air was rich with pollen and salt. The horizon softened. A red crescent of sun sank into the sea.

"We left the boat a ways up north." Hannigan pointed past a pale cliff ten miles up the shore. "We'll camp here tonight, get to the ship and gear it up tomorrow, and shove off the day after that."

"How long's it been out here, a month?" Walt said. "I hope you hung onto your parking slip."

"We left a couple men with it."

"Hmm."

Hannigan eyed him. "Hmm what?"

"I wonder if we should be looking for more leather tarps."

They made camp in a farmhouse with a missing front door. Skeletons rested in three of the beds. A dog had gotten in at some point; sharded bone littered the floor, marrow cleaned out. The sun went down and they lit candles and ate potatoes baked the night before, which reminded Walt to check the kitchen for tinfoil. Tinfoil would be one of mankind's great losses. There might never be more of it, but it made a world of difference in keeping the grit and ash off your dinner. He lucked out and found a roll. Not that he expected to do a whole lot of cooking on the boat. Well, maybe they'd brought down a converted yacht or something. He added it to his pack.

He was plenty tired, but that made little difference to his body, which didn't seem to like the idea of closing its eyes on the desolate beach. After an hour of tossing, he got up, found his shoes, and wandered into the warm night. Insects buzzed from the boundary of the advancing jungle. Walt walked down the road until it dead-ended, then continued across the grassy dunes to the water's edge. A silhouette waited above the tideline. The moon and stars showed the man's gun.

"That you?" Walt called.

"Yep." Hannigan put the gun away. "Though if I'd known it was you, I wouldn't have bothered drawing down."

"Are you saying you could beat me down barehanded? I wouldn't argue. You look like shaved Donkey Kong."

"I used to play that game." The man grinned and spat into the surf. "What're you doing out here?"

"I think," Walt said, "that I'm scared."

"Scared?" Hannigan gestured to the starry night. "What's there to be scared of? Besides the panthers, pythons, and poisonous frogs?"

"Of Los Angeles. The aliens."

"After you damn near eradicated them?"

"Obviously I missed a few."

"Yeah, and they ought to be shitting their alien pants about you."

Walt snorted. "I was terrified the whole time I was on the ship. Anyway, the months of my life leading up to that point were pretty intense. I was in the right place for it. I haven't tangled with anything scarier than a barracuda in years."

"Barracuda are pretty nasty."

"I had a spear. And I think it was sick."

Hannigan scrunched his brow. "How do you know what a sick barracuda looks like?"

"Because when I cut it open it was more worms than meat."

"That's a thing I would rather not have heard." He tipped back his head and gazed at the shameless spread of stars. "Hard to believe something so pretty brought us something so nasty."

"Ah, those things don't care about us," Walt said, and instantly felt better about his place in the cosmos. "What brings you here?"

Hannigan shook his head at the sky. "Nothing."

"Then why don't you combine that nothing with another nothing and go to sleep?"

"It's my wife."

Walt glanced down the beach. "Married to the sea, are you?"

"She's out there on a mission of her own." Hannigan gestured vaguely. "I shouldn't complain. The world's still so far from safe. We ever want peace, we all have to absorb some risk."

"Be that as it may, how much would you pay for a cell phone right now?"

"You got one?" The man laughed. "Trade you for all the coffee beans you can carry."

Walt grinned, then walked down the beach until he got tired enough to sleep. The others got up early, clumping around on the hardwood floors. Walt woke groggy and angry. He supposed he could sleep on the boat.

They pan-fried bananas and boiled a few bivalves and small crabs someone had collected from the rocks. There was no proper walkway along the sea—turned out rural Mexican waterfronts were slightly less developed than Brooklyn boardwalks or the strands of Los Angeles—so they hiked along the grassy, hard-packed sand. Before the sun climbed to noon, they made their way around the northern cliffs where Hannigan had left the boat.

The sun beat down on an empty shore. Small gulls floated on the wind. Round gray birds waited for each wave to come to a stop, then darted into the foam and pecked at the water-softened sand. Walt shielded his eyes against the glare and got out his binoculars.

"Dude, where's your boat?"

"Must be further up," Hannigan said. "Around the next bend."

It wasn't. It lay in pieces across the shore, white foam lapping charred fiberglass and tangled rigging. A foot tumbled in the surf, bone sticking from a soggy calf, neatly sliced below the knee.

5

"Where did you go on your trip?" Raina said.

She stood at the railing, watching the fins of the dolphins arc through the waves. They weren't very playful today. No leaping or chasing. All business.

She had waited until they went out fishing together to ask her dad these things. She wanted to see what he said when her mom wasn't there. Parents were much better at lying to you when they were together.

"To stay with friends," he said.

"Did you have a good time?"

"Very."

A dolphin swam alongside the boat, turned on its side, and stared up at Raina. "Where do they live?"

"Up north," he gestured. "Along the bay."

"Close to the ship?"

"The mothership? Sure. You can see it from their front yard."

"They must be weird," she said.

Her dad laughed. "It's just a bunch of old metal."

He was wrong. And she thought he was lying. He reached for the crank to the winch. She picked up her club. When they finished and sailed home, she brought the coolers to her mom and lingered at the fire in the smell of woodsmoke and fresh fish.

"Where did you go the other day?" she said.

"Friends." Her mom glanced up from the grill's lattice and smiled. "They want to see you. Maybe another time."

"Where do they live?"

She waved north. "Marina Del Rey, I think? I'm not really sure where the old borders are."

"How did you meet them?"

"At the Dunemarket. Couple months ago. I swear I see new faces every time we go there."

Raina went around front to wash up, suddenly doubtful of herself. But two days later, she came back from the ruins and didn't let the screen door slam. She caught her parents by surprise in the kitchen; her dad saw her and stopped mid-sentence. He grinned at her, eyes lined with lies.

Raina went to the mall to talk to Martin, but he wasn't there. She walked downhill past the park where the skeletons sprawled from vast concrete pipes. She didn't know what the pipes had been for—they were big enough to funnel torrents of stormwater, but they didn't lead anywhere—but they had wound up as mass graves.

A flock of parrots flew past, red heads vivid atop their green bodies, cackling madly. She hid behind a tree and waited for them to go away. You couldn't trust a thing that laughed at the dead. Once it was safe, she trotted through the silent houses. Most were fenced, but their pickets and chain-link hadn't been able to keep out the only thing that mattered.

Martin and his mother lived on the south coast in a house that looked like a shrunk-down fairy-castle. Statues of angelic babies grew mossy in the yard. A high, peaked roof cast plenty of shade. There was no one out front, so she peeked through the porthole cut into the door to the side yard. Martin was down on the beach with a weathervane flapping in the wind.

"Hey," Raina said, padding through the sand. "Did your mom leave on a trip last week?"

Martin glanced up from a little black box connected to the vane by a string. "How'd you know that? Are you always stalking me?"

"Because I think they're planning to stand against the men from Catalina." She explained how her neighbors left at the same time as her parents, about the stranger on the road, and the single question he'd asked Wendell. "They're lying. They're lying but I can't prove it."

"Wait, they want to fight? What should we do?"

She gazed at him steadily. "Help them."

"That's crazy. We'll get killed."

"My parents are already involved. Already in danger. I won't sit by while they risk their lives."

Martin wiped his nose on his sleeve and twiddled a knob on the little black box. "I might have something for you. Watch my stuff while I go get it."

He set the box on the weathervane and ran through the yard to his house. She stared at the weathervane's churning wind-cups. Did he expect a shark to wallow up on the sand and eat it whole? Martin was strange. He worried too much about the wrong things. He came back a minute later and handed her a black device riddled with buttons.

"What's this?" she said.

"A tape recorder." He grinned. "So you can hear what they talk about when you're not around."

"It still works?"

"A lot of the purely mechanical stuff does. This one was probably ten years old before the plague hit. All you do is push these buttons." He clicked down two of them at once, then showed her how to shut it off. "The tape only records for an hour. You'll have to set it when you know they'll be alone together."

She tried the buttons for herself. "What about the batteries?"

"I put in good ones."

"What if they run out before I catch them?"

His face crumpled. "I don't have many good ones, Raina."

"What are you going to use them for? Is it more important than my parents' lives?" She held out her hand. "I'll bring them back if I don't use them up."

"You have to look for more for me, too."

"Fine."

He nodded unhappily and ran back to the house, reemerging with a clear plastic sleeve of four. She put them in her pack and wrapped her spare shirt around the tape recorder.

"I'll try not to drop it."

"Don't!" he said, reaching out.

She laughed and walked home. Out of sight beyond the trees, she got out the recorder and clicked it on and off, murmuring into it, testing it. Hearing her own tinny voice was uncanny, as if she were long dead and listening to her own captured spirit.

Her parents made a ritual of brushing and flossing their teeth before bed; except in the winter, they did this out back, where they could spit into the yard. Raina used the time to hide the recorder in their room. The first night she got nothing but the noise of the tape itself, a faint hiss like a wave forever sweeping up the shore. She had started taping too early. The second night she heard low murmurs and then laughter and fleshy smacks and moans. She listened for two minutes, then fast-forwarded; when she started it up again, they were speaking. She rewinded to the beginning of the conversation, which was dreamy and largely inaudible, clusters of words fighting to be heard from beneath the chair cushion Raina had zipped the tape recorder inside.

"...worried..." her mom said. "...so wild..."

"Not wild," her dad said. "Independent...fine."

"That's what worries...even need us?"

"These days? ...hope not." He coughed. "...showed her she doesn't have to live like some..."

Her mother laughed. "...had to cut the dirt off with an axe. Oh well. She'll be..."

The rest was indistinguishable. The recorder shut off with a click.

The third night Raina heard goodnights and the thunk of a glass set on a table. The fourth night she set the recorder wrong and taped nothing at all. On the recording of the fifth night, she could hear them crisply—she had snuck the tape recorder into the bookshelf, and learned to turn the volume all the way up. Aside from the constant low hiss and occasional warble of the tape, she could hear them as easily as if she'd been crouched in the room herself.

"When do you leave?" her mom said.

Her dad grunted. "Three days."

"Same as before?"

"Yeah. Bryson's."

"What this time?"

He chuckled. "What do you think?"

"Is that even plausible?"

"If we can make it look like an accident."

Her mom was quiet for a while. "It sounds dangerous."

He laughed. "You think it sounds dangerous to sabotage a gang of heavily armed killers?"

"My question is why it can't be someone else."

"It is someone else," he said. "It's half the shore. Listen. It's this or we leave."

"I know."

"After the tribute, we're barely making ends meet. We don't have enough left to trade. That means old clothes. No shot at gasoline. No medicine—"

"I know," her mom said.

Her dad gentled his voice. "I don't want Raina growing up in this. We either leave or get rid of them. I don't think starting over in this world is any less dangerous than fighting for what we've already built."

Her mom got very quiet. "I know."

"I love you."

"Yeah, yeah."

The wet noises followed. Raina clicked off the tape. The screen door banged closed. She pocketed the tape recorder and went to the kitchen, where her dad took hard flatbread from the counter and dusted it with salt.

"I want to go with you to see Bryson," she said.

He set down the salt shaker. "Bryson who?"

"Bryson who's going to attack the Catalinans."

"God damn it. Did your mom tell you that?"

She shook her head. "I listened."

He tipped back his head and stared at the ceiling, hands on his hips. "You are the sneakiest little rat. What did you do, hide outside the window?"

She smiled. Rats didn't reveal their secrets. "I want to help fight them."

"Then you're going to be a disappointed little girl."

"I'll follow you to Bryson's."

"So I won't go." He raised his eyebrows. "You don't like them, do you? The islanders?"

She stared right back at him. "I hate them."

"Then stay out of this. Don't try to follow me. Don't try to help. If you do anything to put yourself in danger, I'll cut my involvement on the spot."

Anger shook up from her bones. "That's not fair."

"Fair." He turned to the window. "I should ground you."

"What's ground me?"

"It's what parents used to do to kids who were having too much fun." He laughed, then covered his mouth.

She glared at him, fists clenched. "If it's that important, we should all help."

"What's important is that you have a future. The kind of future we imagined when we took you in." He raised his tanned and rope-roughened hands, silencing her. "This isn't a discussion. Bring it up again, and I'll never see Bryson again."

Raina glared more, but it did about as much good as she expected. She got to hear about their talk again when her mom got home from Wendell's. Her dad left three days later and her mom hung by her shoulder, watching, refusing to let her stray from the yard. Raina thought about going anyway—her mother couldn't stop her physically, and unless the woman nailed the windows shut and stood over her all night, she had no way to keep Raina in bed. But unless she made an offering to the moon, it would be hard to track her dad's cold trail, and if she tried, it would mean her mom would wake to the knowledge she had a husband who couldn't protect her and a daughter who didn't respect her.

Instead, Raina decided to work harder, to fill the cellar with canned perch and mussels, to mend the nets and scrape the hull, to prove she was no longer the child she'd been when they found her. He had decided to fight after all. If he wouldn't let her help directly, she could still pitch in by freeing up his time to prepare with the other rebels.

She brought the tape recorder and the two batteries she hadn't used back to Martin. The men came with their boats twice more. The nights grew less cold while the spring days turned blustery and rainy. Green sprouted from the garden. Her dad left once or twice per week, spending as much time away from the house as he did in it. Her mother went with him every second or third trip and they warned Raina to stay near the house and out of sight of strangers.

The men came again, extracting their portion of food and fuel from her father. By now it was a routine. Neither side needed to speak, though sometimes Trig—the man who'd carried the club—tried to needle her father. He never gave any sign he'd heard.

The raiders shoved off from the pier. Just a week later, they returned.

"Run," her dad told her. She pounded down the planks of their dock. A gunshot cracked the sky above her head and she skidded to a stop on the salt-worn wood. In the boat's prow, Trig pointed a rifle at her middle. He bobbed with the swells as the other men trimmed sails and guided the boat in to rest.

The tall bald man was the first off the boat. He smiled at her dad, deep folds warping the sun-worn skin around his eyes and mouth.

"We're here for your guns," said the man. "Don't make me take more than things."

Trig smiled at Raina. Her dad swabbed sweat from his brow. "We don't have any guns around here."

The bearded man barked. "And I have no lice. Give me your guns and don't make me do evil."

Her dad bulged his cheek. "Seems to me I'm not in much position to make you do anything."

"That's because you chose to have children instead of soldiers." He flipped his hand toward the yard. "Search the house until it feels used."

Trig laughed and jumped to the dock. Ten more men joined him, jarring the planks, bumping past Raina with the smell of sweat and sea. Their boot heels yanked grass from the yard. Her father grabbed her by the upper arm. The men filed inside their house. Wood thumped; glass smashed. The home went silent. Her mother emerged, wide-eyed, teeth bared. Raina's dad glanced at the man with the beard, who ignored him, then pulled Raina across the dock. In the sandy grass, he put his other arm around his wife, holding her in place while the soldiers tore their home to the floor.

The islanders came out with two shotguns, two pistols, and the rifle with the scope, along with a duffel bag sagging with ammunition. They set it all at the bearded man's feet.

He squinted. "Is that it?"

Her father's sad smile confirmed it. "Is there anything else you'd like? My shoes? My teeth?"

The big man stooped, arms spread as if he would rip the dock up by the roots, then picked up the rifle and fitted it to his shoulder. He aimed at a pelican wafting on the thermals, tracking its slow drift.

"Just the one rifle? What if it broke?"

"I don't suppose I'd notice," her dad said. "We never used it."

The man shook his head and rose. "My God, man, you've got to think of your future." He gestured at the boat and the men picked up the guns and took them onboard. "Although it's moot now. Firearms are henceforth banned from the mainland without express writ by King Me. The penalty for unlicensed ownership of firearms shall be death by firing squad."

"What if raiders come?" her mother said, voice shaky and hot. "What should we do, reason with them?"

The man snorted. "We'll protect you."

"While you're safe on your island?"

"Then we'll avenge you." He raised his thick brown eyebrows and leaned down until his gaze was level with hers. "I see what happens on my land."

He turned and hauled himself up the rope ladder to the boat. The house was a mess of shattered glass and scattered papers and upturned drawers. Raina helped sweep the broken water jugs from the garage into a pile and then buried it in the pit in the back where they put the things that couldn't be mulched or burned. They folded away the last of the clothes by candlelight.

Raina left in the night. In the morning, she was the first one up, and went out to scrape salt from the tarps while her parents boiled and drank their tea. Her mom walked uphill to speak to Wendell. Her dad went to the shack by the dock and sat down to mend the net. Raina brought him a small walnut box. He frowned and took it, hands dropping under its unexpected weight. Metal skittered across wood. He slid his fingernails under the lid and removed it. A revolver sat beside red boxes of bullets.

He gaped. "Where did you get this?"

"From a dead man," she said.

He touched the grip. "We shouldn't have this."

"I can get more. Everyone can have one."

Her dad looked up sharply. "No more. You can't be found with these."

"How are you going to fight back without any guns?"

"That's for us to worry about. If I catch you with one of these again, your only worry will be what it's like to spend the rest of your life locked in the trunk of a car." He winced and lowered his gaze to the box, which he refused to set down. "We'll bury it. In case there's trouble. Do not bring back another. You hear?"

She nodded, but he'd taken this one. He yielded. It was what he did. Raina had seem him yield to her mom for a long time and assumed that was what husbands did—bow to the wind, then straighten once it calmed—but he yielded to the Catalinans, too. Even when they hurt her mom. Each time they pressed, he bent. Each time he bent, they came back and pressed harder. Someday he would break.

Unless she pressed back and straightened him out.

She went to bed. She knew from the tapes her parents never stayed up longer than an hour after lights-out. She waited just longer than that, then got up and got her two biggest bags and her travel kit. She crept across the wooden floors in her socks, then put on her shoes outside, where the air smelled like old seaweed and fresh crabs. She cut north up the hill past the ruins of the manors. The signs along the winding road warned her to watch out for horses. The first time she'd seen these, she'd been excited, but there were no horses left.

Often the woods were so deep she saw nothing but trees. A tall wooden fence rose from the wilderness. She climbed through the hole she'd dug underneath it. Behind a screen of grass and weeds, a brick house sat beneath an umbrella of strong-smelling pines. Raina clicked on her flashlight and went to the shed around back and pulled the carpet away from the trapdoor. Before descending, she drew her symbol between her collarbones, tracing a circle, then bisecting it down the middle. She needed its help. The bunker was a bad place.

It was a liar. It had promised the man who built it safety, but caught in the beam of her flashlight, he was as dead as the TV in the wall across from his bed. Half-mummified in the dry, cool air. Jaw hanging open. Lips shrunken from his teeth, which were parted as if in the middle of a silent, stupid groan. Crusty brown spots stained his sheets and the thin carpet, but when Raina had first sniffed them—she hadn't wanted to, but something made her, the same way it used to make her poke dead dogs with sticks—they hadn't smelled like scat. They were bloodspots. He'd set up his fortress and died like all the others.

Which meant this place was hers for the taking.

Some of the cans on the pantry shelves bulged with mold, and most of the cereal and chips tasted stale despite never being opened, but no mice or bugs had gotten inside, and the bags of rice were clean and white. The goods in the adjoining room hadn't been used, either: great racks of paper towels, toilet paper, disinfectant, batteries, soap, shampoo, medicine in nicotine-brown plastic bottles. All of it right there. The armory was lightly dusty but just as untouched.

Rifles stood in wooden racks. Pistols hung on pegs. She knew very little about guns. Except the three times her dad had made her practice with the rifle, she had never fired one, even during the year she'd been alone, because guns made noise, and when you made noise, bad things came for you. Men appeared in windows. The shrieking ships creased the sky and let loose monsters that never tired.

The true way was to become a shadow. To disappear with the daylight. To walk behind without being seen. That was why she liked knives. They were cold and metal and silent and they reminded her to hide in the cracks and strike when the back was turned.

She'd left the bunker virtually untouched, but not from fear or respect of the dead. The dead were there to feed the living. This was the lesson of mushrooms and maggots. She had left it be because of the lesson of squirrels, which she had often stolen fruits and nuts from: when there is plenty, leave it buried. With her new mom and dad, she'd had no need for food or weapons. The man with the beard had changed that.

She picked bullets from the red and green boxes and fit them to the guns to know they were right. On its own, a bullet was light, but in boxes of fifty they weighed her down like little anchors. She took four rifles and two pistols and two boxes of bullets for each, got packages of unworn white t-shirts from the room next to the pantry, and wrapped them around the guns so they wouldn't clank or break. She hiked the long pack up her back and swept the flashlight around the corners of the room to make sure the shadows fled from her, then turned her back and climbed the metal steps. She locked the door behind her.

It didn't feel good to be traveling with something so heavy, but the night was still late, and she walked home in thick darkness. She took the road to the top of the hill and then slipped off the shoulder to cut through the trees and tall grass. She paused once at a clearing to gaze down at her house.

Its windows were as dark as the bay. She hoisted the bag and continued down the hill. Her father had taken the revolver. He would take these, too, because of what the men from Catalina had done to Raina's mother and to him, and he would pass them to his friends and ask for more. Soon, the bay would be free.

She should have known better than to think about the future. The future was a shadow, too. If you were arrogant enough to think you could see its shape, it smiled and slipped the knife between your ribs.

A flashlight snapped on from the pines a few yards to her left. "Stop right there!"

She raised a hand to shield her eyes from the glare.

"I said stop! Hands in the air and freeze!"

Raina lifted her hands. The man turned and shouted to someone uphill, illuminating himself with the flashlight. He had a burn scar on his left cheek, which he'd failed to conceal with a haphazard beard. He was one of the soldiers, one of the men who'd taken the guns from her father.

Raina tensed. The guns pulled on her shoulders with drowning weight.

6

The severed foot surged up the shore on a white tide of foam. The wave pulled away, beaching it on the yellow sand. The bone was cut cleanly, ringed with black on its severed tip.

Walt looked up and gazed across the windswept water. "We have to go."

Hannigan knelt and touched the sea-slick hair on the bodyless calf. "We aren't doing a damn thing until we search for survivors. Find out who attacked us."

"Do you see that bone?"

"No. No, I don't."

"What?" Walt said. "It's right there. The white thing sticking out of the gross thing."

"I see the man it was a part of." Hannigan rose and drew his pistol. "And I aim to avenge him."

"The only thing you're aiming to do is confuse the next local when he stumbles over your foot." Walt jerked his thumb uphill at the shrubs screening the beach. "The boat's gone. We have to get out of here."

"I want two on the beach keeping watch. Everyone else searches."

Two of Hannigan's men waded into the surf, shoulders swaying, and reached for the flotsam swirling in the ceaseless waves. Ken knelt and wrapped the strap of his rifle around his forearm and peered far out to sea.

"Shit," Walt said. "I'm going to head up the hill and get a better view."

Hannigan nodded absently and strode into the water, jerking his knees high to avoid the worst of the waves. Walt turned his back and jogged up the dune to where the grass sprouted from the sand. Three trees deep into the burgeoning jungle, he crouched down and watched. Soldiers staggered through the surf and pulled the wreckage up to shore. He felt suddenly foolish and ashamed in a way he hadn't encountered in a long time. Brush snapped to his left. He gasped and ran deeper into the jungle, swatting at broad leaves and low branches.

A man screamed in fear. Walt whirled. Through the thicket of green, the shoreline boiled. A blue bolt lanced across the water and cut the scream short. Walt lurched forward, ankle turning on the muddy ground. He limped through the pain. Rifles banged and roared. Men wailed. The surf sighed. Very soon, it went dead quiet. He heard nothing but his own ragged breathing.

His ankle creaked and he dropped like a rock. He balled up in the wet grass and slick dirt, grasping at his foot. Leaves shuffled. Walt got out his gun and went still.

Lorna crept from behind a curtain of fronds, face frozen in panic. She passed within eight feet. The green swallowed her up.

Walt gritted his teeth. "Lorna!"

She made a quavering noise. "Who's there?"

"Walt. I'm back here."

She swung into view, breathing in quick jerks. "What's happening?"

"Aliens. You need to run. If you hear one coming, drop and freeze until it goes away."

"What are you doing there?"

"Leg's hurt," he said. "I'm kind of stuck here."

"I don't know the way." Lorna gestured to the wall of trees. "I'm staying with you."

Walt pressed his knuckles to his forehead. He should have let her go without a word. "That's not a great— "

Something heavy sloughed through the grass. An irregular patter of steps followed. Walt bugged his eyes and gestured her down. Lorna glanced back, mouth agape, then crushed herself beside him beneath the bushes. He hovered his mouth over her ear.

"Don't. Move."

The thing sloughed nearer. A gray shape clarified from the ferns and trunks, seven feet tall, a scramble of wavering, snaky limbs and hard, spidery legs. Two fist-sized eyes bulged from an oval head. Silver tools winked from its pincers. It slid past, tentacles whispering in the muck.

Lorna shuddered. Walt clamped an arm around her, pinning her still. A second creature followed, two thick tentacles bobbing above its head, oscillating side to side like long, lumpy radar dishes. Walt knew he could bellow the National Anthem in perfect safety—the things were as deaf as a stump—but he couldn't make himself speak until the rasp of their passage faded into the trees.

"We're just going to stay here a while," he murmured.

"What if they come back?"

"Then that's how we know they truly love us."

"What?"

"Keep playing possum. That's our best chance."

She gave him a look like he'd just swallowed a live and very warty toad, but she stayed put. His ankle throbbed. Something crawled across his neck and he stiffened against the instinct to slap it. Lorna's breathing slowed against him. A long time later, distant appendages trudged overlappingly toward the beach.

Lorna lifted her head once they were gone. "Are they gone?"

Walt stared at the horrendous orange caterpillar undulating along the underside of the leaf above his face. "While longer."

After another couple minutes, he glanced toward the beach, saw plenty of jungle, and got the duct tape from his bag to wrap a long strip around his ankle. He was no doctor—although if he decided he was, there weren't exactly any boards around to challenge his qualifications—but he was pretty sure the tape would help. He glanced around for a straight and sturdy branch.

Lorna gestured beachward. "We have to help them."

Walt looked up from his work. "If you think that's a good idea, it's no wonder you need my help."

"And you think it's a good idea to just leave them there?"

"Hang on a minute." Walt trimmed the twigs from a thick stick and used a pair of shoelaces to lash a short, fat crossbar to one end, forming a crooked T. "This is weird. Like, highly coincidental. Any chance they followed you from L.A.?"

"Why would they do that?"

"Maybe you weren't the only ones looking for me."

She tore her gaze away from the direction of the beach and met his eyes. "How would they know to find you here?"

"They're aliens. For all I know, they know my Social Security number and that the first CD I bought was Kris Kross." He thumped his improvised stick against the ground, testing its handle. It could function as a short crutch, a long cane, or, if things got truly desperate, as a pretty good club. "Okay, let's get out of here."

Lorna gestured at his crutch. "I thought you were getting ready to help them."

"Help who, the dead people? Do you think they need us to tell them how to lie there?"

Her mouth swung open. "We have to do something!"

Walt laughed "You just spent two hours lying in the dirt. By now they'd have bled out from a paper cut. You didn't go down sooner because you knew there was nothing to be done."

She lurched forward, hand hardening into a fist. "What a hero. Sitting there in your own filth."

She hunkered down and crept toward the beach, vanishing behind the crush of stems and leaves. Her feet swished through the undergrowth. After a minute, he heard nothing but the whir of insects. A minute longer, a long, pained scream ripped through the moist air. Walt flinched. The bugs droned on.

Leaves stirred on the ground. Walt went still, pistol held on his knee. Lorna wandered to a stop in front of him, her face as frozen as the caterpillar's still eating the leaf above his head.

"I thought you'd been shot," Walt said.

"They're gone."

"Back into the water, probably. They look like they could survive there fine."

"Hannigan. Ken. Reynolds. My people. There's nothing left but sand and blood."

Walt moved his blunt black pistol to his pocket. "I'm sorry."

Her eyes brightened. "How did you know they were coming?"

"The leg on the beach was cut off with a laser. In my experience, that's a general hallmark of a non-human presence."

There wasn't much more to say. He used the crutch to lever himself to his feet, then started back into the jungle. His ankle hurt, but supported by the stick, he could walk well enough to get by.

Lorna followed. "Where are you going?"

"Away from the monsters who may have been trying to kill me. Ideally to someplace with a roof. If I'm very lucky, there will be a bed."

"Nothing's changed."

"Except the transportive qualities of the boat that was supposed to get us there. And the lifelike properties of everyone who was supposed to go with us. Alone on foot from here to California?"

He walked on. Wordless, she followed. When he looked back, her face was wild and tear-damp, infinitely more wretched than her silence would indicate. He paused a few times to rest his ankle and listen to the jungle. Sometimes the birds shut up when big mean things were moving around, but he didn't hear any eerie silences. Either the birds were too stupid to recognize an alien when they saw it, or he wasn't being followed.

Except by Lorna, of course. But if she wanted to follow him all the way to Chichen Itza, that was her business.

After a few miles through the humid, deeply shadowed jungle floor, he followed a path to a road to a house with broken windows and peeling paint. He went to the bathroom around back, then plunked down on the back porch to rest and think. Afternoon sunlight sliced through the trees in coin-sized beams. It had been a long time since he'd run into anything like what had happened on the beach. He was surprised by his reaction to it. Troubled, even. He knew he wouldn't always have hidden in the jungle while the others died.

His vague guilt didn't last. The idea of "bravery" was a social construction meant to save people who couldn't save themselves by sacrificing those who could. Anyway, there were fights you could win and those you couldn't. The latter certainly included being ambushed on a strange shore by laser-wielding tentacle-horrors.

Mostly, he was annoyed that it had happened at all. It would have been fun to sail up to Los Angeles and smash up the last remaining alien bastion. Now that the boat was gone, along with the team of well-armed and trained men to lead the way...well, it just seemed like an awful lot of effort. Too much risk, too little reward.

"I'm going home tomorrow." He repositioned his muddy shoes on the scuffed wooden porch. "If I were you, I wouldn't go back to the beach."

Lorna glanced up. Her face was still locked in that awful, soundless grief. With perverse effort—like a shattered glass pulling itself back together—she smoothed out her face.

"I told you," she said flatly. "Nothing's changed."

"How much talent does it really take to shoot up a bunch of alien eggs? Hell, Ripley was just a crewman on an unarmed ship."

Lorna laughed. "Let me replay what just happened. We were attacked by the same things we're fighting up north. We had trained soldiers. A couple ex-Marines. And you're the only one who survived."

"Am I? Then I'd kindly ask you to quit haunting me."

"I lived because I followed you." She stood and shuddered, clamping her arms across her chest. "You think this is proof we don't need you?"

He gestured at the jungle. "Even if that were true, our ride got blown to smithereens. Unless you know some friendly dolphins, we're out of luck."

"They say you walked all the way across America."

"They do?"

"It's no further from here to L.A."

"Walking across a continent is the sort of thing you really only need to experience once." He glared across the red dirt and unkempt weeds of the back yard. "I'm out. I'm sorry. You'll find a way without me."

Her eyes flashed. She hugged herself hard enough to snap ribs, but something else in her broke first. She sank to her knees on the porch, face disintegrating into anguish.

"We're the last generation of the old world. My people are trying to preserve it. To hang onto what little is left so our children don't grow into animals. What if we're the only ones? What if the aliens snuff out our last candle?"

He shrugged. "Who cares? We'll be dead."

Her cheeks twitched. Grimacing, she fought off the emotions attempting to overwhelm her. "Then do it for me."

"Don't take this the wrong way, because it's also true of literally everyone else on the planet, but I don't know who the hell you are."

She lowered her head, dark hair spilling over her face, and climbed into his lap. Her hand was warm on her neck. Her thighs pressed against his.

"What are you doing?" he said.

"You're the man who saved the world." Her breath was as warm as her skin, buffeting his ear, sending a chill down his spine. The most intense human contact he'd felt in three years had been a handshake. She ran her fingers through the hair above his ear, avoiding his eyes. "I can't get home by myself. I need you."

While his brain attempted to make sense of what was unfolding on top of him, his body took action. He reached up and kissed her.

7

The man with the scarred cheek aimed his pistol and ordered her to drop the bag. She did. He told her to turn around. She did. He tied her hands with a thin cord and yanked it tight.

Finally, she understood how her dad must have felt.

The man made her sit down, then unzipped her bag. Gunmetal gleamed beneath his flashlight. He chuckled, a strange mix of mirth and regret.

"Got us a situation," he hollered into the darkness. A twig snapped. A silhouette approached through the trees. The scarred man waved. "Caught me a young one. Careful, she's armed."

Another Catalinan drew up and raised his brows at the guns. "No kidding. Shit. Well, Karslaw's still in with the family."

"Might ask them outside," her captor said. "Try to keep the why quiet."

The second man tapped his nose and headed toward the house. The burned man nudged Raina with his toe.

"Get up."

"Where are we going?" she said.

He jerked his head toward the back porch. "Where we'll be able to see a little better."

As she decided to run, the man grabbed her bonds and twisted, cutting into her wrists. His strength was bullish, irresistible; he marched her to the well-swept concrete. Candles now flickered through the kitchen window. A pair of soldiers walked out, followed by the tall bearded man—Karslaw—her parents, and one more soldier.

Karslaw eyed the man with the burned cheek. "What's up?"

"Found this," the man said, jerking her by the cord. "And this." He flopped the bag at Karslaw's feet. Rifles clunked.

Karslaw sniffed hard, mouth bunching. "Those look like guns."

"Yep."

"I'm confused. We made it very clear that guns are illegal."

The man nodded. "Yup."

"This poses a problem." Karslaw palmed his beard and turned to Raina's father. "Is this your daughter?"

"I told her to leave them alone," her dad said. "She doesn't know any better."

The bearded man sighed and turned to Raina. "Sweetie, why did you get these guns?"

She shrugged awkwardly, hands tied behind her. "So you could get rid of them."

"Let me provide you an incentive to tell the truth." He bent down, touched her cheek, and pushed his thumb into the corner of her eye. She squealed and squirmed, but the burned man held fast with his implacable strength. Karslaw's nail gouged into the wetness of her eye. "Why did you—?"

Rage reddened her sight. "Because you hurt people!"

"I judge her competent to stand trial and cognizant of her crime," Karslaw said. He drew a gun, put it to her father's head, and pulled the trigger.

Her mom screamed. So did she. So did one of the soldiers. Her dad staggered forward, looked Raina in the eyes, gasped one garbled word, and fell on his face.

Her mom fell too, wailing over the roar of the surf. Raina wrenched her wrists free of the burned man and head-butted Karslaw in the gut. He dropped back a step, cocked his fist, and slugged her in the side of the head. She collapsed, star-sighted. He leveled his gun at her mother's temple. Raina called out. Her mom looked up.

Karslaw's expression shifted. He clucked his tongue and pointed his pistol at the sky. "I've changed my mind."

"They got guns," said the burned man. "The law's the law."

"And I'm the man who made it." The quarter moon lit the cunning on his face. "Execution has its place, but it's very wasteful. Do you think we're in position to be throwing things away?"

The man looked uncertain. "Generally speaking, there's another use for just about everything. Like in the Scaveteria."

"Exactly my thinking. So let's recycle them instead." He holstered his gun and gestured at the ship. "Throw them on the boat."

Hands hoisted Raina. Cords cut into her arms. She kicked out, striking an unseen jaw. A man peeped in pain and socked her in the ribs. Raina curdled in on herself, fighting for breath. Grass whooshed below her face, smelling dewy and sweet. It switched to sand and then the damp boards of the dock. She swayed, breath jolting again as a man slung her onto his shoulders and clambered up the ladder to the boat.

Her mother screamed her husband's name, hoarse and broken. "Will! Will!"

The man carrying Raina dropped her on the deck. She sobbed, choking for air, cheek pressed against the cold, textured fiberglass. Shoes tromped up and down. Men called instructions back and forth. Her mom cried in whinnying jags. An engine burbled—much too weakly for a boat this size; they must only use it for marina maneuvering—and the ship drifted from the dock.

Raina rolled on her back, chest heaving, finally able to fill her lungs. It was the dead of night and the wind was dim and they left the little engine on, pushing the boat out to sea.

It was another minute before she felt well enough to sit up. A candle flickered from the front window of the house, untended. Karslaw's words about wasting things was just empty air. He didn't care if the house burned down.

Nearly half a mile of black water sloshed between Raina and that last light. On the side of the main cabin, a couple of men wrestled with the rigging. Another raider sat up front, binoculars clenched to his eyes. She wriggled around for a better look at the back of the boat and fell on one elbow. The man with the burn on his cheek loomed from around the cabin and gave her the eye.

"You hang right there," he said. He swung from sight.

Raina's mom sobbed somewhere below decks. The boat pitched beneath her. As it dropped down a gentle wave, she bounced to her feet, reeling three steps as she found her balance. The man in the bow turned at her footsteps, binoculars still held to his face. Raina dashed toward the chrome railing and leapt headfirst off the ship.

"Man overboard!" a man yelled.

She hunched her shoulders tight to her neck. Her head hit the black. The water was very cold and swallowed her up like a giant lamprey. She tumbled through the darkness, her momentum turning her belly-up somewhere beneath the surface of the waves. She hung under the water for a moment, telling her nerves to calm and her lungs to wait, then kicked up toward the moon's stingy light. Her nose bobbed into the brisk and open air.

Flashlights swung across the water, dazzling the crests of the waves. Saltwater ran down her sinuses, rough on the back of her throat. She spat and breathed and kicked. Men yelled at each other, voices muffled whenever the water closed over her ears. She kicked hard, knifing up high enough to see the weak yellow flicker painting the far-off kitchen window, then rolled on her back and kicked toward the light.

At times it felt like she wasn't moving at all. Her hands remained tied and she didn't try to use them except when she threatened to slip below the waves. Then, she flapped madly, straining her neck. Her legs threshed the water. The men's voices carried through the darkness with startling clarity, whole sentences preserved above the background hum of the departing engine.

She kicked and kicked and kicked. When her legs burned too hard to go on, she rolled onto her stomach. Before their first time fishing from the boat, her dad had taught her the dead man's float for if she ever fell overboard. It was scary, but if you hung there facedown, you could stay right on the surface, popping up for regular breaths until you weren't tired anymore. The burn in her thighs receded. She reoriented herself to the stars, turned on her back, and continued.

Her face and ribs ached where she'd been struck. Her strokes grew looser, inefficient. Waves rolled and hushed over the sand. She had to float facedown again and the noise of the breakers receded as the current tugged her away from land.

Numbly, she resumed swimming. Waves swelled, surging her closer to shore. One curled over her head, spinning her under the scouring saltwater. Something rubbery tangled her legs. She let the water calm and kicked until her nose hit the air. Another wave slapped her against the hard-packed sand. She groaned out a huff of air, wind knocked from her lungs. Her legs were too noodly to stand.

Using her elbows, she rolled up the beach until her face mashed into dry sand.

Her chest hitched without end. She spat repeatedly, but the taste of salt wouldn't leave her mouth. Cold water dribbled down her nose and the back of her throat. She had to get off the shore. She couldn't see the boat, but if the men turned back and found her, she wouldn't escape again.

She couldn't see the candle or the kitchen, but the framework of the dock projected a couple hundred feet to her left. She crawled there, stopping twice to cry and breathe, then at last wormed beneath its comforting shadows, the homey smell of clams and seaweed and stagnant, brackish water. Her breath echoed hollowly beneath the close wood. She slept.

A shriek woke her. She hurt everywhere. Soft yellow light poured from the sky. She crawled to the edge of the dock and peered inland. A small figure trundled around the side of the house, fell to one knee, and barfed enthusiastically. She wiped sand from her brow and gummy eyes. It was Martin.

She straightened and shambled across the burning sand. Martin unbent and wiped his mouth. He saw her, froze, then turned and ran.

"Martin!"

He stopped and shaded his eyes with the blade of his hand. He took an unsteady step toward her, then sprinted up beside her. He held his arms a short ways from his body, unsure what to do next. Her knee went out. He embraced her, propping her up.

"What happened?" he said.

"They killed him."

"Who was it?"

"The men from Catalina. I brought him guns so they shot him."

"Where's your mom?"

"They took her. They took her back to the island." She pushed away from him. "We have to go, Martin. We have to go get her."

He laughed in disbelief. "Right now?"

"Before they do more to her. Last time she killed it and buried it in the woods."

"What?" He glanced to the sea. She followed his gaze, terrified at what she might see, but the sun glared too brightly from the waves to see if there was a sail. He reached for her shoulder. "Come on. Let's go to my house."

"No!" Her mouth was so dry it was barely a word. She coughed, throat tearing.

He passed her his water flask. It tasted so sweet she drank it all. He looked to the ocean again, then took her upper arm and guided her through the grass to the road. She shuffled on the asphalt until they reached his fairy-story house with its tall peaked roof.

His mother was out. He took a long time cutting the ties from Raina's wrists, careful not to slice her, then got her more water and crackers and hazelnuts they grew in the back. She drank and ate it all.

"Tell me everything," he said.

She shook her head, but found a way, starting when they came for the guns—Martin said the islanders had taken them away from his mom, too—and ending when she woke up under the docks.

"I'm so sorry," he said.

"I'll go back tonight," she said. "I'll get my mom and kill the man who killed my dad."

"You can't."

"I'll find a boat. I'll take my knife."

He leaned forward and almost but didn't quite touch her shoulder. "Raina! There's like five hundred people over there. They'll kill you so much they'd still be killing you next week."

"There aren't that many," she said. "There's only like thirty of them."

"That they bring over on the boat," he said. "There's much more on the island."

She frowned. "How do you know that?"

He shrugged and glanced across his kitchen, which was bigger and better-lit than hers had been, with full windows that climbed above her head and bathed the gold-flecked brown tile with sunshine.

"I've been learning about them."

"Then you can tell me how to kill them."

Martin mashed his lips together and hopped down from his bar stool. He walked across the tile to the windows and stared out at the palms lining the back yard. Heavy fronds drooped from their crowns.

"I don't want to be a jerk. But if they wanted to kill your mom, they would have."

"So I should just leave her there? Let her enjoy her new life?"

"That's not what I mean. But, like..."

She balled her fist. "What?"

He blushed at the wind-rippled palms. "Well, you're just a girl."

"I can kill him if I want," she said with exaggerated calm. "I can cut apart his legs and stand on his chest until his lungs squirt from his ribs."

Martin turned and made a face. "I don't think this is a good idea."

"Everyone's been sitting around for months planning to fight back while the islanders took more and more. That's what my dad did and now my dad is dead."

After everything she'd been through in the last twelve hours, saying the words was what finally broke her. Her face crumbled. Tears ran in cataracts down her cheeks. Karslaw had shot him. Taken his life. That meant her father's spirit belonged to the bearded warlord. He had a new family now. A bad one. He would forget her. Worse, the bearded man would use her father's power to hurt more people.

And the only way to free him was to kill the one who'd taken him.

"They killed him, Martin," she continued. "They shot him in the head and left him in the dirt."

"I know."

"So I'm going to kill the man who did it. And you can't stop me."

"I won't," he said.

She swiped at her clumpy lashes with the back of her wrist. "But you said I was just a girl."

"A girl who'd stick a knife in my back," he laughed. "But what are you planning to do? Row across the whole ocean, land at night in a place you've never seen, and slit his throat in bed?"

"Yes."

"Can I tell you about another idea?"

She crossed her arms. "What's that?"

"Well." He pinched a lock of his hair and dragged it through his fingernails, as if preening himself for lice. "If you go over there yourself, you can kill him, but you can't get back your mom. They'll find you before you get back to shore."

"You don't know that. I could find a boat with a fast engine. Or we'll hide on the island and wait to cross until they give up searching."

"Do you really believe that?"

She slapped the window, rattling it. Martin winced. She hit it again, harder, certain she could break it. "I have to try!"

He reached out to grab her hand, stopping halfway. "But not by yourself. Your parents were part of a rebellion, weren't they? If we can find who they were working with, we can help strike back. Wipe out the whole island. Be free again."

Her head thrummed. As real as a memory, she could smell the smoke of their homes as she burnt them to the ground, feel the heat of the islanders' blood as she cut them to the bone. She shook her head, dislodging the vision.

"I can't. I don't know who they were meeting with."

"Oh, well. That's too bad." Martin smiled the way he smiled when he was about to show her a new gizmo he'd dug out of the ruins. "But I do. Want to go talk to them?"

8

They walked east along the road away from the beach until it forked north, and then they walked north instead. Walt wasn't positive it was the right way—his only map of the region was a broad-level thing you might find at a diner, far too crude to show the two-lane road spooling from the jungle—and when he asked Lorna if she knew any better, she murmured something he couldn't make out and kept on walking.

Neither their course nor her silence was a big deal. If the road dead-ended, or turned the wrong way, they'd get back on track eventually. As for Lorna, he didn't much feel like talking, either. Not that anything had gone wrong the night before. She'd more or less attacked him, riding him angrily, refusing to make eye contact. She'd even come. Yet he couldn't shake the feeling the circumstances of their liaison—woman lost in the jungle two thousand miles from home, reliant on a near-stranger to get her back in one piece—were the sort that would once have landed him on a campus list somewhere. Or a Penthouse Forum, which might be even more disgraceful.

He gave her a furtive look. She walked untiringly, face blank, hair a bit greasy, but the line of her clenched jaw and the sharky draw to her eyes made her look even prettier. She hadn't been snappy or insulting to him, just distant; if she were angry, it wasn't with him. He did mean to help her. Pretty generous, he thought, considering it meant putting his own well-being on the line. And if he was the type of person who wouldn't agree to such a thing until she'd fucked him, well, he'd long since made his peace with himself.

Aside from those concerns, he felt relaxed, but otherwise little different from how he'd felt the day before, when his Ripken-like dry streak was still going strong. Sex was a lot like air or water, he figured. You only get worked up about it when you find yourself without it.

So they walked north for days, slowed by his ankle until it healed up, sticking to the road except once when Walt thought he heard the keen of an alien ship and twice when they saw smoke curling from homes along the way. Then they returned to the world of leaves and muggy air and whining bugs. Two days into their revised travel plans, the jungle opened on a small town. Walt knelt and watched through his binoculars. Pigeons fluttered around in the cobbled square, but he saw no humans.

Lorna had lost her bag back when she'd followed him away from the beach. Walt looted a nice map from the glove box of a Volvo, then explored the pastel yellow and off-red houses for several hours, helping Lorna pick out clothes and hiking shoes and her own binoculars and machete and drinking jugs.

Inside a sprawling stucco villa, Walt tossed a pan down on the patterned rug. The piece was durable iron and reasonably small, but he already had a good one—a little too small, maybe, but at least he knew how it cooked, and it had high enough rims that it could double as a bowl.

"You know, we'd save ourselves a lot of trouble if we just stripped down to knives and strings of varying thickness." He leaned against the plaster wall. "That's all you need to get by, isn't it? Stuff to cut things, and other stuff to tie it back together."

Lorna picked up the pan and added it to her pack. Wordless, she entered the shadows of the hallway and lost herself in the bedrooms, footfalls echoing on the stone floors.

They found some canned goods, which Walt didn't entirely trust, and a half-full swimming pool, which convinced him to camp at that house for the night, strain the pool water through a fine-woven sheet—the water was unchlorinated, old rainwater—then boil it over the fireplace, where Walt cooked corn and tomatoes and peppers from a neighbor's garden gone to seed. He let the tomatoes char on one side and didn't toss in the peppers until the last couple minutes. He thought it was pretty good, but waited the whole dinner without a compliment.

"We could probably find some bicycles," he said. "The only problem is trying to balance with five gallons of water and full packs. Maybe we can find bike trailers."

"So we can throw them away next time we have to cut through the jungle?" Lorna said.

"What we really need are sled dogs. And a couple thousand miles of snow. Or we could just put little wheels on the sled and have a dog-drawn carriage." He spooned corn from his all-purpose metal bowl/ cup. "Then again, feeding the dogs would be problematic. Unless we also rigged up a few teams of sled chickens. In fact, forget the dogs. With chickens, we could make the food carry itself."

She set her metal thermos on the red tile so carefully it didn't make a click. "What are you talking about?"

"Forget it."

In the morning, he tried to start a few cars, just for fun, but none even attempted to turn over. One had grass growing from the dirt that had blown into the seams of the hood. He didn't bother trying to rig up something involving bikes. He didn't have a good solution for that yet. They were carrying too much weight. There was no way around it. The less food and water they carried, the more they would have to forage. The more they foraged, the less time they'd have for travel. On an unfamiliar road, it was best to grab up all the goods in front of you than to rely on more to materialize further down the path. They could get around this if they could find some good bike trailers, but like Lorna said, they'd have to abandon them the second they went off-road. The jungle was far too thick.

So they walked on. Lorna cut a quick pace down the blacktop, one that left her sweating freely and ready to collapse into sleep each night. He thought she was punishing herself. Survivor's guilt. He'd probably had some of that himself after the plague. Two days out from the village where they'd restocked, they heard a car grumbling down the road and ran into the bushes to watch, but its engine faded the other way.

Along the road, they made good time. Their feet and legs had been hardened by the passage through the jungle and they sometimes managed forty miles per day. With no major delays, they might make L.A. in two months. Walt had the impression the timing wasn't completely critical. Even crazy alien hive-babies needed some time to grow up. As long as they finished the trip in less than, say, five or ten years, he imagined they'd arrive with plenty of time to make a difference.

The jungle was regularly interrupted by wide patches of tall grass and short trees, the corpses of former farms being devoured by the forest. Lorna wasn't proving much of a travel companion. It wasn't that she was unwilling to help. She pitched in on all the essentials: scouting towns, kindling fires, traipsing around for water, setting snares in the jungle at night and checking them at dawn. With her around—more specifically, the second pair of eyes and extra set of shoulders she provided—he bet they were covering more ground than if he were alone.

He was lucky if he could get her to say more than four sentences a day. That had its upside, of course. It meant she never complained, and that he didn't have to worry about her yakking on and exposing them to anyone who might be lurking behind the tree line or the doors of old homes.

But the flipside to that coin was she never admitted when she needed to rest. For all he knew her toes might have fallen off inside her tennis shoes. If she wound up with an infection, a broken bone, or even a bad case of blisters, they might be stopped for weeks on end.

For that matter, there was just something vexing about running around with somebody who wouldn't speak to you. It ran contrary to the idea they were in this together. It meant he had to make all the decisions for himself. Not a huge deal, considering the bulk of their decisions boiled down to "Should we keep going? Y/N?" But even so. Annoying.

Nine days into their trip, they camped out in the ruins of a foundation a few hundred yards into the jungle. Walt put together a fire while Lorna added water to the cornmeal she'd been grinding up from old kernels over the last couple days. After a dinner of fried bananas and somewhat undercooked cornbread, he hung up his socks to dry. Leaves rustled in the darkness. Walt whirled. Two round yellow eyes stared from the shadows.

"That is totally a jaguar," he said.

"Good for it," Lorna said.

Walt backed up and got his .45 from his bedding, keeping his eyes on the disembodied pair all the while.

"That's crazy. That thing's like right there." He waved his arms. "Hey, cat! Go be-feline someone else!" The eyes blinked slowly and disappeared. Somehow, that made it worse. Walt stood and turned in a slow circle. "Holy shit!"

Lorna had stayed seated all the while. "All you've been through and you're afraid of a cat?"

"Well, I was crazy back then. It helped."

"You went crazy? Why?"

"Oh, the usual." He seated himself, staring into the black trees. "Girlfriend cheated on me, then everyone in the world coughed up their lungs and died."

"Including her?"

He set down his gun. "Yeah."

"How'd you take it?"

"I told you. Went crazy. Genuinely sick. I hated her, so I was happy she'd died—I found her in our bed; this was in the early days, before we knew what was happening—but I loved her, and that made me want to die too. Killed a lot of people instead."

He stopped to think for a moment, then laughed and shook his head. "It was surreal. My world ended right along with this one. Sometimes I thought the two were linked. That Vanessa dying had caused the plague. That I was walking across my own brain, and there was nothing outside it, and when I reached California, instead of reaching the Pacific, I would find myself in front of a smooth bone wall curving from the sea to the sky."

The fire popped. He took a sharp breath of woodsmoke, then smiled at Lorna. "But I got better."

"I can tell," she said. "Squatting on ruins. Running back to war the first chance you get."

"I said better, not well." He'd kept his crutch/cane around as a walking stick/bludgeon. He poked its scarred foot at the fire. "What about you?"

"What about me?"

"Who'd you lose?"

The light undulated over the hard planes of her cheeks. "Husband."

"What did you do?"

She stared into the fire for a long time. "Went on."

He woke several times in the night to screeches that were far too close, but there wasn't much he could do about them. After a while, the creature quieted down, but started shrieking again at dawn. Unusual. Walt swore, rinsed out his mouth, shook out his boots, then went to check it out. One of their snares had caught a small brown monkey with limbs as long and spindly as pipe cleaners. The snare noosed around its neck and right arm flapped weakly against the dead leaves. Walt rubbed his mouth and got up to go.

"What are you doing?" Lorna said behind him.

He jumped. "Checking the other snares."

She hoisted a lolling rat. "Already got it. Why don't you take care of that one?"

"It's a monkey."

"So? You've killed humans before, haven't you?"

"Well, for one thing, they tried to kill me first," he said. "For another thing, it's a monkey."

She cocked her club, arched her back, and whacked the monkey's skull. The beast howled, voice penetrating the canopy. She struck it again and it went silent. She hit it a third time, mashing the side of its head.

"Doesn't look like a monkey to me." She hunkered down and slipped it from the tangle of thin rope. "Looks like meat."

"There's something wrong with you."

"Why are you coming to Los Angeles?"

"I'm generally opposed to the hostile takeover of Earth by outside forces."

"Are you in love with me?"

"We've only known each other a few weeks. If I fell in love with every woman I just met, we'd be having this conversation in southern Utah, not southern Mexico."

She smiled a hard smile. "Answer the question."

"I'm going because I gave my word!" He stepped up to her, then considered the treetops instead. "Wait, that's not right. I don't care about my word."

"Then why, Walt?"

"Because I'm still mad."

She smiled broadly, slung the monkey over her shoulder, and walked away. They ate it for dinner that night. It was on the greasy side, but it was meat.

He feared what her increasingly bizarre behavior foretold for the rest of the trip, but after the bludgeoning of the monkey, Lorna seemed to normalize, as if she'd at last plucked out whatever pieces of shrapnel had been worming their way into her guts. She replied to his questions. Made suggestions. Two days later, while he was cleaning up the camp, she returned from up the road to let him know there was a town ahead.

"Good," he said. "I'm down to my last good pair of socks."

She shook her head. "Chimneys are smoking."

"Oh. Back to the jungle with us, then."

"I found a trail through the woods. Looks like it circles around town."

"Nice work." He zipped up his pack and beckoned forward. "Lead on."

She walked for a quarter mile, sticking to the shoulder of the road so she could jump into the brush at a moment's notice, then swerved onto a muddy little path weaving through the undergrowth. It was too short for humans—an animal trail, wild pigs or something—forcing them to duck and dodge and slash with their machetes. Slow going and too loud. Between hacks of his blade, Walt froze and put a hand on Lorna's arm, stilling her. He cocked his head.

"That is a guitar," he whispered.

Notes trickled through the leaves, acoustic and melodic. It had been months since Walt had heard music. Maybe a year. Not since the Maya had invited him to one of their harvest festivals. To Walt's ears, the song sounded very Mexican in style, but the feelings expressed through it were universal: a bittersweet yet gentle regret, the sort of song you'd play six months after your lover has left you, when it's been long enough for the ache to soothe, but still recent enough to sting.

In the middle of the jungle in the middle of a broken world, the music was like magic, a slice of order coaxed out of the chaos. A portal to another place. One where you had the luxury of spending thoughts and calories on love instead of finding the next meal or staying out of the jaguar's claws.

"Let's sheathe the machetes for a minute," Walt murmured.

"Don't want to interrupt?"

"Did you just make a joke?" he said. "I'm more concerned about being noticed and killed."

He put on his leather gloves to push aside the branches and thorns by hand. The going got even slower. Half the trail was cleared by the passage of animals, but over the last few days the jungle had clearly gotten younger, trees bursting out of reclaimed farmland, and with a less-developed canopy blocking out the sun, the undergrowth sprouted all the more fiercely. After three miles and two hours negotiating the trail, they cut brush back toward the road and walked on.

They spent another night camped off the road in the young jungle. No fire this time. They still had the other night's monkey meat, along with flat slabs of cornbread just beginning to go stale.

"What were you doing out here, anyway?" Lorna said as dinner wound down. "All you've done for the planet and you wind up sitting on a crumbling pyramid like a forgotten king."

"So?"

"So there's much more work to be done."

"For who?" Walt said. "I'm not part of society. I'm just an animal. Eat, shit, sleep. I don't see lobsters and armadillos building houses and getting the power lines hooked up again. They seem pretty happy anyway."

"You don't have to do things for others. You could do them for yourself. But you came to rest like a fallen fruit."

"Like I'd be the first to lead a meaningless life."

She gave him a flinty stare. "That's what you expect from yourself?"

"Come on." He washed out the taste of monkey with a swig of water. At least the monkey was something new. He was getting so tired of water. Jugs were almost empty, too. Would have to find more tomorrow. "I would say I've already accomplished more in my life than some civilizations. What should I do for an encore, enslave the sun? Invent a time machine that runs on grass clippings?"

Lorna shrugged and smiled, mocking, but with the first warmth he'd seen out of her since the night after the beach. "You peaked young. You don't always have to top yourself, Walt. Sitting out on your own life is the best way to make sure the rest of it's disappointing."

"But it might be a very long disappointment," he said. "I think I could live with that."

"How long had it been since you'd been with a woman?"

"A while. Several whiles."

"You're right. It's quite a life you had going."

"There's more to life than that, you know. Sex and romance was just a cynical invention of the greeting card-industrial complex."

She laughed. "You don't believe any of this. You're here with me. You're on your way to L.A. You can't wait to kill them again."

"Here's what happened: I got someplace comfortable, and I let myself stay there." He knew better than to reach out to her. "Isn't that what we're all trying to do?"

He got up with the daylight to wander around and try to scare up some water. His empty bucket banged against his back, rope coiled around his shoulders. Birds whooped. Like always, it was hot, but maybe a little less hot than the heat he'd grown used to in the Yucatan.

Within a few hundred yards of the camp, he spotted a gap in the trees. It might have been a house, or your everyday, run-of-the-mill clearing, but he could smell the fresh water, and he wasn't surprised to find a cenote sunk into the forest, easily a hundred yards wide and god knew how deep. The water forty feet below the rocky rim was a bright, frosty blue, opaque with minerals. It looked like the sort of thing that would get an elf drunk.

He nudged a hefty rock with his foot, sat down on it, braced his soles, and lowered the bucket hand over hand. It donked against the limestone facing, spinning awkwardly. Back at the cenote at Chichen Itza, he'd rigged up a whole pulley system—one of the many projects he'd spent a few days cooking up, although in this case, it had been one of the rare bits of labor that had saved him more time and energy than it cost—and ever since traipsing off with Hannigan and Co., reverting to hauling in a bucket with his own two hands felt like an incredible pain. From this high up, most of it would slosh out anyway. What he ought to do was try to dip just the lip of the bucket into the stagnant rainwater, get himself a good gallon or so, bring that back to the camp, then come back here with Lorna to—

With the sickening give of a loose tooth uprooting from its gums, the rock slid from beneath him. He cried out and fell toward the bright blue water.

9

"Who is it?" Raina said. "Who were they working with?"

"I'm not telling," Martin said, index finger and thumb pinched together, other fingers splayed. "Not unless you promise not to run after the islanders with a knife in your teeth."

"Do these people mean to fight back?"

"Yeah."

"Then I'll see them."

"Great," Martin said. "Okay, then you have to get cleaned up first. I promise not to look."

"Do you normally?"

"No," he blushed. "But you need it, Raina. No offense, but you look like something coughed up by a dolphin. We'll only have one chance to make a first impression with her."

"Her?" Raina said. "My parents were seeing a man named Bryson."

"I'm talking about Jill at the Dunemarket. She organized the whole thing. Bryson must be working with her."

"How do you know Jill will see you? You're just a boy."

He shrugged, smiling. "I fixed her walkie talkies. She'll do anything for me. Come on, I'll set up the tub and get your clothes. Which ones do you want?"

"What do you think Jill will like?"

He shrugged again, not meeting her eyes, and went to the garage and pulled out the big plastic tub they used for a bath. She grabbed sun-warmed jugs of water from the back porch; he brought her green bar soap and a big black bottle of shampoo and a towel that didn't smell too bad, then headed up the shore toward her house. She stripped while he was still within eyeshot, but he didn't turn around. Out in the breakers, black dolphin fins scythed the water and disappeared. She poured the water into her salt-locked hair, scrubbing the sand from her scalp with her nails. The water was nicely warm, offsetting the cool morning, but she knew better than to waste water or time. Her hair hung down her back like beached kelp. She dried off and went inside, rattling around the kitchen for scissors. Martin got back a few minutes later with a bundle of her clothes, including white tufts of underwear.

She held out the scissors. "Cut my hair."

Martin tucked his chin, staring at the scissors as if they might leap for his tendons. "What?"

"My hair. Cut it."

"I don't know how to cut hair."

"You open the scissors, then close them. Do that until my hair is shorter."

He looked up in horror. "Seriously, Raina, I don't know how. I'd make you look crazy, like one of those little dolls with the—"

"Fine. I'll do it." She twisted a clump of her hair, snugged the scissors against her scalp, and closed them with a crisp clasp. A long black chunk of wet hair tumbled to the tile floor.

He reached for her hand. "That's way too short! You'll look like a boy."

"Then do it how you want."

He mashed up his face, cheeks red, then accepted the scissors. "Let's go outside. The light's awful in here."

He brought a chair to the back porch. She dressed, then sat outside while he trimmed her hair in careful snips. He didn't understand. Now that her wrath had gelled and cooled, she wasn't sure she could kill them all. There were so many. They had guns. Boats. Lived isolated on an island across the waters. She had to become a different Raina, but she knew too firmly what Raina looked like to do that.

But if she looked in the mirror and saw a stranger, that stranger could become anything.

Birds peeped from the trees. Martin snipped and mumbled to himself. Hair coiled around her bare feet. He took a long time. With the sun close to noon, he stepped back, returned for one last cut, then brought her a mirror.

Raina's hair had hung down her back like a cape. The girl in the mirror had visible ears, her shiny black hair stopping short at her chin. She turned her head, examining.

"Well?" Martin said.

"I don't know who I am."

"Did I cut it too short? Didn't you see the stuff on the ground? Why didn't you say something?"

She handed him the mirror. "It's perfect."

She stood. He brushed stray hair from her shoulders, confused. Finished, he put together food for the long walk to the Dunemarket.

"I'm going home," Raina told him. "I'll be right back."

"What for?"

"My knives."

"Why didn't you tell me to grab them when I got your clothes?"

She gave him a look. "Because you don't tell someone where your knives are."

She headed to the house, jogging to work out the stiffness in her legs, but didn't press herself too hard—the trip to the market would take a few hours and she was already bruised and sore. Crows cawed from around back. She approached from the front. The house looked the same as always—the wind-chapped paint, the windows greasy from the constant seaborne mist—but it no longer felt like home.

She kept her three best knives under the particleboard on top of her bookshelf. One of the blades was longer than her hand. The others were finger-length, one double-edged, the other serrated. She put them on and returned to Martin, who had two packs ready and a walkie talkie on his belt.

Raina had gone to the Dunemarket a couple times a year with her parents, but she let him lead. Once they got past the first hill, the sunny day got hot. They drank warm water as they walked. Blind windows watched them, doorsteps sheltered by tall tangles of grass. She knew of a few families who lived in the neighborhoods west of here, but the homes along the main road were all abandoned. Even in the peaceful years before the Catalinans arrived, no one wanted to be obvious to travelers.

They detoured around the makeshift graveyard at the bottom of the long hill. There, sun-mummied bodies and gnawed bones showed the scorches and shatters of a gunfight that had erupted in the middle of the jammed-up cars. Martin hiked up a residential street nestled between two clusters of supermarkets and coffee shops and veterinary offices.

The long, shallow valley between the next two hills had been burnt to the ground. Black timbers leaned from foundations. A crater rested on the far slope, its hundred-yard hole finally healed with vigorous green grass. Houses stood half-collapsed, paint blackened, windows broken. The homes and shops on the other side of Gaffey St. had mostly survived, but half the city had been erased, reduced to rubble, much of it already reclaimed by hungry grass, coastal scrub, and young trees.

But the straight road through it was the best route between the ruins of Long Beach and the whole Palos Verdes Peninsula. A market had been inevitable.

That's what Raina figured, anyway. It already existed in a smaller version of its present form by the time her second parents had brought her to the hills. The market itself had sprung up on the road, where it shifted daily, a fluxing quilt of tents, tarps, and stalls bracketed by a canyon park of tall palms and a shuffle of perpetually brown undergrowth. The permanent merchants lived in these small, undulating hills, but Raina didn't know why people called them dunes. They weren't sandy at all.

They walked in from the south, the road sloping down into the canyon. Travelers and locals mingled among the spreads of lemons and oranges, the fresh fish and bread, the scavenged jeans and seeds and cans of coffee. Martin put his walkie talkie to his mouth, repeated his name and "Over" a few times, but got no response.

"They must not have theirs turned on," he offered.

A man with sunglasses and a crossbow watched from a platform shaded by an umbrella. Martin waved. The man nodded. A couple of the marketeers glanced Martin's way; they must have recognized him, because they didn't bug him to buy or barter. He turned off the paved road to a dirt trail leading up the serpentine hills.

Raina watched his plodding back. It was weird to see evidence he knew people. He usually spent his time alone in the ruins. Even around Raina, he could be shrinkingly shy. Then it came to her: it was the road that brought him here. The information. Wires and outside news were his two great loves.

Palms fluttered overhead. This part of the interior could get blazingly hot in late summer and the merchants had dug new homes into the sides of the hills, for protection from sun, fire, and hostile travelers. Martin passed by three wooden shacks that served as foyers to the underground homes, then knocked on the door of a fourth.

It was opened by a heavyset man with a drooping black mustache and arms as tan as Raina's. "What's up?"

"It's Martin Grundheitz," Martin said. "Can I speak to Jill?"

"She's out."

"When will she be back?"

"How should I know? She doesn't tell me nothin'." The man scratched his bristly cheek. "You want, you can wait down at the tent." He gestured to a blue tarp strung between the scraggly trees lining one of the canyon folds. "I'll let her know you're there."

"Thank you," Martin said. The man closed the door, stirring the smell of dust. Martin brought Raina down to the tent. The shade was cool and the trees smelled like pollen and sage. At the very bottom of the fold, dried white mud promised a creek would return when it rained.

"Do you think she'll see us?" Raina said. "You might do work for her. That doesn't mean she'll tell you about the rebellion."

"She thinks I get so wrapped up tinkering with an engine or a solar panel that I can't hear her talking to her people. I know what they're planning. She can't just brush me off."

Raina had her doubts, but after an hour in the shade, feet crunched across the layers of fallen brown palm fronds. A middle-aged woman with a sun-blond ponytail stepped into the shade and offered them a bottle of water, which they accepted, as was polite.

"Hey, Martin," Jill said. "What brings you up from the sea? Got another machine part you want me to watch out for?"

"Not this time." He glanced at Raina, fiddling with his hair. "Can I ask you something?"

"Is that what you walked all this way to do?"

"Yeah."

She grinned. "Then I think you'd better."

"Well, it's just kind of secret. Like, it isn't something where I want you to get mad, or think I've been prying, and maybe I'm not even right, but—"

"We want to join the rebellion," Raina said.

The woman's mouth twitched. "The rebellion?"

"The one against the Catalinans. The islanders. The ones who want to take us over."

"I think they've gone from 'want' to 'did,'" Jill grinned wryly. "Now, Martin."

"What?"

"You're too smart for this," she said, earning a blush from him. "You're our little technowizard. Rebellion? Even if one of those existed, you wouldn't want to get dragged into something like that. What if something happens to you? What do we do next time the radio breaks?"

"They're not that hard to fix," he muttered.

She turned to Raina. "As for you. I don't know you."

"You knew my parents," Raina said. "Kate and Will Ambers. They were working with Bryson and Bryson works with you."

"Were?" The woman shook her head. "Say a fight's brewing. Say people don't want to become the subjects of a bunch of savages. Such a resistance might be considered noble. But what kind of people would they be if they used children to fight rapists and killers?"

"But Jill—" Martin said.

She cut him off. "Keep your heads down. Move inland if you need. Whatever it takes to stay out of trouble. Good seeing you, Martin."

The woman strode uphill. Martin watched her leave, dumb with disbelief.

"You said she'd listen," Raina said.

"It's not fair. I help her all the time."

"Are you going to just let her go?"

"What's the point?" He flapped his hands. "We should go home. She'll never listen."

"Not to words," Raina said. She exited the tarp into the post-noon heat.

Martin hurried after her. "Where are we going?"

She almost didn't tell him—the storage was her place, her secret—but Jill hadn't even let her speak. Martin was her way into the rebel ranks. She needed to trust him, and more importantly, for him to trust her.

"To prove we're useful."

She took him to the dead man's bunker, detouring along the way for trash bags from a hollowed-out grocery store. The walk took most of the afternoon. At the metal steps leading down from the trap door, Martin clicked on the pen light he never left home without. He swept the beam over shelves of food and soap and coats.

"Dude," he breathed, "this place has everything."

"This is where we go if we ever have to hide," Raina said. "It's my most secret place. You have to promise not to tell."

"Promise," Martin said. "Are those vacuum tubes?"

She yanked him away from the glassware. "Stop it. Jill doesn't care about vacuum-tunes. She cares about guns."

Dozens still stood in the rich wooden racks. She took six. Enough to command Jill's interest without quenching it or exhausting her own supply. She took no bullets. Jill would have to earn those. Martin looked longingly at the room with the tubes, then followed her upstairs for the trek back to the Dunemarket.

The late afternoon wind was cool and steady. They had a long way to go, so Raina avoided the winding side roads in favor of the PCH. Blocks on end were jammed with cars, but the sidewalks were clear enough.

The sun dropped and went away. A dark blue dome of light rolled into the ocean, dragging a blanket of star-speckled black behind it. But when they reached the Dunemarket, there were still torches flapping in the wind, like she knew there would be, along with a line of solar-powered garden lights embedded along the road, their pale light just bright enough to place your feet by. Jill was there in the road, arguing casually about the cost of a spear gun with a grouchy old man. Similar dickering played out at a half dozen stalls and blankets.

Raina flung the bag at Jill's feet with a clank. A rifle barrel tore through the black plastic, exposed by the torchlight.

"Got a use for us now?" Raina said.

"Sweet Christ!" the old grouch spouted. "Is that a .30-30?"

Traders and travelers turned, wafting old sweat. Jill stared at the pile of metal.

"What you got there, Jill?" said a man who was less old than her, his grin a V of delight. "A bag of suicide?"

"Contraband," Jill said, snapping out of her shock. "From two kids. Who don't know any better." She grabbed up the bag with a grunt, then took hold of Raina's wrist. "Come on."

The woman dragged her up the hill straight for her underground home. A candle wavered in the foyer-shack. Jill used the candle to light two more, handed one to Martin, and went down a short earthen tunnel propped up by wooden beams. It smelled like moist dirt. Jill brought them through a doorless entry into a semicircular room just tall enough for the woman to stand upright.

She hoisted the bag in front of Raina. "You idiot."

Raina crossed her arms. "You need guns to fight them, don't you?"

"I also need them not to hear that I have them. There were a score of travelers out there. You too short to see they had eyes? If one of them tells the islanders what they saw, how long do you suppose I'll get to keep these guns?"

"That depends on how well you hide them," Raina said. "They only took the others because no one knew they were coming."

The fire in Jill's eyes dampened. "Could be. Or it could be they come here and put out my eye to make me tell them the truth."

"So let them take these ones. I can get you twenty more tomorrow morning."

"From where?"

Raina tipped back her face. "That information is reserved for my superior officer."

"For God's sake," Jill muttered. "Stay right here."

She left the room, footsteps crunching down the gritty floor. Martin cleared his throat. "Was that smart?"

"It got us inside her house," Raina said.

"A dirt house. That's like the best place to bury people in."

Minutes dragged on. Her confidence flagged. A flat black beetle wiggled along the wall. Footsteps scuffed down the hall.

"I have talked," Jill said. "And I have decided to make an exception."

Raina grinned at Martin, who grinned back. She stepped forward. "So we're in."

"As long as you can keep scrounging up guns? Hell yes you're in. I want you combing the city 24/7."

Raina didn't understand that last part, but she got the rest of it. "I don't want to scavenge. I want to fight."

Jill's smile bent. "We've got trained people for that. It's not all about warriors. What are we going to fight with if we don't have any guns?"

"I don't want to find guns! I want to kill Catalinans!"

The woman gaped, then extended her hand to the south. "Then go and kill them. Nothing's stopping you. But you want to join my group? Then you follow my orders."

Raina clenched her teeth. Martin edged beside her. "I think we should do it. We can help. That's more than we can do on our own."

"This is a waste of what I can do," she said.

"You're what, fourteen?" Jill said. "This won't happen overnight. We've got a lot of work ahead of us. Recruiting. Supplying. Training. They've got a huge head start on us and it could take years to close the gap. If you're ready then, I'll let you on the front lines."

"I can't wait that long. They've got my mom!"

"Come on," Martin said. The pleading in his voice made Raina want to punch him. He moved close enough to feel the heat of his skin. "They're not going to kill her. We'll only have one shot, remember? We need to take our time and do it right."

Raina hated it. She hated the islanders, this woman, Martin's insipid compromises. The Catalinans were wrong. That should be enough. She screamed and struck the wall, dirtying her fist. Jill flinched.

"I'll bring you more tomorrow," Raina said. "Then see what else I can find."

Jill reached out, but she drew away. "Don't be so eager to get hurt. This won't be pretty."

It was too stupid to respond to. Jill offered them a tent in the canyon to sleep in. Raina let Martin lead her into the starlight and the crisp, dew-dust smell of the night.

"Come on," he said. "I'll buy you some tea."

"I don't want it."

"It's good. They make it with real milk."

She sighed; he thought he could make her feel better, but she no longer cared about tea at all. Martin walked up the hill and took the road down to its base, where candles flickered in the windows of the inn. A horse whickered. A torch crackled at the door to the McDonald's on the corner. Martin held the door for her. Inside, men and women stood around the counter holding foaming glasses and small tumblers of clear liquid. Martin settled Raina in a booth, went to the bar, and came back with two black mugs of opaque reddish-brown tea. It tasted like hot candy.

"See?" he said. "Good, right?"

"It's okay."

He stirred the little specks in his tea. "It'll be all right, you know. They're just scared of the raiders because nobody's stood up to them. Once we get enough guns, Jill won't hold back."

Raina doubted that—no one was ever willing to fight, not when their enemy was bigger or meaner or willing to hit first—but she was too tired and frustrated to argue. Resentfully, she drank her tea, which was very good.

At the candlelit bar, two men separated, glaring at each other. One of them was the man with the V-shaped grin, the man who'd made fun of Jill when Raina brought her the guns. He faced a bearded man who was half fat, half muscle, and half a foot taller.

"I said," said the man with the grin, "that you took my drink." He motioned at a glass on the bar. "This one is yours. You might identify it from the fact it is empty."

"So quit bitching and buy another," said the man with the beard.

"My thinking, which I feel is quite reasonable, is that you should buy me another."

"How about I give you yours back?" The bearded man snatched the empty glass, unzipped his pants, and hauled out his penis. The bartender gaped as the man urinated into the glass and, penis still dangling, sloshed it at the thin man, whose V-shaped grin had long since inverted. "Drink up, motherfucker."

The man squinted at the glass. "As long as we're getting to know each other, I've been fucking your wife. She's not very good."

The bearded man's face darkened. He stepped forward. The thin man slapped the glass from his hand, dousing the man in a rain of urine, and followed it up with a straight punch to his nose.

The other man bent halfway, roared, and straightened, blood flowing from his nostrils. He looped his fist at the smaller man, who had just enough time to look sad before the big man's fist slammed him to the ground. He tried to squirm away, but the other man punched him again, rattling his head against the sodden linoleum. The big man smiled, lifted his boot, and stomped the unmoving man's ribs.

Raina screamed loud enough that the whole room winced. She flung herself onto the big man's back, her longest knife flashing in her fist.

10

Walt threw himself flat as the earth slid beneath him. He hardened his fingers into claws and stabbed them into the dirt, but the dirt kept going away. His feet kicked into empty air. He went off the ledge.

He slid close to the rocky wall, shoes stubbing along its outcrops. A jutting rock bashed his chin. He groaned, pain exploding across his body. Something slid beneath his fingers. He grabbed on hard. His feet banged against the sinkhole wall.

"Help!" he shouted. "Lorna!"

Below, the tail of the rope splooshed into the vivid blue water. Walt shouted again, his voice hilariously faint in the chasm of the cenote. Well, this was terrible. If he slipped and fell to the water waiting forty feet below, there was no guarantee he'd be smashed to bits—most of these pools were dozens if not hundreds of feet deep—but there existed the chance he'd land wrong, knock the wind from himself, and quickly drown. Or sprain his shoulder, be unable to haul himself onto the rocks, and slowly drown. Or land fine, get halfway up the limestone face, find there were no handholds left, and finally, in his exhaustion, plunge back into the waters to tread water and drown slowest of all.

Generally speaking, it was not good to fall forty feet onto anything. So he shouted again, as loud as he could, groped for a higher hold, and pulled himself a foot up the wall. That put him about six feet from the rim, he figured. Five or six more holds until he flopped over the lip onto good, old-fashioned, not-moving flat land.

He only found two more.

Tantalizingly close to the top, the rock wall angled toward him, its surface forbiddingly flat. His fingertips scraped over stone, but he couldn't find a grip. Carefully, he edged laterally, toes probing, dislodging pebbles and snot-slick moss, but the climbing was no better over there. His biceps quivered. He tensed, preparing to leap up as high as he could and scramble for a new hold, but sanity prevailed. He held there, relaxing as well as he could to give his muscles a break.

"Son of a bitch," he panted.

Lorna's face appeared above the rim. "You've fallen."

"By one definition. By another, I've still got a long way to go."

"Can you get back up?"

"No. Tried. Give me a hand?"

She regarded him coolly, the way he might regard an unidentified beetle trundling up to him on the steps of Chichen Itza. "Do you think you'd die if you fell?"

"I think I fucking might!"

She nodded to herself, watching for another unbelievably long couple of seconds, then retreated behind the ledge.

"Hey!" he yelled. "I have a phobia about things that could kill me!"

His foot slid from the ledge. He swore and gasped, hanging tight as he tapped around, searching for a new foothold. A pair of jeans flapped over the edge, one pant leg hitting him in the face.

"Grab on," Lorna said.

He grabbed tight to the jeans, twisted his forearm to wrap the leg around his elbow, and tested his weight against it. He drew himself up by the jeans, found a grip for his left hand, lifted his right foot, searched for and found a new ledge. Lorna pulled the jeans tight. He hauled himself up to another set of holds. His chest scraped the upper edge. He wriggled up onto the wet grass and rolled on his back, gasping for air.

"Thank God," Lorna said.

"What do you mean, 'Thank God'? You acted like you wanted me to drop!"

She shook her head sharply. "I was thinking."

"Of me bashing my head into raspberry yogurt?"

"I panicked, Walt. Like you did at the beach."

"That was a perfectly level-headed tactical retreat." He searched her face. Her bare legs were folded beneath her. He tossed her the jeans.

"What happened?"

"I don't know!" Her eyes went bright. She twisted her hands in her lap. "It should have been me, you know? How did I make it out when Hannigan was so much stronger? Or Ken, for that matter? They were real soldiers. But I'm the one who made it out. There you are on the ledge, and if you fall, all I have to do is follow you over. Make everything right."

"Shit." Walt stood up, staggered, and found his balance. "Nobody's dying today. Let's get back to camp and on the road."

He'd torn up his hands pretty bad on the rocks. Lorna poured some clean water onto a cloth and wiped away the dirt. He spread Neosporin, applying Band-Aids to the cuts and scrapes that looked likely to reopen.

Back on the road, she didn't speak. Except to suggest rests, neither did he. It was hot again. Big fucking surprise. Yet it wasn't the heat that was so bad. Sit around in the shade all day and you'd hardly notice. But get up and walk around, and you'd be miserable all day.

Meanwhile, they still hadn't found fresh water, they were rationing what they had left, and he'd lost his bucket. This wasn't a complete disaster—they were well out of the Yucatan, and he believed this part of the country had things like "rivers" and "streams"—but he wasn't exactly the master of Mexican geography. He'd only come this way once. Years ago. When there had been a lot more farms. The jungle had regrown massively since then.

But not all the way. Rainy as the area might be, proper agriculture couldn't rely on something as fickle as the weather (and if the rain were that reliable, they'd want to exploit that, too). As he walked along the road, he kept one eye on the jungle, searching for rows among the trees, gaps in the canopy. After four false alarms and five hours of walking, he found what he was looking for: a concrete ditch half-hidden by a bank of shrubs. Its water was low and its sides silted, but it had a bit of current to it, and wasn't the green sludge he'd been expecting. He called a stop and asked Lorna to put together a fire.

"What, now?"

He considered the jungle. "You're right, we should probably unwind first. Think Seinfeld's on?"

"It's afternoon," she said. "Light illuminates things. Like smoke."

"So what? If we don't get the water boiled, next week we'll be shitting parasites so gnarly they'll make the aliens look like Elmo."

She snorted. "You're the one who's paranoid about being seen. If you're not concerned with being kabobbed by cannibals, neither am I."

"Look, I just don't want to go stumbling around a ditch at night," he said. "I've had enough of falling into water for one day."

Lorna tightened her mouth, ready to say more, then shook her head and smiled. "Just saying. I'll get the kindling."

He raised his eyebrows in exasperation, then got out his machete and started whacking at the wall of foliage blocking off the ditch. It was much too wet to burn and he flung the choppings in a messy pile. While he worked, Lorna set bark and grass at the base of a tree to flume the smoke away from unwanted eyes.

In addition to their canteens and jugs, they each carried a waterproof canvas water bag, with a third held empty in reserve in case they expected dry spells or damaged one of the others. Walt had found this one in the deserts of Northern Mexico. It was old and beaten and featured an illustration of an old-timey, Model T-ish car, and he was fairly certain it was a good seventy-plus years old, something 1930s motorists used to sling over the hood of their car on trips through Death Valley or Chihuahua. He'd seen cleaner, stronger bags since picking it up, but had hung onto it anyway. It was well-traveled. Good juju. Not the sort of thing you threw away.

He filled it and lugged it to Lorna, who had managed a small and smoky fire, which she stoked as he set up the pan to boil. The smoke tasted verdant and sharp.

"I'm going to wash up," Walt said. "I look like I stumbled in from 1970s Times Square."

He grabbed his soap and shampoo. At the mouth of the tunnel he'd carved through the brush to the canal, he stripped down to his hole-riddled jockeys, glanced over his shoulder, then ditched those, too. Insects thrummed from the trees. He climbed down the canal and stepped in to his ankles. It was mucky and slick but the water was warm. It was too murky to see the bottom, however, which was very troubling. He didn't like the idea of things swimming past him unseen. Especially the parts of him that would soon enter the water.

Well, whatever. It wasn't like he was getting so much use out of them anyway. He waded in ribs-deep, careful not to stub his toes. The canal leveled out. He ducked underwater and listened to the bubbles, then burst up and slicked water from his face.

Something darted between his legs. He yelped and dashed forward, falling awkwardly into the water, thrashing in panic. Behind him, Lorna laughed lowly. He started to yell at her, then took much greater interest in her bare hips and teardrop-shaped breasts; she had an athlete's body, any excess fat sweated away in the jungle. She strode forward, water closing over her navel.

"Do you always thrash around this much when you shower?" she said. "I hope your tub is made out of steel."

"Lately it's been made mostly out of ocean." He was already hard by the time she reached him. She pulled tight, legs brushing his under the sluggish, silty water. He rested his hand at the top of her ass. She moved in and kissed him, lowering her hand below the water.

After a minute, he pulled back. "Can we move it up to the shore?"

"Why?"

"Because I'd rather not have a piranha bite off my balls."

"We're a thousand miles from the Andes."

"Then how about the fact water makes terrible lube?"

She smiled darkly and ran her hand down his back. "Now that's a legitimate concern."

She turned and led him up the algae-slick curve of the canal, water dripping wonderfully down her back. As if she could feel his gaze on her skin, she turned and grinned.

That was the night they became a team. The panic she'd shown as he dangled over the cenote didn't return. Often, she was up before him, cleaning whatever they'd caught in the snares or packing fruit plucked from roadside trees. She smiled. She laughed. She talked. Not excessively—he got the feeling she wasn't much of a talker under any circumstances—but after the laconic, grief-stricken stranger he'd been traveling with the last couple weeks, it felt like living with the Micro Machines man.

She erased the physical distance, too. Sometimes the day's travel left them too tired to move, but most nights they made love or fucked or both, her cries competing with the nocturnal birds. He had missed it. Lots. She was more than just a warm body; she was a part of a team there, too, as dedicated to getting him off as he was to her. At times, she took it like a sporting challenge, and if he took too long she rolled him onto his back and straddled him with a look of renewed dedication and amused but friendly contempt.

The road began a gentle rise. After a few days, the jungle gave way at last, opening to low green hills under a too-warm sun. When they had to go off-road for water or to avoid strange towns, the thinner vegetation made for easier travel but tougher foraging. If anything, their progress slowed.

But they still made good time, crossing a hundred miles every three or four days. Bladelike ridges knifed from the horizon. They skirted villages, a few abandoned cities. There was no pattern to which places showed the smoke or noise of human life, but it was rare, and never organized. The census on his map was dated 2005 and claimed Mexico was populated by 106 million people. Something like half a million must have survived the Panhandler, but either the last five years had not been kind or the survivors had melted into the wilds, fleeing the attacks of aliens and their fellow former countrymen.

And then the road reached Mexico City.

It filled the whole valley between two mountain ranges, sprawling, endless, incredible, a gridded mass of labor and matter, some sections scorched to ruins, others pockmarked and cratered but largely intact. Sporadic towers spurted from the blanket of pastel houses and grim apartments. Snow lay on the mountains. Trees grew in the parks. It would have been smarter to go around, but Walt didn't have a choice. They were running low on food, and the more time they spent gathering it from the wilderness, the less time they had to travel. He entered the city, Lorna at his side.

Most neighborhoods could have been from any other big city on earth, gray-brown housing blocks fronted by shops with yellow signs. Walt's Spanish was good enough to recognize most of them and they were able to find weighty bags of long-term, durable food, the dry corn and wheat and beans that took extra prep time to mash, grind, or soak, but would stay edible as long as they kept them clean and dry. They supplemented this with cucumbers and peppers and avocados and strawberries from the parks and weedy backyard gardens.

Abruptly, even the most dour neighborhoods transitioned to bright, airy, gleaming places. A glass-fronted tower with a permanent scaffold of blue and red rectangles. A bizarre restaurant wrapped inside what looked like a wavy blue net, its interior paneled with solid bamboo, as if they'd stepped inside the forest's oldest trees. Yawning plazas with baroque churches capped with gold domes. Stone saints in dried-out fountains. Walt walked through one square blinking sudden tears. He hadn't thought much of Mexico, back in the day, disregarding it as cartel-racked and grossly impoverished, but despite the miles-wide slums, its capital was a jewel, an achingly beautiful tombstone to a people now departed.

Somewhere past its center, they took shelter in a tile-lined subway entrance to eat a toasted mash of avocados, corn paste, chilies, and wild Mexican oregano that Walt called waltcakes.

"I'm glad we came here," Lorna said.

Walt nodded, gazing across the way at a fountain headed by a faux-Aztec ziggurat complete with intricate pictographs of serpents and birds. "Are you Mexican? Were you? Wait, how do we talk about this now? Is Mexico still Mexico now that the Mexican government's gone? It's not like there's a patrolled border anymore. Mexicans and Americans can switch countries whenever they want. It's one big Amexada."

"My father was of Mexican descent. My mom was white."

"Oh. Ever been here before?"

"Why would I come to Mexico?"

He screwed up his face. "Friends? Family? A quest for the perfect cilantro?"

"My great-grandpa was the last born-in-Mexico Mexican in the family," she said. "This place wasn't any more special to me than Ireland would have been to you."

"I'm Scots-Norwegian," Walt said.

She shrugged. "Think either of those places exist anymore?"

"Just in myth," he said. "Same as here. Same as America. If we have kids, let's not tell them there were different countries."

"We're not having kids."

"Good. I never wanted them. Even in the halcyon paradise when you could summon a pizza to your front door. Parents couldn't get their kids to mow the lawn once a week. How would we motivate them to grind flour every day?"

"Violence?" Lorna smiled.

Walt crammed down the last of his avocado-cake. "How do you do it in L.A.? Some of you must have kids, right?"

"A few. They've adapted. Parents are less lenient now that not picking up your trash means being eaten by bears."

"I wonder what sucks more: being born into the wonderland and having it torn away from you as an adult, or growing up not knowing anything else?"

Something scraped softly in the darkness of the tunnel. Walt turned. It shuffled again. He clicked on his light. Tucked in the corner where the floor met the wall, the black eyes of a rat glared back at him. Behind it, a spongy orange layer of matter globbed the mosaic wall.

"Oh," Walt said. "Oh shit. Oh, grand, sloppy piles of shit."

"What?"

He pointed at the orange and dropped his voice to a murmur. "I've seen that stuff before."

Lorna leaned forward, lips parting. "It looks like fungus."

"Could be. I don't know if it's food or bio-insulation or carpet or what. But it's alien. It's all over their homes."

She drew her pistol. "Are they here?"

"I don't know. But we shouldn't be."

They hurried quietly down the street, guns out, the magic draining from Mexico City. His wonder had probably never been genuine in the first place. Just a projection of a mind overwhelmed by weeks in the blooming chaos of the jungle. Walt jogged at a casual pace that, even loaded down as he was, he could sustain for several miles. They weren't out of the city before he ran out of breath. Or before darkness fell. They walked on anyway. Crickets and beetles chirped from the bones of the churches. He smelled no smoke, heard no cars. The city was a graveyard. Like everywhere else. Humanity could never grow large enough to reclaim it before the wind and rain took it for themselves.

Long after midnight, they stopped at a gas station at the very fringe of the city. For the first time in weeks, they took watch. Walt saw nothing during his term. He didn't catch up on his sleep for a couple more days. He kept one eye on the skies and the other on the hills. It had been shortsighted to assume every single alien who'd survived the destruction of the mothership had stayed cooped up in

L.A. So much of the world had been forfeited by humans. The invaders could claim any of it.

The land rose. The air dried out but stayed hot. Within the span of a couple days, the green hills became a yellow plateau. The canvas water bags grew lighter and lighter. Outside another sprawling city—Zacatecas, claimed the signs on the highway—Walt stopped and dug out his binoculars.

"Water's running out," he said.

Lorna shrugged. "There's always some in the city."

"Yeah, but I'm concerned about what we find in the desert on the other side."

"Or what we won't."

"Right." He lowered the binoculars and wiped his bare arm across his gummy mouth. "I like walking. I think it's safer. But the equation inverts when you walk across a wasteland."

She unscrewed her canteen and swigged. "So why don't we get down there and steal us a car?"

11

If Martin had asked later, which he didn't, she wouldn't be able to say why she did it. Maybe she had too much rage and pain to keep to herself. Maybe she simply needed, in a deep-down, thirst-level way, to hurt someone. Or maybe she could no longer stand to watch a strong man hurt someone weaker.

She jumped on a table, vaulted onto the bearded man's back, and stabbed him deep in the shoulder.

The man hollered like he'd been set on fire and slapped at his shoulder. She pulled out the knife and stabbed between his shoulder blades. His holler became a scream. He turned his hips and slung her off. Raina landed in a controlled but painful fall, rolling to her feet, knife out and dripping blood. The man yelled and charged. She held her ground and crouched down, flicking the knife at his knee. He hopped back.

"You set down that knife, girl."

"So you can stomp in my face?" she said. "Come and get it."

He feinted. She flinched but didn't fall back. He straightened, glancing around him to see how the crowd was taking his fight with a teen girl. They gazed back, drinks momentarily forgotten.

He smiled and made a fist. "You got a knife. Good for you." He raised his left forearm. "How many times you think you'll have to cut this before the other one strangles you dead?"

He lumbered forward. Raina edged back. Behind the bearded man, the small man swayed to his feet, produced an icepick, and inserted it into the base of the bearded man's skull. The man stopped and waved an unsteady hand. He opened his mouth and vomited a puddle of blood. He thudded to the streaked white tile of the McDonald's floor.

Across the bar, a man shouted and stood. The thin man with the icepick grabbed Raina's wrist. She raised the knife.

"Hey now," he said. "Time to run."

She did. Martin followed them into the cool night. Back inside, a man yelled. The thin man darted across the street between two strip malls. The McDonald's door banged open, spilling firelight into the street. The thin man laughed in exasperation. Raina fought to keep up. He vaulted a low chain-link fence, ran up the back porch, and yanked open the door. Raina put her knife in front of her and followed him into the darkness.

Martin pressed in behind her. The man was silhouetted in a room of couches and speakers and a big black TV. He gestured them over and popped down behind the couch. Raina crawled around its arm and hopped to the floor.

"Probably ought to just sit here a spell," the man whispered. "Think I might have hurt that guy."

"You stabbed him in the brain!" Martin hissed. He grabbed Raina's sleeve. "What are we doing with him?"

"Not getting hanged," she said.

The thin man chuckled, then leaned forward. "Hey, it's you. Little Annie Oakley."

"What?"

"The girl with the guns. Threw them at Jill's feet. Yeah, everyone was talking about you. Aren't you getting ahead of yourself? Teenagers are supposed to rebel against their parents, not murderous pirates."

Feet pounded the asphalt outside. Men jabbered back and forth. A flashlight beam whisked over the window, lighting up the ceiling. Raina pressed her back against the couch. The men continued down the alley, footsteps fading.

"I don't have parents," Raina said. "The pirates took them."

"Ah. Revenge. My favorite form of venge." The man stuck out his hand. "I'm Mauser."

She shook it. "Raina. That's Martin."

"Funny, he looks like a Martin," Mauser said. Raina snickered. The man straightened his light leather jacket. "So what did Jill say? Are you in or out?"

"Out," Raina said.

"In," Martin said.

"She wants us to get stuff for her," Raina said.

The man gave her an owlish look. "And you'd prefer to kill."

"That's what they did to my dad."

He held up his hands in mock innocence. "Did I say there was something wrong with that? I'm just clarifying."

"We won't be scavengers forever," Martin said. "Jill made it sound like you could be a soldier later."

"She was lying," Raina said. "I'm not too young to shoot a gun. She just doesn't want me to get hurt before I get her guns."

Mauser drummed his fingers against the back of the couch. "I'm trying to decide if this would make me a bad man, and if so, whether I would care."

Raina raised her knife to her knee. "What are you talking about?"

"Helping you," he said. "Possibly by hurting you."

"You're talking like a fool."

He burst out laughing, then glanced toward the window and made a face like he'd been bad. "Here's the thing. If you show Jill you know how to get guns, she's going to use you to get more guns. If you show her you know how to fight, she'll use you to fight."

"I don't like this," Martin said.

"You think we should attack the islanders," Raina said.

"That would be insane," Mauser scoffed. "I think you should attack some total strangers."

"Like kill the first stranger who walks into town?" Martin said. "You're crazy!"

"Keep your voice down. Anyway, they might not be strangers. You kids heard about the O.C.'s?"

"The Osseys?" Raina said.

"The O.C.'s. As in, from..." Mauser paused, then shook his head. "From one of the many places that no longer exists. Anyway. They're from down south, and they've been giving trade on the eastern roads a hell of a time. Jill and her dude are right mad about it."

"Robbers?" Martin said. "Bandits?"

"When they're feeling nice."

Raina wiped her bloody knife on her pant leg and put away the blade. "So we should get rid of them. Clear the road. Prove to Jill that we can fight."

Mauser scrunched up his face. "Well, I'm not sure I'd go that far. There are kind of a lot of them, although they aren't super well-put-together. What I think is that if you can get them to stop attacking Jill's messengers and merchants, she'd be inclined to upgrade you from delivery boys to special agents."

"Then let's go."

"What, me?" Mauser said. "I'm not messing with the Osseys."

Raina leaned in close. "I saved your life."

He laughed, barking with it, abruptly stopping. "Oh hell. You're serious."

"That makes you mine. I want your help."

"I feel like I'm on the verge of being forced to swear a blood oath." The man pinched the bridge of his nose. "Okay. All right. On one condition: I get half."

"Of what?"

"The cash. The loot. The wonga, in whatever form or avenue that wonga may take: anything we steal, beg, or bargain. Point is, I'm not going to tangle with a violent tribe-gang unless it's going to make me rich."

"Take their ears for all I care," Raina said. "I just want to prove myself to the rebels. I can't fight the islanders by myself."

"Which I convinced you of," Martin said. "So you should listen when I tell you running off to fight a bunch of bandits is just as crazy as running off to fight a bunch of pirates."

"Sure, but at least the bandits will negotiate," Mauser said. "They just want money. Stuff. Things. Far more reasonable than those idiots with the boat. They want power. Not a lot of bargaining to be done there."

Martin folded his arms. "What if we go to them and they rob us?"

"Won't happen. Not if we handle them right."

"Like you handled the man at the bar?"

"That man stole my drink! That's not the sort of thing you just let slide."

"When can we leave?" Raina said.

Mauser shrugged. "As long as we steer clear of pursuit, we can head out now. Won't make it there tonight, but we'll have a good start on tomorrow."

"Do you need to get your stuff from the inn?"

"Inn?" He gave her a blank look. "No, I wasn't staying at the motel. I was going to sleep in a ditch somewhere."

He got up, padded to the front door, slipped outside, and looked both ways down the street. He beckoned the two of them out. Raina didn't hesitate. Martin sighed theatrically and followed her out.

They walked swiftly down the starlit streets. Voices drifted down from the Dunemarket, from the inn across the boulevard. Mauser headed north, taking them away from the men who'd followed them out of the bar, glancing back and forth between the dirty little houses sitting on the scruffy hillside. After a few blocks, he angled back toward the main road and followed it past a park on one side and a bunch of huge stores on the other. Raina had been into those stores a few times—the Home Depot still had a few useful things, and the Wal-mart had so much stuff on the shelves you could still find good food until late last year—but another few blocks marked the furthest she'd been toward Long Beach since the plague.

She kept one eye on Mauser, hand near her knife. She needed his help, but if this was a trap, she'd be ready to cut him instead.

"Is it safe to talk?" Martin said.

"What kind of a question is that?" Mauser peeled off the road and jogged up a freeway onramp. "Well, what did you want to talk about?"

"Are the Osseys really bandits?"

"You keep using this word 'bandits.' They're not Robin Hood's Merry Men. They won't rob you at sword-point and send you on your way with a swat on the butt. They'll take whatever you've got—food, weapons, virginity. They prefer to let people go, because you can always fleece a sheep again next year, but they don't mind killing. It gives them street cred."

"Street cred?"

"Respectability." Mauser gestured outward, puffed his chest. "Badness. The reputation of a crew you don't want to fuck with." He glanced at them. "Pardon my French."

"French?" Raina said.

"Where are you from?"

"Why doesn't anyone stop them?"

"Who's going to do that? Jill?" He laughed. "She doesn't have the manpower for that."

"But she's going to fight the Catalinans."

"With the help of every fisherman, farmer, and scavenger in the South Bay. Even then, it's dicey. If you didn't have the personal revenge angle going, I'd tell you to steer clear of the whole damn thing."

Martin jogged to keep up with the man's quick strides. "If Jill can't fight the Osseys with the whole Dunemarket behind her, how are we supposed to fight them with three of us?"

"I've been thinking about that," Mauser said. They reached the top of the freeway, which swung east over a canal dug between the star-gleaming ocean and the fractal piers of Long Beach. "Seems to me we should offer them a bargain. Take half the guns you were going to give to Jill and offer them to the Osseys instead in exchange for free trade-related passage. Don't give them everything at once—just one or two at a time. Like slinging drugs. You got to keep them coming back for more. Don't want to blow the whole stash on them just to see them PCP-Hulk out on you and eat your liver."

Raina didn't understand half the things he said, but she picked up the gist. "What do you get out of it?"

"Some of the guns and bullets, duh. Unless you have something even more interesting." He gazed out to sea. From atop the bridge, the dark blot of Catalina was clear on the horizon, many miles away. "Sound good?"

"Do the Osseys always travel together?"

"No. They do this thing where a few of them split off, go their own way for a while, then gather back up into one big pack. Why?"

"Then we don't have to fight all of them," she said. "We can find them by themselves and kill them and take their heads back to Jill. That will prove who we are. And the more of them we kill, the more powerful we grow."

Mauser frowned at her. "Let's call that Plan B, Hannibal. I think they'll listen to greed."

The road ran straight across the waterfront, overlooking a thicket of masts, many sunk, some still bobbing on the sheltered swells. Cranes jutted from the docks, climbing a hundred feet into the night. It felt like the graveyard of great and horrible beasts. A place where the ancient things had come to die. Raina drew her circle between her brow and chest and hoped they'd be away from it soon. Music played across the black waters, spiked by bursts of men laughing. A lantern shined between the buildings. Once it was behind them, Mauser led them four blocks off the freeway to a uniform store where the stairs to the second story had collapsed.

He took them to the upper floor, climbing a metal shelf and a series of spikes someone had driven into the walls. "You see? Untouchable as a nun's twa—heart. Because she's married to Jesus, you see."

Raina made bedding out of mildewed nurse's uniforms. They smelled like dust but were soft enough. Mauser snored like her dad. She didn't like that she was sleeping in the same room with him—she'd only known him a few hours—but the best offerings she could find for the quarter-moon moon were a spider and a cricket. She tore off their legs one by one, then smashed them into goop. The moon gave her no sign of its acceptance, but it was still feasting. It would take whatever it could get.

Even so, she found a yellowed newspaper, quietly crumpled the pages, and set them in a ring around her bed so they'd crinkle if Mauser tried to creep up on her while she slept. He went on snoring all the while.

She got up at dawn and looked out the grimy window. She didn't recognize the empty streets. She felt very far from home.

They left before the sun had climbed over the mountains ringing the basin. The road was snarled with cars but the sidewalks were clear. Mauser's gaze darted among the buildings.

"Should be an hour before we see them, but look sharp," he said. "There's this big long canal, but only one surviving bridge. Aliens probably bombed the others. Dirty sons of bitches. Anyway, that's how they get you—you get on the bridge like 'Hey, no problem, a bridge,' then suddenly there's Osseys on both sides."

"This still sounds really dumb," Martin said.

"What do you know? You're just a kid."

Martin looked mad. Raina smiled. The road forked down a long passage of busted-out bars and cafes. They crossed a short bridge, both shores lined with rusting boats, and soon reached another, six lanes wide and hardly a hundred yards long.

Mauser stopped at its foot and cleared his throat. "Hel—"

Two men and a woman emerged from a copse of trees beside the road. All three had guns and wore blousy black shirts with a picture of a silver pirate with a helmet and two curved swords. The woman pointed her pistol at Mauser.

"Jewelry. Weapons. Drugs. Now."

"It's okay, we're not here for that," Mauser said. "We're here to make a deal."

She centered her pistol at his heart. "Here's my deal: give me your shit, and I don't give you this bullet."

"I doubt Preston will approve of you shooting people when they're trying to make him rich."

She exchanged looks with the two men. Raina touched the knife inside her jacket. The woman tossed her head.

"This way."

Mauser turned to Martin. "See, you big baby?"

The woman took them to a church a couple blocks away. They waited in the foyer, guarded by the two men while the woman went through the great wooden doors at the other end. She came back a minute later. Wordless, she gestured them inside.

Pews ran from the back all the way to a dais up front. Melted candles coated the alcoves. Raina walked lightly to make no echoes. On the dais, a man no older than Mauser sat up in bed, shirtless, and held up a palm to stop them. A portable television played at the foot of his bed. Someone on the screen made a joke. The man on the bed laughed and turned it off.

"You act like you know me," he said, voice booming down the pews. "What do you want?"

"I know of you," Mauser said. "And I'd like to make you a deal. One that will mean you can put a stop to all this exhausting robbing."

"Yeah. Listening."

"We have access to guns. Lots of them. I offer them to you if you'll quit stealing from everyone."

The man laughed through his nose. "No."

"Listen, you don't have to stop robbing everyone. Just the people heading to Dunemarket. We can set up badges for them or something."

"We've got guns. What do you think my people used to capture you?"

"Yeah, but you can have more." Mauser wandered closer to the dais. "Dozens. A couple hundred. With ammo. You can then sell those for whatever you want."

Preston swung his legs off the bed. They were bare. A sheet covered his pelvis and upper thighs. "And you want me to stop holding up those Dunemarket peddlers."

"That's all."

Preston sniffed, scratched his chest, and pointed at Raina. "I want her instead."

"No you don't," Mauser said stiffly. "She's the type to cut off your balls in your sleep."

"Sleep? That's why God invented meth."

Raina went very still. So did Mauser. Martin ran in front of her and barred his arms.

"No!"

Preston smiled slowly and stood. The sheet fell away. He wore nothing underneath. "Are you defying me in my own house?"

Raina whicked out her knife. "Get away from me. I'll split your dick in half."

"I like that mouth." He raised his hand and made a come-here gesture. The woman and the two men advanced down the pews, boots clomping.

"Why are you listening to that shitty little TV?" Martin said, voice quavering.

Preston cocked his head. "Huh?"

"You're listening to the built-in speakers. The bass on those couldn't spook my little sister. Meanwhile, you're letting those go to waste." Martin pointed to the wood-paneled speakers at the back of the dais. They were as tall as Preston. He pointed up at the smaller speakers set into the corners of the ceiling. "I can patch all those in for you. All I need is a couple of tools and a couple of hours."

The interest faded from the man's face. He bent over the bed at a regrettable angle, retrieved the little TV, and lobbed it at Martin. "I can wire up some speakers, man. But this thing is battery-powered. Cabs back there run on juice."

"So what? You've got solar panels up on the roof. Might even be a battery for them in the attic."

"You know solar?"

"Sure. Let me take a look."

"Hold up," Mauser said. "In exchange for stopping the attacks on the travelers."

"Nope," Preston said. "Here's how it is. You rig up my speakers, I let everyone walk out of here with their hymens intact."

"That's not much of a deal. That's the same state we walked in here. Figuratively speaking."

The naked man stepped down the dais and leaned his forehead closer to Mauser's. "Sounds like a pretty fucking good deal to me, man."

"It's a deal," Martin said. "Just don't touch her."

"Want her for yourself, huh?" Preston flipped his hand at the woman. "Come upstairs with us. Dave, Hector, you keep these two right here."

He yanked the sheet off the bed and wrapped it around himself toga-style, then brought Martin and the gunwoman through the back door. Dave and Hector stared at Raina and Mauser.

"Your commander," Mauser said. "He's a bit demanding, isn't he?"

The men went on staring. Mauser glanced at Raina, who said nothing.

"Can we at least sit down?" he went on. "I'm not sure my heart can handle the strain of waiting around for someone to finish an electrical job."

Hector tipped back his head, then nodded at the pews. They sat. The gunmen took up a pew behind them. Time stretched on and on. Raina wasn't bored. She was thinking. They were going to leave emptyhanded. To get results for Jill, they would have to find other Osseys and kill them. She didn't like that plan. It was a bad plan. It was dangerous, especially now that they'd already come to speak to Preston; if some of his men turned up dead two days later, he might connect it to them. Come hunting for them. Even if he were too stupid to tie the events together, she would have to attack armed men. She could be hurt.

Mauser made occasional jabs at conversation. Dave didn't reply. Hector mumbled with him sometimes. Raina went on thinking.

There had been a lot of dogs after the plague. Hungry. Scared. Unused to hunting on their own. She had been much smaller then, and she must have looked like easy meat, because sometimes the meaner ones harried her, especially when they were in a pack. But they could be useful, too. They had good noses that led them to food. When she heard claws clicking down the street, she got her knife and followed. If the dog were small enough, she could scare it away from its meal—a dead gull, a garden she hadn't known about—but sometimes she shared, too, so the dog would like her, and let her follow it again. There had been one little black dog with big pointy ears that she'd run with for months. She'd called it Dog. Then it disappeared.

The others weren't as nice. One day she had heard claws and gone from beneath the dogs to find a muscly pup with a broad, flat snout trotting down the pier. It gave her a look and growled and jogged on. Its ribs poked from its skin like the masts and hulls of the boats sunk at the marina. She followed at a distance. It sniffed the doors of the French-Japanese restaurant, then the walls of the old seafood eatery where the empty shells of five hundred dead crabs lay piled in tanks long evaporated.

The dog stopped and lowered its head and flattened its ears. In the doorway of an arcade with clowns and stars painted on the wall, a large brown and black dog with a long, pointed tail bared its teeth. Between its paws, a half-chewed fish sprawled across the gum-spotted concrete, huge and silver, limp enough to still be fresh.

The snub-nosed dog circled the dog with the fish, growling, a stripe of fur raising along its spine. The dog with the fish lunged and snapped. The snub-nosed dog juked away, then nipped at the other dog's side. They exploded into snarls, fangs flashing, butting heads and necks, the scrum carrying them both down the pier.

Raina ran in and grabbed the fish. She climbed the stairs to the roof of the arcade, where she ate it. After the dogs finished fighting, one too wounded to stand, she ate the loser, too.

This was the lesson of the lesser dog: all violence is risk. Even the smallest dog can win if it encourages the strong dogs to take all the risk for themselves.

Outside, the sun rose to noon, rays deflecting weakly through the church's narrow windows. Footsteps banged down a staircase. Preston kicked open the rear doors. He was dressed in one of the black shirts with the silver pirate. Martin was behind him, dusty and sweaty, hair poking up in tufts.

Preston grinned a victorious grin. "Let's kick this shit up."

He strode to the back corner of the dais and twiddled a black box of dials and switches. He straightened and gazed dumbly at the ceiling's ribbed beams. Noise thundered from all sides. Raina balled up on her pew. Guitars thrashed. A man gurgled demonically. On the dais, Preston laughed, drowned out by the music, and banged his head.

He clicked off the speakers and punched Martin on the shoulder. "Right on, man. You're a wizard."

Martin smiled, blushing. "It was just patching a few wires into the battery array."

"And knowing how to do that shit in the first place." Preston rubbed his nose and narrowed his eyes. "Maybe I should keep you around."

"For Pete's sake," Mauser said. He rose, drawing glances from Hector and Dave. "You got a boss set of speakers out of the deal. Probably have lights, too, yes? Air conditioning? We can all walk away happy. Don't get greedy."

Preston jutted his jaw and thumbed his upper lip. Martin looked to Raina for help. She didn't know whether she'd run or fight.

Preston nodded, sparing her the decision. "Yeah. Okay. Get out of my joint. If I see you back here, I take whatever I want."

"As ever, your graciousness is without equal." Mauser took hold of Raina and Martin and shepherded them from the church, followed by Preston's soldiers. The sunlight was hard and sharp. Raina glanced back. From the top steps, Preston grabbed his crotch and made a kissy-face.

"Sorry about that," Mauser said. "Dude's gotten more full of himself since I last saw him. The price of success is arrogance, isn't it?"

"That guy was a jerk," Martin said.

"I know. Why do I always think they'll be willing to talk? No one talks these days. All they do is push you around." He kicked a rock down the sidewalk. "If Jill really does wipe out the islanders, promise me you'll make her come for these assholes next."

"So what now?" Martin glanced back and lowered his voice. "We kill a couple of them and bring them back to Jill? Isn't that murder?"

Mauser shrugged. "I don't think they'll put you on trial for murdering snakes."

"No," Raina said slowly. The idea had come to her so clearly it must have been a suggestion from the spirits. Almost certainly a cat. Only cats could conceive such sadistic plans as this. "We'll take care of them all at once."

"Huh?" Mauser scowled at her. "Raina, the ones you saw in the church were just a fraction of the gang. There's no way we can fight them."

"We won't," she said. "We'll make the Catalinans do it for us."

12

Getting a car wasn't as easy as that, though. If it were, they might have done it long ago—that is, if the roads in the jungle weren't snarled with branches, trees, and other cars, or if Walt weren't still suspicious that an engine-hunting alien flier could pop over the horizon at any time to vaporize them, or if he weren't at least a little concerned that human jungle-dwellers might roll out a trap as soon as they heard a car rumbling down the road.

In other words, there were lots of safety-related reasons why they'd come all this way on foot. But there were practical and logistical ones, too. Like the fact there might not be a single working vehicle in the entire metropolis of Zacatecas, and if there were, it would almost certainly have an owner.

"First things first," Walt said. "Where are we going to get a working battery? Can we find a brand-new one? Will it still have a charge?"

"Generator."

"Eh?"

She stared. "Don't you know anything about cars?"

"I'm a New Yorker," he shrugged.

"Then it's a good thing you're shacked up with a born-and-raised Angelino. You can use a generator to jump-start a car. Same way you'd use another battery."

He swabbed sweat from his forehead. "Where do we get a generator? When the Panhandler hit, generators were probably the number one cause of Home Depot-related murder."

"And almost everyone who took one died in the plague."

"Leaving their generators to be taken years ago by anyone who did survive."

She glared at him, as if it were his fault humanity had been reduced to a pack of rag-donning bone-pickers. "Then we check hospitals. Police stations. Power plants. Any place that couldn't afford to lose power."

"This sounds like a lot of work," Walt said. "Then again, a lot less work than tramping across the entire Mexican desert."

He checked to make sure his .45 was still buckled to his hip and that his backup pistol was inside the pocketed vest he wore to keep vital supplies close at hand. They hoisted their bags and headed toward the city.

A dog barked in the distance. Pigeons shuffled on the eaves of red tile roofs. From outside, the plan had sounded very simple, but down in the maze of streets, it took on a more Herculean tone. They didn't know where any hospitals were. If they tried going door to door, they might run into survivors. Survivors who would be understandably upset to be busted in on by a couple of gun-toting strangers.

Skeletons lolled in gutters. Unfamiliar, Euro-looking cars rotted along the curb. Why couldn't all cities post a map at the entrance? How had anyone found any strange place before GPS? Before they had cell phones to call for directions the instant they got lost? It was a wonder the entire human race hadn't taken the wrong left one day and wound up dead in a ditch.

A brick-colored church with two spires and a dome huddled in the distance. Hundreds of feet above the city, a red cable car hung dead on the lines. They passed through a neighborhood of posh houses colored white and pink and yellow and robin's egg blue. After another couple blocks, Walt spotted the first sign for a hospital. The word was the same in English and it was strange to see the cognate after so many names and signs in Spanish.

They found it soon after, a white building trimmed in blue. Bones and shriveled scalps were scattered everywhere, black hair stirred by the breeze. The lights were off, which meant nothing. Clear pools of sunlight flooded white floors stained with old brown blood. Walt got out his flashlight.

"Basement, right? They always keep this sort of thing in the basement."

Lorna nodded. "Check the pharmacy while we're here, too. See if they've got any antibiotics."

The sides of the halls were lined with blue tarps wrapping long-decayed bodies. Some were piled two or three deep. During the plague, he'd been in the hospital for an unrelated stabbing. It had been chaos. They'd had no clue. The treatment of the corpses here looked undignified, but he expected everything had gone to hell in the last 24 hours before the place had shut down for good, when thousands of the sick were stretched out in the parking lot and the staff had to clear the dead from the beds while they were still coughing their last.

They took the stairs down. Their feet echoed in the stairwell. Every closing door boomed like the command of an angry god. After much wandering down halls that were much less dirty than the dusty, bloody floors upstairs, they found the generator room. It was mostly intact, but there was a distinct vacancy where the machine had once been.

Walt shined the light over disconnected wires and a dust-print where the generator once sat. "Well shit."

Lorna waved a hand in dismissal. "Not the end of the world. We'll check the records in reception. Learn where the other hospitals are."

"How's your Spanish?"

"Adequate."

"You do that while I check the pharmacy. What's the Spanish for 'antibiotic'? 'Antibiotico'?"

"Yep."

They returned upstairs. Lorna swung around the front counter and started rooting through the racks of paper records in the room behind. Walt wandered to the pharmacy and found it thoroughly looted. Bottles and pills speckled the ground. Many of the shelves had been completely emptied. A lot of what was left was gibberish, Spanish medical terms and corporate Mexican brands that meant less than nothing to him. Lacking anything better to do, and dubious that he'd be in another hospital today, he rifled through them anyway, turning up two bottles of fat pills he suspected were antibiotics. On the back of a dusty shelf, he spotted a bottle of what was definitely hydrocodone.

He glanced at the dark door, sat down, and removed two Ziploc bags from one of his vest pockets. He shook the maybe-antibiotics into one bag and the painkillers into another so they wouldn't rattle when he walked, placing the baggies in a vest pocket. Back at reception, Lorna examined a spread of records, taking down addresses on the back of a piece of paper.

He passed her one of the empty bottles. "That an antibiotic?"

She gave it a glance. "Looks like. Got a whole pile of addresses here. One's old folks care. Right down the street."

She finished transferring addresses and they walked back into the painfully bright sunlight. They got the number off the building next door, confirmed they were headed the right way, went down the block, and crossed the street to a much shabbier and homey building. Lorna held the door for him.

The generator was there in the basement. Giant and white and slotted with vents. Walt prodded it. It didn't even pretend to budge.

"Okay, that thing weighs hundreds of pounds," he said. "Guess we're bringing the battery to it."

"No shit, it's industrial-grade." Lorna leaned in to examine its outlets and to thumb the dust from its display. "The best way to do this without blowing ourselves up or burning down the hospital is to find a jump box. It'll be dead, but we plug it into this thing, then hook up the battery, charge it up, and we're golden."

"Where do we find a jump box?"

"Automotive supply. They're loot-worthy, but not number one on most people's list. We're going to need methanol, too."

"Methanol?"

"Wood alcohol," she said. "Gasoline goes stale a year or two after it's processed, but methanol should hold up fine."

"Will it hurt the car?"

"Who cares?"

He rubbed his temples. "Where do we get wood alcohol?"

Lorna shrugged. "Auto shops sometimes carry it. If not, hardware stores are a good bet. We'll probably need it for the generator, too."

"I hate errands," Walt said.

"More than you hate being eaten by coyotes?"

"Depends on the errand."

It felt good to have the generator checked off, at least. Before they left the care facility, Walt checked the kitchen and storage, turning up a few silvery packets of freeze-dried potatoes and beans and unopened water jugs. Heavy, but they could toss them in the car.

He hated errands even more after they'd burned two hours wandering cluelessly through Zacatecas' streets and the boxy, pretty little houses and shops. Lorna found a jump box at the first auto shop they stumbled on. It was a heavy black box floppy with cables. No methanol, but there was a big box home improvement store just down the street. Inside, they struck gold. Translucent, liquid gold.

They loaded up a green wheelbarrow with jugs of wood alcohol and rolled back to the care facility, which involved several wrong turns and two arguments, the second quite heated and ending in Lorna marching down the block, pointing her finger, and waiting for Walt to roll his eyes, catch up, and discover that she was in fact pointing right at the building with the generator.

There was a late-model Suburban stalled at the intersection; it had clearly been working until its driver had unfortunately died. Walt opened the door, reached past the sun-mummy in the driver's seat, and tried the ignition for laughs. When that failed, he popped the hood and watched Lorna detach the battery.

She lifted it with a grunt, then set it down and brushed away a leaf, a spider web, and a generous coating of dust. He followed her inside carrying a flashlight and the jump box and lighted the way down the stairs.

Lorna hooked it all up with no problem. He reached for the on switch and she knocked away his hand.

"I put this thing together," she said. "I get the honors."

She fired it up. It wasn't as rackety as he expected, but it had been years since he'd been inside a room with a functional machine of any kind, and the chug of the generator was disturbing, a deep vibration that felt capable of shaking his guts free from their tethers. The air smelled so sharply of alcohol he thought his nose hairs might burn.

Lorna pointed to a light on the jump box. "We're in business."

"The business of standing around while a box does all the work? This is just how I always imagined the future."

She smacked the counter. "Going to be a while. Want to screw? Or get the car ready?"

"What are you, a fantasy woman?" Walt ran his hand over his stubble. "Don't take this the wrong way, but I'd like to get out of the city. Also, I am incredibly filthy, in the unsexy physical sense. It would be like fucking a dustbunny."

"Then you owe me one."

"I'll owe you as many as you like."

She smiled and headed upstairs. He followed, the thump of the generator receding. Once they were outside, he could no longer hear it at all.

"What do you think?" he said. "Find a car outside of town? Past all the snarls?"

She shook her head. "Just take that Suburban. Can bull our way through all the snarls."

"It's got such bad gas mileage. One of these days we have to start thinking about the environment."

She snorted. "Can swap the battery into something smaller down the road. We'll need to siphon out the old gas."

Walt nodded and went back inside the hospital for a length of plastic tube. He fed it into the Suburban's gas tank and sucked. It tasted like chemical poison death. He spat into the street while the stale gas spattered into the gutter.

Something incredibly fast whirred over Walt's head. A bang echoed down the street. Lorna gaped. Walt grabbed her and leapt behind the car. Another shot whumped into its side.

He reached for the blunt alien pistol inside his vest.

13

"Say, that's a pretty good idea," Mauser said. "I'm sure they'll be happy to oblige this little suicide pact of yours."

"It's not hard," Raina said. "All we have to do is kill some of the Catalinans."

"Now we're killing islanders?" Martin said.

"And making it look like it was the Osseys."

Mauser slitted his eyes, slowly smiling. "You are a devil. I am not yet certain whether you're the Devil, but all signs point to yes."

Raina shrugged. "It's something the dogs taught me."

His smile sagged. "Wait, now I think you're crazy again."

"The Osseys all wear the same thing on their shirts. We kill two of the Catalinans and carve that stupid pirate into their faces."

"That's a Raiders jersey."

"Not all raiders wear it. The Catalinans don't."

Mauser rubbed his eyes. "It seems the generation gap has come early."

"The islanders always come to coast on the same day," Raina finished. "We'll dump the bodies on their route the night before."

"Moses on the cross," Mauser said. "So where do we get the Catalinans?"

"I don't know."

"Oh. Well, good try."

She stopped on the sunlit sidewalk and blocked his path. "You're the one who's been everywhere. Who knows everything. You figure out how we get them."

He screwed up his face and sighed at the sky. "Listen, messing with the Osseys, angling for a little loot, that was all a good laugh. But this is starting to get convoluted."

"You owe me."

"In a certain Conan the Barbarian sense, sure, you saved my life, I owe you mine, blah blah blah." He leaned in close, narrowing one eye in a half-wink. "But what would happen to me if I just walked away? What thunderbolt would strike me dead? What pox would fall upon my house?"

"I could find you," she said.

"You're certainly poxy."

Martin scuffed his feet. "Guys."

"If that's how you feel, you should leave right now," she said. "Because the Catalinans won't stop until we're all slaves or dead."

"There is that," Mauser muttered. He glanced back at the church, then shooed them on. He contemplated the dusty sidewalk for half a block, then looked up sharply. "Oh God. Oh, fuck me with a circus tent."

Martin whirled toward the church steeple, tensing to run. "What's wrong?"

Mauser dropped his hands to his sides, helpless. "I've got an idea."

"What is it?" Raina said.

Mauser gestured toward the sprawling waterfront with its bars and hair salons and bistros. "The Catalinans don't always come here in big battle-groups. Sometimes just two or three of them make it over. I know where they go and I can get us in. On one condition."

"You get all the stuff," Raina said.

"Smart kid."

"Why do you even want it?" Martin said.

"Because they're raiders, man. They get all the best stuff. These days, if you've got something good, you can't stash it in a bank. There's no cops to come arrest a thief and give back your things. If you want to keep something, you have to carry it with you. They'll be carrying your weight in treasure."

"But what are you going to do with it?"

"Retire," Mauser laughed. "Some day I'm going to be too old for this shit. When that day comes, I want a hoard built up to see me through my twilight years."

"So what's this place you know about?" Raina said.

He waved his hand. "It's run by some women. Professionals."

"Professional whats?" Martin said.

"Does it matter? Professional women. In fact, it's a law firm."

"Prostitutes," Raina said. "He sleeps with them."

Mauser scowled at her. "It's a business transaction. Mutually beneficial barter. Better for them to earn a living at it than to run around getting raped."

"That's what you'd do if they weren't here for you?" she said. "Rape them?"

"Well, probably not. No. No, I wouldn't rape anybody. I'd probably just be sad, and make my hand cry itself to sleep each night." He shook his head vigorously, as if shaking off insidious temptation. "Anyway, who are you to judge, Killer McGee? You're the one leading us on the South Bay Death March."

"Against bad people."

"And I'm using my legitimate business contacts to help you. Do you want that help or not?"

"Yes," she said. "Take us to your prostitutes."

"Well, it sounds weird when you say it like that." He crossed the second bridge back to Long Beach. Water sloshed in the canal below, light blue in the hazy sun. "Gonna need to gear up first. Get those guns of yours. Food, water. Could be weeks until their next visit. I don't want to interrupt our stakeout over a little thing like starvation."

Raina walked beside him. Part of her didn't want to tell him about the bunker. If she told, it would no longer be safe. But she knew of other hideouts like it, though they weren't as good, and she could survive with nothing if it came to that. She'd done it before. And if Mauser tried to take it from her, she'd deal with him. Right now, his help was worth the risk.

"I know a place," she said. "It has everything."

"I'd like to see that," Mauser said. "How big are the unicorn stables?"

The walk from Long Beach to the bunker took the rest of the day, a sunny slog down broad boulevards between Walgreens and Jack in the Boxes and the Trader Joe's, all of them hollowed out, picked clean, shelled of necessities, the junk left behind for whoever wanted to try to make use if it. She wondered sometimes where it had all gone. Most of the food had been eaten, and she often found caches that had spoiled or been ruined by rats and bugs. Many of the durable items like guns must have been taken away by people fleeing the city, or hoarded in foolish numbers by those who'd outlasted the plague. Many of those had since died, their treasures forgotten. Hunting the troves down wasn't safe. Unless you knew a place well enough to notice a fixed fence or a shifted curtain, it wasn't easy to tell which homes were truly abandoned and which were still guarded by their residents.

The passage was tiring enough that even Mauser shut up. She wasn't sure that Martin could make it in one trip—he was so frail, a walking vase—but he kept up without complaint. At dusk, she led them into the woods, climbed under the hole in the fence, and opened the trap door to the bunker. Downstairs, Mauser scanned his flashlight over the dry, tidy shelves and whistled.

"Place really does have everything."

"Except an owner," Martin said. He lost himself in the room of radios and wires. Raina showed Mauser the basin in the wall where magic new water appeared and they filled their jugs. She opened the great beige tubs and got out crinkly silver packets of freeze dried apples and potatoes and chicken and beef. Mauser's gaze roved between the bins.

"You know," he said, "we could stay down here. Say to hell with the Catalinans and the Osseys and everyone else who's not us."

"They have my mom," Raina said. "I have to get her back."

"Yes, but here's the thing: do you?"

"You're a devil. Stop trying to trick me."

"It's not a trick," he said, annoyed. "The only trick is the one the world played on us when they made us believe we have to be good people. You know what's more important than being good? Being alive. Good little girls try to rescue their kidnapped mothers. Smart little girls understand there are times you have to walk away."

Raina stuck out her chin. "You think I don't know that? I know what you can fight and what you can't. You can't fight a plague. You can't fight the things in that ship in the bay. The Catalinans are just people. I can fight them. I can win."

"Well, I tried." He zipped up a backpack of silver pouches and ran his flashlight over the whitewashed stone walls. "We'll stay here tonight. My feet are killing me. One more mile and I'm pretty sure they'll finish the job."

That was fine with her. Insulated underground, the bunker never got cold, and there were whole shelves of blankets and sleeping bags. They ate oranges and spinach they'd picked along the way, saving the lightweight freeze dried food for travel. When they blew out their candle, the bunker swallowed them in a perfect darkness that always made Raina feel safe.

That meant the moon wasn't there to watch over her, though. She'd have to look out for herself. If Mauser was playing some kind of con, it was a long one—and he could have sacrificed her to save his skin at Preston's—but you could never be too careful with strangers, especially men who were larger than you. Their strength made them weak to the temptations that crawled up from the dark places of their heart.

She had her room to herself. There was no door, so she rolled up a blanket and laid it across the threshold to trip anyone who tried to sneak inside.

Without windows, they slept later than they meant to. The sun was well above the western mountains before they loaded up and headed south. After a few hours, they were back on the highway they'd taken the night before.

"Where is this place?" Raina said.

"Where else?" Mauser said. "The docks."

"The place we passed that was playing the music?"

"That's the one. Nothing helps you feel less silly to have your pants down than a little music."

After the highway, he split off from the piers and set up camp in the upper floor of a house on a hill a couple blocks away from the waterfront. Upstairs, he ditched his two big packs in favor of his small bag with a pistol, medicine, fresh socks, a day's food and water, and toiletries and sundries. Raina did the same and waited for him at the top of the stairwell.

"Where do you think you're going?" he said.

"To the prostitute store with you."

"Oh no you're not. Way too dangerous for that."

She cocked her head. "We're planning to attack experienced killers and you're worried about danger?"

He gestured at her body. "I don't want anyone getting ideas."

She couldn't stop herself from looking down. She was fit from walking and hauling nets and lines on the boat, but she saw nothing exaggerated or to her eyes exceptional.

She met his gaze. "Like what?"

"Like your lack of a Y chromosome. If I brought you inside that place, some dude would try to buy you from me."

"How much would it cost?"

"I am insulted you think I know the answer to that." Mauser moved to the stair landing and barred the way with his arm. "You'd only invite unwarranted attention. Some of these people aren't very good at hearing 'no.'"

Raina bumped into his arm. "This is my fight."

"Yes, and you can rest easy knowing that when it comes time to do actual fighting, you'll be front and center. Right now it's about business, and nobody wants to do business with a fifteen-year-old girl." He scrunched his mouth. "Well, nobody you want to do business with."

"Who cares, Raina?" Martin said. "This is just to set things up, isn't it?"

She backed away from the staircase. "I don't like being left out."

"Trust me," Mauser laughed, "there are times when it's for the best."

He went downstairs. The front door closed. Raina went to the bedroom on the south side of the house and watched him walk down the street toward the sea. He disappeared behind a row of stores, reemerging a minute later on the endless docks. He approached the front of a four-story condo, knocked, and was allowed inside by an unseen doorman.

"Do you think they really buy girls?" Martin said.

"Yes."

"That's so...gross."

"You wouldn't go to a place like that?" she said.

"No. Especially not if the women don't want to be there."

"I don't think any of them do."

"Well, it's wrong. People shouldn't have to do that. I wouldn't want to be with a girl like that."

She frowned. She didn't see how they could like it either but maybe they thought they had no other choice. Maybe they liked it better than fishing. She didn't like Martin's prudish judgment, but she didn't like Mauser's casual acceptance of it, either. She hoped they owned themselves. Otherwise, they were certainly being used.

Mauser emerged from the condos a few minutes later, hands pocketed in his leather jacket. It was a straight walk between the docks and their house, but he turned left, vanishing into the cluster of waterfront shops. What would she do if he left them? Go see the women herself? She'd have to. It was that or go back to Jill and be a delivery boy while the woman's so-called rebellion puttered along.

Mauser showed up a half hour later. Martin wandered to the upstairs landing while Raina intercepted the man in the foyer.

"Here's the deal." Mauser blew into his hands. "They don't know when the boys from the island will be around next. They don't exactly schedule appointments. But they usually come by once a month, sometimes more."

"Do you know what their boat looks like?" Raina said.

Mauser smiled and shook his head. "Give me some credit. I'm not going to spend the next month sitting around on some oyster-smelling dock playing boat spotter. I've got friends there. One of them has agreed to hang a red lantern from her window when the islanders show up." He pointed to a window in the upper floor of the pierside condo. "That one right there."

"And then we kill them."

"You have a one-track mind, you know that? Once we see the lantern, we wait until they conduct their business, get sleepy, maybe a little stoned. Easy prey. Once that happens, my friend will turn the lantern white."

"Then we go in," Martin said from upstairs.

"Exactly." Mauser tapped the side of his nose. "I'm like the Sun Tzu of convoluted whorehouse assassinations."

As usual, she had no idea what he meant. "It has to be close to when the big boat's supposed to come again. We can't hang onto the bodies for days and days. We could get sick. Animals could smell them."

"And when does the big boat grace us again?"

Raina rolled up her eyes, thinking. "Twelve days."

"But they'll be back again next month," Martin said. "Even if we miss them this time, we can try again then."

This was true. But that would mean one more month for her mom to spend in the Catalinans' hands. One more month for their leader Karslaw to go on living. One more month for her father's spirit to be trapped in the bearded man's spell. Raina didn't want to wait. She would have to make the moon another offering. A proper one. The most potent one she'd made yet.

That night, they stayed up late, but she waited yet again for the others to sleep. As soon as they were out, she crept outside and walked up the dark street. The moon liked water. It shined and played on it. She went house to house until she found a swimming pool with a foot of rainwater in its bottom. She kicked off her shoes, climbed down the steps to the empty shallow end, and scooted on her butt down the slope to the collected water. It was slimy and foul, but she had to prove herself. If she couldn't handle a little green sludge and a couple mosquitoes, the moon would never believe her.

She got out her knife and cut the back of her hand. Not deep—she'd need her hands—but enough to draw blood. It dripped down her brown skin in a black line and fell to the stagnant water with tiny ripples.

She tipped back her head. The moon watched her from high in the sky. It was more than half past full and growing more bloated each night. It might not be hungry. But she'd never offered it anything nearly so fat.

"Help me take their lives," she whispered to it. "Help me take their lives, and I pledge them to you."

Had it widened just then? Had its silver eye bulged in anticipation? She grinned and blinked back three times to show she understood. She climbed out of the pool and cleaned off her feet and ran back to the house.

They didn't have much to do besides watch the windows of the condo and keep out of sight. Mauser showed them how to play hearts and gin rummy and bullshit. They gambled with pennies and he cheated constantly. On clear days, she could see Catalina to the south, a high blue bulge of land at the edge of the horizon. Twenty miles away. She could sail her dad's boat there in half a day or less, depending on winds, but she'd probably need help.

A yellow lantern burned off and on in the window Mauser had pointed out. Never red. Days counted down: eleven left until the big boat came to collect its taxes, then nine, then five. The moon reached its fattest and began once more to starve itself to nothing. They had plenty of food, but not as much water, and Raina didn't like not knowing anything about the neighborhood they lived in. She wanted to know where to run. Where to hide. Where to lay in wait if chased. At night, she roamed the blocks around their home in an ever-widening circle, sneaking deeper and deeper into the dead streets of Long Beach. She felt better.

People came and went from the condo every day. Almost exclusively men. She rarely saw the girls except when they went outside to smoke things or wash in the basin screened off in the parking lot. A few of the men were there every day, stocky hulks with tattoos and darting eyes. Bodyguards. Or maybe just captors.

Four nights before the islanders were scheduled to come in force and extract their tribute from the peninsula, Martin ran in from the other room.

"The red light," he said. "It's up."

Raina ran to the window. Down the street, the condo window glowed an unwinking red. She ran to her room to dress in all black and get on her knives. Martin got out his pistol and stared at it dully.

Mauser tossed his icepick into the air. It spun end over end. He snatched it by its handle. "Stick to the plan and we'll all be fine."

He led them out the back door of the house and they circled around the humid streets to the shoe store across from the condo. Amid the smell of leather and rubber, Raina watched the window from the darkness.

A silhouette exited the side of the condo and peered into the streets. A fire flicked at face-height, illuminating the face of a woman a few years older than Raina. A cigarette bobbed in the night.

"That's my girl," Mauser said. "Be right back."

He crossed the street and exchanged a few words with the girl. In no hurry, he walked back to the shoe store.

"Two of them," he murmured to Raina. "If we're fast, we can use the blades." He glanced at Martin. "Anything goes bad, you shoot them. Don't worry about the noise. Worry about us being strangled."

Martin nodded, pale.

"They killed my dad," Raina reminded him.

"I know."

"And if this goes bad, they'll kill me, too."

Martin's brows rose. He nodded, firmly this time.

Male laughter burst from one of the windows. Some minutes later, a woman groaned, higher and higher. It went quiet. The lantern turned white.

Without a word, Mauser led them across the street.

The woman had left a slip of paper wedged in the lock so it wouldn't latch. Mauser closed the door silently and took them up a flight of carpeted steps. Voices droned from behind the walls. Music played from the lobby. On the third floor landing, Mauser took them down a hall to a nondescript door. Martin pressed himself beside it. Mauser knocked softly.

A naked woman answered. Mauser ushered Raina inside. The white lamp barely lit the room. Two men rested in twin beds. One had his arm around another woman. Smoke curled from a glass pipe in his hands. Raina knew the second man. It was Trig. One of the men who had hurt her mother.

"Hope I'm not interrupting," Mauser smiled. "Manager's special. This one's on the house."

The man with the pipe looked skeptical. Trig grinned. "Looks new. Fresh."

Her ears roared. She stepped toward him, remembering to smile. Mauser drifted between the beds, babbling something affirmative. The man swung his legs off the bed. He was naked and his genitals were wet and wrinkled. He patted his lap. Raina reached for his leg, took out her knife, and jammed it into his throat.

He choked on the blood. The other man yelled. From the other bed, she heard a scuffle, a gurgle. Trig fell onto the floor, kicking at her even as blood gushed from his neck. She dodged his heel and slashed at his warding arm. He yanked it out of harm's way, other hand pressed to his throat. She stabbed him again in the side of the neck, wriggling the blade from side to side.

Her chest heaved. The two women watched with wide white eyes, backs pressed to the wall. Mauser had knocked the other man from bed and pinned him to the floor. The man's hand flopped, went still. Mauser pulled off the top sheet and stood up and wiped himself off.

He held out his hand. "Riches."

One of the girls detached from the wall. Mauser got a rag from his pocket and stuffed it in the dead man's throat wound to stop up the blood. He laid out the sheet and rolled the man up tight, then moved over to do the same to Trig. She cleaned her knife on the sheet, hands shaking. It felt different from animals. Better. She considered granting him to the moon, but she'd never taken a human before. In this case, keeping him was risky. Trig was evil. His presence within her might corrupt her.

But maybe she could learn from him. She had the feeling she might need to do strong, dark things on the path to free her father. Trig's whispers might show her to secret roads she'd be blind to on her own. She'd just have to be careful. Keep him locked up in the deepest places of her heart. Only go to him in times of greatest need.

Metal clinked. She whirled, knife out. One of the girls clutched a backpack to her bare chest.

"Easy there, shortpants," the woman said.

Raina lowered the knife. The woman rolled her eyes and extracted a fistful of shining gold chains from the bag. She quickly sorted them into two purses, handing one to Mauser and shaking it to get his attention.

"Do not wear or sell yours here." He accepted his purse and slung it over his shoulder. "Nothing to tip us off to the bossman."

The woman snorted. "No shit."

"Glad we're all professionals. Now get dressed and help us haul these bodies downstairs."

He went to the door and let Martin inside. The boy gawked at the blood-soaked sheets shrouding the downed men.

"Look," Mauser pointed to the brightly-stained sheets. "We made big soppy candy canes."

Martin swallowed hard. One of the girls laughed. The door banged open and a lanky man spilled inside, smelling of a day at sea.

"Hey assholes," he declared, "save any of that for—?"

His gaze flicked between the sheet-wrapped bodies and Mauser and the girls and Raina. He turned and fled into the hall.

"Shoot him!" Mauser hissed.

Martin held up his hands and shook his head. Raina darted into the hall, Mauser pounding after her. The stairwell door clanged.

"If he gets to his boat," Mauser said, "we should just kill ourselves right now."

"I know!"

She entered the stairs a step ahead of Mauser. Guitar music throbbed from the ground floor, washing out the clap of the fleeing man's feet. The downstairs door shuddered open and the man ran into the night. Mauser passed her, leaping down the steps four at a time. He bowled outside. She followed. The air was moist and just cooler than lukewarm and within a few steps she was sweating.

The man ran past the shops toward the docks. Mauser fell back a step. The man turned onto the main road to the marina, Mauser dogging him from a block behind. Raina cut down the delivery lane she'd discovered a few nights earlier. A brick-paved gutter ran down its center. Undistinguished rears of buildings abutted the lane. She burst into the moonlit boulevard right across from the sprinting man.

He was getting away, but Trig's spirit already had a suggestion for her. One so black she nearly laughed out loud.

"Help!" she screamed. "He's trying to rape me!"

The man turned, slowing in confusion. Raina raced toward him. The man looked over his shoulder, trying to spot Mauser, whose feet rang somewhere down the block.

"You all right?" he said to Raina. "Come on!"

She thought she'd seen him on the islanders' boat. She couldn't reach his throat too well, so she drove one of her finger-length knives into his belly instead. He doubled over, shrieking, still running, pinwheeling one arm for balance. She dodged it and lashed at his throat with her hunting knife.

That brought him down. He was still gasping fitfully when Mauser jogged up beside her.

"Nice work," he said. He frowned. "Although as the only adult present, I'm not sure I should be encouraging this."

"We need to get him to the wagon," Raina said.

"I'm not carrying that bloody mess. We need to get the wagon to him."

He dragged the dead man next to the front of a seafood restaurant and headed back toward the shoe shop where they'd waited for the lantern to change colors. Martin was already there, sheet-wrapped bodies piled on a large green wagon they'd taken from a hardware store.

One of the women from the house was there, too. Her teeth flashed in the darkness. "All yours."

"What a lovely gift," Mauser said. He leaned in and kissed her cheek. The woman didn't move one way or the other. Mauser glanced across the street at the whorehouse, which continued to play its rhythmic music, candles flickering behind the drapes. "Won't be around for a while. Try not to miss me."

"Deal," the woman said.

Mauser grabbed the handle of the wagon, heaved, and grunted. The wheels turned soundlessly; they'd had plenty of time to oil it and check its bolts. Raina and Martin shouldered their bags. They got a block away from the condo, putting a row of buildings between them, then circled around. At the slope to the seafood restaurant where the dead man waited, Mauser flipped the wagon around and leaned against its handle so gravity wouldn't pull it and its cargo of corpses down the hill and into the sea.

At the third body, Raina and Martin each took a leg while Mauser took the shoulders. Martin's hold slipped while it was halfway on the wagon and the body's left leg bounced against the sidewalk. Mauser swore and wrestled it atop the others.

"I'm sorry," Martin said, breathing hard.

"No worries," Mauser said. "We're all loaded up now."

"In the room. I couldn't shoot."

"Happens to every man at some point."

"It would have been too loud anyway," Raina said. "It's for the best."

But she didn't believe this, at least deep down where it counted. The man could have gotten away. She'd had to put her life on the line to stop him. Martin couldn't be trusted.

She took point while Mauser wrangled the wagon, ranging a block or two ahead to make sure the streets were empty. When Mauser ran out of breath, Martin took over, leaning against the wagon tongue as if fighting the worst Santa Ana wind Southern California had ever seen. He lasted less than ten minutes before Mauser took back over.

Its wheels thundered lowly. A dog's nails clicked down the street. The condo faded behind them. Now and then when she entered an intersection she looked back and saw its candles burning in the night.

They got off the highway in San Pedro and Mauser called a stop for the night. It was well after midnight. Raina scouted out a house while the men watched over the bodies. She found one with no signs of recent squatting—no food scraps or fire ashes, no telltale stink of feces from the corners or the yard—and they wheeled the wagon into the garage, hauled down the door, and went to sleep. Martin and Mauser took rooms upstairs. Raina laid out her blanket in front of the door to the garage. They had come too far to risk something coming for the bodies in the night.

Mauser got up late that morning, rotating his arms and grumbling about stiffness.

Raina almost smiled. "You wouldn't complain if you saw the guys in the garage."

He looked pained, then sighed. "You can't toy with my morbid curiosity like that. It's like peanut butter to a dog."

He squared his shoulders and opened the door to the garage. Raina trailed him. The men lay on the cement floor, covered by a crusty, bloody sheet. She swept it away. Their fingers were curled. Trig had his mouth open in a frozen scream. His eyes had been put out (and offered to the eye of the moon, though Raina had no intention of telling Mauser that). The three men were shirtless and a rough icon of a helmeted man with an eyepatch and two swords had been sliced into their chests.

"Well, no one can accuse you of lacking initiative," Mauser glared.

"I thought it would be best before they got stiff."

"Spent a lot of time around dead bodies, have you?"

"I used to eat them."

"Not going to ask." The lines around his mouth deepened. He leaned down. "What did you do to their shoulders?"

Raina reached into her pocket for a bloody handkerchief. She unfolded it, revealing two-inch squares of skin inked with black. "They had tattoos. I cut them off to give Jill proof it was us."

Mauser opened his mouth to say more, then shook his head and walked away. They waited until night to move again, wheeling the wagon down lesser-used streets paralleling the main roads. It wasn't yet dawn when they hit the southern coast at the base of the hills.

It was two days before the islanders were supposed to arrive. As the sun rose, Raina climbed up to the crotch of a tree and watched the sea through her binoculars. Mauser and Martin kept watch on the land, hiding out in a lifeguard shack standing on stilts in the sand.

The bodies went slack and began to smell. Their faces and bellies swelled. The night before the Catalinans were scheduled to arrive and take their tax, she and Mauser wheeled the bodies above the tideline and dumped them face-up in the sand. They took turns standing watch in case of animals or strangers.

The tide sighed, coming and going. In the early morning, Raina spotted a sail on the sun-shattered waves. They retreated to a high house a few blocks from the beach. The Catalinans made landfall at the pier and started down the beach. When they found the bodies, they gazed east toward Long Beach.

They claimed the bodies and returned to the boat. Raina struck out toward the Dunemarket, matching strides with Mauser.

"They looked pissed," he smiled grimly.

"They should be," Raina said.

At the top of the long hill leading down to the merchants' blankets and stalls, Mauser stopped and clucked his tongue. "Know what, we can do better. I'm a man who likes to make an entrance. Right now all we've got for Jill is a story and your three bloody postage stamps. Why don't we wait a couple days and see how the Catalinans respond?"

They had been away from the Dunemarket for a couple weeks and Raina wanted nothing more than to go straight to Jill and demand a place at the table. But Mauser was right. And waiting a few days more wouldn't cost them anything.

They turned off the road and found a new house a few blocks away. Their water was low again and they collected some from a canal and boiled it.

Mauser was right. Righter than Raina would ever have believed. Three days later, the Catalinans declared war on the Osseys.

14

"Stop!" Lorna yelled in Spanish. "We're not here to hurt anyone!"

Another shot cracked from the buildings. A bullet crashed into the sidewalk behind Walt and whined away. Windows stared by the dozens. Walt peeked around the bumper of the Suburban. A rifle roared again, smashing the rear window in a sharp-edged shower.

"We have to get off the street," Walt said.

"They'll steal our car," Lorna said.

"So what? It'll be easier to set up a new one than to try to steer that one using ghost-hands. Count of three, run to the hospital. Zigzags. Don't give them an easy shot."

She gritted her teeth and nodded. He counted down. On three, he dashed from the safety of the car, arm held over his head, reeling in unpredictable vectors. Two shots chased him up the sidewalk. Lorna hollered. He glanced back to make sure she was unhurt, then yanked open the hospital door and held it for her.

He followed her into the deeply shadowed lobby. She vaulted the reception desk and dropped behind it. He did the same, banging his shin in the process.

He clutched his throbbing leg. "Couldn't see where they were shooting from. There's like a thousand windows out there."

"They'll just wait us out," Lorna said. "Shoot us as soon as we step outside."

"Sounds like we should stay in here. Start a new race of hospital-people."

"Sun sets in an hour. If we haven't figured something out by then, we might as well bring ourselves to the morgue."

His pistol hung from his hand. "If I know where they are, I can take them out."

She laughed dryly. "Such confidence."

"More in the weapon than myself."

Lorna's gaze dropped to his gun. "Get to an upstairs window. I'll make them show themselves."

"By dressing up as a target?"

"Any better ideas?"

"Not unless you saw a tank in the basement." He leaned in and kissed her. "Don't get shot."

"Then don't miss."

He winked at her, stomach sinking, then ran to the stairwell. It was pitch dark on the stairs and he flicked on his Zippo to light the way. The echoes of his footsteps chased him to the fourth floor. He ran into a room with two skeletons sharing the single bed, a third in the armchair, and a fourth dragging the sheets on the floor. He went to the window, careful not to disturb the blinds.

The hospital faced banks of dusty offices. The sun had sunk behind the buildings, leaving little glare, but most of the windows were too dark to see through clearly. He let his eyes drift, seeking movement. The window had a crank that allowed it to open just far enough to extrude his pistol.

Lorna screamed from downstairs. Across the street, a gun flashed in a window on the fifth floor of a pastel yellow office. The report sounded an instant behind it and echoed from the buildings.

The nice thing about a laser was that it provided its own sight. Walt depressed the trigger-buttons wrapped around the handle. A blue beam licked across the air, incinerating particles of dust. It sent smoke curling from the edge of the shooter's window frame. Walt moved his wrist fractionally, sending the beam swooping into the silhouette in the office. A man screamed in pain. Walt moved the laser up and down, then let go of the triggers.

A second gun went off three windows over from the first. Glass splintered, hailing into Walt's face and bare arm. He flinched, swearing, bleeding from several small cuts. Across the way, the woman in the other window pulled back the bolt of her rifle. Bright brass caught a beam of light and spun toward the pavement. Walt steadied his elbow on the sill and fired back. The laser struck her somewhere in the upper body. She collapsed from sight.

The street was silent. Walt scanned the office for any more shooters. A door banged in the hallway behind him. Lorna jogged into the room, struggling to keep her expression composed.

"Now that's fucking teamwork," Walt said.

She pointed at the blunt black gun in his hand. "Did you have that at the beach?"

"Never leave home without it."

"You had a laser. And you didn't use it."

He pulled back his head. "Hang on. I had a laser. They had lots. Not to mention whatever crazy alien submarine they must have sailed up in. Under those circumstances, I couldn't have turned a Big Wheel, let alone the tide."

Lorna shook her head, composure cracking into cold fury. "You could have tried!"

He fumed. "Can you walk and chew bubblegum? Pat your head and rub your belly?"

"What are you talking about?"

"Can you?"

She spread her palms. "Sure."

"Great, you can do two things at once. So yell at me while we drive."

He tucked the gun inside his vest and headed down the stairs. After the darkness of the stairwell, the lobby's deflected sunlight felt positively lush. At the front doors, he stopped to stare at the dumbstruck windows across the street. No one fired. Nothing moved.

He jogged toward the Suburban. Lorna followed with the jump box and the battery, which she fitted into the engine while he watched the street. She dropped the hood with a metal clunk and got behind the wheel. Walt loaded up the back. The engine turned over, coughed, revved, and steadied. Walt pumped his fist and leapt into the passenger seat. She lurched forward before he could close the door.

"North," he pointed. She said nothing. He rolled down the window to better watch the street.

The drive was hell. Every few blocks, wrecks clogged the next intersection. At times, Lorna was able to climb the car over the curb and maneuver around the smashed cars. Others, she had to back up and try another route through the unfamiliar streets. Once, after two unsuccessful detours, she clenched her teeth and forced her way forward, bulldozing through a yellow Beetle with a squeal of scraping metal.

"Was driving always this much fun?" Walt said.

She cursed at another blockage, three low sedans crunched bumper-to-bumper by a burnt-out ambulance. "This is moronic. We should have scouted our path. Or taken a car at the edge of the city. We're sitting ducks."

"We feel more like Godzilla on wheels to me. You're doing great. We'll be fine."

She backed up, swung around, and headed away from the wreckage. "You don't know that."

"Yeah, you're right. But no matter how much time you spend worrying about it, there are only two outcomes. Either you'll be fine, or you won't."

"Dr. Phil? When did you get in the car?"

"Lorna, I'm not bullshitting you with mind-magic. If you'd been through what I've been through, you'd know it doesn't matter."

"What makes you think I've been through anything less?" She fiddled with knobs until the headlights came on, bathing the dusty streets in yellow. "Like you don't get worried? You're pissed off all the time."

"Because terrible shit keeps happening," he laughed. Light glinted from the upper floor of an office, drawing his eye, but it was just the last of the setting sun. "But it doesn't get under my skin. Those problems aren't chiggers, they're flies. They land, irritate me for a minute, and then I wave them away."

"That must be wonderful." Lorna hauled the wheel right, diving around a tipped and half-flattened bus. "What heights of self-improvement. And all it took was going Rambo on an alien species."

A veritable horsefly of irritation landed on Walt's neck and bit down hard. "If you don't like what's happening, do something different. Park the car. We'll track our way out on foot, then come back and drive out."

"Right. We'll grab our compasses and draw a little map. This is all so much smarter than planning ahead. I totally get why Karslaw sent me 2500 miles to find you."

"Just drive. Let me concentrate on not getting shot by paranoid locals."

He turned to the window. The truth was that he was stung. She wasn't a fly, she was a hornet. He wasn't sure he liked that. Was he coming all this way, risking his life just so he could be in the presence of a woman who often acted like she couldn't stand him? Because that would be kind of crazy. Not fun-crazy, either. The kind of crazy that manifests after sitting on a pyramid for too long with your hand down your pants.

He glanced across the cab at her. She kept her eyes on the way ahead, cornering down a long hill of square and tidy houses. From above, the neat rows of homes must have looked like Easter-colored teeth.

Like that, the city stopped. The Suburban coasted down the black stripe of the road. To each shoulder, yellow weeds poked from the hardpan. The silhouettes of cactus and desert shrubs lurked in the highland night. It smelled like sweet pollen and dry air. It had been a long, long time since he'd traveled any faster than running speed, and as Lorna accelerated down the highway, he rolled down his window, stuck his face out into the night air, and smiled.

Lorna drove for a couple of hours. Without discussion, she pulled off at a ranger station on the edge of a national park. Dim rocks climbed the horizons. Lorna parked behind the station and opened the back of the SUV. While she unloaded gear, Walt entered the cabin, feet clunking on the wood floor, and checked with a flashlight for any obvious families of rattlesnakes, skunks, or tentacled horrors.

He turned up nothing but dust. He lit a candle and dug the Tupperware of waltcakes out of their bag. The mashed avocados had begun to brown but tasted edible enough. He went outside and passed one to Lorna, who accepted it with a nod and chewed slowly, dribbling crumbs.

"Sorry," she said. "I was stressed."

"Yeah, where did that come from?" he said. "We were only trying to flee a strange city after a running gun battle."

"You were trying to help."

"And by this point in life I should have learned that in times of stress, that only makes people angry."

She laughed, touching his arm. "Think the aliens are any better? Or did the pilot only decide to smash Earth after her husband nagged her the whole trip?"

Walt shrugged. "During my encounters, they looked less like enlightened beings and more like the Ten Thousand Stooges. But they must have emotions. They're made of meat just like we are. Chitin and slooshy stuff, anyway."

"It will be better when we're home." She tipped back her head to the burning bed of stars. "I don't know this place. Its people. You and I are all there is. Spend too much time alone and you become a savage."

Walt laughed. "Are you calling me a savage?"

"Aren't you?"

"Who isn't? Aren't we all pretty much shitting in buckets these days?"

"But you tried to massacre an entire species. That puts you into a special, Attila the Hun category of savage."

"Yeah, well they started it." He slipped his arms around her waist. "We're good?"

"We're fine."

That was comforting, but after all the walking, hauling, running, and shooting at Zacatecas, he was too tired to make use of that fineness. They slept in each other's arms. The cold woke him in the middle of the night; they'd gone to bed under a light blanket, but the desert air had cooled drastically, seeping through the cracks in the unheated cabin. It was the first time he'd been cold in a couple years. It felt good, bracing and exposing. Lorna slept on, untroubled.

She looked as pretty by starlight as daylight. Despite all his free time, he hadn't yet taken a close look at his feelings toward her. Now wasn't a good time, either. Not since they'd gotten the car. With any luck, they could finish their journey in three or four days. That wouldn't be nearly long enough to plumb the depths of whatever was inside him.

That was the other advantage to walking. It gave you time to think. To explore things down to the roots. If a voyage was a transition from one place to another, it made sense for it to take place over a transition in time, too. Cars, planes, they obliterated that transition, making a separation in space less real. Less meaningful. It removed the chance for growth. No wonder everyone had been so damn confused and angry before.

He went back to bed. The morning warmed up fast. They packed up and drove out between dusty fields studded with lumpy cacti. The Suburban burned through their fuel fast; they camped outside the next major city they encountered and spent the next day foraging for wood alcohol and moving the car battery to a hybrid.

By the end of the day after that, they were in spitting distance of the border. The landscape stayed hot and dry and vast. Less than 24 hours later, the air turned gentler. Cooler. Damper. The meaning of this still hadn't dawned on Walt by the time they broke over a ridge and looked down on the peopleless sprawl of Los Angeles Basin.

II:

SCOUR

15

Smoke toiled in thick pillars from the shores of Long Beach, stretched over the downtown in gauzy sheets by the constant offshore breeze. The wind blew parallel to their position on the hill above the Dunemarket, but the rifle shots were loud enough to survive the trip, hard cracks followed by echoes that faded out like the slowing of a dried-out, dying machine. Sometimes there was just one shot. At other times, they crackled like strung fireworks, one after the other, overlapping into a fray of bangs. An orange flame climbed from the wick of a pierside building.

"Dumb as hell," Jill said, camo binoculars clamped to her eyes. "What do they do when those flames spread into the city? Call 911?"

"They had the wisdom to survive a plague," Mauser said. "Providing them with many unburnt yet unoccupied sections of city to relocate to."

"The wind's about to stop," Martin pointed. "It always does this time of day."

Raina thought she could taste the smoke. "The Catalinans started the fire. They don't care what it burns."

Jill wiped her sleeve over her mouth. "And you three are to blame for this mess."

"Well, who says who's to blame, really?" Mauser answered. "We wouldn't have gotten involved at all if the Catalinans weren't squeezing our balls off with taxes while the Osseys rob everyone coming to bring us new goods."

"But you're the ones who set them at each other's throats."

"Again, though, is that our fault? If they weren't so touchy, we never would have been able to light this little fire. Surely they must share the responsibility."

"Did you have a reason for starting this war? Or was it just for the fun of setting things on fire?"

Mauser gaped, affronted. "Do you think we're here to brag? Of course we had a reason."

Jill nodded, wiped dust from the lenses of her binoculars, and set them away in the case on her hip. "Guess we'd better go inside."

She trudged down the hill to the shack opening to her underground home. After the dazzling daylight, the cave was total black, and Raina stood in the entrance waiting for her eyes to adapt. Jill hung a right down the hall. Boards creaked; sunlight flooded into a round room walled and floored with mortared brick. Indirect sunlight lit the room through a square window in the roof, making for a kind of courtyard. Possibly the only natural light the underground home allowed. A sturdy table painted Chinese red sat in its center. Jill sat at its head, grabbed a small black box from it, and fished out a brown cigarette. She lit it and blew a pillar of blue-gray smoke at the hole in the ceiling.

"Well?"

Mauser leaned his elbows onto the table and pressed his palms together. "Well."

"We killed three Catalinans in a whorehouse," Raina said. "We carted the bodies away and made it look like the Osseys did it."

Jill let smoke drift from her nostrils. "To set them up. To spark a war."

"Yes."

"Why?"

"Because we hate them both?" Mauser said.

The woman tapped ash onto the brick floor. "'We.'"

"You wouldn't let us help you," Raina said. "So we had to do it ourselves."

Jill nodded, tapping her nails on the painted wooden table. "How do I know you three caused this?"

Raina delved into her pocket. She withdrew three pale, yellowing scraps that had already gone hard and scratchy along the edges. She spread the three pieces of skin on the table so Jill could see the tattoos.

"These belonged to the Catalinans."

Silence enveloped the room. Martin glanced at Raina, as if seeking permission to speak. "It's compelling proof, isn't it?"

"That you're reckless?" Jill said. "That you don't listen to orders?"

"That we're more than delivery boys," Raina said.

"Right. You're also liabilities."

"You're messing with us," Mauser said, tone halfway between a declaration and a guess. "Back in the good old days, these two couldn't legally drive a car. Don't tell me you're not impressed with the Game of Thrones shit they just pulled."

"If there's no blowback? Sure. You've got my ear." Smoke curled from her mouth. She squinted against it. "Tell me. I know why these two are involved. What's your angle?"

"Moi? Maybe I'm just a keen evaluator of talent. A manager, if you will. Or maybe I believe that in these trying times, a man of action, cunning, and results is well-positioned to be rewarded for his talents."

"Talent. It's true. We need that." She leaned back in her chair and drew on the cigarette, cherry blooming in the gloom. "So let me bring you up to speed. Best estimate, we've got a thousand people living in the greater area. A good piece of everything they're taking out of the ground or the sea is going to the islanders. A lot of the locals were already struggling. Under the tribute, they're scraping."

"Isn't that why there's a rebellion in the first place?" Mauser said.

"But that thousand people is just a guess. There are a lot of ghosts out there. People who want to live their lives and don't want any part of a fight. Of the people who might help us, the Catalinans' tributes mean they have to spend much more of their time farming and fishing than learning how to fight. Meanwhile, the enemy can strike us at any time and retreat to their island at the first setback. They only have to commit their soldiers. If we fight, we risk entire families."

She sat back and pursed her lips. "What this adds up to is slow growth. We stock up—food, medicine, weapons. We keep recruiting and we train our people to be effective fighters. We're not going to turn this into a guerrilla war. Not when so many are fighting just to put food on the table. We wait until we have the strength to end this with a single blow."

"That sounds...dynastic," Mauser said.

Jill tapped her cigarette with her index finger, dumping ash. "It could take months. If things break wrong, it could take years. But I'll tell you this. The less time our people have to spend working and foraging, the more time they have to train. The sooner we drive the Catalinans back to their island for good."

"You still want us to be delivery boys," Raina said. "After all we've done."

"Wrong. I want you to be hunters." The woman smiled. "Of gear. Of guns. And, when the opportunity presents itself, of the enemy."

The conversation continued, but Jill just rehashed what she'd just said. It stung. Raina had imagined she'd become a warrior. One of Jill's frontline fighters. But it didn't sound like there would be a frontline for a long time.

At least Jill no longer regarded her as a shovel, something you used to turn things up. Instead, Jill wanted her to be a knife. You could dig with a knife if you had to. Knives were versatile. But the main use of a knife was to cut. To harm. To kill.

And Raina could live with being a knife.

She moved with Martin and Mauser into a house south of the Dunemarket. The gunshots in Long Beach continued through the night. By morning, the smoke had cleared. After breakfast, figuring that while she worked to advance the rebellion one wagonload at a time, she might as well work to advance herself, too, Raina asked Mauser to teach her to fight.

He raised a brow. "What makes you think I know how to do that?"

"The way you stabbed the man in the bar."

"Then the first lesson is to always keep a psychopathic teenager around to distract your enemy."

"This isn't a joke. This is my life."

He sighed and gazed across the hills toward Long Beach. "You want to learn? We need some gear. White t-shirts. A bunch of them. And two red markers. Felt. Fat-tipped."

"What for?"

"The markers are your knife. The shirts will show you how easy it is to die."

She drew back her head, then jogged off to the ruins. It was a very simple thing to find the shirts and simpler yet to find the markers. Safe in their bubble packages, they retained their ink. Mauser took her to a park down the hill to the west of the market. Skeletons crowded a concrete culvert but there was no smell.

"Pretend you're about to stab me." He handed her one of the markers. "Not that you need to pretend."

She dropped into her stance and tensed to lunge. He closed his eyes and waved his hands. "Come on, Raina. You're left-handed, aren't you?"

"It's in my left."

"You're leading wrong. You've got your knife out front. You stab at me, maybe I grab your wrist. Bend it into an unwristlike configuration. Take your knife away and stab you with it." He mimicked her knife-first stance, then reversed it, drawing his marker close to his body. He waved his empty hand in her face. "See this? It's my hand. You better not ignore it, because it can punch you in the throat. Poke out your eyes. So I strike with it first."

He did so. Reflexively, she grabbed for it, neutralizing it. He flashed in with the marker, slashing a broad red smear across her gut. "See? That red splotch represents you, quite dead. Because I lead with my free hand."

She reversed her footing. It felt strange, reserving her blade, extending her naked hand first, but after a few minutes of dancing around in the grass, slashing and stabbing, marking each other's arms and guts with red, it felt much safer. More dangerous. Mauser couldn't afford to ignore either threat. If she landed her empty hand, he would be hurt or knocked back, vulnerable to the knife; if he tangled up her free hand with his, that left him open to a swift stab to his belly or ribs.

"You take to this with disturbing ease," he said.

She lowered her marker. "Where did you learn?"

"Jail."

"You were in jail?"

"Nothing that exciting. Some drug charges. My celly claimed this was San Quentin shiv-fighting. I don't know about that, but it's proven effective enough."

They danced back and forth, shuffling across the grass. He showed her four ways to grab the enemy with her free hand: a noncommittal, thumbless hold; a death grip; a grab for the enemy's fingers; a wristlock. He showed her how to jab at the eyes and rake the face. Some was instinctual, but there was a crispness to his technique that she was greedy to learn. To replicate it, she had to slow down to a frustrating crawl.

The sun sank. They went home and slept, picking up where they left off right after breakfast. Martin watched glumly from the shade of a palm. After a couple hours, she suggested they go take more guns from the bunker to bring back to Jill. Martin brightened. He had some ideas about the rainwater-collection system and how to apply it to the underground homes of the market.

At the bunker, Raina left a few guns and dozens of boxes of ammo behind. She wanted a fallback plan. They loaded the wagon with twenty firearms of all shapes and sizes and a thousand rounds of ammo. It was a tough drag and it took most of the night.

"Nice work," Jill said in the doorway of her home, groggy-eyed; it wasn't yet dawn. "Can you get more?"

The gunshots and smoke rent Long Beach for two more days. Jill had scouts who returned with stories that it was mostly sound and fury. A few people had died on both sides, but they were mostly feeling each other out, dancing the same way Raina danced with Mauser in the grass of their yard, markers held close to their bodies, waiting for an opening, a mistake. Raina took Martin and Mauser into the ruins to plumb more arms. When they came back, with just two pistols, a rifle, and a few boxes of bullets, the scouts said the east had been quiet all day.

Men and women came and went from the Dunemarket. Most wandered among the tents and blankets, but a few found Jill, murmured with her, and followed her up the hill to her home. Raina watched each one, memorizing faces.

Raina continued combing the old homes. On their previous trip to the bunker, Martin had drawn sketches of its water collection and filtration system, and while Raina searched for weaponry, he looted tools and materials from garages and piled them in the wagon.

Raina didn't keep any of the guns, but she took her knives everywhere. As she scavenged, she thought about how she would use them—if a man attacked her like so, she would block and stab like so; if he came in from her left, she envisioned slipped past him, slashing and stabbing at his guts as she tried to get around to his back. When she thought no one was looking, she practiced on the trees, attacking low limbs, visualizing them as aggressive arms waiting to be gripped and cut and broken.

But someone had been watching. A couple days into her makeshift, constant practice, she returned to the Dunemarket with a wagonload of mesh screens and bags of charcoal for Martin's water barrels. He intercepted her on the road and grinned.

"Want to see something cool?" he said.

"No," she said. "I hate cool things."

For a moment, he looked devastated, then laughed and blushed. "Then you're going to really hate this. Come on."

"Let me get the wagon to the market."

Martin glanced dismissively at the pile of material. "That stuff made it through the last five years. I'm pretty sure it can handle five more minutes. Come on!"

She glanced up the road to make sure no one was around to take it, then pulled the wagon to the shoulder and let the handle clank to the ground. Martin jogged down Gaffey St., burnt-out foundations to his right, untouched homes to his left. He hung a left down a narrow side street that led to their home, a pink stucco place with two couches on its shaded porch. He hunched down in front of the one-car garage, heaved, and shoved the door up its track with a rickety clatter.

A wooden post jutted from the middle of the floor. A pair of thick sticks poked from the post at knee- and shoulder-height, padded with foam and wrapped in cloth. Sanded wooden knobs capped the limbs' ends.

"It's all yours," he smiled.

She stepped forward. "You got me a scratching post?"

"But it's not for cats. It's for Rainas." He walked around it, striking at the padded limbs. "It's a practice dummy. So you can train when Mauser isn't around."

"Cool."

"It is cool. You should try it."

She got out her knife and, feeling foolish, jabbed at one of its "arms." The blade sank into the foam. The attack took her uncomfortably close to the other arm. The two angled legs threatened to tangle her own. She pulled out the knife, grabbed its arm with her open right hand like Mauser taught her, and swung to the dummy's side, stabbing at the body of the post. She stepped back, considering the sanded wood.

"When did you have time to build this?"

"Mornings," Martin said. "Afternoons, too. Sometimes at night, so long as I didn't have to make any cuts to the wood. I guess I spent pretty much the last three days on it."

"It's cool. It's like a body. It makes you think about how you'd fight a real person."

"Cool," he grinned. "Let me know when you cut the foam up too bad and I'll replace it."

She nodded and attacked it again, rattling its arm. Mauser had shown her a few steps to use, short, shuffling things he claimed would let her react faster and move in or out without commitment—that was a big thing for him, committing. He said it was one thing to commit to a punch, but when the other guy had a knife, too, you didn't want to make any big clumsy moves where he could stab you right back. She found the steps unnatural and had to think about each one, but the dummy gave her the perfect target to slow down and visualize what each step meant.

When she finally looked up, Martin was gone. When she got tired she toweled off with a bit of the unboiled water they kept in the garage and went inside to eat dinner. She returned to the garage and resumed, practicing without end, a slow dance that left her shoes dusty and the floor littered with bits of foam.

"What's that?" Mauser said. She whirled. He coughed into his hand. He smelled like beer and his eyes were puffy. "Find yourself a scratching post?"

"Martin made it," she said. "So I can practice when I'm by myself."

Mauser chuckled and touched the slashed-up foam of one of its arms. "That kid. He'd take a bullet for you. And then take the bullet and build it into a bullet-spitting robot. We're wasting his potential."

She lowered her knife, sweating in the half-cool night. "What do you mean?"

"That he's handy. We should get him to work on a trebuchet. A mangonel, even. Blast the holy hell out of the enemy's stupid yacht."

"About the other thing. Taking a bullet."

Mauser raised his eyebrows, which barely widened his glassy eyes. "You really don't know?"

"Know what?"

"That he pines for you like the taiga. Yearns like young Werther."

It took her a moment to translate. She shook her head. "He's too young."

Mauser scoffed. "Like them older, do you?"

"Maybe I don't like them at all."

His eyebrows shot up, then his face pinched in on itself. "You're messing with me."

She laughed at him. "Why do you care? Are you jealous?"

Mauser's expression clouded. He stepped closer, as close as she came to the dummy as she stabbed at the vitals between its arms and legs. "How old are you, really?"

"Would it matter?"

He smiled, eyes half closed, breath whistling through his nose. He moved toward her. Her pulse leapt.

He halted and bared his teeth at the dummy. "Does it matter to the law? To this little society we've got here? No. Thirteen, seventeen, eight, eighty, it's all the same."

"You talk a lot," she said.

"And I wasn't finished." He patted her face. "It doesn't matter to the law because there isn't one. But call me old fashioned, it still matters to me." He winked at her and lumbered past. "Good night, Raina."

The garage door slammed. Her candles wavered. She flushed with a lowdown shame. She whirled on the dummy and jammed her knife into its neck.

Mauser wasn't around in the morning. Not in the house. Not in the yard. Not in the Dunemarket, either, when she was offloading flares and binoculars onto a trader's blanket and three Catalinan soldiers strolled up and asked for her by name.

16

Lorna drove with purpose through the buttery sunshine and dried-out streets of outer Los Angeles. Or maybe it was still Orange County, Walt didn't know. All he knew was that the ocean glittering far below wasn't as pretty as Mexico's shores. Not the southwest coast they'd reached after their first leg through the jungle. Certainly not the pale blue glow of the Gulf. It wasn't just a loser in the looks department, either. According to Lorna, it was more dangerous here, too. A downgrade in pretty much every way from the life he'd left behind.

Yet Los Angeles still felt like a homecoming. He hadn't spent more than a few months there, but those months had been big ones. Seeing the city again was like revisiting the city where you went to college. Bumping into your first girlfriend and going out for drinks. Returning at midnight, after retirement, to the field where you hit your first home run.

"This is weird," he said.

She braked the car, jolting him forward. "What? Do you see something?"

"Yeah," he said. "The place where I saved the world."

"How nice." She gassed the car downhill. They drove through nondescript strip malls and apartment complexes, then hit stucco Spanish-style houses and palm-lined streets. She only had to detour around two blockages of wrecked and abandoned cars on her way to the shore. The marina lot was half empty and she pulled into a spot, stopped, idled for a moment, then switched off the car and hopped out into the warm air. Walt stepped onto the grassy parking barrier and stared out to sea.

"We should garage this." She traced her hand over the car's hood, drawing finger-lines in the grime, a thousand miles of Mexican dust and a few hundred of the American kind. "It would be wrong to abandon it."

"Don't you have any on the island?"

"It's more than that. It took us this far. We can't just cast it off."

"You're right. It would sulk for months."

"It could be useful. I don't know how many working cars we have on the mainland."

"That's the thing about our brave new world," Walt said. "The old one isn't really gone. If you spend a little time searching for it, and a lot more time restoring it, you can bring a piece of the old ways back to life."

She turned to him, her desert-tanned face an unguessable mixture of emotions, then nodded at the boats still berthed at the docks. "Here's the big question. Do we row to the island? Or do we sail?"

"Do we have something against engines now?"

"You think it's easier to get a boat running than a car?"

"Rowing or sailing it is," he said. "What's less likely to get us killed?"

"Do you know how to sail?"

Walt laughed. "I bet I make a mighty fine passenger."

Lorna smiled wryly. "Is that a no?"

"That's among the no-ingest noes you've ever heard."

She walked over the grass divider to the concrete walkway to the docks. "I know just enough to know that it would be tough to get us across by myself."

Walt swung his arms, limbering up. "Then we row."

She stepped onto the wooden pier. "It's twenty-plus miles from here."

"We just walked a thousand."

"On our legs. Unless you were doing handstands while I wasn't watching, this will exhaust an entirely different set of muscles. You'll wear out a quarter of the way across."

"The Hawaiians did this all the time. On a diet of poi, no less."

"They had canoes. And crews of rowers. We'll have two of us, unfit for duty, in a rowboat." She stopped in front of a mast angling from the placid marina waters. Kelp swayed in the shallows. Finger-length orange fish drifted between the fronds. "If we row, we know our arms will give out. We don't know that's true of the wind. We'll sail."

"Aye-aye, captain. Does this mean I'm your first mate?"

"Eighth."

"Then I'll settle for being best."

"Third."

He snorted. "Then I'll settle for being the one who's still here."

She walked from boat to boat, sizing up rotted sails and green-tinged ropes, kicking hulls, muttering to herself. Walt grew progressively more bored, feeling unusually useless. After an hour of searching, she clambered onto a small sloop whose sails only had a couple small holes and stomped her foot on the deck.

"This'll do."

"Great," Walt said. "I think I could have swam there by now."

They went back for their goods from the car and loaded up. Lorna unfurled sails, yanked on ropes, rubbed her jaw. "This is going to be ugly. Good chance we'll crash before we're out of the marina."

"Good god. We'll have to swim dozens of feet."

Lorna gestured at the cleats and the ropes holding them to the dock. "Mates work the ropes. Untie us and jump aboard."

He saluted, jumped down to the pier, and unknotted the lines. The boat bobbed at an angle from the dock. He stretched for the ladder and climbed back up. She hauled hard on the sails, trimming them tight against the wind. The sloop swung slowly about. With a grating roar, its rear end hit the dock and knocked Walt to the deck.

"Is that standard?" he said.

The boat ground harder, juddering Lorna's voice. "Get out and swim. We'll see who gets there first."

With a lurch, the rear yanked free. She had chosen a ship near the end of the piers and it wafted toward the jetty of black rocks that pincered the entrance of the marina. The sail flapped against itself and Lorna adjusted it, swinging the boat around to face the way out. It overcorrected, nose pointed toward the rocks, drawing closer by the second.

"Lorna," he said.

"Who drove a thousand miles to get us here?" she shouted into the wind and the slap of waves against the hull.

"You did."

"And I can fucking sail us the last twenty to get home."

He strapped himself in to one of the fishing seats and gripped it hard. The boat bobbed closer and closer to the rocks. When it came parallel, the jetty was so near he could have jumped down and landed on it. The wind bore them past into the open ocean.

Walt stood and cheered. "Now there's the girl I married."

She smiled vaguely and went back to work on the ropes. The sun banked from the waves. The shore receded behind them. He thought he saw a darker blue blur on the horizon but couldn't be sure. He offered to help and she brushed him off. He returned to the fisherman's chair, plunked down, and enjoyed the sun on his skin and the scent of the salt.

The blur coalesced into a blob and then into a solid lump. Walt hadn't been on a proper boat since trips off Long Island with his childhood friends, but he thought they were making good time. The sun climbed and peaked. He napped, waking with sweat greasing the folds of his skin. His mouth was dry. He went into the cabin for a drink of water, then approached Lorna near the mast. She gazed at the approaching island.

"I'm concerned," she said.

"Isn't that it?" he pointed. "The big island-shaped island?"

"About us."

Walt blinked, stung. "The part where we have fun together? Or the part where we went through some amazing shit down in the jungle but came out alive because we had each other?"

"My people won't understand."

"Will they understand my middle finger?"

She smiled tightly. "You won't be able to help us if they don't trust you. This thing I brought you here for is bigger than us."

"You're serious?" he said. "What are you suggesting? That we break it off?"

"Maybe just for a while."

He sniffed at the ocean. "Nope."

"What do you mean, nope?"

"I mean," Walt said, "that I'm much more concerned about a resurgent alien menace than the judgment of your friends. If they don't like it, I can always head right back to Mexico."

"Walt."

"Lorna."

She rolled her eyes, wind whipping her hair. "This is a different world than the Yucatan. There are rules."

"No there aren't." He stood, spreading his hands, the breeze drying the sweat from his armpits and the crooks of his elbows. "If you think anything's changed, then you don't understand what the plague was all about. It didn't change the rules. It just proved they never existed."

"Great speech," she said. "That won't change how they feel. They're good people, but they're very wary of outsiders. That's what kept us alive."

He stripped off his shirt and slung it on the deck. "Okay."

"What are you doing?"

He stepped to the railing. "Swimming back to shore."

"Walt."

"Lorna."

"You don't understand what it's like there."

"Do you care about me?" he said.

"Of course I do."

"Then act like it. It's that simple."

"No it isn't!" She grabbed his arm, fingers prying into his biceps. Her eyes burned brighter than the sun on the sea. "But what I care about most is saving my people. I don't want to give them any reason to distrust you."

"It wouldn't matter," he said.

"That's right. I forgot. You're the man who saved the world. How's a little thing like a society going to stand in your way?"

"Here's the thing: I don't give a shit about these people. I give a shit about you."

"Were you always this romantic?"

"It's the reason any of us are alive."

She shook her head, black hair streaming across her face, and glared at the island. "It would have to be a secret."

"Us?"

"We don't have to stop. But we do have to pretend like it never was."

He shook his head. "I don't know what you're so afraid of. But this isn't my home. If that's what it takes, then I'll keep my mouth closed."

"Good."

"Until it's on your body."

She gave him a look. "You ran off by your lonesome. You don't know how things changed. When the plague took our families, we formed new ones. Hundreds of people on that island see me as their sister. Their niece. Their daughter. Six of our men died and I'm coming back holding hands with a stranger. How's that going to look to them? Do you think people judge women less now that everything's gone to shit?"

"You'd think the total collapse of everything we knew would be a pretty good time to reevaluate old prejudices." He leaned forward and set his elbows on his knees. "Know what, I have no problem lying. If that's what it takes, for all I care we can tell them I'm a eunuch."

"Speaking of." She adjusted the ropes and turned to him. "Take off your pants. It could be a while."

He grinned and unlatched his belt. The pitch of the ship made things tricky even after they were lying down, threatening to slam him onto her with far more force than his anatomy could stand, but that just made it better. He barely held off long enough for her to finish. After, he lay on top of her, taking great gasps of salty air, sweat trickling down his sun-baked body. She winked and pushed him off and got a towel from the cabin.

The island congealed from a blue-black lump into a green chunk of land. Lorna adjusted the flapping sails. He dressed and wandered back onto the deck.

"Is the wind always like this?"

She shrugged, clothed again. "Sometimes it blows the other way instead."

He retreated inside the cabin with scissors, knife, rag, water, and his remaining can of Gillette. By the time the island was close enough to make out its ridges, trees, homes, and docks, he'd carpeted the floor with his long hair and middling beard. His chin was reasonably smooth, his hair cut short enough to bristle his palm. He had shaved himself down to the scalp a few times in the jungle—sometimes he got so sick of the heat and humidity he couldn't handle a single hair on his head—and as always, the act was cathartic, redefining. Lorna gave him a long eye as he stepped back on the deck.

"Who's that?" she said. "A stowaway?"

"Have to look tough for the locals. Long hair is for poets."

The island loomed nearer. A quarter mile out, a mirror winked from the shore. Walt shielded his eyes and leaned forward. A rifle boomed across the ocean.

"Jesus!"

"Get down and try not to get shot," Lorna said.

Walt had already crouched down. He dropped to the pitching deck, shielding his eyes against the blinding waves. "I thought these were your friends. What did you do, skip out on the rent?"

"Give me your shirt."

He peeled it off and flung it at her, not bothering to ask any questions. This was her show now. She pounded up the metal ladder on the side of the cabin, braced herself against the rise and fall of the waves, and twirled his shirt above her head.

"What's that, your distress signal?" Walt said. "Or just trying to convince them we're friendly strippers?"

"They don't know it's me," she said. "They were expecting Hannigan's boat. Weeks ago."

Walt rolled on his belly. The island neared, a mass of craggy green hills fronted by rocky beaches. The remnants of a small town waited to the right of their present course. Fingers of smoke climbed from chimneys. The mirror on the shore winked again. Lorna whipped the shirt to her sides—three times right, twice left, once right. The mirror flashed twice and disappeared. A figure waited on the sandy shore.

Lorna drove the boat straight into the beach. Sand scraped the hull, groaning and squeaking under the mass and momentum. Walt sprawled forward, landing on his elbows, pain stinging up his arms.

"Lorna?" a man called.

She grinned, strode to the railing, and vaulted over the side, landing in the surf with a splash. Walt followed her over. It was a warm day but the water was cold. He gasped, sucking in a mouthful of salty water. He coughed and kicked, beginning to panic, but his shoes struck sand beneath him. He lurched up and walked to shore.

Lorna embraced a youngish man with a wormlike, angry scar running front to back down his scalp. He pulled away, laughing in the sunlight.

"We thought you were dead!"

She smiled wryly. "Just about."

The man's smile cracked. He glanced at Walt and the boat beached in the surf, then rubbed his mouth. "Is this it?"

"We were attacked. Aliens."

"Hannigan?"

She shook her head. The man embraced her again. After a couple seconds, she drew back and nodded at Walt. "But we got what we came for."

The man with the scarred scalp smiled and frowned at the same time. "That's him?"

"Tell Karslaw we're here. We're going to my house to clean up. We'll call on him in an hour."

The man nodded, smiled sympathetically, and jogged toward the town down the beach.

"Karslaw," Walt said. "Sounds like a Russian horselord."

Lorna hiked up the beach toward a road. "He was a contractor. Now he's our king."

"Should I wear a tie?"

"Subtract the sweat and the dirt and we'll be fine."

She led him up a grassy hill to a Cape Cod-style home painted bold blue and trimmed with white. L.A.'s houses always threw him. This one could have been right at home on Long Island or New England. As usual, the neighboring houses were a jumble of Spanish, Victorian, Tuscan, and '50s modern, though the island town was decidedly more beach town/tourist than what he'd seen on the mainland. He still couldn't decide whether this schizophrenic diversity was an awesome display of artistic freedom or a pathetic attempt to appropriate the status of older places.

Lorna's front door was unlocked. She strode through it, glancing casually at a kitchen and living room, as if to reassure herself it was still there. She brought him to the back patio, which was dusty and crusted with old leaves. She told him to wait there and brought a plastic kiddie pool, a bar of soap, a towel, and sloshing jugs of clear water. He washed up. She came back with some beat-up but clean men's clothes—jeans, t-shirt, white socks.

He stood up, dripping. "Want to join me?"

"Dry off and get ready. I've been gone for months."

"So what's five minutes more?"

"Walt."

"Two minutes."

"The boat wasn't enough?" she said. "Get dressed. Let's go. Or I'll bring him here instead."

Walt stepped out of the kiddie pool and grabbed his towel. He got on his clothes, his shoes. Once he was ready, Lorna climbed an unpaved trail into the hills. A herringbone marina extended from the bay. Pastel Mediterranean houses crowded the slopes above the beach. Lorna dipped off the ridge into a valley, putting the town a mile behind them. At a lonely hill across the plateau, a vast structure spread against the horizon.

Walt pointed. "What is that?"

"Karslaw's home," Lorna said.

"It looks like a..."

"Fort?"

"I was going to say castle."

"It should. It is one."

"Okay," he said. "What is a castle doing on an island twenty miles from L.A.?"

"Exactly what it's supposed to do," she said. "Protecting us."

"From aliens?"

"Mainlanders. We started building it before we knew the aliens weren't all dead."

High wooden walls thrust from an earthen rampart. Wooden towers flanked the gates and the corners of the outer walls, rising another three floors into the sky. A keep waited behind the outer fortifications. From across the valley, it looked wooden, too, but as they crossed the plowed-up farmland surrounding the dirt road, he saw the keep was brick and stone.

"I feel like I could use some etiquette lessons," Walt said. He glanced back at the shacks spotting the fields on the approach to the castle. "Do I call him 'Sir'? 'Your Majesty'?"

"Karslaw."

The wooden gates were open. A figure moved in one of the towers. Walt wasn't sure what to expect as a way of greeting—trumpets, men with pikes, a hail of arrows—but nothing met or challenged them as they thumped across an actual drawbridge spanning a dry moat. A flagstone path led to the keep.

A tall, burly man exited into the grassy bailey. He was bald and bearded and his shoulders rolled easily as he walked. Lorna laughed.

The man ran the last few feet, crushing her to his chest.

"We thought you were dead!" he bellowed.

"Almost." She grinned the same wry grin as at the beach, tugging her shirt smooth.

"So Chad said. I'm sorry to hear—"

"Later," Lorna said. "I'll tell you everything later. Once I've had gin. I miss gin like it were air."

"Whatever the returning hero wants." Karslaw stepped back from her and regarded Walt. "Who's this?"

"Walt," Lorna said.

The big man jerked his thumb toward Santa Monica Bay. "Is he the one—?"

"Yep. That's him."

"Huh. A man never looks like his reputation, does he?" Karslaw extended his thick hand to Walt. Across the blue waters, Los Angeles rested in the haze. "Welcome to Catalina. Care to finish what you started?"

17

She wanted to run. Hide. No one knew the ruins like her. The three soldiers down the street could hunt her for years and never find her. But she didn't feel like running anymore. Not from the Catalinans. She might still fear them, but she hated them more.

The soldiers were at a stall speaking to the woman whose two boys used bikes to deliver messages and packages across the city. Raina walked out from the shadow of the shack she'd been watching from.

"I'm Raina," she said. Heads swung her way.

"Is that her?" a dark-haired man asked another whose windbreaker sagged over his basketball-sized paunch.

"Yup." The paunchy man smiled at her. "You don't forget eyes like that. They look ready to leap right out of her skull and stab you."

"Why aren't you at your house?" said the dark-haired man.

"What house?" Raina said.

He waved his hand west toward her old home. "Down on the shore."

"I moved."

"Why didn't you let anyone know?"

"No one told me I had to let anyone know."

"Made it damn hard to find you."

"I had to move," she said. "I can't run my boat by myself. Was I supposed to starve?"

The paunchy man glanced at the people milling around the blankets and merchants, several of whom watched their conversation. "Maybe we should take this somewhere more private."

"I'm fine here," Raina said.

"We're getting off track," said the dark-haired man. "Where were you last Friday?"

"When was Friday?"

The other man rolled his eyes. "Were you at Pokers?"

"What's Pokers?" she said.

"Whorehouse." He gestured east. "In Long Beach."

"Why would I be at a whorehouse in Long Beach?"

The dark-haired man laughed. "Do you have an answer for anything?"

"I wasn't at a whorehouse in Long Beach. I'm just a girl. Who would ask such a disgusting question?"

He pulled back his head, flustered. The man with the belly smiled, mirth in his eyes and contempt on his mouth. "Because one of the pros said she saw a skinny little Mexican girl hanging around in the parking lot that night."

"I'm not Mexican," Raina said. "My parents were from Costa Rica."

The first man ran his hand through his black hair. "Hold on, did Heather mean Mexican-Mexican, or of the general appearance of a Mexican?"

The other man shrugged. "Hell should I know?"

"What's this about?" Raina said.

The third soldier hadn't spoken the whole time. He had doleful eyes and the build of a utility pole. He leaned down to her level. "Murder."

"Someone died?"

The man straightened, judging her from on high. The fat man wiped his nose on his sleeve. "They didn't drop dead. They were killed. Know anything about it?"

She shook her head. "I was moving here last week. Hauling stuff with my friend Martin. Why would I know anything about a murder?"

"People kill for many reasons," said the tall and quiet man. "Greed. Pleasure. Revenge."

Raina let out a shaky breath. "Well, I don't know anything. Am I under arrest?"

The three soldiers looked between each other. The paunchy man reached out and tapped her chin. "Not yet. But don't go anywhere. We might want to talk to you again."

She wanted to bite off his fingers. "I'll stay right here."

The Catalinans walked up the road, stopping to talk with another vendor, who pointed up the hill toward San Pedro. Raina watched them until they climbed over the rise, then ran to her new house to tell Martin about her alibi.

"Do you think they'll come for me?" he said.

"Don't look so scared. You just have to lie."

"What if they can tell?"

She snorted. "If they knew anything, they wouldn't be asking."

"What if they're trying to trick you? To get you to lie? We'd better tell Mauser."

"Why?"

Martin gaped at her. "Because he could be in trouble, too."

"He can take care of himself," she said. "But you're right. We have to get our stories straight."

They asked around the market and Dana the ironmonger said Mauser was speaking to Jill at her house. They caught him closing the door to the hillside home and, isolated in the dusty, palm-studded field, Raina explained how the three soldiers had come to her about the murders.

After, Mauser grimaced and dabbed sweat from his brow. "They said this woman saw you at Pokers?"

"Yes," Raina said. "Is that really its name?"

"Tragically, yes," Mauser said. "And Heather who works there said she saw a skinny Latino girl on the scene."

"Yes."

"Which describes, oh, ten percent of the surviving populace of Los Angeles County."

"But what if she can identify Raina?" Martin said.

"Should we kill her?" Raina said.

"Should we kill—?" Mauser tipped back his head and spread his arms, beseeching the sky. "Raina. Killing can't solve all your problems. Well, unless you kill everyone, anyway, at which point you probably would be rid of all your worries. Except what to do about the smell."

"But they came straight for me."

"No, they didn't. It's been what, a week since they found the bodies? Since the war began? If they had any real leads, they'd have been here six days ago." He cracked his knuckles. "This is a new golden age for violent criminals. The police don't have any DNA to trip you up with. Of course, there aren't any proper cops either, so those fellows who came to see you could, if so inclined, beat the shit out of you until the truth spilled out with it." He picked at something on his neck, looking thoughtful. "So don't piss them off, I suppose. Did you piss them off?"

Raina shrugged. "I played dumb."

"They were looking for you to slip up. Or for an excuse to smash your skull. If they come back, stick to your story and it will all be cool."

"But they knew my name."

"Yeah, because they came to the market with your description and someone said, 'Oh sure, that's Raina.' Trust me, they don't have shit. Know how I know that? Because you're talking with me instead of drowning in the bilge of their boat."

Raina wandered off, convinced, but in the morning, the hand-cranked siren yowled from the Dunemarket. She jogged from the garage where she'd been practicing on the dummy. Down the hill, twenty of the Catalinans marched into the market. Some carried axes and machetes. All carried guns. She threw herself behind a rusted pickup and waited for them to call her name.

But they weren't there for her. Their leader strode to the middle of the street and cupped his hands to his mouth. Wars were costly, he declared. In order to fund the ongoing battle against the violent gangs to the east, they required—to their own regret—increased tributes. More food. Bullets, if such things could be found, although they would accept raw lead as well. They needed soap, too, which they knew the merchants knew how to make, or at least import. Condoms. Toothpaste. A host of minor things. Raina didn't listen too close. All their soldiers would soon be dead.

There was a lot of grumbling among the merchants. Less so among the travelers who'd been bartering at their stalls. After the soldiers left, Jill announced a meeting for the following afternoon. She wrote a batch of messages and handed them to the bicycle boys.

Sixty-odd people showed up for the meet, sitting under umbrellas and a tarp stretched between two stalls to shield them from the sun. It wasn't the entire population of the Dunemarket; Raina figured there had to be at least a couple hundred more in the hills of the park and the surrounding ruins. Raina had brought Jill enough guns to arm half the people in the street. Assuming they were willing to fight. Seeing how few they were, Raina understood why Jill waited.

But the war with the Catalinans didn't have to be a fight to the death like the dogs she'd stalked on the pier. There were hummingbirds, too. They fought off much larger birds with no more than a sharp bill and raw anger. However small their numbers, if they struck back with enough force, it might be enough to convince the Catalinans to stick to their island.

"So the islanders want more," Jill said from a small platform set up in front of the tarp. Her voice was hoarser than normal. "I don't see much choice. We have to give them what they want."

"How much further do we bend?" called Velasquez, who ran the herb stand. "What if the next thing they want is my left nut?"

"Then be grateful you've got a right one." Some laughter, but Jill didn't have to wait long before it ended. "All they want is a little food. A little stuff. A little of our time. And you know what? All that time is borrowed. They won't be here forever."

"How do you know that?" Velasquez said.

Jill surveyed the crowd. Her face was composed, but Raina could see the calculation. The rebellion wasn't an open thing. Was every face in the crowd of sixty a face Jill could trust? Raina didn't think Jill would think so. She leaned forward.

"Over the last few months, we've been assembling a trade union," Jill said. "We're still working on logistics. A way to ensure that when we speak, they listen. In another couple months, we'll be ready to offer them a proposal. Their island keeps them safe, but it also keeps them poor. If they want what we've got, they'll have to negotiate."

"From the right end of a gun," an old man grumbled.

"We'll see. I think they'll listen. Keep your heads down and we'll see how it shakes out."

"Why not just blow up the damn boat?"

Jill laughed humorlessly. "You think that's the only one they've got? You think that's all their manpower? If you blow up one boat, what do you do about the three that come after it?"

They talked more, but that was the end of it. Raina waited for the crowd to break up and for the last of the hangers-on to leave Jill alone. She approached then, gesturing up the bare hill where they could talk by themselves. Jill sighed but followed up the summer-browned grass.

"What is it, Raina?"

"Is that true? About the union?"

The woman gazed downhill. The market had resumed. Vendors entertained travelers and crafted small wares. "The union's a pipe dream. A cover story. We will make a legitimate proposal. I don't expect the islanders to accept it."

"And when they don't, we fight."

"That's the plan."

"Why don't we ambush them tomorrow? How many more of them are on the island?"

"Lots," Jill said. "Enough to squirt us between their toes even while they're dealing with the gangs over in Long Beach."

Raina gestured vaguely south. "How do you know? Have you ever been to Catalina?"

"I know because a different batch of soldiers steps off that boat every time it comes for taxes. Two months, three, we might have enough people to stand up to them. Is that so long to wait?"

"Not for me," Raina said. "But it might be for my mom."

"This is ridiculous. I used to be a substitute teacher." Jill sighed and shook her head. "You want to make progress? Guns, Raina. Lots and lots of guns."

Raina left her on the hill. She was tired of hearing about guns. It was all these people thought about. Carrying them. Using them. Fighting over them. Such stupid things. Anyone could use them. Anyone could pull a trigger from across a field. They rewarded cowardice. They made people think that violence was a quick and clean and easy thing. If the men on the boat had to kill with their hands, not one in ten would have the stomach for it.

The bunker was nearly out of guns and she was keeping the few that remained in reserve for herself. Reduced to aimless scavenging, she wandered up the coast from her old home, checking houses methodically. There was no telltale sign or pattern for where you might find a gun. Most had been looted, hoarded, or lost. Taken from one place and abandoned in another. Even so, she went first to the rich houses of the Beach Cities. People with wealth would have wanted to protect it.

She climbed the winding roads in the green hills of Palos Verdes, rummaging through lavish homes that looked stolen from Spain or Boston or Italy. She stayed away from houses she wasn't sure were empty. The afternoons were hot but cooled as soon as the wind turned. It took as much as an hour to search each home—you could do it faster, but the true valuables, the guns and jewels and dollars owners once yearned to protect, those were often hidden or locked away in safes and closets, some of which she could find keys for if she looked hard enough. Most times these stashes were empty, but now and then they turned up a pistol or bullets.

Some houses searched must faster. Some had been completely hollowed out, dust resting in the scratches on the bare wood floors. Others had been used for squatting, chairs burned for heat, rooms cleared to eliminate hiding spots for rats and roaches. At such places, she spent five minutes searching for secret compartments, then headed to the next house down the street.

This part of the coastline was miles away from the market and she traveled alone and slept in empty houses. Over the course of seven days, she turned up twice as many guns. She brought them back to Jill and returned to the hunt in the hills. She resented the time lost when she could have been training with her knife—alone and away from her dummy, she could only practice her more rudimentary and abstract skills—yet it was this time away from her training that gave her the opportunity to revolutionize it.

She exited a shed in the back yard of a house on the edge of the sea. The patchy grass sloped into a decline that was almost but not quite steep enough to call a cliff. Black rocks ringed the shore below it, buffered from the ocean by a narrow beach. Light flashed from the sand.

The man was shirtless. Tanned as brown as herself. Two streaks of gray in his dark hair. The skin on his face and arms and belly looked old, but his muscles moved smoothly. He had a knife in both hands and she thought he was dancing.

But that was only because his movements were so fluid. Flowing like the ocean washing up and down the shore. Knives flashing. Slow rolling motions that exploded into blurs of light and steel. She knew as certain as she knew her own name that he had been doing this for longer than she'd been alive.

For a minute, she did nothing but watch, hunched in the wild weeds at the edge of the decline. Something came alive in her. All the while she'd been training, she'd had to keep a persistent doubt at bay. Karslaw was so much bigger than her. So much stronger. Mauser's lessons were practical, effective, but she feared they weren't powerful enough to overcome the bearded man.

But nothing could stand against the man on the beach. His knives could split the wind.

At once, he stopped, bounced down to his haunches, and wiped his palms in the sand. Her heart lurched—was he about to leave?—and then he drank from a blue plastic bottle and started his practice again. Raina backtracked to a trail down the cliff, ran to the beach, and walked up behind him.

"I want you to teach me to do that."

He whirled, knives out. He was at least fifty years old. He lowered one blade. "Why would I want to do that?"

"Because I want to learn," she said. "Because I want to be the best."

He smiled, pulling wrinkles around his eyes and mouth. "No."

"Because someday you will die but your skills can live on."

He sheathed his knives and bent to pick up his bag. "Are you appealing to my ego? I don't care about my ego. Or yours."

She dogged him as he headed up the beach. "Because I can give you anything."

"You've already given me a headache." He gave her an amused look. "Just what do you think you have to offer? All I see is a pair of shoes and a flagrant lack of shame."

"I find things. I know this place. Whatever you want, I can get it for you."

"Do you imagine I'm so busy I can't poke around the rubble for myself?"

"What will take you less time?" she said from beside him. He was only a couple inches taller than her. "Ferreting out the treasures from all this sprawl? Or teaching me to do what you do?"

He glanced over at her for the first time since walking away, squinting against the wave-reflected sunlight. "There's nothing I want."

Her heart beat harder. "Then I'll make you teach me."

"If you could do that, what more could I possibly teach you?"

She jogged around front of him, got out her knife, and lunged, leading with her open hand. His mouth tightened. He slapped her wrist away, stinging it. She flicked her knife under their crossed hands, going for his gut. He pivoted on his heels, pulling his body out of harm's way. She jabbed toward his face. It was just supposed to be a feint, an uncommitted strike to rattle him, but he intercepted her forearm with his palm, guided it away from his body, and, still holding her arm in place, slammed the extended knuckles of his other fist straight into the soft flesh of her inner forearm.

She yelped and dropped the knife into the sand. He hit her with a flurry of blows, dazzling her, knocking her to the beach. She tried to get up and her elbow folded. Her face skidded into the sand.

He set his hands on his hips. "Now you have blood on your nose and sand on your face and I'm still not going to teach you."

Raina pushed herself up to her knees. Too many parts of her hurt to locate them all. "Teach me because I want to kill the man who killed my father."

"Do you think I just stepped out of the 36th Chamber?" He walked on. She jumped up and got her knife and put herself in front of his path.

"Teach me again, sir."

He laughed, pressing his palms to his cheeks and then dragging them down so she could see the wet red lids below his eyes. "Are you that devoted? Then here's my deal. Bring me a Chagall, and I'll teach you."

"What's a shoggle?"

"Who."

"What?" she said.

"It's not a what, it's a who."

"Who is Shoggle?"

"Chagall," the man said. "He's a painter."

"You want me to bring you him? How do you know he's still alive?"

"He's not. He's very dead."

"Do you want me to bring you his body?"

He stepped back and shook his head at the sand. "This is absurd. I retract my offer."

"No! Tell me about Chagall."

"Bring me one of his paintings. Not a print. Not a replica. One of his. If I like it, I'll teach you kali."

"Where can I find you when I do?"

"If you can find a Chagall, you can find me."

"Then I'll find your Chagall," Raina said. "And then I'll find you."

He smiled. "Sure you will."

She ran up the slope. At the top, she crouched in the brush and spied on him. He lived three blocks from the beach in a house half the size of his neighbors. She went back to the basement where she'd concealed the guns she'd scrounged and ran back to the Dunemarket, arriving at sunset. At the house, Mauser pan-fried sausage links while Martin pointed at the pan and babbled about ideal heat levels.

"Why does he want a painting?" Mauser said when she explained. "Who's he hoping to impress, the Empress of The Burnt-Out Ruins That Used To Be Los Angeles?"

"I don't know," Raina said. "But he wants it. I'm going to get it."

Martin nodded and backed off from the fire pit. "When do we leave?"

"Tonight. We're going to Malibu. Crossing the entire city. Best to travel at dark."

"I'll go get packed."

Mauser's mouth hung open. "You can't just run off on some ridiculous quest. We're in the middle of a rebellion here."

"Jill moves as slowly as mold. She won't miss us for a few days."

"In case you forgot about the war we started, the Catalinans and the Osseys are at each other's throats right now. Don't you think we'd better stick around for that?"

"No," Raina said. "See you later."

"At least eat dinner."

She went to her room to add a few long-term items to the travel pack she'd carried while hunting for guns on the coast. Freeze-dried food. A third lighter. Spare safety pins. Martin met her in the hall.

"I've never been to Malibu," he said. "Is it far?"

"It's on the other side of the bay," she said. "Thirty or forty miles."

"Do you know what the paintings look like?"

"Don't all artists sign their work?"

Martin adjusted the strap on his pack. "Probably. But it will probably be faster if we know what we're looking for."

"Brilliant thinking, chief," Mauser said behind them, legs churning to catch up.

"I thought you weren't coming," Raina said.

"And I thought you were bright enough to know about the magic of libraries and museums. We're not going to Malibu. We're going to the Getty. It's time you two got cultured."

"That sounds ominous," Raina said.

Wind shuffled the palms, carrying the scent of the smoke of the Dunemarket campfires. Raina kept one eye on the dark streets, but thought mostly of the man on the beach, and all the ways she would hurt the Catalinans once she learned to make her knives dance.

18

"We've seen them on the shores," Karslaw said. "Little ones. Children of the stars. Offspring of our murderers, raised by the gravekeepers of our world. Monsters with clapping beaks and more limbs than a spider."

"Sure," Walt said. "Aliens. I've seen a few."

"Of course," the man smiled. "After all, that's why you're here."

"Well, in my official capacity as your military advisor, I would advise you to shoot them."

Karslaw laughed, baritone whoops echoing off the stone walls of the keep. A small fire crackled in the hearth, smoke drawn up the flue. The stone was worn, dusty. Naked beams upheld the high ceiling. Outside, the wooden palisades were new and blond. The mortar in the stones of the keep walls was only lightly stained and showed no moss. But this place, the heart of the keep, it felt much older, decades if not centuries, as if Karslaw and his people had built their fort around a venerable mansion. A museum, maybe. For all Walt knew, it was the former main hall of an Ivy League college. Whatever it was, they hadn't built it—they'd found this place, this hilltop estate, and adapted it into a castle. Taken the bones of the old world and made themselves a new home.

It was like this everywhere, he suspected. People were scared, tired, eager for anything to shelter them from the storm of the end. They didn't have time to build from scratch. They'd hole up in the empty shells of anything they could find. And not just in the literal sense of old buildings, but in everything, picking up old beliefs and dreams and judgments. Hermit crabs of the Earth.

Karslaw drank from his stein, a pewter hulk with an attached clapper-lid. The smell of coffee wafted through the breeze-cooled room. "Shoot them. Sure. It sounds so easy."

"Isn't it?" Walt said.

"Gets a lot less easy when they shoot back. Here's the problem, Walt. I'm not running a squad of SEALs over here. I got a whole people to worry about. A nation. A small one—Vatican City with fewer miters and more guns—but I'm responsible for hundreds of lives nonetheless. It isn't just aliens I have to worry about. I got gang problems on the mainland. My people are patrolling the shores and the city every day. That's manpower spent keeping the peace instead of tilling the earth. I got to ask taxes from the settlers on the peninsula just to keep my people in salt and soap."

"'Ask'?" Walt said. "As in, 'Would you prefer to pay my taxes or be shot?'"

Karslaw made a face. "Somewhere in the middle. The citizens like paying them about as well as anyone has ever liked paying taxes, which is to say they'd feel less violated if I knocked on their door and actually fucked them. These people would be wiped out without us, but do they care? All they see is my men leaving with their food. They don't see our tireless work to keep them safe."

"Sounds like a heavy crown," Walt said. "How did you come to bear it? Pander to the Ohio swing voters?"

"Hah. Long story. When the virus hit, I saw the writing on the wall damn quick. I lived in Hermosa. Took my family here. Figured we could quarantine it. Wait out the Panhandler."

"Smart. But it didn't work, did it?"

Karslaw smiled wryly. "I wasn't the only one with smart ideas. We lasted three weeks longer than the mainland before someone brought the virus here. Within another week, it burned through us like a fire."

"I'm sorry."

The man narrowed his eyes, smiling the sharp smile of a man examining a hopeless fight. "My losses were no more special than anyone else's."

Walt shook his head. Impossible as it seemed, he took for granted that the natural state of the world was to be ruined, but there were times when it all came flooding back. "It's all so fucked up."

"So was I. Then, on a trip to the mainland, I found a man half-dead on the beach. Brought him back here. We nursed him back to health. It made me feel like there was hope after all. For months, that's what we did. Found survivors and brought them here where twenty miles of ocean could keep them save from thugs and gangs. We planted crops. Gathered medicine. Built a life.

"Then the aliens came, and we quit going to the mainland. Even after you brought them down. At that point we had more mouths than food. It was time to consolidate and care for those of us who were already here. We'd become a people."

He drank from his stein, coffee dribbling into his beard. "But I think long-term, Walt. This island won't protect us forever. Not if we let the aliens breed their foul hives. That's why I sent for you. We need to wipe them out now. While we still can."

"Cool," Walt said. "Except we totally can't do that."

Annoyance flickered on Karslaw's brows. "Don't be so fast to doubt my men's resolve."

"What I doubt is their ability to secure the whole planet. The aliens are everywhere. We ran into them in Mexico, too. Unless you're planning one hell of a crusade, you can't get rid of them all."

He shook his head and leaned forward, reaching toward Walt with a scarred hand. "I'm not insane. I know we can't save the world. But we can save Los Angeles."

"Maybe," Walt said. "Here's what I can tell you, anyway."

He dropped all he knew. How they appeared to be deaf but could sense motion instead. The vulnerability of their heads, especially their oversized eyes. How they'd established towns during the invasion but seemed to have abandoned them all after he downed their ship. Their apparent loyalty to each other. When he told Karslaw about the hot air balloon, the man laughed until he cried into his beard.

"Outrageous," Karslaw said when he'd sobered enough to speak. "And obsolete. Here is our challenge: the ship may not be able to fly, but they're still using it for their home."

"Big deal. Sail over there, toss one of those big rubber circus tents over it, and exterminate them."

"We've tried. Something has changed since you dropped it into the sea, Walt. Anything that tries to approach it now is destroyed."

"What? Like how?"

"Like in a great big explosion."

"Well, that's weird. How many times have you tried to come up on it?"

"A dozen times or more." Karslaw sipped his coffee. "The most recent attempt was less than three weeks ago. When our boat got within half a mile, a missile arced from the ship and destroyed it."

Walt glanced up at the naked beams and did some thinking. "What kind of stuff have you sent toward it?"

"Unmanned vessels. I wouldn't send my people on suicide missions."

"Yeah, but like Predator drones? Origami boats? What?"

"Sloops and cutters, primarily. Once we tried a speedboat loaded with explosives. Even at full throttle it couldn't get close. Does it matter?"

"The reason the balloon worked is because it was so stupid," Walt said. "Too stupid to defend against. So here's the question. Is this defense system something new? Did the aliens who survived the crash amend it to hit even the dumbest targets? Or have your approaches just not been stupid enough?"

"You have an idea." Karslaw grinned. "Perhaps sending for you wasn't my worst move after all."

"It's time to drop some science on their ass, man. See what there is to see. And even if it's bad news, it should be pretty fun to find out."

Wind tousled his hair. The boat pitched on the waves, turning Walt's stomach. A mile away from them and several hundred yards from Santa Monica Beach, the disc of the mothership projected from the ocean, cracked and skewed.

"Can we get any closer?" he said.

Karslaw shook his head. "Not a good idea. God invented binoculars for a reason."

The man called out to the raft floating beside them, tethered by a single rope. On it, Lorna and another man hauled up the sail and trimmed it to the wind. The sail flapped raggedly, then went taut. The raft drifted toward the downed vessel. Lorna untied the lines to the yacht and flung them into the sea. Men on the yacht hauled in the lines.

A wave flooded over the raft's deck, slopping over Lorna's bare feet. The vessel was as simple as they could make it: wooden logs roped together, a square-sailed mast rising from near its center. No metal at all, and aside from its mast, its profile climbed less than a foot above the water.

It separated itself from the anchored yacht, moving so slowly over the water that Walt could have overtaken it at walking speed, assuming he had Jesus-like powers. Lorna adjusted the sail and turned to face the mothership. The raft dawdled another hundred yards nearer the aliens. Lorna and the second sailor dived off the edge and swam for the yacht.

Karslaw lowered a rope ladder and helped bring them in. Walt offered Lorna a towel. She took it with the polite smile of a stranger and closed herself in the cabin to change clothes.

Walt sat and dangled his legs between the rails. "Think they can see us?"

Karslaw shrugged his broad shoulders. "If they do, they don't care enough to shoot us. Their system has limited range or it's completely automated. They don't blast anything unless it comes within a half mile or better. You'll see."

Waves sloshed against the hull. Pelicans and gulls winged on the breeze. The raft pulled further and further away. Lorna's reading of the wind and tide was perfect; the downed ship made for a big enough target that there was plenty of room for error, but the raft headed straight toward its center.

It was a sunny day and the reflected light had Walt sweating and squinting. He took off his shirt and wrapped it around his head. The raft continued its maiden and final voyage. Walt held the binoculars to his face, wiping off the sweat whenever the eyepieces grew too slick. The little boat closed halfway to the other ship.

"Is this going to work?" Walt said.

Karslaw scratched his beard. "Too soon to tell."

"I mean, it must not shoot everything. Unless you've noticed a sudden upswing in dolphin funerals."

The man laughed. He had the sort of easy, booming laughter that felt like a reward. Walt wasn't surprised Karslaw had wound up in charge. He was a natural leader, wholly at ease with his position, inhabiting the mantle of command as casually as most people sat on their own toilet. The kind of man you wanted to please. Walt had only been around him a few days—it had taken two to rig up the raft, and a third to haul it out here—but he already believed in the man's cause. He had a good thing going. A few hundred people who were already self-sustaining and protected from the mainland while having ready access to its abandoned treasures. Karslaw had vision, too, and the will to carry it out. If they could scour the last of the aliens out of the area, Walt had no doubt the man would cultivate Catalina into a walled garden safe from the chaos and entropy of the rest of the world.

The raft bobbed nearer the ship. The breeze tugged at the sea, hazing the horizons. Something flashed from the ship, sped through the air in a line drive arc, and slammed into the raft. White light burst from it in a vast semicircle.

Walt pulled away from the binoculars, grunting. "Was that a missile?"

"Hard to say from here," Karslaw said. A rolling boom crackled over the waters, the noise tinny and distant, like an old movie played over bad speakers. "Would you like to take a closer look?"

"Well shit."

"Lost five men the first time we came too close."

"Guess this rules out an approach through air or on water. Got any submarines parked back in town?"

"We may have one stashed beneath the aircraft carrier."

"Um," Walt said. He blinked against the negative-flash still tingling on his retinas. "Can your men swim?"

"While keeping their rifles dry?" Karslaw laughed his rolling laugh. "I've chewed this problem in my mind's teeth for months, Walt. I hoped you'd know something I didn't."

"Well, either I got lucky or they learned from their mistakes, because they weren't using missiles before." Walt rubbed his eyes. Since destroying the raft, the enemy vessel had been utterly silent. If he'd just stumbled out onto the deck, he'd never know the mothership wasn't the corpse it appeared to be. "There's got to be some way to get at it. Give me some time to think."

"Take as long as you need," Karslaw said. "The only thing riding on it is our future."

He hollered to his men to turn the boat around. Back at the island, Walt spent several days yutzing around with alternative designs to try to slip past the crashed ship's defenses, including a raft with a long, narrow, ribbon-like sail just a couple feet tall and another with an outboard and no vertical profile whatsoever. Both were demolished around a quarter mile from the ship.

In a sign of less than perfect trust, they housed him at Avalon, the port town where Lorna had made landfall. By the standards of the day, it was a hustling metropolis: boats came and went from the piers at the rate of three or four a day. Sometimes when he sat on his porch and gazed downhill, he could see actual pedestrians in the streets. Dogs barked. When the wind blew in the right direction, the bleats of sheep carried from the valleys.

He didn't see Lorna much. Friends dropped by her house every day to catch up and console her about the loss of her friends. When he wasn't too busy tying logs together and doodling sketches on his porch, he missed her. When he missed her, he worked harder. What if they ran it out of resources? Flung raft after raft at it until its missiles dried up? Or just overwhelmed it Zerg rush-style, launching a hundred boats at it at once, with Karslaw's soldiers hidden in motorboats ready to zoom in while the cannon fodder tied up the defenses?

Problem was, if it had the power to launch those missiles, or whatever they were, then maybe it had the power to manufacture new ones, too. And as for oversaturating it with targets, there was no guarantee that would work even if they had the ten thousand men required to pull it off.

"So we bomb the hell out of it," he told Karslaw. "Find a plane and just blast it to smithereens."

"Know any pilots?" Karslaw answered. "Any warplanes that survived the invasion? We've checked the nearby Air Force bases. Aliens laid them to waste. Are there jets left in the interior of the country? Maybe. But here's the problem, stranger. Unless we atomize every square inch of that ship, we have no guarantee we've got them all. I want to go inside. Gut them like a fish. Ensure their threat is ended once and for all. Only then will my people be safe."

Walt frowned and went straight to Lorna's, entering without knocking. She was in her living room with a young woman who shared Hannigan's chin and deep-set eyes. Sister, maybe.

Lorna rose without a smile. "Walt. I have a guest."

"Is she going to be here forever?"

"Not unless something goes terribly wrong," the woman smiled.

"Then I'll wait."

"What do you want?" Lorna said.

"For you to show me around the island," Walt said. "I'm going crazy trying to draw up Karslaw's battle plan against that stupid squid-infested mountain growing out of the bay. I want to see something new. Jog my brain."

"You've already seen Avalon. The palace."

"Come on, Lorna." The other woman nudged her. "Has he seen the Scaveteria? The fort?"

"The Scaveteria?" Walt said. "That sounds horrible. I have to see it."

"I'll show myself out," the woman smiled.

The door clicked behind her. Lorna folded her arms. "Do you really want to see the island? Or are you here to see me?"

"I can't do both? I've got two eyes, don't I?"

"The Scaveteria's not nearly as interesting as she makes it sound." Lorna laughed. "Grab your pack. It's a full day's hike to the fort."

Walt grinned and ran to his house in the hills for his day-pack. When he returned, Lorna led him down the winding roads to the base of town. A longhaired black cat lay across a stoop, tracking them. A few blocks from the piers, in a downtown of boutiques and inns, real live people strolled around, chatting and going in and out of open, operational stores, which were marked by sandwich boards out front. At a corner cafe, a couple shared a table. Grilled pork wafted from the doorway.

"I don't know if you guys know this," Walt said, "but you appear to possess a civilization."

"That's the goal."

She brought him through the tourist waterfront to the esplanade. The shops ended, replaced by open fields of grass and trees. On the other side, a bike path lined a short, rocky beach. A quarter mile ahead, the land curled into a small, short point dominated by a single building: round and orange-roofed, easily a couple hundred feet across. A few small boats were tied up at its piers.

"There's the Scaveteria," Lorna said.

"Isn't it kind of fancy?"

"Formerly a ballroom. Who knows? Maybe it will be again."

The road led all the way to its steps. The front doors opened to a gigantic single room. Walt stopped and gaped. "You guys did this on purpose?"

Shelves lined the walls and divided the floor into a city-like grid of rises and avenues. Two-thirds of the shelves were full, crammed with shoes, jeans, blankets, scrap metal, boxes of screws. A thousand different things. Walt spotted a box of red Christmas ornaments. A handful of people wandered amongst it all. A couple appeared to be browsing, picking up items and turning them over, examining them for cracks or wear, but other people were adding things to the shelves, pulling flatbed carts through the aisles and transferring debris to the racks.

"What is this place?" he whispered.

"Some of our people go into the city on a regular basis." Lorna wandered forward, taking a pair of pliers from a shelf. "Some do it because they need things. Others do it for fun. Whatever the case, Karslaw passed a law requiring them to bring back more than they intend to keep for themselves. It can be anything people might need. When they sail back home, they check in with the dockmaster, who goes over their goods and brings everything they don't want back here. To the Scaveteria."

"And then what?"

"Then, when people here need something, they see if they can find it here."

"And they just take it? Like a library for stuff?"

"Pretty much."

"Huh. That is incredibly cool." Walt picked up a pack of pens still in its bubble packaging. "What do you do with people who take too much? Whippings? I bet public whippings are a major deterrent."

"Nobody ever has."

"How lucky that you've built an entire society of the only honest people on earth."

She pointed to a man at a desk beside the front doors. "The clerks keep track of what leaves and who takes it."

"Is he wearing a visor?"

"Anyone who takes more than a reasonable person might need is sentenced to a month of scavenging. So far, nobody's exceeded reason."

Walt set back the pens. "What does a person do if he can't find what he's looking for here?"

She raised a brow at him. "Same as everyone else. They go without. Or if it's something that can be crafted, maybe they go to the blacksmith."

"You guys have a blacksmith?"

"Where else would we get our black?"

"Really, what does he make?" Walt said. "Horseshoes?"

Lorna shrugged. "Whatever. Karslaw keeps him occupied, but sometimes his apprentices have spare time. When the clerks here aren't busy, they'll haul a wagon of scrap up to the palace."

"And Karslaw just came up with this?"

"Just because he looks like Attila the Hun doesn't mean he burns books and drinks fermented goat spit."

"I bet he'd try it, though." Walt glanced outside to check the sun. "I can't wait to see the fort. Does it have cannons?"

"Not yet."

She took him up the hills past the valley and the palace. A couple of lakes filled the crevices between the rocky green hills. The land got browner, scrubby grass and tough shrubs. The road snaked along the sides of the ridges. Once, Walt looked down on a green plateau studded with shuffling brown lumps as big as boulders.

"What is that?"

"Bison," Lorna said.

"Karslaw brought bison here, too? What's he planning next, a gold rush?"

"They were here before we were," she said. "Don't ask me. People do strange things when they get their hands on an island."

As far as remote, semi-mountainous roads went—and in the last five years, Walt had seen more than a few—Catalina's were good and walkable, and they made good time, sweating in the moderate heat. Even so, the sun dropped below the hills before they'd made it to the fort. Lorna walked on for another hour anyway, traveling down the middle of the road, lit by the stars and a quarter of the moon.

They slept beside the road. At dawn, they got up and continued on. After a slow trek over rolling hills, the road dropped down into a flat shelf of tree-heavy fields. Waves pounded the shore a couple hundred feet to their right. After less than a mile, they entered a clearing. At the beach, a tall wooden fence surrounded a five-story wooden tower.

"That's it?" Walt said.

Lorna laughed. "You were expecting another castle?"

"Sort of."

"Do you have any idea what a pain it is to haul lumber someplace as remote as this? We brought it in by boat. Took six months to erect it. Project like that gives you a whole new appreciation for why homes used to be so expensive."

"You know what would have been a whole lot easier? Building it in Avalon."

"We wanted a view of Santa Monica Bay." She pointed northwest toward the hazy hills of Malibu, then swept her finger to the right along the curve of the city, past the black blot of the mothership, all the way to the high, mounded hills of the peninsula to the northeast. "Including the ship. It's got one of two radios we leave on permanently. Other one's at the palace. Batteries are getting hard to find. Don't know what we'll do when we run out."

They watched the fort for a while longer, then turned around and headed back the way they'd come. Other than the roads, and the occasional crumpled, sun-faded can of Coke along the shoulders, much of the island showed no sign of habitation. There was lots of room here. A bit on the dry side, but plenty of potential. They'd walked through several different climates on the way here—warm coastal, dry upland, hills, light forests. He liked that.

Lorna called it quits a while after sundown. "Thought we could make it back today. Palace is just ahead if you want for try for it."

"Nah. I'm enjoying it out here," Walt said. They unrolled their blankets on the side of the road and ate the last of the dried fish they'd brought with them.

"I don't know what's up with that ship," he said. "If it had been doing that missile shit when I came for it, you'd still be finding bits of me washing up on the shore."

Lorna got out a towel and tipped a water bottle into it and scrubbed off the worst of the day's sweat. "Think you can do it?"

"I don't know. I want to. This place is pretty cool."

"Were you thinking of staying?"

He looked up. "Would you have a problem with that?"

"I haven't had a lot of time to think about the future," she said. "Not when I'm still dealing with past lives and present troubles."

Walt frowned. It was the perfect time to broach the subject of their future together, but he lost his nerve. He knew why he didn't want to push things—because there was the chance he'd push them into a place he didn't want to go to, would uncover truths he'd prefer to leave as imagined fears—but that didn't help. Now wasn't the time to push. Not when things were so unsettled. It would be best to wait until she was ready to talk.

"We'll see," he said. "Maybe I should help stamp out those aliens before I set down roots within sight of their watery fortress."

They laid down together, but he was too tired to do more than sleep. He woke while it was still dark. He'd heard something. Something wrong. He lay under the stars, warm where Lorna's sleeping body touched him, cool where he was exposed to the raw hilltop air.

Another boom crackled over the hills, a long, rumbling explosion. From the east. Toward Avalon. Lorna's breath caught. She jumped up, eyes bright in the darkness. They grabbed their bags and ran.

19

"Did you ever think of this stuff not in terms of ruins," Mauser said, "but as just another form of terrain?"

Raina glanced up from the empty houses. "No."

"People used to call it the concrete jungle, and that's not a bad description. There's all kinds of goodies if you know where to look. There's also horrible things that could kill us at any moment, but at least there are a million places to hole up in, too."

"Did you see something?" Martin said.

"What? No. No, it's totally clear. But the fault in the whole jungle analogy is that there are roads in a city. If you were in a hurry, you could walk across the entire L.A. Basin in a day. How long would it take you to cross thirty miles of the Amazon? Eternity, because the poisonous frogs would get you first."

Martin swirled his canteen and took a drink. They were a few miles inland and it was notably hotter than along the coast, heat simmering off the asphalt. "It's kind of like a prairie. Except you can't see more than a couple blocks ahead of you. And there are lots of places to hide."

"So it combines the attributes of both the jungle and the wasteland," Mauser said. "Does that mean it's unique? Raina, what do you think?"

"That you should shut up and watch the road," she said.

"Oh really?" He gestured to the barren streets. "Think we'll angry up the ghosts?"

She did, in fact, but knew better than to say as much. The old people didn't believe in those things, but the old people had grown up apart from death. She had grown up within it. She was sensitive to it in a way these people never had been. Maybe their senses had been drowned out by being surrounded by living cities rather than the waste-jungle they were currently crossing, but she could feel the places where the dead had dropped their bones. That's why the ship in the bay was no good. Maybe that was why there was so much fighting back on the peninsula. The spirits were angry. You couldn't see them, but you could feel them, and they made you angry too. Maybe it would be best to move to a place where no one else had ever lived.

She just shook her head. "Time spent talking is time not watching."

"That's a weird thing to say," Mauser muttered. "That's one of yours, isn't it? A little Raina-ism."

They reached a stretch of burned-down houses and charred apartments. Raina detoured around it. Too little cover there. Too many spirits. Sun slammed down on parking lots and dusty cars and neighborhoods with scrawny yellow lawns hardly wide enough to separate one house from the next.

Mauser pointed to a green sign at an intersection. "405's a few blocks from here. If I'm remembering my cultural institutions, that should take us all the way to the Getty."

"It's a raised highway." Raina jerked her head at the lanes strung over the road to the east. "You'll be able to see us from a mile away."

"Only for another couple miles. Then it's ground-level. Barrier walls on both sides. If we walk along those, we'll be as stealthy as ninjas."

"What's ninjas?"

"Are you kidding me? You are one." He looked both ways, then jogged across the intersection. "Here, we'll compromise. Once the highway drops, we'll merge and ride it all the way to the Getty."

That sounded fair enough. She was about to exit the lands she knew well anyway. The wide boulevard led them past a stately white mall and hotel towers pinstriped with windows. She doubted many people still lived here. There was too much pavement to have space to grow things and all the canned food would have been eaten or spoiled long ago.

If there were any survivors making a go of it here, they didn't trouble the three travelers. Raina continued north until the angled highway crossed overhead, then followed along in its shadow. When it descended and became one with the ground, they hiked up its curling onramp.

Dead cars clogged the northbound lanes, but the shoulders were largely clear. They walked along the corrugated barriers. Bugs twirped in the grass. The highway unspooled for miles, curving and rising and falling with the contours of the land.

"Airport used to be right over there," Mauser pointed after another hour. "The runways are just on the other side of the highway and planes would come in not three hundred feet from the ground. It's no wonder Hollywood turned out the way it did. Passing under that was like driving through a Michael Bay movie."

"Does anyone ever understand what you're saying?" Raina said.

"Those raised in America and currently between 25 and forty years of age," Mauser said. "Anyone else, and communication is admittedly spotty."

The road ran on and on. They stopped for dinner and Raina did some light scavenging of the nearby cars. Most were locked and abandoned; the few that opened tended to have bodies, sun-dried skin wrapped around untouched bones. She found nothing of interest.

At dark, they slept in the grass beside the concrete walls. She woke to quiet shuffling noises down the road. Mauser was already sitting up, a knife gleaming in his hand, but it was only an animal. Raina didn't fear animals. She had many of them within her and they would tell the live ones that she only killed for food or to sate the demands of the moon.

"Don't worry," she whispered. "Just possums."

He snorted. "Is that right? How polite of them to inform you they'd be passing through."

He continued his vigil, staring into the darkness. A moment later, a fat shadow waddled from the shoulder, the size of a small dog. Mauser's foot jerked, scuffing. The thing turned to face them, its white face standing out in the moonlight.

"Told you."

"How the hell did you know that?"

"Skunks walk faster. Trot-trot-trot, they make. Raccoons coo and fiddle with things. Possums just trudge along. Want to eat it?"

Mauser laughed and shook his head. Martin got up to go to the bathroom. With everyone awake, they rolled up their beds and walked along the lanes, going slow to avoid tripping in the darkness. This was perhaps Raina's favorite feeling, traveling when she couldn't be seen and no one expected her to be awake. It made her feel wise. Mauser and Martin made too much noise—Martin had forgot to put a cloth between his bowl and his pan and they made a low metal scrape with each step—but even if there were strangers ahead on the highway, the others would be sleeping, confused and alarmed even if the shuffles and coughs were enough to wake them. The deepest night before the dawn was her world, and for a few hours every day, she belonged.

The night became pre-morning. It was no lighter but she could tell it from the way the birds woke and cheeped. She could feel it in the air, too. The night had cooled but never truly gone cold. It was going to be a hot day.

Dawn broke. A tattered woman smiled from the billboard of a Spanish TV headquarters. She was used to buildings being two or three stories tall and the rising city made her feel uneasy. Mismatched buckets and tarps littered the roofs. Water collectors. She had no way to tell which ones were recent and which were abandoned.

Around noon, they got off the road to catch up on sleep and wait out the worst of the sun in an apartment above a hamburger stand. Before heading on, she and Mauser drilled with sticks to practice their knifeplay. Near the end, she worked out a new unarmed move with him that involved blocking an incoming high strike with her wrist, then letting her forearm collapse and driving her elbow into his jaw.

"Can you show me that?" Martin said.

She smiled. It was the first time he'd asked to join in. She walked him through it motion by motion and found the act of teaching someone less skilled forced her to visualize dynamics of movement she took for granted. He was clumsy and stiff, but she hoped he would continue training.

They walked on. Towers climbed to their right, impossibly high, fantastic sentinels over the endless city. The highway began a shallow climb between glassy, glossy buildings with elegant curves and then through parks and tidy homes and a golf course gone feral.

"There you go," Mauser said.

Across a spotty, brownish field, a white palace grew from the earth the way coral grows from the sea. Banks of bluish windows tiled its sharp-lined levels. The trees and shrubs had outgrown their careful cultivation, and some had withered to elderly, waterless husks, but their placement still evoked a logic and beauty.

"It looks like Lothlorien," Martin said.

"Huh?" Raina said.

"Elves," Mauser said. "It's going to burn down some day. We should have forced architects to build everything monumental out of rock. Now there's a material with staying power. You ever tried to punch a rock? I wouldn't."

"Why did they make it so pretty?" Raina said.

"It's a museum. Looking pretty is the only thing it does."

They crossed an unkempt lawn. An amphitheater-like park was recessed in the grass. At its bottom, a burst of bushes crouched atop a swampy mire of rainwater. The doors were tall and stood open. As she went inside, Raina said a silent prayer to all the old things.

The place had been looted. Ransacked. Vandalized. Shattered glass flanked the displays in sharp-edged skirts. On the walls, pale rectangles showed the ghosts of departed paintings. Statues lay toppled, marble pebbles strewn over the floor. Sunshine streamed from the skylights and illuminated dust and trash and dried-up feces.

"This is a disgrace." Mauser's voice echoed in the still and empty space. "You can't just rob a museum. These are everyone's treasures!"

"You were about to steal from it," Martin said.

"Just one painting for Raina! And maybe a jade elephant for my trouble. That would leave at least 99.9% of the place unstolen."

Raina moved quickly through the airy rooms, jogging up stairs with steel wire railings. There were no paintings left. In the upper floors, some statues remained, too heavy to lift, although several had been toppled. Some carvings and foreign artifacts remained, too, wooden masks and painted figures. Everyone else had considered them unworthy of the bother, but that didn't stop Mauser from scooping a few into his pack. Past the vast windows, Los Angeles spread out for miles, bowled in by the mountains, smudged by ocean-haze and the coming dusk.

Mauser waited downstairs. "Well, the trip wasn't a total waste. Found this in the gift shop."

He handed her an oversized book. It was a collection of Chagall prints. Vivid explosions of color. Surreal images of a bull with an umbrella and angels climbing a ladder to heaven. She could see why the man with the knives wanted one.

Martin found a door to the basement. Its lock had been bashed in and it had been looted, too, stripped down to statues and carved trinkets. Raina's lantern flashed on a red lacquered stick a foot and a half long. She stooped for it. It had metal caps on both ends and the handle wiggled in her hand. She tugged on it and a single-edged blade slid free from its wooden sheath.

She touched it to the back of her hand and drew blood. She gasped, lantern wavering. Colors rippled on its blade like molten moonlight. It was hundreds of years old she could feel its presence like she felt the beat and rumble of her own organs—the cut on her hand was not the first time it had tasted blood.

She sheathed it with a click and tucked it in her belt. They stayed in one of the upper rooms overnight and slept without incident.

"Well, here's the question," Mauser said in the morning. Yellow daylight flooded through the dusty windows. "What now?"

"We keep looking," Raina said.

"If you're bound and determined, I say we try to find another museum. This is one of the biggest cities in the world. It could take years to dig your needle out of this haystack."

"Not if we go to Malibu."

"Well, a week of fruitless searching should convince you better than I can. In the meantime, can we try Beverly Hills first? It's right here. Much closer than Malibu. And I guarantee you its former owners were just as wealthy."

She hesitated, then agreed. They took the highway back to the city, then hung left onto Santa Monica Boulevard, passing glinting hotels and clothing shops on their way to the homes nestled in the hills and winding roads above the city. The houses were massive, some Spanish-style with orange roofs, others hard-cut modern things of glass and metal. Many had pools, now empty, or green and slimy from past rains. Some had tennis courts, too. Raina walked along in envious shock. Some of these homes, places people once lived, were as pretty as the Getty.

Something scurried from a side yard. Raina glimpsed a shaggy beard and stained clothes. The sound of the man's feet faded in the distance.

"Stay away from any house that looks clean," she said. "Anywhere with a garden or a way to gather water."

"Sounds like you mean to split up," Mauser said.

She nodded. "I don't want to be here any longer than we have to."

"I brought these." Martin knelt and let down his pack. He extracted three plastic rectangles with blunt rubber antennas. "I don't know how great their range is, but we can let each other know if we see anything funny."

"Walkie talkies?" Mauser laughed, taking one up. "I haven't had one of these since I played spy games as a kid. Well, for the record, I think this is very stupid, but let's meet back at that intersection. Dusk. I'm not busting into strange homes after dark."

Raina intended to do just that—she didn't need as much sleep as they were getting—but agreed. She padded down the street.

She had no problem opening doors. Breaking windows. She didn't think of them as homes. Homes were places people lived. These were just caves. Pieces of land closed off from the world. In each one, she paused in the doorway to listen, then walked quickly from room to room in search of the startling colors of Chagall. There were lots of stone and wooden floors and she didn't like the way her feet clapped through the high-ceilinged rooms. After three houses, she took off her shoes.

There were bodies in some. Giant flat-screened TVs in all. Palatial kitchens with islands and multiple faucets. Sometimes there was clothing flung across the bedroom floors. Possibly looters, but in most cases, she thought they'd been left by someone moving as fast as possible to get away from the plague. There were many paintings, but no Chagalls.

She walked up the steps to a yellow stucco manor and opened the door. Behind it, a man pointed a rifle in her face.

"You hold right there," he murmured.

"Wait," she said.

"I seen you coming up the street. A little thief. Wants to slobber her mitts over what I got. Well, what I got is this rifle."

"I don't want your things. I'm looking for a Chagall."

His brows bent. "This is my home. Seems to me that gives me the right to smear you across my front steps."

Raina had raised her hands. As the man spoke, she'd slowly lowered her elbows close to her waist. She pressed her elbow into the walkie talkie, depressing its button. Hurriedly, she spoke the man's address.

He jerked up the gun. "What did you just say?"

"I just told my friends where you live."

"And gave me one more reason to part your skull!"

"Raina?" Mauser asked over the device, voice fuzzy.

She shook her head. "Let me go. I'll leave. That was my friend, and he isn't nice. If you hurt me, he'll put an icepick in your ear."

The man smiled defiantly, then his lip curled into a snarl. "You get away from my house. I see you again, I shoot you. I don't care how many friends you got."

"Agreed."

With her hands still up, she backed down the steps. At the bottom, she turned around and headed straight for the sidewalk, expecting at any second to hear the crack of the gun—or nothing at all, just the abrupt, splinter-like removal of her soul from her body. The man watched her go, a shadow in his doorway, the gun held firm to his shoulder.

Mauser was not happy to hear what had happened. "Communication is always a clumsy thing, but one language is universal: a gun in your face. It's time to go."

"Then go," she said. "I'm finding my Chagall."

"Raina, what's the big deal? You could have been shot. Is this knife-master of yours really that impressive?"

"If you'd seen him, you would know."

"What about that guy we saw?" Martin said. "The guy who ran away?"

"Dude with the beard and the hobo-stink?" Mauser said. "Yeah, he looked like a real art aficionado."

"If he lives here, we can hire him. As a guide. To keep us away from everyone else."

"Martin!" Raina grinned. Martin blushed and smiled back, so pleased with himself she knew he'd do anything for her. She liked that thought. There was one thing all animals agreed on: it was always best to have an escape route.

* * *

Aided by the bearded man—Mauser had convinced him to lend his aid in exchange for a half-empty flask of liquor, two packs of Big Red gum, and a wooden panther nicked from the Getty—they searched the mansions of the hills in relative safety. But after four fruitless days, Mauser had had enough—or, as Raina suspected, had run out of space to carry any more jewelry.

"Okay, this time I'm serious." He jerked his thumb south in the general direction of the Dunemarket. "That's where we belong. We're not doing anyone any good up here."

Raina gathered up her things from the bedroom floor of the boat-like house where they'd centered their camp. "Not until I go to Malibu."

"What is it with you and Malibu? There are no magic fish in its seas. Plenty of antique lamps, I'm sure, but I can guarantee you none of them have wish-granting genies."

"That's where my first mom always wanted us to live." She put her dirty socks in her bag and let her hands hang there, helpless. "She told me that when we made it to Malibu, we'd never want anything again."

"Oh, for the love of criminy, you played the 'my dead birth mother' card. Well, it's bought you one more leg of this idiot's odyssey. Then we're going home."

They took Santa Monica Boulevard all the way to the coast. It felt good to be back on the ocean, away from the July-baked city. It was cooler, refreshed by afternoon breezes you could set a clock by. Ahead, the hills ran down to the sea and the highway curved along their base. It was already close to evening but she thought they could make half the walk to Malibu before bedding down. After an hour, she'd counted three mile markers along the coast-hugging road.

Martin pointed out to sea. "What's that?"

A single strand of houses separated them from the sand. Raina shielded her eyes against the sunlight angling in from the horizon. A hundred yards out from where the waves began to break, a fat black lump sat idle on the surface.

"A whale?" Mauser said.

"It isn't moving."

"A dead whale."

Martin's walkie talkie popped. He started, slapping at his belt. The transmitter clicked rapidly.

"We should go," Raina said.

"I think it's like a boat," Martin said. "Let me get out my radio."

"Martin—"

The brush stirred across the road. Raina whirled and drew her knife from its red lacquer sheath. A man emerged onto the asphalt. He looked sickly—gaunt, ivory-pale, his bare torso tattooed with symbols from a language Raina had never seen—but she knew the look in his eye. A seer. A hunter. A man who's gone to all the worst places and come back alive.

20

Walt ran up the hill, flashlight jarring in his hand, providing him a sporadic glimpse of his footing on the road ahead. "What was that?"

"What do you think?"

"Do you guys have a lot of explosions here?"

"No." Lorna wasn't breathing hard yet. "Maybe it followed you here."

All things considered, his pack was light for a multi-day journey, with maybe twenty pounds of blankets and water and such hanging from his shoulders. But it was enough to force him into an awkward, bouncing stride that battered his back. He pulled up and knelt down.

"What are you doing?" Lorna said.

"Hurrying."

"By sitting down."

He flung away dirty jeans, spare shoes. "Fixing it so I can run without feeling like a duck with gout."

She did the same, putting a pistol and a bottle of water into a small shoulder bag. Walt's laser was with him because he carried it everywhere. He kicked the rest of his stuff off the road, then set a white stone on the asphalt to mark the spot. They ran.

Over the next hill, lights shimmered in the windows of the palace. A man shouted orders. The road ran within a hundred feet of its palisade. Lorna jagged onto the road leading to the drawbridge, which was lowered. A gaggle of men spoke behind it.

Lorna called out her name as she approached. "What's happening?"

"Attack on Avalon," one of them said.

"O.C.'s?"

"Dunno. No radio, just the lanterns." He pointed across the valley. On a hill overlooking the road, two lights burned. "Coming with?"

She shook her head. "We'll see you there."

She raced back to the main road, Walt on her heels. Back when he was an out-of-shape smoker, he couldn't have run to the corner bodega, but that part of his life was six years and many thousands of miles behind him. He ran at just under a dead sprint, spilling over the hill to Avalon minutes later.

A fire burned on the beach. Smoke blew crosswise over the dark shore. People screamed. A blue beam cut across the sands.

"Those aren't humans," Walt said.

Lorna grunted, then started forward. "Come on."

"Did you hear what I just said? About the humans those aren't?"

"I don't care what they are. They're attacking my people. They need to die."

Walt laughed and followed her down. A machine gun opened up, racketing across the beach. Lorna swerved down a back road. Three blocks from the shore, a man slumped on the corner, holding his forehead and dripping blood onto the sidewalk. Lorna hit the esplanade and crouched beside the corner of a Peet's coffee house.

Walt got down beside her. Lasers flashed from the other side of the beach, focused on a makeshift barricade of debris strung across the road. Rifles boomed from behind it, orange flashes answering the blue beams of the attackers. Directly across from Walt and Lorna, a young woman hobbled up the beach, limping heavily. A tangle of limbs rushed behind her. The thing straightened a tentacle, aiming.

Lorna ran from the corner, firing her pistol at the alien as she went. Her first shots showed no effect; the fifth or six staggered it. It continued after the limping woman. Walt charged behind Lorna, but her body did a near-perfect job of blocking his shot.

The limping woman screamed and collapsed. The alien shot her with a short flick of light and turned its tentacle toward Lorna. She shot it somewhere in the body, knocking it back a step. Its blue beam splayed over the roofs behind the esplanade. Dust popped in small white bursts. Lorna closed on the creature, emptying her pistol and flinging it in the enemy's long, ovoid face. It slapped a tentacle at the incoming gun, distracted. Lorna bowled right into its body.

Metal flashed in her hand. A line of light lanced from the alien, searing the sand into glass. Walt swung around it, aimed his laser at its thudding feet, and pushed the trigger-buttons. Lorna screamed. He jerked back his hand and stopped shooting. Her knife winked again and plunged into the thing's chitinous hide. It didn't make a sound. It scrabbled for her neck with a pincer and she ducked her chin and stabbed again, the blade skittering off its side. It backhanded her with a tentacle, bashing her into the sand.

Walt shot it in the head. One of its bulbous eyes ejected in a jet of superheated steam. Its body slapped to the ground, twitching dumbly.

Lorna wasn't moving. Her eyes were half open, showing their whites. Walt checked her wrist and found a pulse. He glanced down the shore. The fighting remained concentrated around the barricade. The other woman moaned, pawing at the sand. Walt got down, rolled Lorna onto his shoulder, stood, steadied himself, and slogged back to the road.

He carried her two blocks down the street, not certain where he was going except away from the danger. Footsteps rang out ahead. Walt leaned against a wall and drew his laser.

A man skidded to a stop, mouth wide. "Is that Lorna?"

"She's hurt," Walt said.

He nodded. "Come with me."

Walt followed him down the street, breathing hard. Just as he was ready to call for help carrying her, his guide held open the door to an unmarked building. A light wavered down the hall.

"Doctor's inside," the man said. "I'll take it from here."

"I'm not leaving her," Walt said.

"If we don't drive those things out, we're all dead. Get your ass to the beach."

Walt wiped his forearm across his face, slicking off some of the humidity-induced sweat. "Right. Well, if I die and she doesn't, tell her I love her."

The man looked up sharply. "You do?"

"Not like that," he said, feelingly incredibly stupid for bothering to keep up her ruse at a time like this. "We bonded on our trip. Look, just tell her. She'll know what I mean."

"Yeah," the man said slowly.

Walt exited into the street. Men hollered over the roar of gunfire. He ran within a block of the esplanade, then turned parallel to it, making for the barricade. Chairs and boards and tables cluttered the street. Fires burned in several places. Twenty-odd men took cover in the less-flaming parts of the rubble, firing out to sea. Walt poked up his head. No aliens. No lights.

Bullets plowed white roostertails from the calm waters of the bay. Bubbles roiled the surface. A naked man as pale as unworked dough dashed across the sand, laughed, and plunged into the waves. Steam rose from a black shape waiting offshore.

"The ship!" a man shouted. "Shoot the ship!"

Bullets pinged against the vessel, ricocheting away with drunken whirrs. The shape vanished into the sea.

Half the men fanned out, jogging down the nearby streets, sweeping the strand along the beach.

Walt tapped the shoulder of a man whose face was half-masked with soot. "What happened?"

The man's mouth hung half open. "They hit the dock. Blasted our flagship before we knew they were here. Boom, firewood. Then the boats next to it—pow. Fleet's crippled. We got our people down here just in time to catch them crawling up the beach. They dived back into the water as soon as they saw us." He grinned, teeth bloody. "Guess we scared 'em."

"Doubt it," Walt said. "They're not human. Their brains are filled with yellow muck and alien ideas."

"You're an expert?" The man tipped back his head, recognition dawning on his face. "Hey. You're the guy Lorna hauled back here. Been flinging rafts at the mothership one after the other."

"You really think that's a coincidence?" said a second man, bearded, his long hair tied behind his head.

The first man gave Walt an angry smile. "You can't seem to stop getting my friends killed, can you? Hannigan. Ramon. Ken. How many more you think you cost us tonight?"

"Like how many did I personally shoot?" Walt said. "Zero. These things have been trying to kill us for five years now. Are you actually blaming me for fighting back?"

"Bullshit. We ain't been attacked once those five years. Not here on the island. You been stirring them up. You're the one who took down their big ship, huh? Maybe they came here for revenge on you. But they didn't see you, so they ran off."

"That's the stupidest thing—"

Knuckles pounded into his eye. White light blinded him, pain spiking his skull. He crashed to the asphalt, scraping his elbow. The longhaired man grinned down at him. Still on his back, Walt slammed his heel into the man's knee. The man howled and dropped. Walt rolled to the side, popped up on his knees, and jabbed the man's chin, bouncing his head against the road.

The first man kicked at Walt's head. He flung himself back, staggering to his feet, and put up his guard. Other soldiers circled him, faces grim in the light of the fires burning from the barricade. Walt's head pounded, nausea pooling in his gut.

"What the fuck!" Karslaw bellowed.

The man across from Walt took on a sober look. The other men and women froze. Walt blinked heavily. His eye was already swelling.

"Is your blood thundering so loud you forget our dead are lying on the beach?" Karslaw bulged his eyes. "Get ours to the clinic basement. Get theirs on a wagon and take it to the capital. Everything they brought, too. I so much as see an alien toothpick in anyone's hands but mine, I dangle you off the pier and see what I can catch."

He seemed to shrink a couple inches, softening his voice. "You fought with pride tonight. They tried to step on our land and you beat them back—but we don't know they're gone. Watch the water until we know Avalon is safe."

He raised his fist. The troops matched his salute and scattered for the beach. The man who'd first spoken to Walt crouched beside the longhaired man and shook his shoulder. The downed man groaned.

Karslaw turned to Walt and crooked a finger. "Walk with me."

"What's up?" Walt said.

Karslaw strode back up the street. "You tell me. I bring you here to stop those things. Not two weeks after you arrive, they're bombarding my shore."

"Are you claiming the two are related?"

"I'm claiming I'm mighty fucking mad that half a dozen of my brothers just died."

"Lorna was hurt, too," Walt said. "I have to see her."

He turned toward the triage center. Karslaw grabbed his shoulder and bent down to his eye level. "Where are we at, Walt?"

"Confused. Worried. And not too happy about earning a black eye when all I've done is try to help."

The big man sighed, straightening. "I'm not being fair to you. I'm angry, Walt. It's my cross to bear. Judging by my shoulders, it's a god damn big one, too." He grinned wryly. "No more rafts. I don't know if they caused this attack, but we can't ignore the timing. Put that big brain of yours toward a new plan, son. Prove I didn't sacrifice good men in vain."

"Nice speech," Walt said.

Karslaw chuckled huskily. "I'm sorry. In leading, I've discovered the higher you elevate your words, the more gravity there is to push your people to action. Sometimes I forget to turn off the rhetoric when I'm speaking face to face.

"But I mean what I say. Figure it out. Our asses are on the line."

He clapped Walt's shoulder and walked away. Walt rubbed his face and went to see Lorna.

She had bruised ribs. A possible concussion. No laser burns. She was awake and aware enough to speak, though she didn't give him more than monosyllables. After five minutes of one-sided conversation about what had happened on the beach, Walt rolled his eyes and walked away.

On his arrival in Avalon, Karslaw had offered him a bottle of clear, home-brewed liquid and the assurance it was vodka. Walt grabbed it from his house and trudged back across the hills to where he and Lorna had ditched their stuff. It was a childish gesture—going back to get her clothes and gear would only make her feel worse about not speaking to him after saving her life—but after several drinks from the bottle, which tasted like vodka inasmuch as it tasted like throat-searing alcohol, it seemed like a pretty swell idea.

The sun rose somewhere along the way. By the time he found their bags, his skull felt like it was sharing two headaches. Home was much too far away. He tied a blanket between the shrubs to form some shade and went to sleep.

He wasted one day nursing his hangover. He wasted a second waiting for her to come to him. On the third, he went to her home and knocked on her door. She answered. She had a bruise on her cheek and moved stiffly but otherwise looked no worse for wear.

"Take me to the mainland," he said.

"You're leaving?" Her eyes went blank. "Is this about the other night? I was so tired. In pain. I just wanted to sleep."

"Did you know the woman on the beach? You attacked that thing with a knife. What were you thinking?"

"You of all people should understand," she said. "I wanted revenge."

He laughed. "There's a lot of that going around, isn't there? It's more virulent than the Panhandler."

"I'm sorry."

"It's okay. I do understand. It's like a fire. The only way to quench it is with death."

"About us." She touched his shoulder. "I know I'm hard to be with. Now more than ever. I used to make jokes. I bet you don't believe me, but I did. It just doesn't feel that funny anymore."

"Really? To me it feels like the biggest joke ever told." He glanced down the street. A woman was walking a fat black dog. You would never know aliens had bombed the docks three days earlier. "You gonna take me to L.A. or not?"

"Please don't go. You just got here. We still need you."

He let out a long sigh. "I'm not leaving. I just want to take a look at the ship. See if I can figure out a new way to stuff a potato up its tailpipe."

"You want to go see the ship." She smiled. "Of course. I'll need a couple days to square things away."

"Whatever you need."

Once she was ready, the trip was completely uneventful. Lorna brought another woman with her to help her sail. She anchored a short ways off the north flank of the peninsula and rowed him to shore in a dinghy. He flung his stuff above the tideline. She hugged him.

"Three days?"

"Should be enough," he said. "See you then."

She rowed back to the boat. He hoisted his bag and walked along the ribbon-like bike path at the base of the cliffs between the beach and the buildings. Fifteen miles away, the broken ship bulged from the sea.

A couple hundred yards away, a man stood on the sand, casting his line into the breakers. He turned to watch Walt pass. Walt raised his hand. The man hesitated, then waved back. Gulls sat on the flat sand above the tide in packs of fifty, beaks pointed toward the sea. Heat baked off the beach. Walt wiggled off his shirt, wrapped his head with it, and had a couple drinks, one of water, one of moonshine.

He wasn't too happy with himself. His thing with Lorna was a mess and his progress vis-a-vis the aliens was underwhelming at best. Each problem felt equally impossible. One was a half-mile-wide vessel with an automated defense system more advanced than any human had ever dealt with, and the other was a woman.

He laughed. Where was a rimshot when you needed one.

The trail took him past rock jetties, kelp-strewn beaches, two more fishermen, a woman surfing, a marina/pier complex, another pier, a small fishing boat, loads of garbage, evidence of three campfires, and several dozen sets of footprints, most of them weathered by the wind. The few people watched warily until he passed down the concrete trail. People used to throng to these beaches every day, completely untroubled by the hundreds of strangers playing volleyball and sunning themselves. Funny how a little thing like the end of the world put everyone on edge.

After a detour around another much larger marina, he found himself in Santa Monica. The beach was hundreds of yards deep. He plunked down just above the upper wash of the waves, got out his bottle, and screwed it into the sand.

Excluding his recent bender, it had been a long time since he'd been drunk. He felt good, relaxed. People had used to say that drinking alone was the true sign you had a problem, but he disagreed. There was no better way to think through an unsolvable problem than to grab a bottle and go get shitfaced in the wilderness by your lonesome. If nothing else, it was a good way to remind yourself that you chose to be wherever you were; that there were always other options; that if things got really, really bad, you could always walk off into the woods, metaphorically or literally. Put it all behind you. Become a whole new person. He'd done it himself.

He pulled the bottle from the sand and had another drink. It was high summer—August, probably, although who gave a damn—and although he'd been traveling all day, first by boat, then by foot, the sun was just now setting behind the wreck of the mothership, yellow beams catching its black edges, painting deep shadows across the valleys of its deadened hull. A tremendous chunk of it had broken off and settled just above the surface; water coursed through the channel between it and the body of the ship. He squinted through his binoculars but couldn't see any movement.

He woke, which meant he was alive, which meant he had stuff to do. He watched the ocean churning along. After a while, a black fin cut through the waves and he got a little thrill, imagining there were big old sharks right out there, but then its back rose from the water, followed by its fluke. A dolphin. He sighed.

Others swam with it, fins breaking the surface at predictable intervals. They swam parallel to the shore, unhurried, then disappeared. A minute later, much further out, closer to the ship than to him, one leapt clean of the water and splashed back down.

He frowned. He took a drink to cut the phlegm and clear his head. Bottle was almost empty. He resolved to do a bit of scavenging in the restaurants back at the strand. Must be a bottle of something somewhere. He went for a swim, toweled off, then poked around the cafes until afternoon.

The next morning, a figure walked up the beach, black hair fluttering behind her. A sailboat sat at anchor a mile further down the shore.

"Can't you count?" Walt said. "You're a day early."

Lorna glanced at the fallen ship, as if afraid it might spring to life then and there. "There's been another attack. They wiped out the fort. You have to come with me."

21

The pale man's hand drifted toward his pocket. Raina drew her knife. Mauser produced a pistol.

"Don't even think about it," he said. "Because the act of thinking about a thing makes you feel like you have tacit permission to do that thing. But what do you think will happen if you reach into your pocket?"

"You'll shoot." The man's voice was hoarse and broke on the last word. His eyes hardened. "Don't you dare threaten me."

"Then don't move," Raina said.

The man blinked against the breeze. Scars laced his arms and chest and face. A gull cawed and Martin flinched.

"Well, what we have here is the typical impasse of two strange parties away from home," Mauser said. "In the interest of both parties, why don't we just smile, back away, and—"

"Are you from the island?" the man said.

"Catalina?" Raina said.

The man went for his pocket.

Raina lunged forward and pushed her knife against his corded neck. "I hate every man there! I want to wade in their blood. Burn down their houses and throw their bones in the ocean."

Ignoring the knife against his neck, the pale man laughed, a croaking, awful sound. "After all that's happened, you're still trying to kick the shit out of each other."

"Right," Mauser said. "Who are you?"

"I don't know."

Martin frowned. "Are you all right? Do you have amnesia?"

"My name is from a language that's never been spoken." He shifted his eyes to Raina. "Get that damn knife off me."

She moved it sideways a fraction of an inch, daring the killing steel to draw blood. "Why should I?"

The man looked to the black shape in the sea. "If you harm me, my brothers will never stop hunting you."

"Your brothers," Mauser said. The man didn't move. "You're talking about the pilots of that submarine over yonder? Did you capture it from the invaders?"

"The aliens?" Martin said. "What's it like? How did you figure out how to get it to go?"

"Because the aliens are still in it," Raina said. The pale man smiled. She relaxed the knife from his throat. "Why did you ask if we were from the island?"

"So I'd know whether to kill you."

"Implying you wouldn't otherwise," Mauser said. "Excellent. I propose we shake hands, tip our hats, and toddle our separate ways."

"Are you going to fight them?" Raina said.

"Soon," the man said.

"So are we. We could fight them together. Wipe them out."

The man was silent for a long while. "Can't trust you. When the fear comes, humans break down. Collapse. Betray each other to save their own skins."

"But you were thinking about it?" Mauser said. He had a strange gleam in his eye. One that Raina wasn't sure she liked.

The pale man nodded. "I want them dead, too."

"I don't suppose you've got a cell number in case you change your mind."

"Sure, but I prefer Skype."

"Oh well, neither do we." Mauser smiled brightly and extended his hand. "Are we at least agreed not to murder each other?"

"For now."

They shook. Mauser leaned in and clapped him on the back. The man looked uncomfortable. Not to be touched by another man. To be touched by a human.

Mauser withdrew, rocked on his heels, and jammed his hands in his pockets. With his chin, he gestured across the road to the ocean. "After you."

The pale man walked across the road, crossed a half-dead lawn, reached the sand, and walked straight into the water. The waves swirled over his head. A minute later, steam boiled from the black vessel, snorting in twin gouts like the nose of a dragon in the cartoons Raina watched as a child. It sank into the sea.

"Why did you let him go?" she said. "We could have slaughtered the Catalinans together."

"Are you serious?" Mauser said. "He looked like a cross between a Maori warrior and a dead lamprey."

"That's how I know he'd make a good ally."

"The thing about getting into bed with the devil is that it's the devil. Nothing but spines down there." He shuddered and waved his hand down the road. "Anyway, if you'd gone all Voltron with him, you'd have to end this ultra-important quest for a dead guy's doodles."

Martin's walkie talkie spewed clicks and pops, then went silent. He turned the volume up until the static hissed. Hearing nothing more, he put it away. "I don't think we should stay."

"There you go, two to one, Raina," Mauser said. "Unless you fancy a swim, let's extract ourselves from Dodge."

She gazed over the sea. Far to the south, the black shell of the main ship loomed like an island. She drew a circle between her shoulders, brow, and chest, then traced a line down its middle. The moon wouldn't help her here; she was hunting, but not for blood. She would have to be extra careful.

They reached Malibu the next morning. After the way her first mom had spoken of the place, Raina expected more than the beaches, canyons, manors, cafes, and brush-clogged hills. It was pretty, but no more so than the south shore of the peninsula where she'd lived with her second family.

Virtually all the town hugged the coast, with a few tentacular roads probing into the canyons. That made for an easy search. They split up, each taking a walkie talkie, and went door to door, watchful for any signs of people lurking behind the boldly painted doors. Half of the front doors were unlocked. All the houses were desolate. Plenty of things. No people.

Few of the things were worth caring about. Some cans of food that might be good if they were cooked long enough. Assorted batteries, although most of them were leaking juice, corroded by time and sea air. Plenty of paintings. Just like Beverly Hills, none were what she was searching for. In one marble-floored villa, she found a hanging of an abstract swirl of flower-bright reds and yellows. With the help of a chair, she got it down and radioed Mauser and Martin, but Mauser dismissed it as something called a Kandinsky.

"Which is amazing," he said. "Any right-thinking person would happily settle for a Kandinsky. 'Settle' isn't even the right word. This thing might have cost more than the house it's in."

Raina shook her head. "He wants a Chagall."

"Well, what the grumpy, demanding, would-be kung fu master wants, the grumpy, demanding, would-be kung fu master gets."

Martin and Mauser's luck was no better, although their bags grew lumpier by the day. After two days of steady westward searching, she discovered why none of the homes were inhabited. Just past a college campus, a rampart of rock and mud lay piled across the road, running all the way down to the sea. Above it, the hills were charred, young brush sprouting from the sooty soil.

Raina stopped and glanced back down the highway. Was this a sign? She'd seen mudslides before at Palos Verdes, but this one was right across the road. As if the earth itself were warding people away from what waited beyond. But that could be a trick, too. A ploy to turn back seekers before they found the treasure. If it were a ruse, and she fell for it, the earth would surely frown on her. It might even close the way forever.

Before she could make a decision, Mauser hopped on a rock and climbed up the rubble. She followed him. On the other side, a man and a woman stood on the highway below the mudslide. They had rifles in their hands but hadn't yet aimed them.

"My name is Mauser!" he called. "There, we're not strangers. Now it would be a crime to shoot us."

A white-haired woman tipped her head. "You don't know my name."

"April? You look very much like an April." He glanced down to ensure his footing, then presented the couple with a smile. "You saw us on the other side of town. Busting in doors and such."

"Yep."

"And you're here to tell us to turn around and go back the way we came."

"Yep."

"We're not here to cause trouble. All we want is a painting."

"Looters," the man grunted. Like his wife, he was old, with a salt and pepper goatee. But the woman was as lean as Raina. The man had a doughy gut that would collapse under a punch.

"You have us all wrong," Mauser said. "We're not wanton robbers stuffing our pockets with anything that sparkles. We are the agents of a highly respected man—a master martial artist, once renowned both in America and in his home country—and at his behest, we are here to find one of the works of Marc Chagall." He lifted one shoulder, stirring his heavy pack. "I have a book of his paintings right here. Would you like to see it?"

The woman shook her head, shifting her rifle. "Nope. We got a community to look after."

"You see, our employer— "

"Doesn't draw shit around here," the man laughed. He had a gravelly, musing voice and leonine silver hair. "We all used to be somebody, man. Things changed."

"Sweet strikes and gutterballs," Mauser murmured. "Are you—?"

"What did I just tell you? None of us is anyone."

"Well, Mr. Person I Might Truly Have Once Adored Like Your Own Mother, then understand what I'm about to tell you isn't a threat, but rather a gesture of my deepest appreciation for you or the man you resemble." He jerked a thumb at Raina. "See this girl here?"

"Yeah."

"See that knife on her belt? Big red Japanese one?"

The man raised a shaggy brow. "You're sure this isn't a threat?"

"Those pirates on Catalina killed her father. Kidnapped her mother. She's here to become the pupil of the aforementioned martial artist, who refuses to teach her stab-one unless she brings him a Chagall. If she does, then once her training is complete, she can sail to the island and defeat all who stand between her and her mother. This must sound like a fairy tale, but on Donny's grave, I swear to you it's the truth."

"What it sounds is crazy," said the woman.

"But not half as crazy as this girl is." Mauser shot Raina a worried look. "She's got it in her head we'll find the painting here. If she isn't allowed to search, I don't know what she'll do. That isn't a bluff. I seriously have no fucking idea."

The woman laughed. "Get shot, most likely."

"Well, possibly. These days, that's a likely fate for anyone. But I've got a proposal that will leave all of us unshot and unstabbed. Let us have a look around. We won't take a thing. Not so much as a sip of water. All we want is the painting. The painting that will let this little girl rescue her mother."

"Chagall," the man muttered. He turned to his wife. "Didn't Willis used to have one of those?"

"For Pete's sake, you're not actually considering this."

"Well?"

The woman put her hands on her hips. "No one's coming into town with a gun."

"Agreed," Raina said.

"Wait a minute," Mauser said.

The woman counted off points on her fingers. "Second, you don't touch any homes that got a person in them. There aren't many, but the few there are are sacrosanct. My husband will show you what to avoid. Third, you get three days. When time's up, no sob stories about how you're homeless or you're too sick to travel. You see the sun?" She pointed up. It was nearing noon. "When it reaches that spot three days from now, you march on back to L.A."

"Deal," Raina said.

With a sigh, Mauser turned over all three of his pistols. Martin handed his over without complaint. Raina didn't have one but the woman wanted to take away her blades. When she clung to the one from the Getty, the man allowed that maybe she could hang onto it—there were coyotes around, you know.

The woman showed them to a house where they'd be allowed to stay. It was very nice. Raina didn't care. They dropped off their bags and followed the man around town. He went to the Willis place first, but if it had once held their painting, it wasn't there any longer.

Raina's spirit endured. She went door to door, skipping only the houses the man warned her away from. Martin helped comb the sprawling estates while Mauser spent most of his time chatting about movies with the old man. Raina's annoyance mounted. Movies were part of the old world. They were wasting time.

One day ticked by like nothing at all. The second slipped away just as swiftly. The third night, Raina didn't sleep, escaping the house while the others slept. She ranged into the canyons north of town, remotest from the road. The waves thundered below her. She ran from room to room and house to house. Light peeped over the eastern mountains, bouncing from ten million waves, failing to penetrate the misty haze enshrouding the city halfway across the bay. She ran back to the house and threw herself down in her bed. Not five minutes later, a door creaked open in the hall.

The old man came around. Raina ran back to the canyons. Her steps echoed in tomblike foyers. Her heart thudded in her aching head. She willed the sun not to climb. It denied her.

"Raina!" Mauser's voice rang out from the beaches below. "Raaaina!"

She wandered into the mansion's yard and plopped down beneath a naked cliff. It wasn't fair. She had searched for so long. Traveled so far. Effort was supposed to yield reward. All she had for her work was sore feet, a pounding head, and a belly that was growing more and more angry eating so much freeze dried food.

"Raina!"

She wiped her eyes and stood. Motion stirred on the rocks above her. A gecko sat in the sun. It was yellow with a bit of blue on its tail. Black spots dotted its skin. It jerked its head and stared her in the eye.

She froze, overwhelmed by the power of the omen. Every beast and man in her family of souls held its breath.

The gecko dashed into the rocks. She flung herself at the cliff, clawing for purchase. A stone clattered away from her hand. Mauser yelled from way down below, joined by the gravelly bellow of the old man. Raina gritted her teeth, found a new hold, and spidered up to the ledge where the gecko had been. It startled again, dashing up the scarp.

She followed it, running awkwardly up the pitched slope. It scrambled over a ridge. She reached the top and froze. She could no longer hear its tiny claws ticking on the stones.

Before her, a white palace claimed the plateau, more hills mounded behind it. The sunlight blared from its white marble pillars. Half blind, fingers bleeding, she walked toward it.

* * *

They dragged a wagon back with them to the south. Between it and Raina's insistence that they only travel at night, which hardly lasted nine hours at this time of year, it took three days to return to the peninsula. Mauser and Martin came with her to the cliffs at the southwestern sweep of the point, but she stopped them out of eyeshot of the man's home.

"Thank you for coming with me," she said. "But the next step of my journey I must take alone."

Mauser laughed and rolled his eyes. "At least I can say I knew you when."

Martin hugged her. "Good luck."

She rolled the wagon down the street, parking it on the sidewalk in front of the house. She picked up the painting, staggering under its awkward, doorish size, propped it against the wooden post holding up the roof above the man's porch, and knocked on the front door.

The man from the beach answered. He had a knife in one hand. His jaw dropped.

She began her training.

22

"You realize how little sense that makes," Walt said. "If you're being attacked over there, the safest place to be is anywhere else."

"What are you doing here?" She kicked an empty bottle slanting from the sand. "Getting drunk?"

"It's pretty fun. Ever tried it? You could use it."

"Excuse me if I don't laugh. My people are dying."

He almost walked away. He grabbed his pack instead. "Don't you want to know what I learned?"

She'd been walking toward the faraway boat. She stopped and turned. "Do you have a way to get onto the ship?"

"No."

"Shocking."

He trudged behind her. He couldn't figure out whether the rift between them was her fault or his. The fact of the matter was he'd agreed to come here. Agreed to help. Both he and the islanders had expected him to do just that. Instead, his suggestions backfired. Drew down the assaults Karslaw had feared all along.

He knew this wasn't his fight. So what if they'd pinned their hopes on him? If this had all been a stupid idea, that was Karslaw's blame, not his. He ought to leave before things got worse and the islanders—or their leader—turned their anger on Walt. The only thing he stood to gain from this was Lorna, and she looked like less of a prize every day.

But that was because she resented him for failing. She was scared. They all were. Scared of an enemy that just wouldn't go away.

That was why he followed her to the boat. He still had work to do.

They rowed to the sailboat and cast off. He stood on the deck and watched the gulls circling over the mothership. It must have its own ecosystems by now. Barnacles and mussels on the hull. Crabs scuttling over the anemones stuck in the tidepools of its crevices. Fish taking shelter in the wreckage, nibbling algae while predators lurked in the waters beyond.

Meanwhile, people harbored in the city and the islands, hiding away from the threat growing inside the ship itself.

Avalon's main pier had been damaged during the beach raid and Lorna guided them into the smaller one at the Scaveteria. Karslaw had a runner waiting for Walt. His presence was requested immediately. Walt sighed and followed him over the hills to the palace.

Karslaw saw him in the same room they'd first spoken in. There was no fire in the hearth today. Spiderwebs hung between the naked beams of the ceiling. At their first meeting, Karslaw had been invigorated, swollen with fight and fury, laughing with the life of it all.

Today, he sat in a stuffed chair, his feet tucked under it like a child at school. His eyelids were puffy, sleepless or hungover or both. He directed Walt to a chair and combed his fingers through his beard.

"I'm going to tell you some things. Dangerous things. Things I would never tell an outsider except when I had no other choice."

Walt rubbed the back of his neck. "I'll wait to be honored until I hear what they are."

"My motives for this are many. Foremost, I need to know where we sit so I can decide how to move forward. Second, I need to light a fire under you. And lastly, if things keep on as they've been keeping on, it won't matter who knows what, because none of us will be left to act on that knowledge."

"That's dramatic. If it's that dire, why don't you pile into those boats of yours and sail some place less infested?"

Karslaw shook his head vaguely. "It took five years to build this island. Much as I may look like the king of the castle, not all my people would follow. And I will not leave a single one of them behind to die."

"Really? So a few of your people decide to commit suicide, and your response to that is to condemn everyone else to death with them? If that's leadership, it explains a lot about the former American political process."

Karslaw chuckled, regaining a little of his old light. "I wish I'd had you sooner. As it is, here is where we stand. We are withdrawing from the mainland. I won't waste my troops on Long Beach street gangs when I need them here at home. That means abandoning the mainlanders to the gangs instead. I'd hoped to make them one with our people. But hopes are will-o-wisps leading us away from truths, aren't they?"

"Indeed, my liege," Walt said.

"Watch yourself," he chuckled. "So we withdraw. Regroup. But this island isn't safe from the enemy in the bay. They will continue to hound us. They will continue to breed. As we grow weaker, they grow stronger."

Karslaw leaned back and pressed his palms together, fingers splayed. "That's the logic of it. Hit them while we're still strong enough to throw a punch. And the sooner we act, the better my chances of hanging onto the mainland, too. But you don't use logic to fire up the troops. What do I say to convince their hearts? Better to die as warriors than as our conquerors' cattle? Nobler to stride into the grave than to lie in it?"

"That sounds a lot better than 'Rush in willy-nilly and hope it's alien nap-time.'"

"We may be overthinking this. Getting into the ship is a Gordian knot. If you can't unravel it, I'll cut straight through it."

"By flinging your men face-first into missiles?"

He shook his head. "We don't know that it's capable of destroying more than a single target. If we send in decoys first and follow them in with our fastest boats, we may confound their defenses."

"Or you wind up as shrimp food," Walt said. "I hope they like beard."

Karslaw grimaced, patience deserting him. "Then soothe my stress-itched mind with a better idea."

Walt screwed up his face. "How many pistols you got?"

"Plenty. The mainlanders have been passing along the spares to help deal with this menace." He frowned, bristling his beard. "Pistols are no good. You can hardly hit what's right in front of you. We don't know how many of those things are onboard. We need firepower.

Rifles. Automatics."

"Yeah."

"Then why would you want pistols?"

"Tight quarters in there," Walt said. "I'm still thinking. That's the third option besides charging in ASAP or abandoning L.A., you know. Give yourself the time to hammer out a solid plan."

"How many weeks have I already given you? When thought hits a rut, action is what frees you. You have three weeks to give me something better. Any plan that takes longer than that to work out would be too complicated for us to execute in the first place."

Walt left angry, mostly because Karslaw was right. Not necessarily about the timeline or the ludicrous suite of external pressures he appeared to be dealing with. But because it sounded like a lot of people were about to die, and if Walt were just a little smarter, they could be saved.

He didn't see much of anyone for a while. He spent most of his time in his house doodling or taking notes. At night, he wandered around the shrubs and grass in the hills behind Avalon, turning the same set of questions over in his head. When he did step out during the day—sometimes to get food, sometimes to pull things from the Scaveteria and see what it took to make them float—he saw change. Soldiers standing guard in the streets and on the beach. Boats massing. The rasp of scrapers on hulls. Men tinkered with engines, wiping oily hands on their pants. Karslaw was assembling his fleet. Soon, it would make its first and likely last attack.

Avalon threw a party. Walt wasn't quite sure what it was for. Possibly something war-related, but between the fireworks popping over the bay and all the drunken singing rolling up from downtown, he had the impression it was independence-related, maybe the anniversary of New Catalina's founding. He didn't join them in person, but went back to his house for a bottle to join them in spirit.

More singing. Bonfires on the beach, complete with public displays of dancing. They'd even rigged up an electric guitar to go with the drums, horns, and singer, who had to shout as loud as he could for his unaided voice to be heard over the instruments. The crowd joined in to help him out. All together, their tones sounded better than the lone man's harsh strain. They covered up each other's off notes. Blended together in surprising and pleasing ways. A bit sloppy, falling out of time, having audible difficulty hitting the more extreme notes, but overall far prettier than any but the most talented singers could manage on their own.

How many places like this were left in the world? Where there were enough people—and they were safe enough—to throw a dance party/kegger? A couple of the Maya groups had held festivals and holidays. There must be other groups scattered around the planet, too. But they must have been vanishingly rare, especially on the scale of Avalon, which had done more than survive. It had rebuilt. Hung onto the luxury of culture. Because Karslaw had had a vision of bringing the survivors to a new land.

And now he was about to let that vision and the feelings it kindled be snuffed out.

Walt woke with a hangover. Lorna was out, so he hung around on her porch until she wandered in. She offered him a brief hug.

"Late night?" she said.

"A lot of thinking."

"Turn up anything useful?"

"I swam out to it, Lorna. When I was in Santa Monica, I got good and drunk, swam out to the ship, and climbed aboard. I sat on its hull and I walked around and then I swam back."

She gaped. "You swam to the ship?"

"The dolphins were doing it."

"That's your excuse? The dolphins did it first? While you were out there, did you also eat raw sardines and ram sharks with your nose?"

He waggled his arms. "Look at me. One piece. No missile-wounds. I don't know if it's not programmed to shoot at organic targets because of all the animals or if their gunner fell asleep at the wheel or what. But if I made it there, maybe your whole army can."

The derision faded from her eyes. "That's a long swim."

"Less than a quarter mile. Anyone fit to fight can swim that far."

"Not with all their gear. You can't swim through a quarter mile of waves holding a rifle above your head."

"I know. And if we try to float it over on a raft, the aliens will just blast it to bits. That's what I've been stuck on. My best idea is to stick pistols and ammo in Ziploc bags and send the troops for a swim. I'm going to give all this to Karslaw and see what he can do with it."

Lorna folded her arms. "He won't go for it. He'd rather send his men on an all-or-nothing charge than to knowingly send them in with inferior weapons."

Walt went to see Karslaw at the palace anyway. The man chewed his beard a moment, then shook his head. "I don't like it. Send them in naked with a handgun and thirty rounds apiece? Why not save the ammo and shoot them myself?"

Walt rubbed his eye. "That's exactly what Lorna said you'd say."

"That I'd shoot my own men?"

"That you'd rather stick with the Charge of the Light Brigade."

"Do those close to me find me that predictable?" Karslaw rumbled. "Very well, then I am consistent. As long as you can pull a surprise from your sleeve now and then, consistency is a virtue in a leader."

Walt went for one last walk around the island. It was a warm day and it felt good to sweat. He thought it might be fun to settle on an island for a while. Just really get to know every bend of the beach and fold of the hills. None of that desert island crap, though. A place where stuff grew on its own and you could pick fruit from the trees without spending all day busting your ass. Nothing too jungly, though. He'd had enough of jungles for a while.

He had nearly a week until Karslaw unleashed the Catalinan Armada, a growing collection of sloops and speedboats, and, possibly due to logistical concerns, more of the former than the latter, which hardly infused Walt with optimism. Part of him wanted to stick around for the big battle. There was still the off chance he'd come up with something better than popguns in baggies, and he would love to see if Karslaw could actually pull this shit off.

But Walt knew they couldn't. And he couldn't think of a plan. Sticking around to watch the fireworks would only be depressing, considering that the fireworks would be made of people. It was time to leave. Before his departure could pose a distraction from Karslaw's grand plans to get the entire island killed.

He was unimpressed enough with Lorna that he thought long and hard about leaving without a word. But rowing all that way would be a serious pain in the arms, and anyway, if he smacked her into the concrete wall of an ultimatum, maybe it would finally knock some sense into her.

He went to her house and had to wait again. She approached from the road leading to the castle. He hugged her, then asked if she wanted to go for a walk.

"Why? I just got done walking."

Walt was too tired to drag it out any longer anyway. "Because I'm leaving."

She cocked her head. "What do you mean?"

"I mean I am departing this island, never to be seen again. Because you're all going to die."

"You can't."

"Sure I can. If you want to give me a ride, that would be wonderful. Want to come with me? Even better. But if neither of those options rings your bell, I'll steal a rowboat and paddle back to L.A. on my own."

"No," she said. "You can't leave me."

"Lorna, it's a bit late for the 'I'll love you forever' crap. You've been ignoring me for weeks. You're going through some shit? I'm sympathetic. Deeply. But we're all going through some shit. If you want to work it out, you've got to work it out with me. Keeping me at arm's length won't solve anything."

Her face worked in several directions at once. She bared her teeth, then touched her stomach. "I'm pregnant."

"What?"

"The situation that results when a man and a woman have unprotected sex."

Walt reeled. That much was true, although he'd made sure to pull out since their first couple nights together. And they hadn't had sex since they hiked out to see the fort. Not that that mattered, though. That was recent enough that she might not even have missed a period. Then it must have happened before the gunfight in Zacatecas. The long walk through the jungle when they'd been at their closest. They'd been pretty busy then.

"You're sure it's mine?"

She punched him in the face. "Very."

He straightened, rubbing his sore cheek. "How do you know? You don't look so pregnant to me."

"All the ways you tell without looking. The fluids that stop. The others that start up, primarily in the morning. You don't have to swell up to a blimp to know what's going on."

"Okay, well, first things first. There are teas, you know. Herbal shit. I mean, are you sure you want to—?"

He stopped dead. His head hadn't yet come back to earth after her announcement, and with the formation of his new idea, it blew away again, spinning off into the dizziest mental clouds.

"Want to what?" She sneered. "Get an abortion?"

"Yeah," Walt said. "But that can wait. First, I'm going to save your people."

23

He didn't want to teach her.

His name was Carl and his father came from the Philippines, a place Raina didn't know about. He told her it was an island chain far, far away. The islands had been conquered and reconquered for centuries. First by natives too old to name. Then by Muslims from Indonesia. Then the Catholics of Spain. Then, not so long ago, by Americans. Most recently of all, by the aliens.

Like all disputed places, its people learned to fight. Like all conquered peoples, their new masters tried to stop them. The people turned to weapons anyone would have. Knives. Sticks. Bare hands. It didn't look like much. Nothing to arouse suspicion.

It was deadly.

Carl's father learned kali in the Philippines. He moved to America. Carl was born, and the father taught his son until he exhausted his own skills, then sent Carl to the academy in Torrance, a place Raina did know—it was one of the cities just north of the peninsula. Its training wasn't like the Philippines, Carl said. Not as traditional. But in some ways better, because its masters were as famous as they were skilled—one had worked with Bruce Lee, who even Raina had heard of—and open to the ideas brought in by the students their reputations drew from around the world.

"And none of this matters," Carl told her, "because you should be learning to use a gun instead."

"I know how to pull a trigger."

"Why do you want to learn this?"

"To learn how to kill."

"You believe a fist or a knife kills better than a gun?" he said.

"I believe a gun is loud," Raina said. "I believe a gun is messy. I believe it jams and misfires and needs ammunition and gunpowder and cleaning. Guns rely on many things. Knives don't. Fists don't. I don't, either."

Carl snorted. "Then carry two guns. Learn to make bullets."

Raina scowled at the spray of color on the canvas Carl had hung on his living room wall. "I brought you your painting. You said you'd teach me."

"Did I say I won't? I said I shouldn't. If you really want to learn an obsolete art so badly, I have nothing better to do."

"Then let's start."

He smiled, amused in a way she would have found intolerably insulting from anyone else. But he had earned it. He knew how to kill in the old ways.

"We start with empty hands," he said.

"Because they're the most basic," she said.

"Who's teaching who? We start with hands because I don't have the right sticks and I'm not giving you a real knife." He smiled in that way again. Soon, she'd see it two dozen times a day. "And yes. Because the hands are most basic. In kali, one thing is everything else. A stick is a knife is a hand."

She stayed until nightfall. He allowed her to return at noon the next day. She did nothing else for a week straight.

The style was aggressive. Flurries of quick, staccato strikes at whatever target presented itself. The body or the head, if you could attack them safely, but the legs or the hands if you couldn't. It felt like it was built for her.

On the walk back to her house, two columns of men and women marched down the middle of the road. Jill was at their head, calling time. She barked a single word and the columns dispersed, scattering into the bushes and houses on the sides of the street. Raina stayed hidden in a hedge until the columns regrouped and carried on down the road.

Carl began with single actions. A punch, a slap, a jab. But from the beginning, he made her work with two hands and often both feet at the same time. She found even the simplest coordinated movements infuriatingly clumsy, her slow-motion gestures appalling.

"Why is this so hard?" she said. "I've been using all four limbs at once since I was born."

"But you're only now learning kali."

"It shouldn't be this hard to learn. A style should be natural."

"Nature doesn't come from within," he said. "Nature is something you put inside yourself."

For no good reason, he laughed.

But after her first week, it seemed to come together. She often moved without thinking, slapping away his fist with one hand and striking his arm with the other. Mauser's original training made it easier. Some of the concepts were similar, and once she understood the purpose and flow of a move, it nestled with the others in her muscles, waiting to be used.

When she wasn't with Carl, she trained on the dummy in her garage. Its limbs made good targets. The rattle of her blows spilled into the street.

"Is it really that much fun?" Martin asked her.

"It isn't about fun."

"Well, you sure seem to enjoy it." He shuffled his feet. "Can I learn, too?"

"No."

"Why not? I helped find the painting."

"You should learn from Mauser first." She struck the dummy's padded head. "Then we'll see."

Martin frowned. She resumed her flurries, advancing to wallop the dummy's arms, then scooting behind it and striking its back. After a while, Martin left.

Carl cut sticks of bamboo from the once-decorative thicket of it overwhelming the neighbor's yard. She took for granted that sticks were for hitting, clubbing, and bashing, but he showed her how to poke, how to rap, how to whip the tips of the springy sticks into thighs and knuckles and eyes.

"The enemy retreats from pain," he said. "So you give him lots of it. You hurt him until he can't hurt you back."

"But hurt animals are most dangerous."

"You have to take what is given," he said. "Do you know what it means to take what's given?"

She nodded.

He smiled, but interest glimmered beneath the mockery. "Do you?"

"After the plague, I lived on my own for two years," she said. "I ate what I could find. I had to fight with dogs and other children and even a few adults. I learned to see when they were hungrier than I was so I could run away. Even if a dog had a bird and I was starving, it was best to let the dog finish and take whatever it left."

"You lived on your own that whole time? You couldn't have been more than ten years old."

She spread her feet, sticks in hand. "I used to pretend I'd forgotten what it was like, but I remember everything."

Carl had skinned a finger showing her how to block with the stick. He stuck his knuckle in his mouth and sucked away the blood. "I want you to learn with me with the same hunger you learned to survive."

She rushed at him. He knocked her to the floor.

A couple days later, Mauser shook her awake. The sunlight cut flat through the window, not yet touching her mattress on the floor.

"What?" she said.

"I want to show you something."

Her ribs and arms were bruised and welted from the lash of bamboo. "I don't want to be shown."

"Yes you do." He nudged her with the hard toe of his shoe. She slapped at his foot and he danced back. "Believe me, Raina, I don't take waking a person up lightly. If it were up to me, people-waker-uppers would be beaten with the bluntest and heaviest item at hand. But you're going to want to see this."

She rolled over and opened one eye. His hair stuck up from his head. His eyes were bleary. She doubted he'd slept. She sighed the sleepy sigh of morning and got up and found her shoes. Mauser led her down the road to the Dunemarket. The sun rose from the hills, painfully bright. Merchants unfolded stalls and rolled out blankets.

"If it's too early for the market," she said, "it's definitely too early for me."

"Wrong as Raina," Mauser said. "Oh, that's good. I'm making that a thing."

He took her through the market to the inn at the base of the hill where they'd first met. She watched the McDonald's warily. He jogged up to the second story of the motel and knocked on one of the doors. A redheaded man answered. He wasn't much older than Raina. He let them inside and locked the door. Heavy drapes muffled the sun.

"Raina," Mauser said, "this is Luke."

"Good for him."

"He's from Catalina."

She reached for her knife—Carl had told her it was called a tanto—and whipped it from the lacquered sheath.

Luke stumbled back against the bed, shielding his face. "Hey!"

"Stop!" Mauser moved between them, scowling at her. "Must you always stab first and ask questions never? He's seen your mother."

The point of her knife shook. "You have?"

The boy glanced at Mauser. "Are you sure? Was her dad—?"

"She's adopted," Mauser said.

Raina took three tries to put away her tanto, its point scraping the mouth of the sheath. "Where did you see her?"

"Is she kind of short?" Luke said. "Dark hair she wears tied back? With the little strands of it hanging past each ear?"

"Yes."

"Kate?"

"Yes!"

"She's on Catalina." Luke slid off the side of the bed, standing several feet away. "In Karslaw's castle."

"He has a castle?" Mauser said.

"With a drawbridge and everything."

"Has he hurt her?" Raina said.

Luke's eyes went guarded. "I don't know."

"She's alive, Raina," Mauser said. "She's still out there. That's all that matters."

Raina's vision smeared with tears. She pressed her elbows to her chest. The room pulled away from her. She ran to Mauser and bowled into his arms.

"Gracious," he said, patting her hair. "The little wasp has feelings after all."

She only let herself cry for a few moments. Mauser dug into his pocket and handed her a cloth that was almost clean. She wiped her face.

"Thank you," she said to Luke.

"For your troubles," Mauser said. With two fingers, he passed the boy a rolled-up baggie of ovoid green buds. "Don't smoke it all in one place."

Luke flushed, pocketed it, and smiled at Raina. "I hope you find her."

Mauser took her outside into the brilliant sunlight. The asphalt glittered. The mountains stood to the north, feet hidden by the haze, crests suspended in the air like a reachable heaven.

"We have to go get her," she said.

"Have you heard what's going on?" Mauser said. "Or have you been too busy twirling your batons to keep up with local events?"

She carried her bamboo sticks at all times now. She pulled one from her belt and menaced him. "Does this look like a baton?"

"Well, the last time tax day rolled around, the Catalinans demanded twice as much as ever. Mostly in food. And they were very insistent on being informed of any contraband guns that may have showed up in the last couple months. There was a beating or two. Most locals had to hand over more than they'd been taking in. A few went—how do you put this—food-rupt? About to starve. Some of the merchants started up a collection to ensure nobody went hungry. Let's just say the Catalinans didn't go home with a lot of fresh admirers."

"So what?"

"I'm not finished. Meanwhile, in the ongoing Period of the Warring Assholes, the Catalinans have pretty much chased the Osseys out of Long Beach. Some guerrilla fighters rolled around now and then to take a couple potshots at the occupying islanders, but by and large the whole gang skedaddled back to Orange County."

"Did they hurt the Catalinans any?" Raina said. "Or did we do all that for nothing?"

Mauser laughed. "Oh, the Catalinans were hurt. Repeatedly. Not a lot of casualties—the Catalinans torched a few buildings, but they weren't exactly eager to fight house to house; lots of sniping back and forth—but, to paraphrase a guy so smart he got streets named after him, every death counts. More importantly, we drew the focus off the Dunemarket. That gave Jill a lot of time and freedom to organize and train her people. Things really came together while we were out gallivanting after that painting."

"Is she finally ready to stand up?"

"I wouldn't go that far. You know Jill. She moves about as fast as a banana peel."

"What does that mean?"

"Have you ever seen a banana peel move?" he said. She shook her head. He splayed his palm. "Precisely."

He went silent as they reached the Dunemarket. He smiled at three or four different women, touching the tip of his finger to an imaginary cap. He didn't resume talking until they were past the vendors and travelers and halfway up the hill.

"Where was I? Nevermind, I know exactly where I was. About to tell you that three days ago, the Catalinans evacuated Long Beach."

Raina smiled. "The Osseys struck back."

"No," Mauser said. "That's the thing. Nothing about the battlefront had changed. They just left. Pulled everyone out and sailed back to Catalina. Which raises the question: if nothing changed in Long Beach, what changed on the island?"

"Did you ask Luke?"

"How do you think I found out he'd seen your mom?" Mauser shook his head. "He didn't know anything. Was visiting the island as an envoy from a kingdom in San Diego."

Raina glanced downhill to ensure they weren't being watched. The sun poured down between the palms. "What does all this mean for the rebellion?"

"That's the thing. Nobody knows. Are they gone for good? Can we stop busting heads and start busting champagne? Or did they catch wind of what we're up to and fell back to regroup? If so, how long do we have before they return to go all Gallagher on the watermelon of our little society?"

"We need to know more."

"That's exactly where I was going with this longwinded bit of exposition. You fancy a trip back to Long Beach? I'd like to see how the prostitute store is doing."

"How long will it take?"

"Just a day. Think you can tear yourself away from the color guard for that long?"

She didn't like it, but she went to Carl and asked if she could skip the next day of training.

He gave her a long and unreadable look. "Do whatever you want."

"Are you mad?" she said.

"Why would I be mad? I never trained as hard as you have."

"I'll only be gone for a day."

"I heard you." He folded his arms behind his back and turned to face the painting hanging from his wall. The Chagall was so vivid it looked like it was stepping right out of the wall. "Anyway, it will finally give me the chance to appreciate my new art."

"The Catalinans just took off and left," the woman said. "Sucks, too. Best business we've done since opening our doors. They made sure we didn't get touched by the fires or fighting, either."

"See?" Mauser said to Raina. "You act like this is such a terrible job, but listen to those fringe benefits. Meanwhile, if they'd fought the war in San Pedro, they'd have probably used the Dunemarket for target practice."

The woman's name was Belle and she had agreed to see them in her room at Pokers. The building looked no different from when they had ambushed the men in their beds. The same couldn't be said for the rest of the waterfront. Bullet holes pockmarked the storefronts. Broken glass carpeted the streets. Several buildings were scorched; one had been burnt to the foundation, with two more beside it reduced to gutted shells. If the fire hadn't been isolated by a curve of the waterfront's quirky streets, half of Long Beach might have burned down.

"So you don't know anything?" Raina said.

"Just one thing." Belle lit a rolled cigarette and geysered smoke from her nostrils. "One of the guys who comes to see me said he won't be back for a while."

"Maybe he doesn't like you anymore."

"Raina!" Mauser said.

The woman exhaled smoke. "You skinny little bitch."

"You'll have to excuse her," Mauser said. "It's a miracle she's housebroken."

"I don't care what some john thinks of me. But I'm trying to help you, God knows why, and she's insulting me to my face."

Martin raised his hand for peace. "She just meant that doesn't necessarily mean they're leaving." He avoided Raina's gaze. "She sees things different. It's hard to explain."

The woman tapped ash from her cigarette. "That right?"

Raina still didn't see what all the fuss was about. "That's all I meant."

"Whatever. They all left. Either every trooper they had decided to pack up their cocks and find a better place to spend the night, or they got sent home."

"Right." Mauser clapped his thighs and stood. "Thanks, Belle. If you hear anything else, you'll let me know?"

She laughed. "Anything for a friend."

On their way out, Mauser chatted with a couple girls in the lobby. Outside, he shook his head and started back toward the market. "Well, that was a bust. And what the hell was that, Raina? Belle's a friend of mine. Even if she weren't, did you forget the part where we wanted information from her?"

"She was acting superior," Raina said.

"And knocking her off her high horse is more important than discovering what the hell is going on? So what if she gets a kick out of male attention? Don't be so judgmental. It's bad for your cholesterol."

Raina kicked a pebble down the road. This whole thing was stupid. Mauser's woman didn't know anything. The whole trip had been a waste of time. None of that was her fault.

"Well, what now?" Martin said.

"Now?" Mauser dabbed sweat from his forehead. There was a breeze off the bay but it wasn't doing much good. "I report in to Jill. Barring something very stupid, I think we're out of options except to wait and see how things shake out."

Martin started to speak, faltered, then cleared his throat and started over. "We could ask the Osseys."

"That would fall under the heading of 'stupid.' They just got their asses kicked out of Long Beach by hostile barbarians. You show up to ask them how that went and they're likely to regain their pride by beating you to death."

"What do you think, Raina?" Martin tried. "Can you think of a better way?"

"Mauser's right." But she wasn't sure of that at all. She just didn't want to waste any more time chasing answers when Jill wouldn't act on them anyway. Not when she could use that time learning from Carl. Her faith in the rebellion waned with each day it failed to manifest in battle. Like the moon, the slimmer her hopes became, the hungrier she got. She couldn't look to others. No one wanted this as much as she did. If she wanted to take Karslaw's head and free her father's spirit, she would have to hone herself until she was as sharp as her tanto.

It was dusk by the time they got back. Too late to go to Carl. She got up at dawn. To kill time before noon, she went out foraging in the ruins for avocados and corn and strawberries. Their supply of freeze-dried food was getting low and she didn't want to walk all the way back to the bunker.

She went to Carl's as soon as the sun neared the middle of the sky. They worked with the bamboo for a while, playing through combinations, welting each other's arms.

She broke for water. She didn't want to put it off until the end of the day when he could shrug her off. "I want to learn how you use the knife."

"You are," he said. "A hand is a stick is a knife."

"No. A hand is a hand. A knife is a knife."

"And I am the teacher."

She gestured south toward the island. "But it's all useless if I don't learn before it's time to fight."

Carl laughed and pointed across the room. "There's the door."

She picked up her bamboo. If he thought she wasn't ready, then her only choice was to work until she proved him wrong.

She didn't get the chance. Three days into a schedule that involved nothing but training and sleeping, Mauser flung open Carl's front door, breathing hard. Someone had found Martin in Long Beach. He'd gone there by himself. The Osseys had beaten him half to death.

24

Waves came and went, swelling beneath Walt with tidal and terrifying force, lifting him as effortlessly as a flake of skin on a shaken blanket. The moon moved on the water, but couldn't penetrate the shadows of the island-sized vessel three hundred yards ahead. He wore nothing but jockey shorts and every kick of his legs reminded him how naked he was. A few other swimmers kept pace with him, the foam of their strokes gray-silver in the moonlight, but most of the scores of soldiers were strung out in loose lines behind him.

Finally, the fat drone of an engine drifted down from somewhere in the sky. Walt laughed, glancing up between waves, trying to spot it in the darkness.

It had taken an amazingly long time to get the Goodyear Blimp up and running. Just tracking down the airfield in Gardena where they housed the thing had tied up a dozen scouts for nearly a week. That accomplished, Walt had overseen its revival, but while the blimp was in theory not so different from the hot air balloons he'd grown up with, in practice, it was more difficult by an order of magnitude.

First off, it was giant. And rather inconveniently stored in a hangar. They'd had to get the airfield tractor up and running just to drag the thing out into the open. Second, the blimp floated via helium rather than hot air, and while the airfield still had plenty of canned gas, they'd had to lug in a generator to get the pump going, at which point Walt discovered that one of the cables tying the slowly inflating vessel to the mooring mast had come free, causing the whole thing to angle from the scaffold at a potentially destructive angle.

Even after he sussed out the basics of inflation and deflation, he found himself faced with an entirely new concept: steering. While the maneuvering of a hot air balloon was based on the simplest and most passive systems—make air in balloon hot, causing it to rise; climb until you find the air stream blowing in the direction you want to travel in, then stabilize altitude and enjoy the ride—the blimp's steering was active. It had engines. Scoops. Valves. Little balloons inside the main envelope that could be filled with colder, heavier air to help keep the blimp level and maneuver it up and down.

There had been several points in the whole endeavor when he'd contemplated scrapping it in favor of a balloon instead. But delivering all their materiel would require multiple balloons, each with their own rookie, Walt-trained pilots struggling with the balloons' clumsy, passive steering. Coordinating an attack would be a nightmare.

So he learned to fly the blimp. And he not only had to learn it for himself. He had to teach it to a young woman named Lacey, the intended pilot of this semi-suicide mission. No way in hell was he flying the thing when he figured it was 50/50 odds that it would ever make it to the mothership in the first place.

Because quite frankly, the plan was moronic. Lacey and her team had done three or four dry runs to work out timing and coordination, but there was no telling whether the alien ship would allow the blimp to maneuver into position, let alone how it would react to phase two of the aerial operations. Walt didn't even know for sure the amphibious end of things would make it. Bringing the blimp into the mix had let him convince Karslaw to try swimmers instead of boats, but the only thing Walt knew was that the ship hadn't shot at him when he'd swum up to it alone. He had no idea what would happen when they approached it with a hundred soldiers. He might be a father soon. One of these days, he was going to have to start acting responsible.

Walt paddled down the backside of a wave, grinned, and got a mouthful of seawater for his trouble.

He spat it out and paddled on. Swimming out to open ocean in the middle of the night was nothing short of terrifying—given how his bowels were taking the experience, there was more than one advantage to being stripped to his skivvies—but if he took what the currents gave him, easing his pace when the low but steady waves hit him and then picking up speed when the incoming water stopped pushing back, he made steady progress toward the waiting ship. The summer air was still warm, too. Overhead, the blimp droned on, barely audible over the splash of the tides and the men and women swimming around him.

The ship filled more of his vision with each passing moment. It slanted from the sea at a low angle, its uppermost heights projecting some three hundred feet into the air. Its flat surface was runneled with canyons and studded with short towers. He was having a hard time keeping his breathing steady. Every flicker of the moon or the stars on the waves made him imagine a magnesium-bright missile arcing from the silent enemy and blasting a foamy crater into the ocean. All that was left of the swimmers would be mangled limbs and strung-out guts wheeling down into the deep parts of the sea.

The ship neared. Walt kicked harder. The last moments were the worst. His fingertips brushed an algae-slick surface that felt like the hardest rubber or the softest metal. He pulled himself aboard.

He crouched down to catch his breath and wipe off the worst of the water. He helped a few soldiers clamber up beside him, then jogged up the gently angled ship. In a few minutes, if everything went according to plan, each of the soldiers would receive a map drawn from the best of Walt's memory and copied precisely by Karslaw's personal scribe. But it would do all of them exactly zero good if Walt couldn't find the way inside.

He ran up the inclined hull in a low crouch, feet slapping the hard surface. Sudden chasms delved into the dark surface and he detoured around, keeping one eye on the crevices, as if an alien horde might boil from the shadows at any moment. Bird droppings freckled the matte black ground. Now and then a blunt tower stuck up from the plane like the weary thumb of a hitchhiker a long ways from home.

And then he spotted it, the metal spire that marked the staircase down to the landing bay. He ran to the opening and lay flat. He got his flashlight from the plastic bag dangling from his back and aimed it into the gloom. A couple portions of the spiral stairwell had collapsed. Better hope the supplies made it down from the blimp intact.

He stood and waved his flashlight downslope, passing his hand in front of the beam to make it wink twice, repeating the signal a few seconds later. Down at the base of the ship, a flashlight blinked three times. Walt tipped back his head. Moonlight sliced through the strings of a parachute descending from the unseen blimp. A box dangled beneath the dark fabric of the chute, swinging through a tight circle.

He tracked it all the way down to the deck of the ship. It landed with a clunk a couple hundred yards away; men and women ran to it, prying it open and passing around assault rifles, pistols, ammunition, dry shoes, and maps.

That was where the blimp came in. Most balloons were only good for carrying three or four people. Between the pilot and two men strong enough to chuck boxes of supplies over the side, that only left room for a couple hundred pounds of cargo. Armaments added weight fast. Especially bullets.

The blimp, on the other hand, was good for a dozen passengers—or three soldiers and a literal ton of gear. And instead of battling the winds to achieve position like a balloon—let alone getting four or five of them to occupy the same general airspace at once—it could be counted on to maneuver overhead at the same time the troops swam aboard.

One by one, the boxes floated down from the sky. No missiles lanced up to meet them. Were the targets too small to trigger the defenses? Was the missile system only activated by water-borne threats? What the hell kind of sense did that make on a spaceship? Had he knocked out its radar-equivalent in the crash, and all it had left to track threats with was sonar? Walt hadn't been certain that any of the boxes would land safely. Getting all of them would be a coup. Soldiers swarmed to each package, dim shapes dwarfed by the vast landscape of the ship.

After the last package thumped to the deck, Karslaw's chute deployed against the stars.

A few scouts joined Walt at the spiral staircase. The rest waited to move until Karslaw landed. Bare legs marched over the metal ground. Rifles and machine guns flashed in the moonlight. Walt didn't know what waited for them below. Even before he'd dumped the ship into the sea like an old tire, the thing had been run by a skeleton crew. And the crash had been catastrophic. The kind of thing that converted healthy bones into dog treats. Most of the crew must have died on impact.

But the damn things looked like bugs. Crabs or crickets or ants, with a lot of squiddish space-horror thrown in for good measure. If they bred like bugs, there was no telling how many of their children lurked in the city-sized interior.

Karslaw strode up and clasped his hand. "This has all gone too well. Could we be walking into a trap?"

Walt shrugged. "Or a ghost town."

"The question is not whether the enemy is here. The question is how many."

He turned to face the gathering of troops. Faces of both sexes and all races went sober.

"I don't know what awaits us in the darkness." Karslaw kept his voice low, but his baritone words resonated through the damp, warm air. "Perhaps I'm leading you into folly. It could be that we'll never see the sun again. This ship could become our tomb.

"But if so, we will rest in it together. Just as we fought in it together. Just as we built our community together. We can no longer allow this threat to mount on our doorstep. If we turn our backs to it, we invite the knife. And so we take the plunge. We step through the doorway into darkness. And when we reemerge, it will be to a new world. A world that is finally ours. A world we can leave to our children knowing they will grow up as we did: safe. Secure. Able to pass it to children of their own."

He smiled, teeth standing out in the night. "You are the bravest men and women I've ever know. I would ask you to do me proud, but you already have a hundred times over."

He raised his fist in salute and took the first step down the stairs.

Along with guns and ammo, the blimp-dropped boxes had been packed with basic exploratory gear. A team of knot-versed sailors rigged a rope ladder across the gaps in the staircase. Troops climbed down to the catwalk overlooking the blackness of the former landing bay. Walt wasn't certain it was the same one he and Otto had used to penetrate the ship five years ago, but if not, it was virtually identical. After the stairs, soldiers snuck along a platform into a short tunnel overlooking a chasm of space where smaller spacecraft had once entered and left. It was too dark to see the bottom clearly, but he didn't think there was any water down there.

Walt followed the foremost scouts across the catwalk. He knew there was no sense in trying too hard to be quiet—he was 99% certain the aliens had no sense of hearing—but he found himself creeping around like a cat burglar anyway. A set of circular doors rested in the wall, seamed down the middle. A couple of troopers went for the handles while others knelt and readied their guns.

The doors opened to blackness. Walt shined his flashlight into the tunnel, illuminating high ceilings and rounded walls. Unmarked doors sat in the walls at regular intervals. Karslaw assigned a couple pairs of soldiers to check each door while the main body of troops moved on, scouts jogging ahead.

The tunnel ran on and on, curving gently, pitched downward by the slant of the ship in the ocean outside. A thin layer of dust lay undisturbed on the ground. On his first and only other visit to the ship, motion-sensing lights had flicked on as he passed, illuminating his way down the halls. Dozens of different hums and rumbles had fought for the full spectrum of his hearing. This time, all he could hear was his own breath, the scrape of his feet on the rubbery floor. The only lights were the ones they carried.

The tunnel hit a six-pointed intersection. Walt played his flashlight over the inscrutable glyphs written around its steeply pitched ceiling.

"I don't have the first clue where we went from here," he murmured to Karslaw.

"Not to worry," the big man said. "This is why the good lord invented scouts."

He gathered ten men and women and sent them down the branches of the hall, redirecting the bulk of his forces to retreat a short ways down the tunnel. His soldiers knelt, guns ready, waiting for the scouts to return. Walt crouched beside a doorway in the intersection and watched the hall for lights.

The scouts filtered back. Most hadn't seen a thing, but one reported finding a ramp leading deeper into the ship. It showed tracks in the dust.

Karslaw motioned the troops onward, leaving two behind as a rearguard. The new tunnel led past several open doors to small, sparse rooms of no obvious function, then to a great hall of some kind. Debris lay piled against one wall, thrown there by the crash, but most of the stools and spindly chairs were stuck to the ground and remained in place.

At the end of the tunnel, a wide blue ramp spiraled down into the darkness. Walt thought he recognized the material—he'd seen it inside the alien settlements established during the invasion—but previously, the substance had been slightly yielding and tacky, assisting the climb up and down. This ramp had gone as hard and brittle as old coral.

But the air rising from it smelled briny. A little rotten. Like something the flies would flock to on the tideline. Lines as thick as Walt's wrist traced the dust leading to the ramp.

Karslaw led his people down the long spiral. Another tunnel stretched into the darkness, but the ceiling here was thirty feet high. A scout waited in the gloom.

Karslaw spoke with her, then beckoned Walt over. "Do you know where we are?"

"I don't think I saw this level," Walt said. "If I did, I was running away from it at top speed."

"There is a chamber ahead. A very large one." He glanced at the scout. "Amanda believes it is inhabited."

"That's what we're here for, isn't it?"

Karslaw smiled grimly. He gathered the leaders of his very basic platoon system and sketched out quick orders. The hallway was wide enough for five men to walk abreast. Those at the front clicked off their lights. They advanced down the tunnel.

After fifty yards, a wide, semi-circular door opened in the wall. The troops crept in two by two, dispersing to either side of the door. Walt slunk through. Dim light filtered from irregular patches on the far walls and high ceiling. The space was large enough to have been a hangar or repair bay; mangled machinery was heaped against one wall.

The middle of the room was filled with houses. Round, orange mounds twelve feet high and twice as wide. Some of the doors appeared to be nothing more than sheets or curtains. A few dozen of them filled the space. The house walls were lumpy. Parts were patchwork, plastic and metal plates scavenged from the ruined machinery. Huddled within a ship the size of a town, one that had crossed light-years of space and smashed humanity to splinters, this makeshift village was so pathetic and low-rent it made Walt's heart feel small.

The curtains parted in one of the doorways. A bulbous oval head poked into the dusky room.

A rifle shot echoed through the cavernous room. The head snapped behind the curtain. A body thumped. Tentacles writhed.

"Take no prisoners!" Karslaw bellowed. "Fight for the lives of your families on the island!"

Ten squads rushed ten separate houses. Walt charged alongside his assigned squad. Machine guns rattled through the hangar. A man kicked open the door of the house and two soldiers rushed in before Walt. Their shots knocked two aliens to the ground. Walt lasered a third, severing claws, its yellow, gloppy blood spattering the bare floor. A fourth creature rose from a pocket set into the wall and the men behind Walt riddled it with bullets. It was half the size of the others.

Outside, aliens streamed from the orange mounds, firing blue beams. A man screamed. Others fired back, knocking the monsters from their spidery legs. They fell with unnerving silence. Walt followed his squad to another home. A laser licked from the doorway, spinning a woman to the floor. She grunted and curled into a ball. The air stank of old seawater and burnt meat.

Another woman knelt and fired a long burst into the doorway. Walt moved beside the entry. As soon as she ceased shooting, he swung around the frame, joined by another soldier. Blue light crackled past his shoulder. He dropped prone and returned fire, punching a steaming hole in the alien's head. His partner opened fire, filling the room with noise and smoke and blood.

It was over within another minute. Most of the enemy had been shot unarmed, or caught in the open as they attempted to flee. The few who tried to hole up were shot in their dens. In the shocking quiet that followed, Walt wandered the grounds, turning his flashlight on the bodies. He counted up to fifty, then ballparked the rest. Two hundred, tops, perhaps a tenth of them obviously smaller than the others. He had expected...more. A thrumming hive. Eggs sitting in countless rows, hatching even as he watched.

Instead, it had been like stumbling into a third world village. And then slaughtering it.

Karslaw's side had suffered just four deaths. He'd brought a former nurse and a veterinarian and the pair treated the handful of wounded with limited supplies. Men walked among the dead aliens, stooping to pick up weapons and gather them into backpacks.

Walt headed over to Karslaw, who knelt beside the woman who'd been shot in front of Walt, hand on her shoulder. Her eyes were tightly shut and sweat glistened from her pale face. She'd been hit in the stomach and it smelled like burning garbage.

Karslaw murmured to the woman the whole time the vet and nurse bandaged her up. After, he straightened and waved Walt away with him.

"That went about as well as we could've hoped," Walt said.

"They were unprepared," Karslaw said. "No one has made it inside this place since it went down. It's tough to keep your people vigilant when the threats are so distant."

"Yeah, but look at this place. It's a shit heap. They're attacking Avalon with submarines and their home base is a shantytown?"

"You act like it's already over. How much of this ship have we yet to explore?"

Something was wrong. It didn't add up. Karslaw left two squads among the houses to protect the wounded, provide a base of operations, and take out any aliens who wandered in from elsewhere in the ship. The rest of the troops advanced methodically through the ship, scouts ranging ahead and coming back to report what little they'd seen. They surprised and massacred another twenty aliens, finding most of the creatures scuttling around alone or in pairs. Once, they walked into an ambush—a hastily-arranged mine, followed by a barrage of laser fire. Karslaw lost four men in moments. But there were just two of the things holding them off behind the scorched doorway. They fell quickly.

Down in the darkness, lit only by flashlights and the luminescent mold that seemed to grow wherever the aliens had set up settlements, time lost its meaning. They searched the ship for hours on end. Karslaw rotated out the squads at the base, allowing two to sleep while a third kept watch and the rest continued working their way across the ship.

They encountered little but wreckage and death. Smashed equipment. Desiccated bodies broken against the walls. They found three functional banks of computers and destroyed them all.

Karslaw's scouts did a banner job locating the creatures' tracks and hunting them down, but the warlord knew it was impossible to check the whole ship. The lower sections were slanted below the waterline.

Some were flooded. It was possible for some of the aliens to have taken refuge there, alerted by the gunfire. And the vessel was just too enormous. Scouring all of its inner holds would take weeks. They'd only brought enough food and water in the blimp-boxes to last them a few days.

But when at last they emerged into the brilliant sunlight of a gorgeous Southern California late afternoon, they had not seen a single alien without cutting it down where it stood.

25

It took nearly a day for Martin to wake for more than a few minutes at a time. A bandage covered his broken nose. Both eye sockets were swollen and bruised. The doctor Jill had sent them from the Dunemarket thought he had a concussion and a couple cracked ribs. When the woman asked Mauser about the state of their medical supplies, he danced around the issue for a minute, then allowed that he might have some painkillers stashed away after all.

"I don't think he suffered anything internal," she said. "But if you see any neurological symptoms—dizziness, confusion, memory loss, ataxia or impaired motor function—come see me at once."

"That's it?" Raina said.

"There's no pill to cure a beating." The doctor stood up from the bed and picked up her bag. "Make sure he gets plenty of rest. Try to limit his exposure to angry gangsters. He'll be fine."

Raina watched him for a while, then went to meet up with Carl. Martin was still asleep when she returned that night. In the morning, she ate breakfast in his room. With a spoonful of oatmeal halfway to her mouth, he sat up and groaned.

"Am I going to be okay?"

She swallowed. "What were you thinking?"

"Huh?"

"We said not to go to the Osseys. We told you it was too dangerous."

He frowned, tried to pull the blankets down from his chest, and gasped in pain. "Well, we needed to find out what was going on, didn't we?"

"Did you?"

"I tried."

"And almost got killed," Raina said. "One of the couriers found you in a ditch."

He shrugged, ignoring the pain. "So what? If you'd thought it was worth doing, you would have done it no matter what I said."

"But you're not me."

Martin clenched his jaw. "I'm going back to sleep."

"The doctor said you'll be fine," she said.

He rolled over. "I'm tired, Raina."

She stared at his back for a moment, then got up and left. She walked out the door and bumped right into Mauser's chest.

"Such bedside manner," he said. "It's no wonder he's devoted to you."

She walked out of earshot before replying. "Well, he could have been killed."

"Because you treat him like a child. He was trying to prove he's not."

"You thought it was a bad idea, too!"

"Yeah, but I wasn't all grumpy about it." Mauser glanced across the house. "Anyway, I'm not the one he's got a crush on. I don't have to be responsible for his feelings."

She went to the door. "It's not my fault how he feels."

"I suppose that's true. But a good person would act like it was anyway."

Annoyance spiked through her chest. She walked out. Their pantry was getting bare again and she had worn out her best socks. She headed down to the ruins to cast around and clear her head before it was time to see Carl.

Martin recovered well. Raina kept an eye on him for any signs of brain injuries, but he was walking fine, if stiffly, by that night. He didn't talk to her much, but a couple days later, she offered to help re-tape his ribs. It had been months since they'd swam together and his chest didn't look quite as sunken as it had before their last few months of racing around the L.A. Basin.

Everything stayed quiet. After the market closed one night, Jill held a meeting in the shelter of the hills. Raina wasn't invited. Mauser was, but wouldn't go into detail.

"It would only bore you," he claimed. "It was primarily a discussion of the logistics of maintaining communications across a diverse group spread across the greater city. At one point, they actually spent ten minutes discussion the feasibility of capturing and training a team of passenger pigeons."

"That sounds awesome," Martin said.

"What's a passenger pigeon?" Raina said.

"See?" Mauser said.

Jill held another meeting a couple days later, but beyond that, and the reports from a few travelers that the Osseys had returned to trolling the bridges of Long Beach, the entire area seemed to be holding its breath. Waiting to see what the Catalinans would do next. That was fine with Raina. Quiet time meant more time she could spend at Carl's. Preparing for war—whether that war came as a troop in Jill's army, or alone in the fields of Catalina hunting Karslaw by herself.

The day came and went for the Catalinans to come collect their taxes. The ship and its crew never showed up.

The following night, Mauser called a meeting of his own. A household meeting, just the three of them. They sat in the warm night on the back porch, three candles wavering on the glass end table.

"I expect you're wondering why I gathered you all tonight," Mauser said.

"Yes," Raina said.

He gave her a pained look. "Nevermind. Look, something strange is going on. The Catalinans had a sweet system set up and they're letting it decay. It should take a second apocalypse to prevent them from coming to collect their being-alive tax from us. Now, maybe something happened with their boat, but it's not like they just have one. So what's the hold up? Did the alien sub from Malibu get them? Did they lose more people to the Osseys than we realize? Are they vulnerable?"

"Maybe we should just go ask them," Martin said sourly.

"That's exactly what I'm thinking. Except I intend to ask the questions with our eyes. And without alerting them to the fact we're asking questions in the first place."

"You want to go spy," Raina said.

"If they're planning an attack, it would be nice to know about it before they roll in the cannons and cavalry." Mauser yawned and sipped the tea he'd brewed from some of the mint and herbs they'd planted in their paltry garden. Abruptly, Raina remembered it had once been among her chief worries to find a way to grow tea so her parents would never run out. It had been less than a year since those days, but it felt like a lifetime.

"And if they've sailed away for greener pastures," Mauser continued, "it would be awful nice to know that, too. Bet they left all kinds of interesting things behind."

Martin rolled his eyes. "No wonder you want to go there so bad."

"I make it a habit to align my personal interests with my professional ones. That's how I accomplish so many big important things, Martin."

"When?" Raina said. "How long will it take?"

"If we leave tomorrow, we can be back by the following morning," Mauser said. "I don't think it's a great idea to stay on the island past daybreak. Can you take that much time off your busy air-fighting schedule?"

"Can we look for my mom?"

"We can sure keep our eyes open." He turned to Martin and raised his brows. "You feel like holding down the fort while we're gone, chief?"

"No," Martin said. "I'm coming with you."

"Can you even lift your arm without pain?"

"Why? Were you planning to surrender?"

Mauser snorted. Raina cut him off. "If he wants to come, then he can come."

"This is my plan," Mauser said.

"We just took a vote. Two to one. You lose. We'll take my boat."

"You have a boat?"

"And I know how to use it."

Mauser did some grumbling, but the issue was settled. The next day, Raina went to Carl to let him know she might be gone a couple days.

"Where to this time?" he said. She didn't want to lie to him. Instead, she said nothing. He glanced out the southern window, as if he already knew, and folded his arms. "Wherever it is, you're going there for the same reasons you're coming here."

"I'm not going to get in any trouble."

"Really? Then why are you working so hard to learn to fight trouble when you do run into it?" He smiled at her and gestured at her belt. "Let me see your knife."

Her heart skipped. She handed it to him, sheath and all. "Are you finally going to teach me it?"

"Not really." He pulled the knife from the lacquered wood and ran his thumb along the part of the blade that looked like magic: the oily, swirling pattern that ran parallel to the cutting edge. "My father would shit himself if he heard me say this, but Japanese blades are the best. Do you know why?"

Raina shook her head. "They're the oldest?"

"The perfect blade is a contradiction. Hard steel makes the best cuts. It's sharpest. But its hardness makes it brittle. Prone to breaking. So the toughest, most durable swords are made of springy steel. Flexible enough to survive the shock of battle. Yet a springy sword wears down faster, dulling its edge." He thrust the knife at her face. She danced back. He flipped the blade so she could see the swirling pattern. "The Japanese found a way to meld hard steel to spring steel. To make the sharpest blade also the toughest."

He sheathed it with a click. "You're a very hard girl, Raina. Don't think that makes you the strongest."

She took back her knife. "Are we going to fight more or what?"

Carl laughed. "Of course. And if you make it back from wherever you're going, I'll show you how to use a knife."

She spent the rest of the day readying her boat. They shoved off when the sun was a couple hours from the horizon, tacking east past Long Beach, then swinging back to the southwest at dark. The island was a black, steady mass. When they drew close enough, she could see lanterns flickering on the eastern shore. She swung back to the east to keep them out of sight of the settlement, then turned sharply toward the island, anchoring just off the shore of a rocky beach.

They jumped in the cool water and swam to land. Martin had found a waterproof bag for their stuff and they toweled off and dressed in dark clothes and shoes. Mauser checked and pocketed his pistol. Raina had carried her tanto and a bamboo stick while she swam. Martin removed several layers of baggies from a palm-sized black object. He glanced up the silent shore and pressed a button. Its screen lit up blue.

"A camera?" Mauser said. "Now there's a smart idea. Don't suppose you have a printer."

"At my old house," Martin said. "But I don't want to go there unless we have to. I haven't been back to see my mom in like three weeks."

Raina laughed. Mauser scanned inland with his binoculars, then led the trio up the shore toward the town they'd seen from sea. The scent of kelp washed in from the rocks. Around a bend, a toppled crane rusted in the grass. Two sheds sat beside a dirt road, paint peeling from their sides. Raina liked the thought that she was here in the darkness and the Catalinans didn't know it.

They walked for a mile until the island curved enough to see the lanterns again. Mauser knelt and watched the quiet town through his binoculars. A lone dog barked from the hills above the small bay.

"They have cute little houses," Mauser murmured. "I expected them to live in lairs of some kind."

Martin took a few pictures, holding his hand over the camera's screen to block out the light. They moved to a blank hill and gazed down at the bowl-shaped valley. A few hundred houses nestled in the winding streets. Smoke curled from three different chimneys.

"Well, they're still here," Mauser said. "No sign of battleships or saddled-up dragons, though."

"Maybe this isn't their only town," Raina said.

"I've only seen about sixty, eighty different faces come around to collect tribute. I'd be surprised if there were more than a few hundred people here. Could all fit in this town easy."

Martin clicked away with his camera. Raina watched a figure strolling alone by the beach. She pushed a clump of damp grass from her sightline. "Maybe we should talk to someone."

Mauser chuckled. "'Hello, old sport! Planning to launch any major invasions soon? Who am I? I'm just an innocent stranger who happens to think black is slimming.' Something like that?"

"We already learned they're still here. We won't learn anything else by sitting on a hill."

"Oh, you'd be surprised what turns up when you have the patience to let the wicked do their thing."

"It's really quiet," Martin said. "I don't even see their ship at the dock."

Mauser swung around his binoculars. "You're right. Maybe there is another settlement. Or maybe they're off hunting for the fountain of youth. God, why can't the enemy just tell us what they're up to?"

The surf rolled across the beach. Crickets chirped from the grassy hills. A whoop of laughter rose from a well-lit store down on the waterfront. Raina's knees grew stiff and she shifted position. As she did so, she caught a glimpse of white not far off to sea. A sail. She took Mauser's binoculars. It wasn't the Catalinans' flagship they used to collect tribute, but the boat came in and tied up at the dock anyway. A man hopped off the ship and ran through town, following the road past the last of the houses and into the hills.

"Where the hell is he off to?" Mauser said.

Men lowered a ramp from the ship and hauled heavy boxes down to the base of the dock. They finished unloading a quarter hour later. One man lit a cigarette. He finished it and stamped it out just as the clap of hooves pealed from the hills. The team drew a large wagon down to the docks. The men loaded it up with cargo.

Mauser gritted his teeth. "We have to follow it, don't we?"

"I will," Raina said. "Go back to the boat if you want."

He shook his head. They crawled back up the hill, standing once its crown blocked them from view of the town, then circled around to where the road fed into the hills, crossing brushy little canyons and a golf course where the grass had gone a bit yellow but was still being mowed.

The road unspooled toward the interior. Mauser brought them into the brush and got out his binoculars. After a few minutes, hooves click-clocked up the way, wagon wheels rumbling behind them. A lantern swayed from a hook mounted above the driver. The team walked by and headed into the rolling hills. Once it was a few hundred yards ahead, Raina and the others got up and followed, keeping off the road.

The path led through a mile of gentle hills before feeding into a wide valley. At the other end, candles shined from the windows of a big and solid building. They crossed the valley, letting the horse team get further ahead to decrease the chance of being spotted.

"That," Mauser said, "is a fortress. Just like the man said."

The wagon stopped in front of a massive wooden door. The driver hollered up to the towers flanking the gate. Raina got down in the brush. The door lowered, spanning a dark pit ten feet wide. The team crossed into the fortress and the door raised back into place with a series of metal clinks.

"More like a castle," Martin said. "That is so cool."

Raina continued across the open field. A tall, blocky building stood behind the walls. Most of the windows were dark, but candles flickered within a few. She stopped and knelt down and took Mauser's binoculars again. She slowly scanned the outer walls, spotting a single face inside the tower above the gate. She moved her gaze to the inner building. In one room, a shirtless man stared out at the moonlight, touching the hair on his belly. Another room appeared to be empty despite the light. Beyond another window at the top floor of the palace, a woman moved back and forth, dark hair tied in a short ponytail. She came to the window, gazed into the darkness, and closed the curtains.

Raina lowered her binoculars. "My mother's in the castle."

26

They returned to the island as heroes.

The people of Avalon streamed from their houses, rushing down the sloped streets to gather at the dock outside the Scaveteria. Their faces were anxious slates ready to be filled in with the news. Sailors guided the ships in to port; others tied down and roped them to the cleats.

Karslaw strode to the railing and gazed down. "We met the enemy, and the enemy is no more."

The crowd roared. Men and women kissed. A teen boy lit sparklers and handed them to the kids, who ran down the beach trailing light and smoke. The soldiers piled off the boat, mobbed and hugged by family and friends. Other citizens watched in rigid silence, scanning the face of each emerging troop.

Seven men and two women hadn't made it back. Karslaw hugged the families, cupping their cheeks as he murmured condolences. He looked very gubernatorial. Walt didn't much care. The only thing on his mind was finding Lorna.

She wasn't among the crowds. She was in her house, sitting in the living room reading a book. Her other hand held a mug of coffee.

"Well, I killed them all," he said. "Again."

She marked her place with a scrap of paper and set down the book. "How many made it back?"

"Almost everyone. It was pretty weird. I honestly thought there was a pretty good chance we'd all die down there, but there were hardly any of the things left. Not many young ones, either. Either they don't breed any faster than we do, or they don't have the food or resources to crank out a hive. Guess they're no better off than us. Not enough bodies to get things done."

Lorna gazed at the wall. "I wish I could have gone."

"Speaking of, how are things?" He gestured toward her middle. "With stuff?"

"With the piece of you and me growing in my belly?" She touched her stomach. "Fine."

"Well. That's good."

"Is it?"

"That depends on us, doesn't it?" he said.

She met his eyes. "Still thinking of leaving?"

"Do you want me to?"

"Stay," she said. "A few more days. I'll have your answer."

He left, less annoyed at her than at the fact he had emotions in the first place. It was senseless. She'd been acting like a jerk to him for weeks, yet he still wanted nothing more than to forgive her right now and go be happy together forever. He'd walked into the jungle with her feeling pretty good. A little wanderlusty, maybe, but content enough. They'd tromped around the wilderness together and he'd somehow walked out of it carrying a messy bundle of affection, lust, tenderness, and care for her well-being. It was harder to get rid of than any parasite. If he had a parasite, he'd want to get rid of it. This, though, he wanted to hang onto. He just didn't know how.

They were partying downtown. He joined them. After his first jar of moonshine and orange juice, he realized it might not be a great idea to mingle with people who'd wanted to punch his lights out just a couple weeks earlier, but it turned out any resentment for him had died along with the aliens in the ship. He was far from the only hero in town—in fact, he was one of about ninety—but as soon as the others recognized him, he didn't have to get up for a new drink for the rest of the night.

Graciously, Karslaw didn't send a messenger to knock on his door until the following afternoon. Walt chugged water and brushed out the taste of last night's booze, then walked across the hills and valley to the castle.

"My general," Karslaw said in the bare-beamed room that Walt had come to think of as the man's throne room. "You should be the one in this chair."

"Hardly," Walt said. "Those things put up about as much fight as a crash test dummy."

Karslaw shrugged his broad shoulders. "There were fewer than I expected. But that doesn't undo the damage they'd dealt to us or the certainty that, given time to breed undisturbed, they would have destroyed us." He smiled ruefully, shaking his bearded head. "How many did we cleanse from that place? Three hundred? Imagine what would have happened if they'd all attacked Avalon at once. It would have been the death of every man, woman, and child on the island."

"Probably. I don't know, man. Imagine it from their perspective—they arrive as conquerors, come this close to annihilating humanity, then when they're on the brink of victory, some fool dunks them like a donut. Only a couple hundred of them survive the crash, which breaks all their shit, leaving them as primitive as we are. Cut off from the battle groups they had scattered around the globe. I don't know what kind of emotions those things have, but down there in the dark, they must have felt scared and lonely and isolated."

"You sound like you feel sorry for them!"

"I doubt they were much of a threat, that's all. Do you really think they were holding meetings to execute their master plan, then giving each other tentacle-fives and slouching back to their hovels to eat some mold? I bet they just wanted to be left alone." Walt sat on the arm of a lush black couch and gazed at the door set into the wall behind Karslaw. It was painted the same gray as the stonework. He hated when homes were painted that boring, safe beige. If he were in Karslaw's shoes, he'd dictate that all doors be henceforth painted red. "What did you want to see me about, anyway? Or was it just to remind each other how awesome we are?"

Karslaw barked with laughter. "I brought you here to get us in that ship. But the aliens weren't the only threat to my people. I have no doubt the gangs have returned to Long Beach in our absence."

"Why bother with the mainland at all? You realize you've got an island to yourself, right? That's the dream of everyone who's ever wanted to be rich."

"There are things we can't get on this island. The treasures of humanity shouldn't be kept away from us by violent thugs. The whole peninsula could be ours. We could bring peace—and with peace comes prosperity."

Walt waved in a direction that may or may not have been toward Los Angeles. "Have at it."

Karslaw's smile faded from his eyes. "I had hoped you would come to believe in this place like I do. That you would wish to continue to fight for it."

"It's one thing to go after a bunch of fucking monsters from space who tried to extinct us. But a squabble with another group of people? One that's shown no interest in fighting you unless you're stomping around Long Beach? Sounds kind of political."

"It's exactly this cold-eyed analysis that would make you such a fine advisor."

"Can I just be a well-wisher? If Lorna wants me, I'll probably stick around. But I don't want to be part of any more wars."

Karslaw nodded, smiling sadly. "Very well. For all you've done, I thank you."

Walt waved and went home. To keep his mind off Lorna, he thought about what else he might do now that the business with the aliens was done. He'd liked the jungle very well—it was pretty, always warm, had lots of interesting old ruins, and once you knew which things could poison you, it was easy enough to keep yourself fed—but he thought he was done with it for a while. After spending time on Catalina, he liked the idea of an island—you could get to know the entire place, and by the very nature of their islandness, there would be an ocean around, which was always good for food—but he didn't have the skills to sail himself to one. Anyway, all the good ones were probably already taken.

He could rule out any place with a real winter, he knew that much. The jungle had spoiled him. Snow and frost and mittens and galoshes were unnecessary hardships. Humans hadn't evolved from snow-baboons. They were warm-weather animals. Know what proved it? Clothes. So he wanted to live somewhere they were optional.

He went to a sandy beach on the north shore to think all this through. The coast of Los Angeles hung in the haze of the sea. There was a thought. Set up shop in those pretty green hills north of the city. Back in days of yore, they must have been within an hour's drive of the peninsula, making it much too likely he'd have awkward run-ins with Lorna and Karslaw. But things had changed. In these exciting new slowed-down times, the hills up north had to be a two-day walk from the ones on the southern flank of the bay. He could live his whole life up there and never see the two of them again.

Assuming Lorna kicked him out, that was his new plan. Six or twelve months from now, when she'd had time and space, he could send her a letter and see if she'd sorted herself out. And if he didn't like the hills, he could always go somewhere else. That continued to be one of the unseen joys of the apocalypse: these days, no life was permanent if you didn't want it to be.

On a personal level, coming back to L.A. had probably been a mistake. He'd walked all that way, put his life on the line a half dozen times, spent weeks assembling their ridiculous attack, and delved into a ship of horrors to do battle, and all he had to show for it was a broken heart and a baby. He still didn't know what to think of that last part, but it certainly hadn't been part of the plan.

On a less selfish level, he'd been a key part of eliminating or at least vastly reducing the local alien population. That was always cool. He supposed that, should Lorna give him the boot, he'd at least leave his unborn son or daughter with the legacy of an alien-free home.

He just wished he could make things work with Lorna. There had been a time when things were good, but he'd let that slip away. If he'd said or done one little thing different it might never have reached this point. Maybe he should have spent more time talking with her about what happened on the beach, but after he'd fallen into the cenote, she'd been doing so well. He'd figured that after she'd spent a while making decisions and laughing at her mistakes and seeing that life went on, she'd be perfectly all right.

Even now, he knew there must be something he could say to get her to stay with him, but there was something unreachable about her. Something broken. Words couldn't get to that place. Maybe nothing could.

It was marvelous, in its way, that it was easier to fight with the aliens than to try to understand another human.

He killed several days exploring the island, poking around the coves and overturning rocks to see what turned up. It gave him a good view of the ship, too. In the summer haze, it looked as dead as ever.

He returned to Avalon one afternoon to discover armed troops jumping in and out of several boats tied off at the piers. Karslaw stood at the foot of the partially reconstructed main dock, regarding his people with folded arms.

"What's this?" Walt said. "Trying to tire them out before naptime?"

"We sail to the mainland tomorrow," Karslaw said. "I am hoping a clockwork display of discipline will help convince the O.C.'s to accept my terms."

"A treaty? Think they'll go for it?"

"Then and there? Perhaps not. They are prideful. But they are cunning enough to conclude that I mean what I say."

"Well, good luck."

"I would like for you to come with me." He raised a furry brow. "Lorna has already agreed to join me."

Walt laughed. "Then I'll be staying here. I'm trying to give her some space. Don't know what else I can do."

"If that's how you feel. But she told me she'd like to see you there."

"Why?"

The big man shrugged. "She's a good woman, but she doesn't tell me anything more than she tells you."

He said yes. Of course he said yes. They launched the next morning with six boats, more than a hundred armed men between them. A warm wind traveled with them across the deep blue waters. The O.C.'s were already waiting for them at Long Beach, standing in a loose cluster a hundred feet up the road from the docks. Walt counted about seventy of them, all armed.

Karslaw's people ticked out from the ships and arranged themselves in tidy rows along the marina, spaced sparsely enough to make anyone with a machine gun work hard to hit more than a couple of them at once. Karslaw stood on a wooden box at the front of his people. Someone among the O.C.'s started to speak, but Karslaw cut him off.

"You will withdraw from Long Beach," he declared. "You will return to Orange County. That is your home. This land is mine."

Among the gaggle of O.C.'s, a man no younger than Walt jutted his jaw, wandering a couple steps closer to the islanders. "Says who? We were here first."

"Even if that were true, you have forfeited your claim. You are thugs. You prey on travelers seeking safety. You do not deserve this place or its people."

Walt chuckled to himself as Karslaw amped up the rhetoric like an Athenian despot. He was going to miss the big guy.

The O.C. leader laughed. "Considering how you treat the place, you're talking some bold shit, man. You said you had an offer I couldn't refuse."

"I do." Karslaw widened his stance. "You leave Long Beach, and I let you keep your lives."

"I got a counteroffer for you. You go run your little island however you see fit, and I do the same with my city."

"Unacceptable."

"Okay, I'll sweeten the deal: go get fucked." He grinned at the man next to him. Most of his comrades laughed.

Karslaw smiled wearily, stepped down from the box, and drew the edge of his hand across his neck. His troops raised blunt black pistols. Lines of blue heat sizzled into the O.C.'s. Their front lines collapsed, mutilated and burned. Men screamed. A third of the gangsters turned their backs and ran. Others went for their guns.

Walt threw himself flat. A bullet whined past Karslaw's head. His people shouted and charged, cutting their lasers into the enemy, who fell away from severed arms and legs.

"What are you doing?" Walt yelled.

Karslaw looked down at him, puzzled. "Protecting my people."

"By slaughtering these ones?"

A shadow fell over the man's face. "I tried to negotiate, Walt. These people are savages. They struck us first. Murdered three of my men and left them on the beach to be picked at by gulls. Do you suggest I turn the other cheek? Let the bad guys win because I don't have the balls to fight back?"

Behind him, blue light pulsed through the streets. Men in Raiders jerseys screamed, scrambling down the pavement, falling as lasers burned holes through their backs.

Walt stood, stomach churning. "So it's time for another slaughter. Just like the aliens."

"Do you think this is how I want it to happen?" Karslaw said. "If given all possible worlds, do you think this one would be my choice?"

In an intersection, an O.C. tried to vault the hood of a crashed car and sprawled on the pavement. A Catalinan strode up to him. The downed man shielded his face with his hands. Light seared. Fingers scattered across the asphalt.

"This world sure as shit isn't the one I'd choose," Karslaw continued. "That's why I'm reshaping it. You're watching a paradox. This is a necessary step to ensure that nothing like it ever happens here again."

"I've killed people before," Walt said. "Shot them down for no better reason than they were making a bad world worse. But this isn't justice. It's genocide, driven by fear and greed. You're just grabbing hold of everything you can take." His jaw dropped. "We didn't go to the ship to wipe out the aliens. We went there to take their guns."

"We were there for many reasons, all of which converged on the same goal: the security of my brothers and sisters." Karslaw closed his eyes. "I thought you had the vision to see as deeply as myself. But you don't understand that the first gains must always be made at the point of a knife."

"That sounds pretty Hitler-y."

"You're hopeless." Karslaw spread his broad hand. "He's all yours, Lorna."

Someone grabbed Walt from behind. He kicked out, but multiple sets of hands dragged him to the ground. Lorna loomed above him. The pain and rage in her eyes was so bright Walt froze in his captors' arms.

27

"You're sure that's her?" Mauser whispered.

Raina's binoculars shook in her hands. "I know my mother's face."

"We could climb the fence," Martin said.

"Might have to knife a guard or two," Mauser said. "Then again, Raina might see that as a plus."

Raina closed her eyes. "We can't."

"Says who? I don't know if it's a good idea. But it's not impossible."

"Because I have to kill the man who killed my dad first."

"He's probably in there, too. Stab him, grab Mom, skedaddle off and find a boat."

"Their boat's gone," Martin said. "He's always on that thing. We don't even know if this is his house."

"Of course it is," Mauser scoffed. "He's the king. This is a castle."

"Because if I get her out, she won't let me go after Karslaw," Raina said. "She'll take us far away to stop me. And if I die here before I kill Karslaw, my spirit and my father's will always be his slaves."

"What are you talking about? Spirits? You're leaving your mother here because you believe in ghosts?"

Her face burned, but her embarrassment quickly became anger and then resolve. "I'm going to Jill. I'll tell her Karslaw and his troops are away from the island. Catalina is ripe for the smashing."

"But she's right there."

Raina put away the binoculars. "She's safe. Much safer than I was after the plague. I survived. She will, too."

"Whatever," Mauser said. "I just wanted to present you with the option. I'd rather not charge in with only the three of us."

They retreated along the road. Raina forced herself not to look back. A deep part of her wanted to run to the castle, leap over the high wooden wall, and fight her way inside, but one way or another, that would put an end to her quest. Karslaw had taken her father's life. That meant her father belonged to the man. The only way to free his spirit was to take Karslaw's life for herself.

They cut overland to their boat, bypassing the town. There was nothing more to see. This land wasn't a place of goblins and monsters. They were simply men, like everyone else, and most of their warriors were gone. If they could find Karslaw on the mainland, perhaps she could convince Jill to ambush him. Or assassinate him herself. If she brought his head to the woman, Jill would have to attack Catalina. Strike its soldiers before they knew their leader was dead. Force the town and the castle to surrender. If they refused, a slaughter.

The winds weren't cooperating on the way back. She tacked back and forth, making slow headway, wondering if she'd done wrong after all.

She made landfall at her old house shortly after dawn. There was so much to do, but she was tired to the bone, and when Martin suggested they sleep there in the house, she agreed with little fuss.

When they got back to the Dunemarket, Jill was off somewhere in the city. Her heavyset husband expected her back that night. Raina asked around the market for any sightings of Karslaw. Someone thought they'd seen his people at an airfield in Gardena, but the news was days old. Raina visited the city anyway, but saw nothing.

Jill wandered in at twilight. She saw Raina approaching, Martin and Mauser in tow, and sighed. "Whatever kooky scheme you've cooked up this time, I don't want to hear it."

"The Catalinans have pulled their warriors from the island," Raina said.

"Maybe," Mauser revised. "Their yacht's away from home, at least. And the town was quiet enough to suggest some troops went with it."

"We can attack the island while they're gone," Raina said. "Or find them here and ambush them."

Jill shook her head. "You won't leave me in peace until we hash this out, will you?"

"We can put an end to everything. Right now."

The woman motioned at the merchants trying to wheedle last sales from the handful of people left in the market. "We can't discuss this here."

She turned and hiked up the hills bordering the Dunemarket, stopping at the top. A warm seaborne breeze tousled the palm trees.

"It doesn't matter if some of them have left the island," she said. "They leave the island all the time. What matters is that we have the strength to guarantee victory."

"It's been months," Raina said. "How much longer do you need?"

"Two months more." Jill pointed downhill. "You notice any new faces down there?"

"Sure," Mauser said. "Place has doubled in size. Dunemarket's booming since the bridge trolls got run out of town."

"The next time the Catalinans come here, we'll offer terms. No more taxes. No more threats and kidnappings. If they're willing to continue policing the roads to keep travelers safe, we'll compensate them fairly for their service, but the extortion and the violence must stop."

Mauser frowned. "People are rarely inclined to accept a worse deal out of the goodness of their hearts. Not unless your offer is accompanied by the waving of clubs."

"Then the next time they come to take their taxes, all those new faces down there will be up here instead. Positioned behind the scopes of rifles."

"And if we kill them?" Raina said. "Then what?"

Jill laughed. "Are you ever not scheming?"

"Possibly when she sleeps," Mauser said.

"If we defeat them, then we take more aggressive terms to the island. Your mom's there, isn't she?"

Heat touched Raina's cheeks. "Yeah."

Jill nodded glumly. "She's not the only one. If it comes to a fight, we'll take all the prisoners we can. Trade ours for theirs. And if we crush them, well, the people left on Catalina won't have much leverage to argue with us, will they?"

"They missed taxes this month," Martin said. "What if they don't come back?"

Jill raised her eyebrows. "Then we've won, haven't we? All we'd need to do is negotiate the release of anyone they've got captive."

That ended the conversation. The three of them returned to their home. Inside, Mauser lit candles and got a fire going for dinner.

He stood up from the hearth, brushing ash from his shirt. "Still happy you left your mom behind?"

"Why would that make me happy?" Raina said.

Martin gave Mauser a doubting look. "You didn't want to break in, either."

Mauser laughed. "She's not my mother."

Martin rolled his eyes. "You act like you don't care about anything but taking cool stuff. Well, you went with us to the island. You're here with us now. And if the Catalinans don't take Jill's terms, I bet you a thousand dollars that you'll be there to fight next to us, too."

"That's not my fault. You two get into the most interesting trouble."

Raina smiled at Martin. He was normally so quiet. So unwilling to stand up. He was angry now. She liked it.

She slept and dreamed of her mother's face in the window. In the dream, there was another face behind her mom, and it was too dark to see clearly, but Raina knew it was a man. She couldn't tell if it was her father's or Karslaw's. She didn't feel good when she woke up. Was the dream a portent? Of what? She went to the ruins to search for more signs among the ghosts, but they gave her no answers.

As soon as the sun peaked overhead, she headed to Carl's. As she walked up the concrete path to his door, the drapes twitched. The door opened before she knocked.

"You lived," Carl said. "Should I ask where you went?"

"Do you care?"

"Depends. If you went to the moon, or 1996, I might care very much."

She rested her hand on the lacquered handle of her knife. "I went to Catalina."

He narrowed his eyes. "Am I teaching you something that's going to get killed?"

"Do you like what they're doing?"

"Do I like being bullied?"

"Why don't you want to fight? You could kill so many of them. If you wanted, you could kill Karslaw yourself."

Carl laughed, then tipped back his head and watched her. "How long were you in school?"

She tapped her knife. "Three years."

"I went to school for twelve. Then four more years of college. Then twenty years of a full-time job. Paid taxes on every cent I made. Maybe I'm just used to being owned."

"I'm not," she said. "I never will be."

"Part of me wants to admire you."

"What about the other part?"

"It wants to tell you to run far, far away." He smiled his smile. "Want to learn how to use a knife?"

She grinned. He went and got his sticks. For a moment her heart sank, thinking he was toying with her, but the things he showed her with the sticks were new. Savage. Moves meant to stab and to slash. But much of it was the same, too, both in technique—short, hard, quick—and in philosophy—attacking whatever was put in front of you with such a relentless tide of blows that the enemy drowned in your fury. By the time she left, bruises darkened her arms and ribs.

She and the others went their separate ways for a time. While she trained with Carl, Mauser spent most of his nights down at the tavern in the Dunemarket trolling the patrons for news from the road. One man told him he'd seen the Goodyear Blimp soar across the moon, but Mauser admitted his source on that had been very, very drunk.

As for Martin, she didn't know where he was off to, but it was away from the house. He had grease under his nails at all times. He was as quiet as ever, but it was a different kind of silence from his usual timid watchfulness. Moody. Thoughtful. Perhaps even angry. One morning he walked out after breakfast without a word and she thought about following him, but she wanted to put in some more time on the dummy before going to see Carl. Besides, if Martin caught her tracking him, she wouldn't know what to say.

Between training, foraging for food, delivering messages for Jill, and the daily drudgework of keeping herself, her clothes, and the home mended and clean, she didn't have much time to worry about them. Not when she had less than two months until the showdown in the Dunemarket. Two months to hone herself to the point where Karslaw's life would be hers, whether she took it in his sleep or face to face in the street.

As it turned out, she barely got two weeks to prepare.

She was in the Dunemarket bartering salt and a few packets of freeze dried food for a second knife—she had a couple dozen others, but this one had a bone handle she liked very much—when Mauser called out her name. He was running uphill from the tavern waving one hand above his head. She picked up her bag of salt, excused herself from the merchant, and went to meet him.

"I'm in the middle of something," she said.

"So is Long Beach," he said. "Like an invasion."

"The Catalinans?"

"That's what it sounds like, but my sources are the type to be drunk before noon. We'd better see for ourselves."

"Where's Martin?"

Mauser flapped his arms. "Out seducing a calculator, probably. If we don't leave now, it could be over before we get there."

She had her knife with her, along with her basic travel bag, so she was ready to leave on the spot. They ran north past the park and the big empty stores until they reached the highway, then jogged east toward the endless docks of Long Beach. Heat rolled off the blacktop. Sweat stuck Raina's shirt to her sides. Without slowing, she drank lukewarm water from her canteen.

Rusty cranes climbed from the grimy docks of the former cargo platforms. At a break in the warehouses, Mauser stopped and pointed. A half mile away at the marina along the closed-up shops and bars, a small fleet of sailboats sat at rest, sails fluttering in the sun.

"Maybe my source wasn't so wetbrained after all."

"I don't hear any shooting," Raina said.

"Typically a good sign, yet I remain strangely anxious." Mauser glanced at the palm trees on the waterfront. "Wind's blowing east. Could have been a showdown without our hearing it."

"Let's go find out."

They walked toward the docked fleet, eyes sharp for movement among the buildings near the shore. At the next onramp, Mauser led them off the highway to approach from the tangle of shops knotting the waterfront.

Raina stopped cold and grabbed Mauser's arm. He grunted, then froze with her. A few blocks down, bodies littered the intersection, blood soaking through their black and silver uniforms. A few men walked among them, dropping to one knee to go through their pockets, stripping off necklaces and ammo pouches and shoes. Raina knew the victors must be the Catalinans even before the big bearded man strode up and passed among his men, clapping them on the shoulders and offering a wide white grin.

"They wiped out the Osseys," Raina said.

Mauser turned off the main street and holed up in the doorway of a smashed-out jewelry store. "Well, let's not jump to draw conclusions. Maybe Karslaw found them like that."

"They were off preparing. This whole time. If we'd acted, we could have hit them before they were ready."

"Could be. Oh boy, that was a lot of dead people."

"If I were him, I wouldn't stop with the Osseys," Raina said. "Where's he going next?"

"I'll stay here and find out," Mauser said. He ran his hand down his face. "You go back to the Dunemarket and tell Jill to prepare for war."

28

They smacked him around until he quit squirming, then cuffed his hands and feet and carried him like a hog into the cabin of a boat. One of the soldiers chained him to a handhold with a third pair of bracelets, then hugged Lorna, went outside, and closed the door behind him. Lorna gazed down at Walt, untroubled by the gentle sway of the tides.

"What's this about?" Walt said.

She laughed once. "Are you really that stupid?"

"Is it the baby? I wanted to stay here."

She kicked him in the ribs. She bent down, face hovering above his, her eyes on fire with contempt. "Hannigan was my husband."

"What the fuck?"

"You could have stopped them. You knew they were coming. But you let him die on the beach."

"He was your husband?" Walt's hold on the world splintered. "What the hell are you talking about? I told him there were aliens. That we had to run. If he'd listened, he'd be alive and celebrating the massacre of the O.C.'s right now."

"He thought there might be survivors in the wreckage. He was a great man. He would never leave one of his own behind."

"Well, it's not my fault he was born without a functional sense of self-preservation."

She spat in his face. He shrugged up his shoulder to wipe it away and she bared her teeth and punched him in the eye. "It's all your fault! You should have killed the aliens when you had the chance. All of them. Instead, you left them to become someone else's problem, and the only man I ever loved is dead."

Walt laughed, eye clenched shut against the pain. "This is probably the single biggest display of ingratitude in the history of humanity. So what was our relationship about? Your revenge? Get me to fall in love, then break me in half?"

"Karslaw was right to give you to me. You don't have any vision."

"Wait. It was all tied into Karslaw's delusions of empire, wasn't it? You were just making sure I'd stick around. Guaranteeing I'd do anything to help your people take down the aliens and get ahold of their weapons."

"Congratulations. You only got smart when it was far too late."

"Damn, that's some cold shit." He blinked. His eye felt swollen. "Know what, I don't believe it. In the jungle, we had something together."

"A fever," she laughed. "A sickness."

"It was real. It was there. Then something broke."

Lorna looked ready to laugh again, then the left side of her face trembled.

"Me," she said, voice cracking. "Because every time I closed my eyes, I saw his. Open. Staring. I didn't even get to bury him."

"We'd been chased into the jungle by pissed-off aliens."

"Just shut up. You make me so sick I can taste my liver rotting from your poison."

For just a moment, Walt had thought he might be able to talk her off the brink. But he'd been letting himself get lost in hope for too long. He leaned against the side of the cabin and lowered his gaze to the floor.

"Are you even pregnant?" he said.

"Why would you care?"

"It might impact my decision to kill you."

She stood, dislodging the tears from her eyes. "Goodbye, Walt. It will all be over soon."

She kicked him in the balls, then went out and closed the door, leaving him alone. He dangled from his shackles, groaning. If he hadn't been handcuffed at the wrists and ankles, he would have hanged himself out of sheer embarrassment.

He wriggled against the cuffs, but had made zero progress by the time the troops returned, unlatched him from the handrail, and dragged him belowdecks to a small room that smelled like stagnant water. They chained him to another rail—the damn things were everywhere—tromped back upstairs, and clapped shut the door, leaving him in darkness.

A bit later, he swayed. The boat was pushing off. The ensuing trip gave him plenty of time to reflect on the enormity of his mistakes. How every time he'd expressed doubts about their quest, Lorna had thrown herself at him, convincing him there was something to go on for, a future to find together. Her act hadn't been some improvisation she threw together after Hannigan's death, either. From the very start, she and her husband had interacted like nothing more than comrades. If that's what it took to lure Walt to Los Angeles, the pair had been prepared to sacrifice Lorna to Walt's love or lust regardless of what it meant to their marriage. Where had they gotten that from? The Maya? Karslaw's "vision"? The simple deduction that a hermit would be particularly vulnerable to sex and affection?

Well, it had worked.

It wasn't all his fault. When a beautiful person strips you down, screws you, tells you they can't make it out without you, you don't generally suspect them of intending to use you as a human lock-pick to break into an alien vault. A tool to be discarded like any other object that's outlived its task.

But he was to blame, too. Lorna hadn't played her part perfectly. Her act had shown plenty of cracks. He just hadn't had to the courage to test them, to push until the whole thing collapsed or proved it had the strength to hold fast no matter what pressure was placed against it. He'd been too afraid to lose her. He didn't know if it was because he'd gotten lonely sitting around on Chichen Itza by himself, but somewhere between when he'd dropped the mothership into Santa Monica Bay and when Lorna and her team had come down to find him in the Yucatan, he'd lost his nerve.

So he'd let her have her space. Her time. And now his had run out.

"This fucking sucks," he said into the darkness.

Waves beat hollowly against the hull. Wasn't that always the way. You mustered up the strength to get off your ass and do a good deed, and the next thing you knew you were party to the slaughter of dozens of strangers at the hands of a crazed warlord deluded by his own success and lofty words. Karslaw's actions still didn't make a whole lot of sense. Walt had the impression the big man had wavered between wanting Walt to become a part of his people and in handing him over for Lorna's revenge. He supposed the surprise attack against the O.C.'s had been the final test. Walt had proven himself incapable of seeing the big picture, so Karslaw ushered him off to the slaughterhouse and washed his hands.

A hell of a thing to get suckered into. And a hell of a way to go out. He figured that bringing down the mothership made him and Otto the undisputed champions of the entire species. But after this, he probably ranked right up there with its all-time fools, too.

The boat slowed. The waves sloshed harder. Feet trampled around upstairs. Things bumped the side of the ship with hollow clunks. Voices spoke back and forth. The trapdoor opened, bathing Walt in hard yellow light. He shielded his eyes. Lorna's face poked into the doorframe, backed by white clouds and a pretty blue sky.

"Come on," she said. "It's time to hand you over to the aliens."

III:

USURPERS

29

She jogged lightly until she was a few blocks away, then ran as hard as she could, footsteps echoing in the valleys of the ruins. Her knife bounced in her belt. After seeing the scores of bodies sprawled in the blood and wreckage of the streets, her blade felt very small.

The Dunemarket was as quiet as when she'd left it. Raina ran to Jill's camping supply booth. Her assistant said she'd just stepped out. Raina scanned the traders and travelers, then ran up the hills toward Jill's underground home, slipping through brown grass and fallen palm fronds. Off to the right, Jill stepped out from behind the tarp strung up around the latrine, still buckling her jeans.

"The Catalinans came back to Long Beach," Raina said. "They brought a whole fleet. The Osseys are dead."

"All of them?" Jill's eyebrows spread apart. "What are the islanders doing now?"

"Mauser thinks they may come here next."

"But they haven't shown any intent to attack."

"You can't sit here when their whole army is right down the highway!"

Annoyance flashed across Jill's face. "I need you to run for me. Visit all the homes east of Gaffey. Let them know to gear up and meet here at once."

Raina nodded and dashed across the hills to the main road. She stopped by their house first, but Martin was out. She left a note on his pillow and rushed down the bungalows packed into the side streets set off from Gaffey, pulling open waist-high gates and knocking on the doors of pink stucco houses. She only knocked at places she knew had residents; often, she skipped whole blocks at a time. Many didn't answer. Maybe they'd moved away from the threat of the gangs and the pirates. She had only found and alerted some fifteen households by the time the horn blew from the Dunemarket.

She ran back. Her water was out and she detoured to the house to refill her canteen, but Martin still hadn't come back. She jogged on. In the road nestled between the hills, merchants rolled up blankets and slung them over their shoulders. Up on the hills flanking the market, men with rifles spoke in urgent tones, pointing down the street toward Long Beach.

"They're on the march," Mauser said from behind her. "Ships are coming this way, too, although most of the troops are coming overland. They'll be here within half an hour."

Raina glanced at a pair of people fleeing downhill from the market. They should stay and fight, not run away. There were maybe eighty people here in the market—enough to fight back, especially if they took cover in the hills—but half of them were packing up to go. A few reinforcements might arrive from the homes she and the other messengers had notified, but they would still be outnumbered. She wanted to leap on the backs of the people running away and pound their faces until they got mad enough to stand up to Karslaw.

"Have you seen Martin?" she said.

"Not since last night."

"He probably ran away."

Mauser nodded. "He's a bright lad. Maybe we should take a cue from him."

She whirled. "We're not leaving."

"Raina, are you even planning to use a gun?"

"Until I get close enough to use my knife."

"I counted about 150 of them. We'll be lucky to have a third as many assembled before they're here. Do you really think the two of us will make any difference?"

"Yes," she said.

"Then I question your analytical process," he said. "There's no shame in walking away from a fight you can't win. And if there is, then I think we need to seriously evaluate whether shame is worth caring about in the first place."

"I don't need to defeat them all. I just need to kill one man."

She turned and crunched through the grass up the hill. Men rested rifles over rocks, squinting down scopes. She found a space near the end of the loose line of rebels and crouched in the dirt beside the trunk of a tall palm. Mauser borrowed a shovel and piled up a mound of dirt to crouch behind. He didn't look happy.

Ever since the day at the house, she'd tried not to think of her father, because she could only remember his death. But she might not have another chance.

She had hated it like poison at the time, but in hindsight, her first days with her new family had been pretty funny. They'd had to tie her legs together so she wouldn't run away. One of them stayed with her at all times. When the chores were done, they both sat with her while she lay in bed, talking to each other, asking her questions about where she'd come from and what happened to her family. In a week of questions, Raina didn't answer a single one.

They gave up on the questions. Instead, her father read to her, a lantern burning on the end table, a paperback folded in his rope-callused hands. Raina nestled under the covers and stared at the ceiling as he told her stories of hobbits and elves and princesses. She let herself get lost in those worlds, feeling the warmth of foreign suns, gaping at the bloom of magic from staves and gestures. For the first time since the plague, she began to sleep through the night.

They took the fetters from her feet. He read to her every night for a month. She stopped thinking about running away. But one night her new dad read her a story about a boy whose parents were killed by soldiers while he was washing their clothes at the stream. When he came back, he found them dead in their home, and with the roads snowed in, he had to make it through the winter on his own—and there were goblins in the night.

"Why do you keep reading those things?" she said in the lantern-light of her new room with its smell of the sea and the flowers on the hill. "There's no such thing as goblins."

Her new dad looked up, book spread on his lap, sudden pain etched in his eyes. "They're just stories."

"They're stupid. None of those things are real. That's the only reason the people in them are safe at the end."

He put away the book and said goodnight and blew out the lantern. She was ashamed then, and wanted to call out for him to come back, but her shame blanketed her more thickly than her comforter, and she rested in it instead; the next night, when her dad tried to read her a story about a boy and his hatchet, she refused that, too.

He never tried to read to her again.

Down in the street, men shouted and pointed. Raina moved in front of the palm. Mauser quit digging and joined her. Below, more than a hundred men marched up the street toward the Dunemarket. Karslaw walked at their front, sun gleaming from his bald head.

Jill stood in the middle of the abandoned market. Her husband stood by her side, arms crossed over his gut, sweat trickling into his thick mustache.

"Just what do you think you're doing?" Jill said.

Karslaw planted his feet. The wind had died and he spoke loudly enough for his words to reach the top of the hills. "I am here to accept your surrender."

"My surrender? Did I sleep through a war?"

The big man smiled, but it was an angry smile, cold and serene. "I know of your rebellion, Jill Benson."

She hunched her shoulders. Raina was too far away to hear what she said next.

"No more lies," Karslaw boomed. "You are traitors, so you can't be surprised that one of your own has betrayed you to me. You planned, with viperish cunning, to kill me and my people. So here are my terms."

He recited a list of names, starting with Jill's. Nine or ten in all. "These are the ones who must die. In exchange for their lives, I will spare everyone else here. The Dunemarket, San Pedro, and the entire peninsula through Long Beach will henceforth be the territory of the Free State of Catalina."

Up in the hills, Jill's people exchanged glances. Jill stood silent in the middle of the road, considering whether to give up her life to snuff out the war. Raina never got the chance to see how she'd respond. Her husband stepped forward. Maybe to shield her. Maybe to threaten Karslaw. That, too, would never be known.

A lance of blue light appeared from behind Karslaw. Jill's husband dropped straight to the street and didn't move. Jill screamed and ran to him. She went for her pistol. A cat's cradle of blue beams knocked her from her feet.

"That's a fucking laser," Mauser said. "No wonder the O.C.'s were all dead."

Rifles opened up along the ridge, ricocheting from the asphalt, striking the front row of Catalinans. Karslaw roared. His troops split into three columns and charged the hill, firing as they went, dispersing to the palms for cover. Mauser knelt behind his mound of dirt and squeezed off a round. Guns crackled from the hills on the opposite side of the road, cutting into the Catalinans' backs, but only a handful staggered or fell.

Raina kept both eyes on Karslaw. He ran up the hill with his people, firing blue burst from the mouth of a fat black handgun. Smoke curled from scorched leaves. The riflemen aimed and fired, picking off a few of the islanders. Most shots plunked into trees or hit nothing at all. It was all happening with terrible speed and she saw no way to get close to Karslaw without coming in easy range of dozens of his men.

From behind a rock, a merchant opened up with the Dunemarket's lone machine gun, shredding the trunks of the palms. Three islanders tumbled into the grass. A searing bolt of heat answered, silencing the automatic fire.

A hundred feet away, Karslaw guided his men to a thicket of trees. They took cover and slashed their lasers across the riflemen's positions in second-long sweeps. Fires sprung up along the hillside. One of the merchants broke cover and sprinted up the hill. Two more followed. Raina could feel it unraveling before her.

She leveled her pistol at Karslaw and pulled the trigger until there were no bullets left. He hunkered behind a tree, shouted angrily, and gestured in her direction. Mauser's shot slammed into the trunk with a spray of splintered bark.

A platoon of men peeled off from Karslaw's lines and charged Raina's position. Mauser shot one down, then swore and ran up the hill. Raina's heart broke. She turned her back and followed.

Heat seared the side of her calf. She crashed into the dry grass. Mauser grabbed her shoulder and hauled her up. Another laser licked past her head. Her wound was just a surface burn; she was still able to run. It wouldn't help. The enemy was too many and too near.

Thirty feet uphill, a figure appeared at the top of the ridge. The man dropped to one knee and leveled a long, fat tube across his skinny shoulder. Fire and smoke blasted from the end of the tube.

"Holy shit, that's Martin!" Mauser screamed.

A rocket sizzled over Raina's head. It exploded a second later, washing her with heat, thundering her ears, kicking her from her feet so hard her organs ached. For a moment, the lasers ceased. A massive crater scarred the hill, bodies flung down around its edges. Dirt pattered to the ground in a gritty rain. She found her feet and ran uphill, ears ringing.

Martin set down the rocket launcher and went for his bag. He withdrew another long missile. A laser flashed between a point downhill and a point on his chest. He looked up, gasped, and fell down.

"Martin!" Raina screamed.

Rifles roared, increasingly sporadic as the rebels retreated over the hill. Raina ran to him. His eyes were open and his chest was still. Fire smoldered around the hole punched through his shirt. Burnt meat wafted on the breeze, overwhelming the smell of smoke. Mauser grabbed Raina's shoulder. She ran with him.

Everything went away for a while. The pain. The noise. The meaning of what was still happening on the hillside. Her feet thudded the dirt, and her knife bounced on her hip, but she only felt these things later, after she and Mauser were a mile away inside an empty house, watching coils of smoke rise from the ashes of the Dunemarket.

The rebellion was over before it had begun.

30

She helped her men haul Walt up into the daylight. The ship was berthed at a dock leading to nothing. Sunlight shimmered on a vast sea. The mainland was a dark blue lump along the horizon, miles and miles away.

"Where are we?" Walt said. "Wait, aliens? I thought we got them all. I thought that was the whole fucking point!"

"We killed the ones we could," Lorna said. "As for the ones we couldn't—well, this will take care of that."

"You're buying them off with my hide!"

She didn't bother to reply. The soldiers dragged him onto a narrow beach. Scraggly grass sprouted along the sand. Behind, sheer cliffs climbed fifty feet high.

"I was wrong," Walt said. "This is history's greatest act of ingratitude."

Lorna reached down and touched his face. "One more thing for you to be proud of. That's what it's always about with you, isn't it? Being admired for all you've done? Now you get to die alone on this beach."

Thirty yards from shore, the water roiled. A dark shape emerged from the sea. Lorna gestured to her men. They ran back onto the dock, untying the boat from the cleats and scrambling aboard.

"Fuck you!" Walt yelled. Not terribly original, but some things were classics for a reason. He rolled to his knees, hampered by the cuffs. He saw no staircases or gaps in the cliffs. No way he could climb with his hands and feet chained together. He tottered up to the grass, found a fist-sized rock, braced the chains on his ankles over another rock, and bashed them as hard as he could. The metal clinked. A small scrape marred the steel.

He laughed sickly. He struck again. Water sloshed from the surf. An alien strode through the breakers. A thin, pale man walked beside it, his chest tattooed with glyphs like the ones Walt had seen inside the ship. Walt stood, stone in hand, and hopped down to meet them.

"Look out!" he said, brandishing his fist and rattling his cuffs. "I've got a rock!"

The pale man laughed but didn't smile. The creature with him clacked its claws rapidly. The man stopped on the sand, waves hissing over his ankles. "Put that thing down."

"No," Walt said. "I'm going to clobber you with it."

"Huh. So you're Walt."

"Walt who? I was kidnapped. Dumped here by a crazy lady. I don't know what's going on."

"Stop that."

"Or what?" Walt said. "You'll kill me twice?"

"Who says we're here to kill you?"

"The woman who brought me here."

"Can you trust her?"

"About this?" Walt laughed. "Doesn't matter. You know damn well who I am."

"To a point," the man said. He stood as still as the alien beside him, making no gestures to accompany his speech or express his emotions. Walt found it very off-putting.

"Then I'm guessing your silent partner there isn't here for my autograph."

The pale man shook his head. "We're here to judge you."

"Like, in court? Who are you to judge me?"

"A man with a gun and an alien brother."

"I guess that beats a degree," Walt laughed. "Which of my crimes am I on trial for? Grand theft mothership? Or the stuff we did a couple weeks ago? Because the former was like six years ago, and there might be a statute of limitations."

"Why would you assume we care what you did to the crash survivors? Or that you brought down the ship?"

"Is this a trick question?"

The man looked like he might shrug, then didn't. "As their killer, there's something you should understand about them. They were convinced to the marrow of their cause. They figured you all were mistreating the world so badly that all they had to do was show up and it would take to them with open arms. But there was more resistance than they expected. And when two assholes literally dropped in and busted their whole operation into the ocean, well, that knocked rifts in the faithful."

At last, the man smiled wryly. "I mean, come on, man. You think just because they're all from the same species, they magically get along? How's that working for humanity?"

"First off, what?" Walt said. "Second, speaking of getting along, how can you do business with Karslaw? He wants you all dead."

"To get the truth from you."

"You're zipping around the world in an atomic submarine, and you can't just snatch me up? I thought snatching was what aliens do best."

"You were elusive. It was decided this would be a good way to put an end to the wild goose chase." The man wiped his nose. "Anyway, who cares what kind of arrangement we made with the barbarian? You think we got to honor that shit?"

"Well, you got me," Walt said. He made a face at the unrelenting sun. "It's a long story. Where should I start?"

"The beginning."

Walt plunked down in the sand, thought for a minute, then started with the plague. How fast it had been. How it killed everyone he knew, leaving him suicidal—

"Slow down, man," the pale man said. "I got to translate."

Walt squinted up. The man was gesturing furiously toward the alien, his fingertips dancing while the alien looked on.

"Like I was saying," Walt said. "Suicide."

And that, of course, transitioned into the story of his long walk, which in turn became a wrathful fight against the invaders. And when even that didn't kill him, he wandered south, traveling with the unhurried interest of a man refurbishing time-worn relics.

After several years in the jungle—uneventful, for the most part, except for a few tangles with the locals and a couple bouts of comically intense diarrhea—Lorna and the others brought him up here to help. Which he'd done, only to be betrayed by lunatics and hauled here to the island.

"So there you have it," he said. Sea lions barked from somewhere down the shore. "The thrilling tale of how loneliness, an almost willful ignorance, a carelessness toward violence, and a lot of shameless deceit resulted in the death of your buddies down in the ship. As for crashing it in the first place, let the record show that they attacked us first."

He had more—a whole sob story ginned up while he spoke, an epic tale of guilt and sorrow for his part in the aliens' death, followed by his resolve to redeem himself, should he somehow be spared—but he stopped cold. He didn't know how the pale man and his alien buddy thought well enough to BS them. Anyway, between Lorna and Karslaw, he'd had enough lies. They were going to kill him no matter what he said. May as well go out on the truth.

"But you know what, I didn't come up here just on a lark, or because of some girl. Or even to try to save the Catalinans. Is it possible for this sort of thing to be a calling? Like instead of a priest being called to serve God, I was called to kill aliens? I mean, not to get all mystical or pretentious. But I was good at it. So when Karslaw sent for me with Lorna and her husband—who seemed like an all right guy, by the way, but who must have had one hell of a cuckold fetish—it felt like something I had to do. Like I didn't have a choice."

He frowned. "I did, though. Everything's a choice. Including the choice to come back here and finish off your maybe-friends in the ship. I did it. I'm guilty."

He sat back, breathed. The sun felt good. The man went on translating for a while. The alien gestured back, tentacles wriggling, claws moving in small, subtle jerks.

When at last they stopped, Walt raised his eyebrows. "So? Have we reached the part where you sentence me to death and I try to choke you with my handcuffs before your tentacled friend rips me limb from limb?"

The man stared at him, expressionless. "My name is Ness. This is Sebastian. We have decided we'd like to talk some more."

"Right," Walt said. "Can I have some water first? I'm about to die of thirst. I'd hate to rob you of the satisfaction of doing it yourself."

Ness gestured to Sebastian, who withdrew a bottle from one of the gray bandoliers strapped to its body. The water tasted strange, like something distilled from a tidepool, or a failed brand of Gatorade. He must have made a face, because Ness laughed.

"Don't worry. Not poison. Took me a while to get used to the taste, too."

"Has anyone ever told you you're a little weird?"

"Since the day I was born. Now. Let's talk."

Walt handed the alien the bottle. It took it back with a prehensile tentacle. The skin glided over Walt's, smooth and dry. He shuddered. "What's up?"

"You spent a heck of a lot of time explaining the why," Ness said. "We believe it's more about the how."

"How did we kill them? With a bunch of guns."

"But you didn't just blow up the ship."

"Turns out none of us had a jet. Or a nuke. Anyway, every boat we brought near it got blasted to splinters."

"The ship thinks it's underwater," Ness said. "Switched its defenses. Its programming isn't doing too well anymore." He gazed toward the mainland, but the ship was too far away to make out from the blur of city and mountains. "I'm not real sure how to put these concepts in human terms, let alone English. But dirt wants to be life. To put it another way, life wants to be. To emerge from matter. If a pool of water lasts long enough, something will crawl from it. Even stars work and dance. We have a saying: the dirt wants to stand up, too.

"But when you make a thing inert, you kill it. You insult the universe's purpose. That's why they came here. To let the Earth live as it should. That, and to take all mankind's shit."

Walt laughed. "So they wiped out civilization because we made too many cars and soda cans? How do they excuse that mile-wide marvel of metal I dunked into the bay?"

"Hypocritically," Ness said. "One of those necessary evils. You seen any of our buildings?"

"Your buildings? The aliens'?"

"Yes."

"Sure. Weird blue things. Sometimes orange. Kind of look like mounds of coral."

"That's because we grow them. Through an accelerated process. Humans, you chip stone out of the living dirt and put the bones in a pile over your heads."

"We got killed because we wanted to get out of the cold," Walt said.

"That's bullshit. I recycled!"

"You're thinking wrong," Ness said. Frustration crossed his face, standing starkly from his usual lack of visible emotion. "It's a hell of a lot bigger than environmentalism, but the fact your civic leaders had to enact recycling programs in the first place only proves how detached you all are from the Way. Dude, you think it's a coincidence the invaders killed mankind through a process that allowed billions of trillions of viruses to find life?"

"I assumed it was just a whole lot more efficient than Operation Entire-Planet-Storm."

"Sure, but that ties in, too. Letting a living virus do the work means they don't have to defy the universe with a whole bunch of tanks and shit."

Sebastian gestured beside him. The two exchanged signs for some time. Ness turned back to Walt. "My brother reminds me we're getting off course. Here's the thing. We find what you've achieved offensive, but we admire the ways you achieved those ends."

Walt laughed. "That absolves me of killing thousands of your people?"

Ness' face remained blank. "Here's the deal. The old ways of thinking is what launched that whole stupid invasion. Got all our people—on both sides—killed. Me and Sebastian, you might call us monks. Reformists. Us and a few friends are trying to do things different. Getting back to our roots. Not being so quick to judge. We're still gonna step in when we see something trying to destroy the Way, but we're doing our best to look at things from a more objective perspective."

"You're not going to kill me."

"We'll get to that."

"Then why did you deal with Karslaw for me in the first place?"

"I told you, to get the truth. And to understand him better. He came to us alone. Unarmed. Big old balls."

"Delusions of grandeur," Walt said. "He uses a lot of romantic speech to get his people to do what he wants. I think it's getting to him. It's like he's writing his own heroic myth in his head."

"Well, despite his balls, I don't think real highly of him. He does bad things and he does them badly." Ness stared off to sea, as if remembering long-gone times. "Lying. Conquering. Taking slaves.

Not that he's alone in that. Sometimes I wish the virus had killed us to the last man."

"Well, we could go beat him up together."

Ness shot him a look of amused contempt. "Just because I've decided not to shoot you doesn't mean I'd ever work with you. You're kind of terrible."

"Can I at least have a ride back to the city?"

The pale man gave him an unreadable look. "We're not going to judge you. We're going to let the dirt do it instead."

Walt frowned. "The dirt? I'd like to check if it attended an accredited law school first."

"We're going to leave you here on this lump of dirt in the middle of the water. If the Way approves of you, you'll find your way home."

"You're going to desert me on an island?" He beckoned at the cliffs. "There are trees up there. I'll build a raft. All that's going to prove is whether there's a current running to the mainland."

"What are you gonna do, chop down the trees with your hands?" Ness stood, knees popping. "Here's the deal. We're gonna cut off your handcuffs. You're gonna give us everything you got. Including your clothes. Then we wave goodbye, and it's just you and the Way."

"So instead of having Sebastian squeeze my head until it goes pop, you're going to let the dirt kill me instead. That doesn't wash your claws of responsibility, you know."

"Sure it does. Now hold still. Lasers are sadly removed from the Way. They don't know the difference between dead steel and a live hand."

Ness gestured to the alien, who produced a blunt pistol and held Walt down with a slew of claws and tentacles. Heat flared at his left ankle, then his right. He didn't dare to move. With gentle strength, Sebastian straightened his arms from his body and lased through the cuffs on his wrists. Melted steel beaded and fell to the sand. A metallic tang hung in the air.

"Do I really have to strip?" he said. "I mean, if anybody's watching, it's just going to look weird."

"As bare as when you were born," Ness said. "Pardon me if I don't turn my back on you."

Walt sighed and undressed. Sebastian collected his clothes and the cuffs and stuffed them into the pouches in its bandoliers. At least it was a warm day.

"What now?" he said.

"I don't know," Ness said. "I hope I never see you again, but if I do, please tell me the story of your judgment."

"Anything for a friend."

Ness gave him a blank look, then turned and waded into the sea, Sebastian beside him, the waves foaming over his hard, shiny legs. Walt thought about rushing them, but other than the possibility of lashing their bodies into a raft, it wouldn't do him a single bit of good.

Sea lions barked from around the cliffs. The deep blue shape of Catalina rested to the east. The city was a blur to the north, miles and miles further away. Walt closed his eyes and laughed.

31

"They killed Martin."

Mauser pressed his palms into his eyes. "I'm so sorry, Raina."

"Did you see who did it?"

He shook his head. "It all happened so fast."

They had broken into a house on a corner with a turreted top floor and a view of the valley leading to the back slopes of the Dunemarket. Empty houses lay below them like rows of pulled teeth.

"Then we'll have to kill all of them," she said. "That's the only way to make sure Martin's spirit goes free."

Mauser looked up. "You little lunatic. You're not still thinking of fighting."

"Why not?"

"Why not? Because your only friend just got shot down in front of you. Because they killed a third of our people and scattered the rest to the winds. Because we almost died ourselves, and what we saw will haunt me until the day I join Martin. So yes. Splendid idea. Let's rush right out and do it again."

"Then I'll go by myself. I'm better off alone."

"I'm sure you'll do very well. One little girl against an army of laser-wielding madmen."

Raina drew her tanto with a hiss of steel and ran the blade across the back of her knuckles. The pain cut straight to her core. She made a fist. Blood fell in slow drips to the thick white carpet.

"I'm going to kill him. Right now. While I still know where he is." She turned from the window.

Mauser moved in front of her. "Grief can turn a person crazy,

Raina. Don't let it drag you into darkness."

She looked up into his eyes. "Get out of my way."

"So you can run off and commit suicide? Why don't you save time and cut your throat right here?"

Raina flicked the knife at his crossed arms. A red line appeared on his forearm. He yelped and danced back. She ran out the door and bounded down the steps. He called after her, but she was already gone.

She ran as hard as she could, crossing the main street and racing into the confused streets of a housing complex, meaning to lose herself from Mauser. Her whole body shook with the purpose of her mission. She held tight to her knife. After a couple of blocks, she stopped to listen for footsteps following her between the small white houses, but the only sound was the argument of crows.

She doubled around to come at the Dunemarket from the south, walking silently beside the walls of houses and shops. She stopped at each intersection to check the roads for scouts, then dashed to whatever cover was on the other side. She approached her house from the alley behind it. It was perfectly quiet. She went to her room to dress in black and get her spare binoculars. Back in the hall, Martin's door was open. She walked through the doorway, half expecting to see him there at his desk hunched over wires and circuits, fingertips black with oil, his hair greasy from not washing it for days.

But it was empty. As empty as everything else. She went to the kitchen for a Ziploc bag, then returned to his room and collected the stray hairs from his pillow. Maybe if she had a piece of his physical body, she could stop his soul from being dragged away.

In case Mauser thought to check the house for her—or in case Karslaw was torturing his captives to track down those who'd fled—she went outside, crept three blocks east, and holed up in an unfamiliar home.

She hid in the closet and waited for night to enfold her before returning to the Dunemarket. Two scouts waited at the head of the road leading down through the hills, rifles in hand. She backtracked to come in through the hills on the east flank, walking as quietly as she could, a snake among the palms. The eastern approach was unburned, but smoke continued to rise from the middle of the market, its cloudy strands turned silver in the moonlight.

"He can be yours," she whispered to the moon. "Help me take his life and I'll give you every drop of his blood. The mightiest warrior in the land. What could be a better gift?"

A gale of laughter swept from the market. Raina hunkered down, spooked. Was the moon laughing at her? Or in anticipation of its feast? But it made no difference to her mission. She advanced step by step until she crossed the final ridge and looked down on the market.

Tents were pitched across the road. Fires crackled on the asphalt. At first she thought they were using the bodies for kindling, but all she could smell was wood smoke. Troops stood around the fires drinking from metal cups. Talking. Laughing. Pointing off into the city. Many of the men were shirtless. She scanned them for Karslaw.

"Where to next?" a woman said, hoisting her cup over her head. Liquid sloshed to the street. "This time can we conquer somewhere with pool boys?"

Troops laughed. A tent flap unzipped. Karslaw strode into the firelight, chest glistening. His teeth glinted. "Our enemies are ruined. Our homeland is safe. Now we consolidate. We know our destiny, but now it's time to prove it to these people—and that our rule is welcome."

"I've had enough with their smoked fish, by the way," the woman said. "I think we should start demanding massages instead."

More laughter. Raina focused on their faces, searing them into her memory. If she got the chance, she'd kill them all.

Footsteps crackled through the leaves. Thirty feet to her right, a man staggered down the hill. A laser bounced on his belt. She waited for him to reach the road and join the others, then crept back up the hill and descended the other side to hide in the brush at its bottom.

Hours later, the last of the smoke cleared from the sky, revealing the stars beyond. She slunk back up the hill and knelt behind a palm trunk. Through her binoculars, the camp was motionless. The fires had burn to low red embers. The tent flaps were zipped. Many of the Catalinans slept in the open, blankets spread beneath them. At the side of the road, a young man was wrapped up in the blanket Jill had been using for her stall earlier that day. There were guards posted at the entrances to the market, but everyone at the tents was asleep.

And she knew which one of them held Karslaw.

She moved down the hill as quietly as she knew how. She loosened her knife in its sheath, but waited to draw it. The steel was so fine it would catch the moonlight like her dad's nets had caught the silvery bonito.

At the shoulder of the road, she paused and looked over the sleeping soldiers. Drunken. Useless. If she'd had a few more people with her, she could have laid waste to them all. She stepped into the gravel. A man rolled over and stared right at her.

"Who the fuck?" he said.

She leapt forward, knife snicking from its scabbard. The man screamed. She plunged the knife into his neck. He gargled blood over the blade. Across the road, men and women stirred, fumbling for guns and eyeglasses, firing questions back and forth. Karslaw's tent was fifty feet down the road.

"Holy shit!" a woman yelled. "Right there!"

She ran back up the hill. Two lasers chased her, scorching the grass. She jagged to her right and another beam blazed through the space she'd just vacated. The weapons cast cold blue light between the palm trees, throwing the world into icy shadows.

Men ran behind her, calling to each other through the darkness. At the bottom of the other side of the hill, she cut sidelong through the brush, emerging into a strip mall parking lot. She sprinted across the street into another block of laundromats and liquor stores and a Brooklyn pizzeria. She didn't stop until she reached the cavern of the Home Depot a mile north of the market.

She hid in the gloom, watching through her binoculars. Far down the street, a lantern bobbed along, carried by three questing soldiers. They never came close enough to spot her.

She burned with shame. She had failed her father. Karslaw's tent had been right there. If she had run to it, she could have reached it before the Catalinans knew what was happening. She could have rushed inside and taken Karslaw's heart, and then her father would be free, and perhaps a better man would take care of her mother, and Raina herself could have died.

Why should she fear so much to die? She was hardly scared of any other thing. She thought she wanted nothing more in the world than to feel Karslaw's blood. Yet the thought of spilling her own scared her even worse. It was a flaw. One she needed to correct.

She circled back to the Dunemarket, approaching through the

western hills. Down below, lanterns lined the street. Men stood at arms, gazing into the night, guns on their hips. She waited all night for them to go to sleep, but she never got the chance. With the men still at watch, and the first hint of dawn peeping from the east, Raina withdrew and crossed the couple miles to the house she'd run to with Mauser.

Inside, he sprawled on the lush living room rug. Dawn broke through the window. A pretty blue bottle was tucked in the crook of his arm, spraying blue-tinted sunlight across the ceiling. He sat up, red-eyed and puffy-faced.

"Did you get him?"

Raina stood there, useless. "No."

"Well, that's a hell of a shame." He held out the bottle. "Fancy a drink?"

"No."

"It's pretty good. See?" He tipped it back and drank, then set it down, wincing, working his mouth to get past the taste. "All right, so maybe it doesn't taste good, but it makes you feel pretty great. It's like a magic potion. They used to use it for medicine, you know. Today's modern doctors could learn a thing or two."

"I killed one of them," she said. "Then the others woke up. I had to run."

"Gosh, are you all right?"

"I could have killed him. Karslaw. But I would have died too, so I ran away. Why did I do that? Why couldn't I kill him?"

Mauser rousted himself from the floor and peered in her eyes. "Maybe because it is incredibly hard to bring yourself to kill."

"I've done it before. So have you."

"I don't think that makes it any easier. Anyway, you're not talking about killing a person, you're talking about killing yourself in the process. And you know what you are? A little survivor. The notion of suicide runs against everything you've got inside you. There's nothing wrong with that. If you were the kind of person who could sacrifice yourself to kill him, you would never have made it here in the first place."

She shook her head. She was tired and her head hurt. She took the bottle from him and drank. It burned her throat, but she felt a little better almost right away.

"So what?" she said. "If I can't do what I'm supposed to, then I'm worthless."

"Or human." He laughed to himself, then saw her face. "Hey. You're not worthless. You're the reverse of worthless. Worthful."

"It's been so long. My dad's still dead. My mom's still gone."

"Yet despite your best efforts, you remain stubbornly alive. After the worst life can throw at you. Perhaps there's a lesson here."

"What's that?"

"That life goes on. Even when you don't want it to. That even if the thing you hold dearest is taken from you, you will survive." Mauser's eyes brightened. He paced around the room, gesturing at the dawn beyond the windows. "It's magical, isn't it? No matter what happens to us, we sail on through it. We're invincible. Immune to everything but death. That's why you fear it, Raina. It's the only thing you can't conquer."

She shook her head. "But it still hurts."

"Because you keep bashing your head into its walls." He crossed the beam of sunlight cutting through the window, swaying toward her. "Let's get out of here. Me and you. Run away to some place peaceful. You don't have to die here and you don't have to hurt. All you have to do is leave."

Her resolve shrank until it got so small it felt like she could pick it up and throw it out the window. She stepped toward Mauser. But as her resolve left her, so did her strength. She staggered to the floor, folding like a jackknife, hugging her knees to her chest.

"I can't!"

He touched her shoulder. "Sure you can. Just get up and walk away. You can walk, can't you?"

Tears burst down her face. She shook her head, rocking on the ground, wailing, remembering her dad smiling at the sun on the sea, her mom waving to them from her chair by the shore. She remembered stalking rats among the pillars of the pier and eating them raw out of sight of the gulls and the dogs. She remembered her first family dying one by one in bed, blood oozing from their mouths and eyes, coughs echoing through the house until she came home from the store to a swift and awful silence. Everything she loved had been taken from her. Perhaps the answer was to stop loving.

The thought sliced straight to her heart. Her first family was long dead. So was her second father. Her second mom was captive, as good as dead. Martin was lost, too. All she loved now were memories. Dreams. Spirits. What was left to fear? She had already lost everything—except her life and her purpose.

One could be taken from her. The other could not. Every spirit inside her spoke up at once, a babel of discordant voices. The rabbits told her to be swift. The cats told her to be stealthy. The dogs told her to be persistent. The fish told her to seek strength in numbers. The people told her to trust no one but herself.

Every one of them agreed on one thing: she must be stronger than she ever knew how.

Her shoulders stopped shaking. Her tears dried up. She unfolded her limbs and stood. Mauser smiled and held out his hand.

She slapped it away. "I won't stop until Karslaw is dead."

The light faded from his eyes. His smile shriveled. He looked tired and suddenly sober. He lowered himself to the ground and drank from the big blue bottle.

"Then there's only one thing left to do," he said. "Rally the troops."

"What troops?"

"Everyone who just lost their loved ones at the Slaughter at the Dunemarket." He reached into his pocket and fished out a small metal object. It was round and smooth and a scintillating silver-gray that reminded her of the forge-line running down the length of her tanto. "Oh, and while we're at it, why don't we give that lily-skinned weirdo a ring? I don't think he liked the islanders any more than we did."

32

Like every young boy, Walt had once dreamed about what he'd do if he were ever stuck on a desert island. Like every boy, most of those dreams had involved wearing an eye patch, not being bossed around by his parents, and lots of beachside snoring under a palm frond umbrella.

He wished very keenly he'd been a more practical kid. Because here he was, stuck on a semi-desert island that wasn't exactly in the middle of nowhere but wasn't within swimming range of anywhere else, and he didn't have the first clue how to get off it.

But that in itself helped refine his decision-making. If he didn't have a plan, the first thing was to buy himself time to form one. He needed to find water and he needed to find food. Once he had that in hand, then he could worry about how to cross miles of open ocean when he didn't have so much as a loincloth to his name.

Something to cut things apart, and something to tie them back together. Other than food and water, that was all you needed to get back on the path to civilization. Before he left the small beach, he searched it front to back, eyes sharp for the glint of broken glass or metal. He found only a plastic bag and a chunk of a large, solid shell. He took both. It was a start.

When Lorna dropped him at the beach, it had appeared to be fronted by sheer cliffs, but on its north end he found a natural path leading up to the heights. His feet were bare and he stepped carefully up the trail. He would very much like some shoes. He didn't like the idea of paddling twenty miles with open cuts on his soles.

The path flattened out. He stood on a vista overlooking a spread of brownish grass and brown-black rocks. A ridgeline ran north-south down the middle of the island, which looked no longer than a mile from one end to the other, and less that in width. In summary, small and brown. Not great prospects for finding running water.

Sea lions honked to the southeast. With a big enough rock, he could probably take out a pup. But he had a better idea. Up north, a cacophony of birds called into the wind. The dirt was mostly occupied by grass, most of it half-dead, but a few weeds and flowers poked from it too, as well as occasional succulents, fat-leafed and waxy green. He filed that away and continued toward the birds. An empty can of Coke was half-hidden in the grass, smashed flat and sun-bleached. He shook off the dirt and added it to his bag.

Something poked into his heel. He winced, then sat down and pulled his foot up to his face. A splinter lay embedded in his skin. From a strictly medical perspective, he wasn't certain whether it was best for a barefoot person to leave it be or remove it at once and risk a bigger, nastier cut, but he didn't like the idea of being in pain with every step. Not when he had so much work to do. He tried to tease it loose with his thumbnail. When that didn't work, he got out the shell and used its chipped edge to scrape the splinter free. There was no blood and little abrasion to his skin. With any luck, he would resist infection. All that time in the jungle had to have been good for his immune system.

The sun warmed his skin. There were a few squat trees along the edge of the cliffs. Their main branches looked thinner than his wrists, but if he could find enough, he might be able to conjure up a raft.

Birds cried ahead. The rock climbed in terraced slabs, terminating in cliffs overlooking the shores. Above the terraces, gray and white seabirds called to each other, flapping their wings, pecking at the soil. Walt walked up with his arms spread above his head, hollering senselessly. Birds took to the air, wheeling over their nests. He got down and gathered their speckled eggs. The birds squawked, swooping at him. He filled both hands and walked away, wary for dive-bombers. At a safe distance, he knelt beside a flat shelf of black rock.

The eggs were maybe half the size of a chicken's. The inside of the first looked just like something you'd take home from a supermarket: a round yolk, lots of gloppy clear stuff that was about the same consistency as the aliens' blood. He'd drank raw yolks as a hangover cure before. He swallowed the egg without a second thought. It tasted good. A little richer than chicken eggs. A hint of fish to it, too.

The second egg contained a fetal chick. He groaned. There was no way he could make himself eat that. Its tiny beak. Its blind eyes like little black yolks of their own. He would have to be a hell of a lot hungrier. It squirmed in the ruin of its shell. He glanced over at the birds. They couldn't take care of something this small. Feeling like the worst person in history, he picked up a rock and put it out of its misery.

After that, he didn't want to open the third egg, but it wasn't about what he wanted anymore. He was naked and the sun was too hot and he was losing water from his body with every breath of air and trickle of sweat. If you want to make a staying-alive omelette, sometimes you have to bash a baby bird's brains out.

Among the remaining clutch, he opened six more yolks and two more fetuses. There had to be a way to figure out which were good before you broke them open. Shake them or something. He resolved to give that a try next time. He hoped the negative karma he'd accumulated in the meantime wouldn't manifest in a case of salmonella.

It was barely a meal, but the calories were low-work. There were hundreds more birds here. Probably more colonies elsewhere on the island. Eat enough raw eggs, and his risk of disease and parasites probably approached 100%, but it would beat starving. He circled around the rookery and checked out the coast. More beaches below, a mix of rock and sand. Slabs of kelp-covered basalt dotted the waves. Shallow pools glimmered between stone upcrops and the beach. Probably some squirmy things to eat down there. Plenty of mussels.

Water was going to be a problem. He continued west along the cliffs and ran straight into a field of wild wheat.

He glanced around, half convinced someone was tricking him. He pulled the head off one of the plants and rolled the seeds between his fingers, shucking them. Tasted like wheat. A little earthier; barley, maybe. Someone must have farmed the place way back in the day.

He stepped on a sharp rock and inhaled with a hiss. He sat down to have a think and a look around. Coastal flies buzzed his face, their bodies antlike and gross. He had pretty good calluses from all the walking, but he needed some goddamn shoes. Why had that stupid alien-lover taken his clothes? He didn't mind the nudity. There was no one around to see him. And considering the trouble his dick had gotten into recently, the flies could have it. But if he hurt himself—slashed himself open on a piece of glass or rock or coral—that could set his work back by days. Without water, he really didn't have any of those to spare. If that pasty idiot had just left him with a pair of jeans, he could have cut them in half and tied one leg around each of his feet.

Being angry felt good, but it wasn't getting him anywhere. Well, if there were crops on the island, maybe there were some old boards or something he could strap to his feet. Or see if the trees had bark that would peel up in one piece. He stood up and glanced toward the ocean. One of the thick, tall succulents clung to the edge of the cliff.

The plant was a good three feet tall with a broad base and a whole lot of meaty leaves. It looked a little like an overgrown artichoke. More accurately, an agave. There had been plenty of agave down in Mexico. He had almost never had any use for them—there were enough abandoned towns near Chichen Itza to bike in for supplies when he was low on shoelaces or underwear—but he'd once watched a Maya use one to catch a fish.

Trying to keep his heart from beating too hard with hope, he moved to the plant and tapped his thumb against the point of its largest inner leaf. It was sharp, snagging his skin. Using the shell as a knife, he cut into the tough, fibrous plant, pulling the needle-like point free of the leaf.

A three-foot strand of natural string came with it.

Walt laughed like a child, cut the leaf and the one next to it from the plant, tried to sit down in the dirt, thought better of it, and went back for a third leaf to use as a seat. He used the shell to gouge a hole in each side of one leaf, then, using a long twig for a lead, threaded the agave-needle through it, looping the string over the top.

The result was one of the shittiest sandals of all time. Walt wiggled it on and hobbled in a circle, arching his foot to keep the makeshift strap from slipping off his foot. The plant matter squished under his weight but the skin of the leaf was fibrous and tough. He sat back down and added a second loop to the shoe, adjusting it to be taut against his heel.

The second shoe went much faster. Within an hour, he had a pair of loose and awkward but effective sandals. The sun was on the verge of diving behind the ridge to the west, and for a moment Walt regretted spending the time to put together a half-assed pair of shoes that were probably going to fall apart in less time than it had taken him to put them together. The simple fact of the matter was that every moment mattered. He had about seven days before he died of dehydration.

And practically speaking, he had a lot less time than that. It was hot on the island and there was virtually no shade. His body would get pretty worthless within four or five days. Catalina was much closer than the hazy mainland, but it was still a good twenty miles away; even if he were able to pull a makeshift raft together, the trip looked like it would take a full day—assuming he could find a current that wouldn't grab him up and usher him into the middle of the Pacific.

All told, if he didn't have a seaworthy vessel or a source of fresh water in the next two or three days, he was going to die.

It had been a long day and he was tired but he couldn't afford to waste the light. He decided to walk around the island before getting too deep in his plans. Maybe he'd find a lake. Or a canoe. Or a fully-fueled helicopter with a copy of Flying a Helicopter for Dummies in the glove box. There was no sense hurrying to patch together a third-rate raft that would break apart a mile out to sea when there might be a real boat just around the bend.

He walked along the edge of the cliff, scanning the shore for boats and glancing inland in search of ranger cabins or old homesteads. Pelicans drifted thirty feet above the waves. The beaches were rocky and slathered in seaweed, black clouds of flies feasting on the rotten vegetation. To his surprise, the sandals held up. The leaves flattened out, dampening the soles of his feet with trapped water, but the stringy, meaty plants held together in a coherent mass.

The island wandered north into a thin spit of cliffs. He made it to the tip and turned southwest along the coast. He didn't find anything more interesting than a sharp wedge of basalt that fit nicely in his hand, which he added to his bag of trinkets. As the sun fled west, pulling a blanket of black behind it, he pulled up bunches of grass and gathered them together for bedding.

The air stayed warm. Sea lions barked in the distance. Bugs

whirred. It smelled like the sea and freshly-torn grass. He'd never been this pared-down before, and while it amused him to be a modern Stone Age caveman, it also lent a clarity to the night, a sense of unconscious understanding and connection so wordlessly profound that it was almost worth enduring everything that had brought him here. After a while, he nestled into the grass and slept. He woke to darkness, sore and thirsty. He was halfway through urinating before it occurred to his sludgy mind that he might want to drink it.

Well, things weren't that desperate yet. While he waited for the sun to rise, he caught moths and beetles, pulling off legs and heads and wings and chewing down the bodies as fast as he could. The moths weren't bad—they tasted fatty and almost sweet—but the beetles were crunchy, and their little bits stuck in his throat. After the fourth beetle nearly made him lose what little lunch he had, he plucked up grass and ate the tender white shoots. The grass was dewy and he emptied his plastic bag and rubbed it around, then licked the film of water on the inside. It tasted like dirt, and there wasn't enough for a proper swallow, but it got his saliva flowing again.

Dawn turned the world gray. He walked on down the shoreline. After half a mile, the cliffs bent into a straight line leading west. In a sandy bay, sea lions flopped in the first light, honking to each other, rolling in the mats of kelp. Something off-white was tangled in the brown, rubbery plants. Walt backtracked to a trail down to the beach, careful not to shred his shoes on the sharp black basalt. At the beach, he pulled a waterlogged fishing net from the kelp, tossing away the salty, tacky seaweed and gathering up the pencil-thin ropes. He grinned. Now all he had to do was find a half-decent paddle. A hammer would be nice, too. Though he supposed rocks were nature's hammers.

He kept one eye on the sea lions while he used his axe-like wedge of basalt to chip mussels from the rocks and smash them open. The insides were snotty and salty and he could only eat a few before he got thirsty. He made himself eat a handful more. He was going to need the fuel.

He walked for a mile without seeing anything more than dried-out grass, the agave-like succulents, scatters of red flowers, and gnomish, gnarled trees no taller than himself. He stopped to pull the ends from the succulents and reel out the thread attached to the base of the needle-sharp points. Using the broken shell, he carved open one of the tough leaves, exposing a clear, goopy liquid inside. He tested it with the tip of his tongue. It tasted soapy but not downright toxic. He allowed himself a few licks, then cut out the meat of the leaf and chewed. It wasn't bad.

There was a small bed of the things and two sported tall stalks heavy with little purple flowers. If these things were agave—and if they weren't, they were certainly from the same family—Walt knew enough about tequila to bank that their flowers weren't poisonous. Far from it. He stripped off the buds and tasted them. They were sweet, sticky with sap. He ate a good handful and cut down the rest. There were several pounds of them and his bag was suddenly quite heavy, straining the plastic handles.

He was no longer hungry and was just a little thirsty, and maybe it was a toxin-induced delirium talking, but he felt pretty good. He continued on, scratching the bug bites he'd picked up overnight on his shins and shoulders.

A shack sat on the southwest corner of the island. Mist-peeled paint crackled from its walls. Inside, there was nothing but a table, a chair, and a greasy old-style lantern. He checked everywhere for the matches it used, but had no luck.

Around back, he struck it rich. A flathead shovel lay half hidden in the weeds. When he picked it up, rust flaked his palm. He jabbed it at the flank of a rock. It clanged but showed no sign of damage.

It was about noon and the sun was at its worst. He went inside the shack and propped the door open to catch a breeze. He was sweating more than he'd like, but at least he was out of the sun. He napped on the dusty floor, waking a couple hours later. He took the chair with him to the beach where Lorna had dropped him off the day before, leaving it there with everything but the shovel, then went back to the shack and broke off the legs of the table and carried it piece by piece to the eastern shore.

His skin was hot and sunburnt and his mouth was dry and his shoes had been reduced to flapping shreds. He rested a minute, then climbed back up the path to find another agave and eat its juicy meat and fashion another pair of leaf-slippers. The nourishment helped, but he no longer felt so good. He didn't have a choice, though. His prognosis looked much better than the day before, but he had a headache and his skin was baking. The water from the succulents wasn't nearly enough. He used the shell to scrape out the remainder of the leaf he'd eaten, tied a loop through its ends, and slapped it on as a hat, pulling the loop beneath his chin.

He still had a few hours of light left, so he decided to get the dangerous stuff out of the way. Some of the planks on the dock were loose enough to pull up with his bare hands. Others he chipped away at with the shovel, prying them up with a squeak of rusted nails and dragging them to the beach. He had enough experience building rafts to fling at the crashed ship that he knew about how much he'd need to keep his body out of the water. By sundown, he thought his pile of planks looked big enough to start construction.

A three-quarter moon hung above the city, a silvery lantern that gave him enough light to lash together the planks and the table, employing the soggy net and the succulent-threads for cordage. After a few hours, he had a decent-sized platform. He propped one end up with rocks and rolled underneath it to sleep.

In the morning, he went back up the path to gather more succulent leaves for the trip across. Feeling quite pleased with himself, he loaded up his bag, dragged the raft to the shore, and pushed off into the gentle waves.

The raft began to pull apart just a hundred yards from shore. The fishing net was holding up fine, but some of the succulent threads had frayed and snapped and the whole thing was threatening to split down the middle. He swore furiously, paddling back to land with the shovel, awkwardly holding the raft together with his left hand.

It took him the rest of the day to gather up enough new threads to tie the raft back together, reinforced triply from his first effort. He ate more flowers and leaves and thought about walking up for some eggs but it would be so little reward for so much work. Instead, he went back to sleep under the raft.

He got up around dusk. As the sun withdrew, the blue lump of Catalina turned black, discretely visible from the ocean and the sky. Well, what the hell. He'd be able to work harder when there wasn't any sunshine beating him down. He shoved off, battling the waves, careful not to take his eyes off the faraway island for more than a few seconds at a time. The tide seemed to be sucking him south, out to open sea; he paddled steadily, trying to convince himself he was gaining ground.

After an hour, his arms were rubbery. He paddled weakly, but even that proved too much, and he stopped to give his burning muscles a rest. But the raft was no longer drifting south. He was being borne east-southeast. If he let himself drift, he'd be swept a couple miles south of Catalina, but if the current held, he might have a chance.

He scooped out the meat of a leaf and chewed down some sticky flowers. It seemed to help. He paddled again, pacing himself, working just hard enough to make a bit of progress north. The island doubled in size. Dizziness rolled over his head. He lay down on the raft until the feeling passed, then took up the shovel and dipped it back into the sea, bubbles churning away from his strokes.

The eastern sky grew light. His lips were chapped and all he could smell or taste was salt. His hands hurt. So did his head. It was still so far away. It would be so easy to lie down and let the ocean take him wherever it wanted. Let the water be his final judge.

Anger stormed through him. There were no judges in the dirt or the water or the air. There was only himself and this big stupid world. He knew which would win in the end, but he intended to give it a hell of a fight.

By mid-morning, the breakers pushed him toward the southern shore of Catalina. Twenty yards from land, a riptide caught his raft, pulling him away faster than he could paddle. He rolled over the edge. The water felt cold and good against his skin but he was so weak he could barely keep his head above water. The tide dragged him further and further from the black rocks and icy panic gripped his spine.

He stopped fighting it and swam parallel instead. The riptide let him go. He thrashed his noodly arms. His foot struck a rock and a jolt of pain shot up his leg. He laughed and stood and hobbled his way up to the beach.

He'd lost his bag as he swam and he was hungry and thirsty but he was too tired to do anything more than crawl up the rocks to the grass and flop under a bush to sleep. He was out for a long, long time. It was night when he woke. He was shoeless again, completely naked, in fact, and he stepped carefully up into the hills. When he finally reached the reservoir he'd passed weeks ago with Lorna, he drank cool water until he threw up, then rinsed out his mouth and tried again.

It was incredible how much strength he'd lost in just a couple days. He was sore and weak and sunburnt and salt-chapped and he took his time recovering, weaving shoes from leaves, skulking around to steal the islanders' vegetables, and sleeping in the treed-over valleys between hills. All that raw food had thrown a riot in his digestive tract, too. He was surprised the smell alone didn't give him away.

After three days of living wild in the hills, he felt good enough to sneak into Avalon from the northwest and, under cover of night, break into the Scaveteria for clothes and real shoes and a water bottle and fishing line and scissors and a few other things to make life less paleolithically low-rent. There were no guns, but there were plenty of knives. He took three.

He was prepared to bide his time for as long as it took, but it was just a couple more days before the ships sailed in from the mainland. Four of them docked at the piers. Walt hung around on the hill just long enough to ensure most if not all of the troops had returned, then retreated and jogged off into the valleys.

He wasn't so sure about his next step. But he knew Karslaw well enough to believe the man would keep the source of his new power close at hand.

Lorna lay on her side in bed, hands tucked beneath her head and pressed together as if she were praying. She smelled like her skin, sweat that hadn't yet gone entirely sour, and the feral richness of a jungle bloom. It was funny. When a person was asleep, you could almost forgive them for anything.

Walt put his biggest knife to her neck. Her eyes snapped open.

"Talk first," he said. "Then you can scream."

33

The metal piece in Mauser's hand drew the gaze as strongly as a dead body. It was an intrusion from another world and you had to keep one eye on it or it might do something bad. The whorled metal looked unscratchable, permanent, wise.

"Where did you get that?"

Mauser smiled. "Lifted it off him after I saw him trying to signal his friends."

"Do you know how to use it?"

"Oh sure, it's just your run-of-the-mill alien tricorder." He closed his palm. "I've fooled around enough to turn it on. Maybe. Look, I can make it show little blue lights. Lights are always a sign of progress."

She gave it a moment's thought, but there was nothing to decide. "Do it."

"First things first. I am so tired you could use my eyelids for doorstoppers, and considering the pale little guy's general surliness during our first meeting—and the aliens—and the fact I stole this from him—I'd say there's a nonzero chance they respond to our call for aid by shooting us. If I'm going to die, I want a good sleep first."

He went outside to pee. While he was gone, she had another drink from the bottle, but it made her head feel swimmy. She went to her room and slept straight through to the afternoon.

They had fled the battle of the Dunemarket with nothing more than their emergency packs, and before they tried the device, they detoured to the bunker to stock up on food and water. Mauser stumbled beside her, eyes hooded. He swallowed a lot and spoke little.

The bunker was untouched. They replenished their water and filled new packs with silver packages of freeze dried meat and fruit. After, Raina led the way west to the beaches a few miles north of Carl's home.

By then, Mauser looked slightly less exhausted and nauseated. He got out the round piece of metal and tapped a couple small buttons on its side. Blue light winked from the eye in its middle.

"Not much of a Bat Signal," he said. "But at least it's something."

She kept both eyes on the piece, waiting for it to speak. It was early evening and a steady breeze brought cool air in from the sea. After a while, they sat. The sun lowered itself to the sea, reflecting from the waves and the wet sand. Flocks of gulls stood on the beach facing the wind. The gold rim of the sun winked away.

Mauser sighed. "Well, when all else fails, hit more buttons."

He poked and prodded at the metal lump. It made no sound, but after a few seconds, the little blue light blinked erratically. Mauser held the device to his ear, then shook it and brought it to his mouth.

"Hello? Alien marauders? We're about to launch a doomed attack on our mutual foe and, well, if you're not doing anything better, we could really use a hand."

More silence. The light flickered a few times, then went black.

"Why isn't it working?" Raina said.

"Let me check the instruction manual."

"Have you tried all the buttons?"

"Yes, I've tried all the buttons."

She reached for it. "Let me see."

Mauser held it away. She grabbed his wrist and bent it sharply. He winced and scowled and handed over the device. It weighed down her palm, as heavy as bullets. She pressed everything there was to press, then scratched at the light in its center.

"Why isn't it doing anything?"

Mauser shook his head. "Fucked if I know. Maybe it is. Maybe they're ignoring us. Or creeping up on us to kill us and take it back. For all I know they sailed to India and they're ten thousand miles out of range."

Black water rolled up the beach, smacking the sand, its foam frosted white by the moonlight. "They won't help us."

"It's only been a couple of hours."

"If they want to find us, they will." She turned to him, hand on the hilt of her knife. "We won't be the only ones who want revenge."

Mauser stared out to sea. "We couldn't beat them when we had an army of our own. Without the aliens, what kind of chance do you really think we have?"

"Any. That's enough for me."

She walked south across the sand, angling toward the paved path that ran beneath the cliffs between the beach and the street. Ragged volleyball nets flapped limply in the wind. Mauser shuffled along behind her. At the end of the path, she climbed the steps to the street and jogged through the dark houses. The surf boomed below. She went to Carl's and knocked on the door.

"You missed your training," he said, backlit by candles. "By two days. Come back tomorrow."

She moved into the doorway. "Did you hear what happened?"

"I spend all day teaching you to fight. Is that the sign of a man who gets out much?"

"The Catalinans massacred the Osseys, then attacked the Dunemarket. They killed Jill and her husband and my friend Martin and everyone who fought back."

Carl glanced past her shoulder to Mauser, then rubbed his mouth. "Are you okay?"

Raina shook her head. "I need you to help me kill them."

"You mean join a fight that's already been lost?"

She looked him in the eye. "Goodbye, master. I have work to do."

"Wait." He opened the door wide and stood back. "I just made tea. Bad luck to turn down tea."

She couldn't say no to that. He found a third chair for Mauser and brought out three matching red mugs. Mauser introduced himself. The tea was hot and black and even had sugar.

Carl slurped and set down his mug. "Tell me you have more people."

"You were the first stop we made," Mauser said.

"For a suicide mission? Such an honor."

"You're a warrior," Raina said. "What's the point of honing a knife if you're never going to use it?"

Carl raised his eyebrows. "Some find the act of honing relaxing. And a good way to keep the fat from settling on your middle."

"It's a waste. You can fight better than anyone here and all you do is go to the beach and show off."

"Show off? You were spying on me."

"All they do is take and kill. And they get away with it because they move while everyone else stands still." Raina clenched her mug of tea. "I won't sit around any more. I'm going to kill Karslaw or die trying. Either way, it means I don't have to live in a world where he's the winner."

Carl ran his finger around the lip of his cup and glanced at Mauser. "And you?"

Mauser laughed humorlessly. "Generally, this is where I'd tip my cap, congratulate him for a game well played, and flee into the night. But his people killed a friend of mine. A kid. I don't think I'd feel right if I ran out on that."

"Even if it means dying?"

"I don't know anymore."

Carl took a drink, holding the tea in his mouth before swallowing. "That doesn't sound all that rational."

"It isn't. They've pushed things past reason. For smart or for stupid, I'm with Raina until the end."

Raina didn't say anything. It felt good to have Mauser's confidence, but there was something frightening about it, too. It made things more real.

Carl nodded. "Tell me more about your plan."

"The islanders are sitting around the Dunemarket celebrating," Raina said. "We're going to find the other survivors. Hit back. We'll attack just like they do—fast, relentless, without warning."

"You should walk away," Carl said. "A place is just a place."

"Not when it's been stained with the blood of those you love."

The man sighed through his nose. "I need to think. See me again before you strike."

"I would have anyway." Raina finished her tea. Mauser said goodbye and Carl nodded. It was full cover of night, perhaps ten o'clock, but that was the best time to do what came next.

She had lived in the Dunemarket for months. Delivered messages between Jill and her conspirators. She had kept her eyes open the whole time because you couldn't trust people. Between all this, she knew the homes of most merchants and rebels within a two-mile radius of the market. Some had died. Many had left. But others stayed, hiding in their homes while the Catalinans camped in the ruins of their former lives.

The first merchant Raina approached was a young woman who lived in a somber blue house on the hill across from the cemetery. When Raina knocked, she cracked open the door and flashed a pistol.

"We're going to fight back," Raina told her. "Take our revenge and take back what's ours."

"Go away," the woman said. There was a crack in her voice that sounded ready to split into a wail. "You think the answer to killing is more killing?"

"No," Raina said. "I think the answer is killing Karslaw."

"This place is damned. You want to die here, you go right ahead."

The woman closed and locked the door. As Raina walked down the drive, the woman's silhouette appeared in the upper window. It was still there by the time the houses cut off Raina's view.

The second merchant they approached was a middle-aged man named Vince. He was fond of puns and had sold toys from a brightly colored stall, allowing them to be bartered away so cheaply that Raina suspected he did it not for food or goods but for the pleasure of handing one of his well-kept dolls or sets of wooden blocks to a laughing child. He lived in the pastel apartments northwest of the market, and when she knocked on his door that night, it was the first time she'd seen him without a smile.

"I thought the whole thing was just talk," Vince said from his doorway. His face was blank and far away. "Rebellion. War. Hooey, I thought—bunch of bluster from puffed-up men with too much time on their hands." He rubbed his eyes. "Then they shoot Agustin dead. Right in front of Jill. Easy as throwing out the trash."

"It didn't seem real," Mauser said softly.

"It's sick. It's a sickness and I can only see one cure." Vince stuck out his hand. It was twice the size of Raina's but soft like well-worn leather. "Tell me where to go."

"Talk to everyone you can trust," Raina said. "We'll be back in two days. Be ready."

Vince held up his hand in goodbye.

Beth lived in a shack in the park two miles down the same street that ran through the Dunemarket. Before the attack, she had delivered seeds and advised people how to grow crops; when she wasn't away, she ran a table of knickknacks she picked up over the course of her journeys. Trimmed berry vines surrounded the shack like natural barbed wire. As Raina neared the door, she heard the unmistakable double click of a shotgun being pumped.

"Beth?" Raina said. "It's Raina. Jill's dead, but the rebellion isn't."

Beth laughed from somewhere in the tree beside her shack. "No? Then who's next on the chopping block?"

"I'm gathering up everyone I can. Do you still believe?"

"Is this a fucking joke? You're not old enough to buy cigarettes."

"There's no more cigarettes being made," Raina said. "No more money to buy them. No more laws to stop me. I'm here to ask you if you want to finish what Jill started."

"I want it all to go away. For the plague to never have happened." Beth laughed again, a sick croak. "I'm done with this place. I'm not following a fucking sixteen-year-old into combat. That's the sign it's over, isn't it? I'll see you in hell."

They turned and walked away. Mauser hiked his pack up his shoulders. "For the good of the recruitment campaign, perhaps we should pretend like I'm the one in charge."

"She didn't turn us down because I'm too young," Raina said. "She turned us down because she's worthless."

"Is that your professional opinion, doctor?"

"She's sitting in her tree like an old crow. All crows do is shriek."

"What we need is hummingbirds," Mauser said. "The silent assassin."

She shook her head. "We need people who are willing to die."

There weren't as many as she hoped. After two days of trudging around San Pedro, Lomita, and the hilly peninsula, she turned up just a dozen recruits. Most of the rebels had been killed in the fighting or disappeared in its aftermath. Many of the survivors disavowed the whole rebellion or meant to move out of the region. Hopes dwindling, Raina went back around to revisit the few who'd pledged support and lead them to the bunker miles to the west.

Down the metal steps, Vince gazed across the concrete walls and full shelves and whistled. "If we've got a place like this, the islanders can have Pedro."

Not for the first time, Raina counted their numbers, as if doing so would magically double them. Seven men, four women, Mauser, herself.

"It isn't enough," she said.

In the flicker of the lamps, Mauser looked skeptical. "I don't know how many more we're likely to get. If we're sneaky, we may be able to take out Karslaw, but let's not kid ourselves."

"I used to fight with packs of dogs for food. The group learns from the leader. If you scare him enough to run, the rest will follow. But if he always fights back, the rest will too. Even after you kill him."

"And I thought my middle school years were rough." Mauser let out a long breath. "There's nothing to stop us from taking a few more days. Who knows. A few more people, and we may be able to escape after the initial attack. Go all Fidel Castro guerrilla-style on their corrupt island asses."

Raina turned to the others. "Find all the guns and friends you can. Be ready to move in three days."

"I know a guy," Estelle said. She was a young woman and she'd lost her husband in the battle. "Girlfriend took a laser to the gut in the market. He'll fight."

"Bring him in."

"One more thing," Mauser said. "If you've been holding back on the tanks and rocket launchers, now would be the time to make them known."

They spread mats and sleeping bags on the dusty cement, speaking of what had happened in the market and what they'd seen since. In the morning, they dispersed, roving to the homes of their friends. Most of Raina's knocks went unanswered. At Mrs. Miller's place, the woman refused to answer the door, her voice coming muffled from the other side.

"Nobody's fighting anyone," Mrs. Miller said. "It's over. They said they're reopening the market. Life goes on."

"Except for the people they killed," Raina said.

"Don't you do it. Don't you stir up trouble. We finally got a chance for peace."

"That's the upside to being conquered."

"Don't you do it," the woman said. "You won't like what happens."

Raina wanted to batter down the door and stab the woman. It hadn't occurred to her that some of the survivors might side with the attackers. The very thought was alien, an affront, something that needed to be killed before it spread.

"You did it, didn't you?" Raina said.

"Did what?"

"Told Karslaw. Betrayed Jill."

"I don't know what you're talking about," Mrs. Miller huffed from behind her door.

"Peace wouldn't be enough for you," Raina said. "You're a fat-cheeked vole. What did it take to buy you? A servant? A home with electricity?"

"All I wanted was peace! Like we'd had for years. Jill was ready to throw all that away."

Raina smiled and walked away. She continued her rounds of the peninsula but was unable to find a single recruit. The moon crept up the sky, less than a quarter full and shrinking by the day, devoured from within by its own endless hunger.

When it reached its highest, she returned to Mrs. Miller's.

The doors were locked, but Raina had spent too many years harvesting the fruit of the apocalypse to be put off by a closed door. As the crickets urged her on, she crouched at the back door and teased the lock open, then took a bobby pin to the deadbolt. After a few minutes of wriggling, it snicked open.

Moonlight gushed through the kitchen windows, flooding over the marble floor. Raina waited beside the staircase to adjust to the deeper darkness of the house, got out her tanto, and climbed to the second floor. Mrs. Miller was a lump beneath the comforter. Raina parted the sheer curtains so slowly they barely made a scrape. Under the slitted eye of the moon, she eased onto the bed and put Mrs. Miller's throat to the knife. The woman thrashed, trapped beneath the comforter, blood soaking heavily into the down feathers.

At the bunker, Estelle had returned with a woman her age with stringy blond hair and the petrified anger of someone who's resolved to die. Mauser brought back two thugs. Raina had seen them at the inn. Quiet men who weren't afraid to be caught staring.

The next day, she ranged south from the bunker, jogging through the rolling green hills with their horse paths and pretty shops tucked between the trees. The day was hot and she doubted she'd brought enough water.

"Raina."

She whirled. A woman wavered from the trees beside the dirt horse path. Her skin was taut over the bones of her face. Her hair was cut raggedly short, white flecks among the black strands.

"Mrs. Grundheitz?"

The woman reached toward her, tendons straining the back of her hand. "Is it true?"

Raina could see it on the woman's face. She nodded.

Martin's mother jerked, her face twitching. "In the attack?"

"Yes."

"And is the rest true, too?"

Raina cocked her head. "That he saved my life? Yes. He killed many of them. He was brave."

"I heard you mean to fight back."

"I do."

A warm wind blew between them, carrying the smell of sun on leaves. Mrs. Grundheitz tipped back her head and watched the smears of white clouds in the rich blue sky. "I want to join you."

"Mrs. Grundheitz," Raina said.

The woman's gaze snapped to her. "You're just a girl, Raina. Don't tell me I'm too old or too weak."

"But if you die, your blood will end."

Martin's mother laughed with the sound of dark things escaping the deep parts of her chest. "After Martin, I couldn't have more kids. My blood will end no matter what I do. Let me spend it fighting the ones who killed my son."

Crickets chirped and chirped. If Raina said yes, she knew the woman would die. "Do you have a gun?"

Mrs. Grundheitz reached into her waistband and produced a .45. "Will this do?"

"Come with me."

She brought the woman back to the bunker. They got a few more people that day. On the third day, they added just one, a boy not much older than Raina who cried when he thought no one was looking. In the concrete walls beneath the surface of the earth, the energy of the bunker felt like an electric ghost, crackling and mad and ready to discharge. Raina got a cup of water from the tap built into the wall. There were gallons and gallons collected from somewhere, but she doubted the system could produce it faster than the twenty people now in the bunker could drink it.

She passed out food. Packets crinkled. People chewed in silence, gazing into their past and future. Upstairs, the heavy door handle opened with a clunk. Raina went for her knife. Mauser's two thugs jogged down the stairs.

"Catalinans are gone," Bryson said.

He was a few years younger than Mauser and had greasy brown hair and eyes that were too small and close together. She wanted to not like him, but while she'd canvassed the hills for troops, Mauser had been working with the others, offering basic training and an explanation of the tactics they would use to assault the camp at the Dunemarket. Earlier that day, he'd told her Bryson was the best soldier they had. She knew the name, too. Her parents had worked with him when they joined the rebellion. She wanted to ask Bryson about them, but then he'd want to ask about the death of her father.

Raina gritted her teeth. "Did you see where they went?"

"Sure. Out on the water, a sail stands out like a flag. They're cruising back to Catalina."

"Cowards," Martin's mother whispered. "Why did they come here at all?"

"What say you?" Mauser said. "Are we ready to strike? They think they're safe there. They'll never expect it."

They all looked to her. Young and old. Martin's mom. Vince. Even Bryson and his quiet, angry friend. Lanterns burned from the tables, casting shadows across the bunker. Raina felt a presence. Not the spirit of a person. The spirit of power. The will to accomplish what would be impossible for one of them to do alone. Raina set down her packet of freeze dried apples and stood.

"We'll take my boat. Storm the castle. Karslaw will be there."

"You don't mean tonight," Mauser said. "How will we get inside the palace?"

"I'll scale the walls. Kill the guards in the towers with my knife so no one hears."

"And what about the big metal doors in the keep?"

Bryson smacked his lips. "Ain't a door can keep me out. Cover me, and I can break us in."

Raina smiled. "They've done us a favor. Most of their soldiers will go home to their own beds."

"Sure," Mauser said. "That only leaves us up against Karslaw's personal guards. His best troops. Armed with lasers that never need to be reloaded in a fortress we don't know anything about."

"I didn't say the odds were good. But they may be the best we'll get." She gazed across the waiting faces. Most were stony. Some were eager. A few were scared. "Are you ready to take your vengeance?"

"Hell yeah," Bryson said.

Vince shook his kind old head. "Don't see as how they gave us any other choice."

"For my son," whispered Mrs. Grundheitz.

"My father taught me the ocean brings both life and death," Raina said. "If you know the sea, you can take life from it. Fish and crabs and clams. You can dry it out for salt and make that food last until you're ready to eat it. The sea has all you need.

"But it can hurt you, too. Its currents can suck you under to drown. Its monsters can bite your flesh and poison your guts. Its storms can smash you on the rocks or pull you down to places so deep your spirit can never get out. You have to always watch the ocean, because the moment you turn your back, thinking you've conquered it, that you know all its secrets, it will send a wave to knock you down and drown you dead."

She whipped her tanto from its sheath. Lantern-light played on the watermark running down the length of the blade, a pearlescent rainbow of steel.

"The Catalinans have turned their back. Tonight, the ocean brings them death."

The bunker was so silent she could hear the ringing of her own ears. After three seconds, Bryson clapped and laughed and snarled. The others joined him, their wordless voices bouncing from the walls. They shook rifles and pistols over their heads. Raina's hair stood up from her arms, a tingle crawling down her spine and up her scalp.

They packed their bags, taking little but food and water and weapons. Raina led them up the metal stairs to the twilight world. The sun was in the place that was neither night nor day and a neutral wind blew in from the sea. As Mauser had trained them, they walked quickly down the road in two columns. They reached her old home on the beach an hour after the last of the light had fled. Hot inland air swirled down through the hills, blowing strongly southeast. This was good. Even with the time it took to rig and ready the ship, they could reach the island well before daybreak.

Martin's mom knew a little about rigging. So did Estelle. Raina left them to prep the ship, then raced northeast back into the hills. The night felt good. Like a thing to be taken. The moon had just begun to rise over the northern mountains, a sliver-thin crescent, its prongs pointed up. It was a claw. A fang. A wicked blade.

Carl opened the door with a vaguely curious look on his face and a half-empty green bottle of beer in his hand. "Is it that time already?"

"It's felt like a lifetime."

"How many of you are there?"

Her gaze didn't waver. "Twenty."

"That many?" He pushed his lips together, impressed, and took a swig of beer, liquid sloshing in the bottle. "It's too bad you're so set on dying young. You could have turned this city into an empire of your own."

"The gods didn't ask me whether I wanted to be born in evil times." She bowed at the waist. "Thank you for all you taught me. I will try to die well."

She turned and dropped down the steps. The bottle smashed in the yard. She spun, knife out.

Carl jogged down the steps, shaking out his arms. "It's a nice night, isn't it?"

"Very."

"I don't know why my dad taught me kali. To live vicariously through me, I suspect. And to hang onto his homeland in a foreign country." He gazed up at the stars. There were so many. "Kali was created to set people free. What if the real reason he taught me was so I could free us from the Catalinans?"

Her skin prickled at the thought of such wisdom. "You think he knew?"

"Who knows." He jerked his thumb at the house. "Let me grab my things."

She smiled. He smiled back, but it was a smile for good things now gone, for facing your fate on your feet. The screen door banged behind him. He returned with a holstered pistol and sheathed knives and a small pack. Together, they ran down the dark streets.

The others had the ship all ready. As she climbed the ladder to the deck, Mauser saluted. "Where to, Captain?"

The island was a blank black mass to the south. The wind blew Raina's hair past her face. She tried to hear her father's voice in its song but all she could hear was the beat of her own heart.

"To the island—and to death."

34

"What the fuck!" Lorna said. "How did you get back here?"

Walt smiled. "I'm not going to tell you. Isn't that mean?"

"You have got to be the luckiest man alive. What did you do? Kill them and take their boat? And now you're here for your revenge."

"Wrong," he said. "I'm here for the guns."

"The guns?"

"The lasers. The sci-fi deathrays I delivered to you people. I did the work. They should be mine."

With his knife at her neck, she sneered up from the pillow. "We're the ones who put our lives at risk to get them. You want them? Go get them."

"Yeah, that's my plan." Walt pushed the blade closer, denting her skin. "I need to know how to get to them. So here's the question you need to ask yourself. Are you better off helping me? Or being a stubborn dick?"

"How am I supposed to help? Every soldier on the island's got one. Good luck getting them all."

"Funny, because I know where you keep your guns, and you don't have one. I'm guessing Karslaw confiscated them as soon as you set sail from the mainland. For all his talk about the strength of 'his people,' he's the only one he trusts to lead you."

She rolled her eyes. "What do you even care? You escaped death. Yet again. Why don't you go take advantage of your luck for once?"

"I had plans to do just that. Then a crazy person broke my heart and threw me on a beach to be murdered by aliens. I thought it was time to adjust my priorities. I'm not sure it's the best idea, but right now, it feels pretty good."

"You won't get off the island alive."

"And if you don't talk, I'm going to find which would win in a fight: my knife, or your throat."

She closed her eyes and sighed through her nose. After a moment, her body relaxed beneath him. "You crazy motherfucker. They're in the palace."

He grinned. "How do I get in the door?"

"Tried knocking?"

"Not the front door. The secret passage in Karslaw's chambers. Where's the entrance?"

She shook her head, heedless of the steel hovering above her throat. "Once I tell you that, you have no reason to keep me alive. You can't leave me here. You know I'll go straight to Karslaw."

"If you don't tell me, you can guarantee I'll cut your throat. But if you help me? Well, you never know what the future holds."

Lorna laughed. "I don't care, Walt. Cut my throat. Blow out my brains. You think I want to live any longer?"

He eased back the knife, keeping his knees pinned to her arms. "Wait a minute, what's the point of a knife if you won't listen to my demands?"

"Sit on it and find out."

Walt bore down again, drawing blood. A pleading look entered her eyes. He bit the blade deeper, then pulled back. "Oh, god damn it. Hold still."

She snorted. "Or what?"

"Or I'll cut you everywhere it hurts and nowhere it kills." He pulled out the gun he'd taken from her dresser and held it on her while he rummaged through his bag.

"What are you doing?"

"I should drag you out to an island to be judged, but I don't have time. This will be my down and dirty equivalent." He set down the gun and produced duct tape stolen from the Scaveteria. He wrenched her right wrist behind her back. She swore and wriggled and he poked her between the ribs just hard enough to part the skin. She gasped. He took the opportunity to clamp both her wrists in his right hand, holding the duct tape under his knee as he peeled it off with his left hand and then tore it with his teeth.

"Here's my best offer, Lorna. I'm not going to kill you. I' going to lug you down to the basement and tie you up. Once I'm back in L.A., I'll toss a message in a bottle into the sea. If you've been a good person, I'm sure someone will find it and let you go."

She squirmed again and he dragged the tip of the knife down the tender flesh of her inner forearm. She yelled and he hit her. He instantly felt guilty, then got mad instead. Just a few days ago, she'd tried to sacrifice him to a hostile alien species. Chivalry could go to hell.

Anyway, it calmed her down. He wound the tape around her wrists, elbows, and upper arms, then did the same for her ankles and knees and thighs. He wrapped it around her mouth multiple times, ensuring her nostrils were clear, then finished off the roll of tape and tied her arms and legs again with thin but sturdy rope.

"You look like a caterpillar," he said.

Her eyes bulged, furious. She tried to spit at him but the tape muffled her face.

"You know who you remind me of?" he said. "Me. That's why I fell in love in the first place. I wanted to fix you. To heal you up. To show you that it really does get better. It does, you know. If you hadn't been a fucking psychopath, you would have seen that."

He tried to sling her over his shoulder, but she bucked so hard he dropped her back on the bed, springs bouncing. That marked the end of his sympathy. He grabbed the cords around her ankles and pulled her off the bed. She hit the carpet with a thump. He dragged her down the stairs to the basement. Her head bumped a couple times, then she had the good sense to tuck her chin against her chest. Moonlight peeped through the narrow basement windows. He shoved her against the cinderblock wall and leaned his face close to hers. She bucked again, nearly driving her forehead into his. He jolted back and laughed.

"Don't wiggle around too much," he said. "You pull those ropes too tight and you might wind up losing a hand or a foot. Do you know you can go for a week without food or water? If you've got any friends, one of them will probably come looking for you before then."

He winked at her and went upstairs. There, he got his pack and rummaged through her house for a working flashlight and more ammunition and double checked all her drawers and closets for lasers. There were none. He stole a jug of water and some dried fruit and ran west up the hills toward the palace.

A large part of him regretted not killing her. It was a major risk and she really, really deserved it. But despite all she'd done to him, he still felt sorry for her. He didn't think she was beyond redemption. There had been points in his life when he hadn't been such a great person, either. He liked to think he'd gotten better. Maybe there was hope for her, too.

Anyway, she'd been on to something on the deserted island. There was something extremely enjoyable about sticking someone in an impossible situation without killing them outright. None of the guilt, all of the fun.

The scant light of a fingernail-thin crescent moon speared down from the heavens. He loped up the hills, then descended into the long valley. The dark shape of the palace squatted in the night. Laughter pealed across the humid air. Probably celebrating their successful campaign. Walt moved off the road and slowed to a walk. He had all night to find the secret passage.

He pulled up a few hundred yards from the castle's wooden outer walls. Lantern-light and songs poured from the windows of the keep. It must be very nice inside. He wouldn't know. He began a slow, wide spiral toward the palace, glancing up from the ground now and then to see if there were any lights in the towers.

He had found the tunnel during one of his many meetings with Karslaw. Big as the man was, his bladder wasn't without limit, and when the would-be emperor had left Walt in the room to relieve himself, Walt opened the plain wooden door in the wall behind the throne. It led into an earthen tunnel. Walt turned on his flashlight, illuminating a long tunnel that sloped gently upward. Wooden beams reinforced dirt walls. He walked inside. A good hundred feet further on, and with no end in sight, he got nervous and ran back to the throne room before Karslaw could return, carefully closing the door behind him. He'd returned to his plush chair and crossed his legs, cup of coffee in hand. Karslaw had gotten back less than a minute later. As far as Walt could tell, he didn't suspect a thing.

But Walt had come away with a few suspicions of his own. Even so, he hadn't put the pieces together until his isolation on the island. There was something about utter solitude that clarified your thinking.

Alone on the island of agave and raw eggs, it had become very obvious that it would be smarter to sneak in through the side hatch than to mount an offensive against the main gates. He'd hoped Lorna would tell him the exact point of ingress to the tunnel, but he didn't need her. All he needed was a little time.

He moved through the grass, walking slowly to make sure he missed nothing in the full gloom of night. Crickets chirped in a steady haze. Surf crashed to the north. Even up in the hills, it was a warm night, and the constant movement left his Scaveteria clothes damp with sweat. After a bit of walking, he found a stick and used that to prod the ground in front of him, listening for any hollow wooden taps.

One by one, the lights in the windows flicked off. The songs and laughter dried up and died. The palace slept. Walt continued his long spiral toward the building, shuffling his feet to feel for anything unnatural. The moon climbed up the sky. An hour passed, then two. He knew it was a long way till dawn, and that the men inside would be sleeping off the night's celebrations until well after daybreak, but his stomach sank. He was stumbling around in the darkness hunting for a door that might not even be there. Each time he circled the castle, drawing inexorably nearer its wooden palisade, he grew further tempted to sprint headlong toward Avalon, steal a boat, and hustle back to Los Angeles.

Around the back of the castle, a couple hundred yards from the walls, a thin strip of grass lay flattened. He followed it. His stick thumped a hollow, wooden patch of dirt. Dust billowed from a two-foot square. He kicked it aside, revealing a trapdoor. He pulled on its ringed handle. It budged, but something was holding it fast.

He swore. Of course it would be locked. He tried again, just in case luck liked him that night, but the door rattled just a fraction of an inch. Which meant it wasn't locked. It was latched.

Candles burnt in two of the keep's windows. Walt set down his little pack, got out the line he'd taken from the Scaveteria, and tied it to a fishing hook. He dangled the hook through the gap, dragging it until it clicked into something metal. The hook skipped right over it. He tried again, finessing the line, but the hook skittered off again. He couldn't see a damn thing. For all he knew, the hook was too small. The latch was only a few inches below the surface, but his big knife was too fat to fit and his small knife was too short to reach.

He tried again, wishing he still had his laser. The hook snagged, then popped loose. Cold sweat sprung up on the small of his back. He couldn't stay out here all night. Going back to the Scaveteria for a thin strip of metal to slide down there would be suicidal. He didn't even know for sure there was a latch.

The hook caught. Gently, he pulled, praying the fishing line had been intended to stand against true monsters of the ocean. It pulled loose with a sharp yank—but at the last second, he'd felt something give.

He opened the door with a squall of hinges. Moonlight poured into an earthen tunnel. Walt climbed down wooden steps laid over the bare earth. A narrow tunnel swallowed him whole. The moonlight faded behind him. He didn't dare turn on his flashlight, so he shuffled along, tapping with his stick. His breath echoed from the damp walls. After a couple minutes, his stick clunked into a wooden door.

He entered the throne room.

A bit of light sprawled through its meager windows, silhouetting the couches and chairs. Walt paused to listen for talk or snoring or fucking. The room was as quiet as a grave. The earthy smell of old potatoes emanated from the northern door to the pantry. He crept to the eastern door. To the stairwell. The treasures were always kept down deep.

In the close darkness of the staircase, he listened for any sound from the upstairs bedrooms, then felt his way down the steps, aided by his stick. He reached the bottom, stopped to listen again, then tapped around until he found the doorway. It fed into a hallway that was just as black as everything else.

He moved into it, cupped his palm over the end of his flashlight, and flicked it on. Reddish light seeped past his palm. He moved his hand partly off the lens, spilling light into the tunnel. The ceiling was a good ten feet high. Unfinished walls extended past the limits of the flashlight's beam. Doors opened into both sides of the hall. The first led to a room of shelves filled floor to ceiling with paper goods: toilet paper, paper towels, Kleenex. The room opposite held cleaning supplies, soap and shampoo and sprays and white jugs of bleach. Further down the hall, the shelves were heavy with medicine, hundreds of amber pill bottles and green liquid cold medicine and opaque white bottles of aspirin. Next came room after room of canned food and bins of wheat and dried corn.

The end of the tunnel fed onto a concrete landing. A staircase descended to both sides. He took the left. At the bottom, a metal door hung open, leading into another tunnel. Dust coated the floor in a solid sheet. On both walls, iron bars fenced off small cells. A bucket sat in each room. An actual fucking dungeon. Walt walked to the end of the hall, then turned back, climbed the stairs to the landing, and took the right fork.

The metal door at its bottom was open, too. Footprints marred the dust. Most of the tracks led to a room halfway down the hall. Inside, rows of blunt black pistols rested on the shelves.

The weapons were heavy, a couple pounds apiece, most of that concentrated in what he assumed was a battery in the grip. He loaded two dozen into his backpack, climbed back to the supply basement, clicked off the flashlight, and ascended to the throne room. Moonlight touched the empty silence. He took the escape tunnel back into the open air.

He stuffed a laser in both pockets, stashed the bag under a shrub, and went back inside. Pillows and cushions of all sorts adorned the couches and wall seats of the throne room. He yanked off four pillowcases, draped them around his shoulders, and returned to the armory for another load. The second trip was done in five minutes. Outside, he tied off the end of the pillowcase and set it down next to his backpack, lasers rattling inside.

He crept back to the throne room as quietly as he knew how, a pistol in each hand, suddenly convinced that guards would leap from behind the curtains. It was as silent as ever. Everyone was drunk or exhausted after the trip from the mainland. Would be a great time to wipe them all out.

It took five trips in all. He was sure he didn't have every single laser—Karslaw was probably spooning with one right now, and the tower guards and most trusted lieutenants might have been allowed to keep theirs as well—but however many remained, it wouldn't be enough for an army.

But the laser closet hadn't been the only room in the armory. The others held racks and racks of conventional weapons: .30-06 hunting rifles, assault SKSes with banana clips, semiauto handguns and revolvers of all kinds. Ammo stacked in hefty blue-gray tins. One room held nothing but swords and axes and quivers and bows.

He returned to the room with the blue-gray boxes and gave them a good stare. There were literal tons of materiel down here. Far too much to carry to the surface one pillowcase at a time. But if he were to rig up a long enough fuse, and then light that fuse with one of the lighters he'd stolen from Lorna's dresser, he could castrate the Catalinans' ability to make war. Shit, with the amount of bullets stored down there, he might well wind up blowing the entire castle to hell and gone.

Fuses were nothing special. Just a length of anything that would burn slowly enough to allow you to run away before the fire reached the combustibles and kicked off the fireworks. There might even be some among all the weapons here. He'd seen a few wooden boxes. The kind that might be used for carrying dynamite. He stepped back into the hall to give them a look.

A shout rang out upstairs. Boots thudded over the ceiling, loosening dust on Walt's upturned face. He swore. They were heading straight for the stairwell.

35

The boat plowed into the darkness. The wind was strong. There were spirits within it and they were hungry for blood.

All their plans had centered on attacking the Dunemarket and were now obsolete. While Raina trimmed the sails and set the ship straight for Catalina, Mauser went inside the cabin of the crowded boat to sketch out maps of the island, the town at its northeast tip, and the castle a couple miles inland to the west. When he finished, Raina asked Mrs. Grundheitz to watch the ship while she joined the others in the wind-sheltered space behind the cabin.

"Stealth and speed," Raina said. "That's how we get to Karslaw."

Mauser tapped the map. "We land on the shore dead north of the palace. Head straight in. A few of us climb the wall and neutralize the guards. If we make any noise at all, Bryson will have a hell of a time picking the front lock while he's dancing the 'Oh God They're Shooting at Me' jig."

"Karslaw lives on the top floor."

"How do you know that?" Mauser said.

"Because he is the type of man who likes to look down on those he rules. And that's where he keeps his women."

"Take one of the stairwells," Bryson said. "Real quiet. Post two people at each landing to hold off reinforcements. Raina finds Karslaw, then we move door to door from there."

Raina nodded. "No matter how quiet we are to the ears, violence is noisy to the soul. The others won't stay asleep for long. Once Karslaw's dead, there's no shame in running."

"What?" Mauser said. "Don't tell them to run away. Then we'll die for sure."

She continued speaking to the troops. "None of you are my hands or my feet or my heart. You can go your own way."

"While that's literally true, I'd just as soon stick together. If we do get split up, however, I suggest we rally down here." Mauser tapped the southeast corner of the island where they'd landed on their initial scouting mission. "That's the opposite way from our boat, but that's why they won't find us. We can steal one of their boats later."

They settled a few more details, then broke apart, each man and woman watching the island growing in the distance. The plan was so simple Raina began to believe they might come out alive. She stamped that thought out as soon as she had it. She couldn't risk a repeat of her failure to take Karslaw's life at the Dunemarket.

The sails began to flap. She trimmed them to the wind, which poured out of the northwest as if scared for its life. The island loomed larger. By midnight, she turned the ship into a bay north of the castle, struck the sails, and dropped anchor. Four at a time, they rowed the dingy in to the sandy shore.

Raina was in the final group to leave the boat. She had no sooner jumped onto the sand when the water boiled behind them.

Her blood went icy. "It's him."

Mauser glanced out to sea. "Huh?"

"The pale man."

"Shit on a griddle, they followed us?"

"Fan out and get down," she said to the others. "In a minute, a man will walk out of the water."

"The fuck?" Bryson said.

Martin's mom gaped. "Is he friendly?"

"I don't know," Raina said. "And he might not be alone. There could be aliens with him. But if you shoot before I tell you to, I'll water this beach with your blood."

Carl shook his head. "Wherever you learned that, it wasn't from me."

Bryson looked like he might protest, then lay prone in the glass, crooking his rifle against his shoulder. The others joined him, spreading out along the beach and taking cover behind rocks and grass. Mauser touched Raina's shoulder. Together, they returned to the sand and faced the sea.

The water stirred. A head broke the surface. Water sloughed and spattered from the man's body. An alien followed him, its crablike claws and squid-like limbs thrashing at the waves. Someone gasped from back in the grass. Raina turned her head and glared.

"You got something of ours," the pale man said. The alien stood silent beside him.

"We tried to give it back," Mauser said. "Where were you then?"

"Watching. You gonna attack?"

"Do you have a problem with that?" Raina said.

The man gazed at the troops bunkered down on the beach. "Not a whole lot of you."

"Then join us. That's why you came here. Quit playing games and help us."

"Is that an official invitation?"

"Hold on a second," Mauser said. "Is this a trick? You've got a submarine out there. If you want the islanders dead, why not just attack their boats in the open ocean?"

The man gestured to the alien for a moment, who responded with quick jerks of its tentacle tips.

"Ran out of torpedoes ages ago. Only weapons we got left are surface-only. Meanwhile, some goddamn fool let these people get their hands on lasers. If they damage our ship, how we gonna replace it? That's not just a sub. That's our home."

"I don't care," Raina said. "Will you stand with us or not?"

The man stared blankly. "There aren't many of us. We don't like these people, but we aren't gonna die to take them down."

"What an inspiring pledge of support," Mauser said.

"We'll help you get inside. We'll watch your backs. Then you're on your own."

"Agreed," Raina said.

Mauser looked pained. "Are we sure this is a good idea?"

"We don't have lasers. If he wanted us dead, he could have attacked our boat." She gestured inland. South. "It doesn't matter. An hour from now, it will all be over."

He sighed. "It's your show."

The man reached into his pocket and removed a device identical to the one Mauser had stolen. "I'll call in the others. Might want to let your people know the score before their fingers get itchy."

Raina explained quickly. Bryson's quiet friend shook his head. "I'm not fightin' with no fuckin' aliens."

Bryson snorted. "You seen their hardware?"

"Sure. They showed it off pretty well when they mounted an invasion of the whole goddamn planet."

"These ones are different," Raina said.

The man raised one brow. "I'd fuckin' hope so."

"I don't trust them completely. But if they mean to betray us, I don't want them skulking around behind us. I want them close enough to cut."

"Jesus," Bryson's friend laughed. "All right. Consider me convinced."

Four more aliens strode from the black waves. They wore bandoliers along their long ovoid bodies. Tentacles carried snubby black guns. The pale man led them to the grass. Most of Raina's people flinched or grew stiff, but some watched the aliens with the amusement of those for whom all life has become a joke.

Raina turned her back and led the group up the hill. The pale man got out a small black tube and held it to his eye. If he saw anything in the darkness, he kept it to himself. His creatures scuttled along in a loose group, several feet of open grass separating them from the line of humans.

Raina moved over to walk beside the pale man. She briefly explained their strategy. "I want you to cover us when we climb up the towers. If any of the guards makes a word, you silence him."

"You givin' me orders?"

"Does it sound like a good plan or not?"

He smiled a bit. "Sure. A laser's mighty bright, though. Hope you brought your sneaking shoes."

She glanced down at her feet. She was wearing sneakers, in fact. The man spoke strangely. She would have chalked it up to living among aliens, but Mauser spoke even less intelligibly, and as far as she knew he'd been among humans the whole time.

Past the hill, the wind died down to a mild breeze, grass swaying around the troops' thighs. She tried to feel for the spirit of her father, but there were too many people around. Maybe there were too many other ghosts, too. She didn't know how these things worked. Just that when you killed a thing, it became yours.

That was what set her apart from the others. Most of them had been raised by supermarkets. When they grew hungry, they went to the stores with the big red letters and the stores handed down packages of meat tidily wrapped in skin-tight plastic. In her early years, she had been no different—her first parents serving her grilled cheese and rice and beans, as if by magic, as if from a place where the food never stopped.

But then everything changed. She killed her own food. Fish. Possums. Cats and rats and dogs and snails. And maybe the others had done this, too, but they were too old, their eyes long adjusted to the light of the old ways, too dazzled by the past to see the other world that had always been there. When you killed a thing, it lingered beyond the flesh. It became you.

In this way, Karslaw had taken her father. If the bearded man killed her tonight, she would become his as well, and she would have the small consolation of being reunited with her dad. But that idea terrified her, too. She would not be any man's. She would kill him. And if fate denied her, choosing to take her life instead, she would kill herself before Karslaw got the chance.

The castle loomed from the hills.

"No more words," Raina said. "Our blades talk now."

The pale man's hands danced as if he were weaving spells. The thick foretentacles of the aliens climbed, swiveling to face the man's hands. Each creature made a quick gesture with their lash-like tentacles.

The castle's gate faced the east and she circled them around its back side to hide them from the towers standing at either side of the drawbridge. As they neared, she crouched lower and lower until the grass swished past her ears. A single tower rose from the back wall. Its windows were too narrow and dark to see inside. Raina gestured the others to stop. They knelt in the grass, the aliens flattening themselves until nothing but their glaring, unwinking eyes projected from the breeze-stirred blades.

"Give me a boost up the wall," she said to Mauser. "I'll flash my knife from the windows when it's finished."

Faced with the hard reality of the palace, Mauser looked ready to turn tail and run, but it was too late. Too many eyes watched him. He handed his rifle to Vince, checked to see he still had his pistol and knife, then gave her the thumbs-up and a manic grin.

They crawled through the grass on their bellies. Dew soaked her shirt. The breeze stopped and she grabbed Mauser's arm. He went still. She waited until the wind once more tousled the grass, obscuring their movement and noise, then crawled on.

The grass ceased. The wooden wall waited a foot from her face. She tipped back her head. She was almost directly beneath the tower. The walls were vertical with no gaps between the boards. Mauser faced the palisade and squatted. She planted her left foot on his shoulder and he grabbed her ankle. She braced herself against the wood and lifted her other foot, wobbling on his shoulders. He grunted softly and stood.

Even when she raised her arms as high as she could, the serrated top of the palisade remained a foot out of reach. She lowered herself, knees bent, then sprung. She grabbed the top of the wall, splinters gouging her palms. Her heels thumped the boards and she grimaced. Mauser got his hands under her dangling feet and pushed. She wriggled up the wall and swung her leg over the side.

A wooden platform fringed the inner edge of the wall three. She lowered herself to it in silence. Overhead, the tower remained noiseless and dark. She entered its base. A ladder extended into the shadows. She loosened her tanto and climbed.

After thirty feet, the ladder reached a square hole in a platform. Raina waited, listening, then poked her head into the room above. Weak moonlight touched an empty chair. A flashlight hung from a peg by one of the windows. A rifle stood propped in the corner. A shape moved away from another window, silhouetted. The man's hair and skin was so dark he'd blended with the night completely. She felt a pang of envy. The man clumped across the platform, passing the hole and leaning into the window beside the flashlight. Raina eased herself up as slowly as a stalking cat, drew her knife, and closed in.

At the last second, he straightened from the window. She jerked the blade into his neck, grabbing his mouth with her open right hand. Blood gargled from the cut, spraying with each pump of his heart. He struggled, shoes thumping, lifting her off the ground, but she held fast. His strength left him in seconds. He sagged to the platform, blood washing down his front. She fought his body's dead weight, lowering it to the floor, and watched until she was sure it would never move again.

She wiped the knife on the man's shirt, put it out the window, and angled it back and forth in the moonlight.

She couldn't see the others hidden in the grass; the breeze disguised their movements. Feet scuffed in the dirt directly below her. She took the flashlight and the black alien pistol on the man's belt. The grip was heavy. She secured it in the back of her pants and climbed down the ladder to the wall.

Carl, Mauser, and Bryson's friend waited for her. Mauser looked anxious. Bryson's friend looked ready. Carl was composed, unreadable. The platform ran unbroken all the way around the inner walls. There was a tower on both the north and south extremes of the wall and two more on either side of the eastern gate. Raina pointed to each man, then a tower. Her people moved in perfect silence along the wall. She no longer felt fear. Just the gut-down need to plunge her knife into those who had wronged her.

Mauser reached his tower and stopped beneath it. Raina continued on, crawling along in the shadow of the parapet. A handful of candles burned in the windows of the keep. A man coughed. She reached her tower. Across the gates, Carl raised his hand. She answered in kind, then gestured across the wall at Mauser, who did the same. They started up their ladders.

She took the rungs one at a time, hands rasping on the metal. This part would be tricksiest of all. They'd all started up the ladders at the same time, but they had no way to coordinate their attacks. Each would have to be perfect or risk alerting the guards in the other towers.

Just below the entry to the tower platform, Raina's foot slipped. She scrabbled, metal ringing under her feet.

"Dan?" a man called from above. Elsewhere around the walls, soft thumps carried on the breeze. A face appeared in the gap above Raina's head. "Dan?"

The man's eyes went wide. She flung herself up the ladder. He shouted in surprise and pulled away from the hole. A whistle trilled, long and loud, splitting the night in half.

Lasers flashed through the gap overhead. The whistle stopped, replaced by a scream. The man staggered, boots thumping. Fat sizzled down on Raina's face. Smoke gushed through the tower. A body banged into the wood. Shouts echoed through the keep. One by one, its windows lit with lanterns.

"The gate!" Raina yelled.

She slid down the ladder and landed on the platform. A winch held the drawbridge fast. She got out the laser and fumbled with its buttons. Blue light licked the planks at her feet, sending up a curl of smoke. She jolted, then lased straight through the rope. The drawbridge groaned, parted like the mouth of a dying beast, and crashed across the span. Her troops sprinted through the grass.

A hot beam sliced from one of the keep's windows, burning into the wall to Raina's left. She flung herself to the grass. The laser whisked overhead and winked off. The pale man and his aliens flanked the gates, returning fire, gridding the courtyard with strobing blue bolts and navy shadows. Raina got up and ran toward the front doors, hustling up the stone steps. Her people streamed across the courtyard, weapons in hand, taking up position at either side of the doors. They were locked. Raina turned the laser on the lock-plate and reduced it to red-hot slag.

Automatic fire rattled from the windows. Lasers lanced at the stone facing.

"Ready?" Raina said.

"Let's fuck 'em up," Mauser said.

She pulled open the left door, leaping off the steps into the grass to the side. Rifles opened fire, bullets and a couple of lasers pouring from the doorway. Mauser and Bryson took cover behind the side of the stairs, edging for position. A metal egg bonked onto the top step and rolled crookedly to a stop.

"Oh shit," Mauser said.

He dived up on the steps, oblivious to the shots blasting over him, grabbed the metal ball, and flung it back inside. Someone yanked Raina down. The ball exploded an instant later. Mauser rolled off the steps in a storm of shrapnel and hot air.

He landed in the grass, limbs flopping. Raina stared. Inside, men screamed and coughed, the noise strangled by the ringing in her ears. Her troops emerged from their crouches, dazed. The world stood still. Waiting to see who would take it.

Raina launched up the steps and ran inside.

Smoke screened the entry of a grand foyer. A couple bodies lay facedown, bleeding on the rugs. A huge, Y-shaped staircase dominated the back wall; a figure ran along its landing and Raina fired through the smoke, laser crackling on the particles hanging in the air. The others followed her in, breaking left and right of the scorched doorway, firing on anything that moved.

Raina ran through the smoke to the left leg of the steps. There were only three men at its top and as they aimed at Raina, Bryson hammered them with shots. Bullets banged past Raina's head, gouging the floor. Her troops barraged the enemy and all three guards crumpled to the landing.

The invaders swarmed up the staircase. It commanded the foyer as well as the doors along the walls of the second floor. Another door stood open in the back wall of the ground floor. At the center of the landing, a separate staircase climbed to the upper floors, enclosed and much smaller than the one they stood on.

A couple of her people were missing. She pointed to half the remainder and gestured at the landing and its view of the first two floors.

"Cover the area. The rest of you come with me to cover the stairs." She glanced up at the ceiling. "Don't shoot the women. My mother's here."

"Your mother?" Vince said. Several others gave her puzzled looks.

"Go!"

They fanned out, kneeling to take aim at doorways and stairs. Raina ran up the enclosed stairwell. Carl, Bryson, and five others followed. Lanterns hung at each landing, illuminating stone walls and thin carpet. Two of her troops posted up at the door to the third floor. She ran up two more bends of the switchback staircase. At the fourth floor landing, the door banged open and a man bowled right into Raina. She flew to the floor.

She knew the man. Holsen. He was one of the two men who had assaulted her mother while her dad held Raina tight on the dock. He leveled a pistol at her face.

Carl dived forward, gun forgotten, and slammed his knuckles into Holsen's forearm. The pistol flew from the man's hand and banged into the wall. He swung a left backhand at Carl's jaw, but Carl moved like the son of the wind, slapping Holsen's arm with his right hand, his left forearm, then his right hand again. The rain of blows arrested

Holsen's movement and staggered him to his right, turning his back to Carl. Carl drove his left palm into the back of Holsen's head. The man staggered, head snapping forward. Carl pistoned his heel into the back of Holsen's knee. While the enemy was still falling, Carl slammed a right hook into his temple. Holsen hit the ground hard.

A gun went off behind Raina, rocking Holsen's body. He writhed and groaned. She planted a foot on each side of his ribs and drove the tanto straight into his back. Its diamond-hard point slipped through his ribs and thunked into the wood below his body. He jerked. His last breath whispered from his lungs.

Raina dislodged the blade and wiped it on Holsen's back. She left one woman to cover the door to the fourth floor, then continued with Carl and Bryson to the fifth and final story.

"Cover the hallway," she told Bryson. He nodded and knelt beside the door, bracing his rifle against his knee.

She jogged onto the rich rug of the uppermost floor. Gunfire exploded downstairs. It had been less than five minutes since the guard had blown his whistle and woken the others. The defenders had had no time to organize and Raina's people had swept in like a scythe. She should have done this long ago—but the others would never have followed. Until the Slaughter of the Dunemarket, they hadn't lost enough to be mad enough to follow a teen girl to war.

She strode down the hall to the elegant double doors set in the middle of the wall. At once, she knew how Karslaw must have felt at every phase of his campaign to take the mainland. The power of it tasted as sweet and thick as nectar. The lesson of people was that they weren't the same as animals. An animal acted because of its fear; people froze from it. If you came at them with all your fury, they would stand in shock while you cut them down. That was what Karslaw had done to the city. And that was what she would do to him.

Silently, she moved to the doors. The handles were locked. She cut through one with the laser. The inner knob clinked to the ground. Carl pressed himself to the other door. She threw hers open and Carl spun inside.

A gun roared. Carl grunted, blood splattering from his shoulder, and collapsed. Raina charged inside.

Her mother stood across the room holding both hands on a pistol.

Karslaw emerged from a door to her left, empty-handed. A laser hung from a holster on a padded red chair by the window.

Her mom gaped. "Raina?"

Raina's hand shook on the laser. "Mom!"

"What's going on here? Are you involved in the attack?"

"I'm here to rescue you."

"Oh honey." Her mother's eyes grew bright. "We need to talk. But first, I need you to put down the gun."

Raina's hand trembled. The gun tumbled from her grasp and fell to the floor.

36

He turned around and ran for the medieval wing of the armory. Whatever their problem was upstairs, they weren't going to solve it with axes. They'd want guns. Lasers. He ran into the back room, hid behind two barrels of arrows, clicked off his flashlight, and produced his laser pistols.

Men jogged down the stairs, feet gritting on the cement.

"What the fuck?" a woman said from down the hall, voice carrying down the blank stone walls.

"What?" a man replied.

"What, what? Notice anything missing?"

"Wait, what? Is this the right room?"

"You think we put up all these shelves for fun?"

"Maybe he moved them," the man said, sounding unconvinced.

The woman laughed. "Without telling us? That's a hell of a way to run a fortress."

"Well, I don't see them."

The woman muttered something Walt couldn't catch. "Just go check the other rooms."

"Why me?"

"Because I'm going to go ask Karslaw. Want to switch jobs?"

"I'll check the other rooms."

One set of footsteps went back up the stairs. The other strolled down the hallway toward Walt, entered one of the other rooms, and was quiet for a few seconds. The man returned to the hall and tried another room. After a minute, the beam of a flashlight cut through the doorway of the medieval weaponry. It hit the wall behind Walt, tracked slowly past the barrels of arrows, and reached the other wall where axes hung from hooks.

"What the hell," the man said. Walt tensed his legs. The light withdrew. So did the footsteps. Walt eased back against the barrel.

A minute later, more footsteps hustled down the stairs.

"He says they're right here," the woman said.

"Well, he's wrong," said the man. "I checked."

"Every room?"

"No, I got tired and took a nap instead. Yes, every fucking room."

She sighed loudly. "This is twelve kinds of fucked up. We're under attack out there. We lit the roof-signal, but it'll be half an hour before Avalon sends reinforcements. Karslaw's barely awake. We need guns and we need them now."

"So we get the rifles," the man said, sounding insulted. "They'll still kill people, won't they?"

"Right. Yeah. Come on."

Guns clattered against each other as if they were being dropped in a sack. The pair ran upstairs. The crack of gunshots filtered down to the subbasement. Under attack? Walt was suddenly deeply confused. He had assumed Lorna had somehow gotten out of the duct tape and ran to alert Karslaw about Walt. Could be Ness had decided to punish the wicked after all, although you'd figure an armada of alien barbarians was the sort of thing the two people searching for the lasers might have mentioned.

Whatever the case, an attack was only bad news for Karslaw. For Walt, it was an opportunity.

He'd already dithered too long to move. The troops would need more than a couple sacks of rifles. He didn't have to wait more than a minute before the pair ran back down the steps. They were breathing hard and they weren't talking this time. Bad sign for the home team. Walt moved to the doorway. As soon as pair thundered back up the steps, he jogged into the hall and took the stairs up to the primary basement.

A man carrying a box exited one of the side rooms and blinked at Walt. Walt shot him in the chest. There was nothing he could do about the stink of burnt skin, but he dragged the body into the room the man had emerged from, shoving him rudely between burlap bags of grain.

Shooting him wasn't the smartest thing Walt had ever done. It cut back on his options quite a bit. That was the problem with running around with a gun in your hand. It just made it so easy to shoot people. Someone insults your mother? Blam, dead. A potentially hostile stranger stumbles out of a doorway? Shoot first and hide the body later. In a way, it was too bad the aliens hadn't blown up all the guns along with the jets and tanks and destroyers.

An explosion burst somewhere upstairs. Walt had enough experience with such things to recognize it wasn't an especially large one, but if he needed another sign that it was time to leave, that would be it. He headed for the stairs. Someone had lit the lantern on the landing and the stairwell looked empty. He made his way up to the ground floor. Candles and lamps blazed from the throne room, glinting from the windows and paintings framed on the walls. He looked both ways, then stepped into the lavish room.

"Walt?" A man goggled at him from the front door. Gunfire boomed behind it. Walt knew the man. He was the one he'd fought when the aliens attacked the beach. "I thought you left."

"Is that what Karslaw told you?" Walt said.

"He said you went to fight monsters up north. That you thought we'd moved beyond the need for your help, but we should be forever grateful."

"How good of him to say." He shot the man in the head. "Then you didn't see that coming at all."

He didn't feel too great about that, either—he probably could have waved goodbye and taken the tunnel to the surface without any problems—but he couldn't afford any witnesses. Anyway, the man might have thought to conscript him. That would have been awkward. He thought about sticking around to take advantage of the chaos and kill a few more assholes, but this wasn't his fight. Anyway, he was already working toward a much grander revenge.

One that would do a little good in the world, too. Or undue a wrong. One that, technically speaking, had been his fault in the first place. But by his math, it was all the same in the end.

More shots banged from upstairs. He ran to the door to the tunnel, entered, and closed the door behind him. He flipped on his flashlight. He ran down the tunnel all the way to the short stairs up to the trapdoor to the outside world.

Uphill from the tunnel exit, lasers flashed up to the keep's windows like a silent and monochrome Fourth of July. After all the traveling, scheming, fighting, and betrayal, it felt anticlimactic to walk away from a party like that, but in the end, that's exactly what he did.

With a bag of lasers on his back and another in his arms.

The ocean was nearest on the north side. He headed that way, weighed down by the weapons, heading perpendicular from the road skirting the castle and, when the buildings fell behind him in the hills, reckoning by the North Star. The breeze did nothing to wick the sweat away from his clothes and skin. It was a miserable, humid slog, and when he finally climbed down to the rocky shore, waves thundering against the land's edge, he resolved to carry a single bag next time, even if it meant extra trips. He deposited the bags behind a clump of shrubs, laid an X of stones above the tideline to mark the spot, and headed back.

In the hour since he'd last seen it, the castle had gone quiet. No lasers lashed from the darkness. Candles and lanterns showed in the windows, and he heard murmurs from behind the wooden walls, but there was no sign of sentries. He slung a pillowcase over his shoulder with a grunt and walked back to the north. After a bit of searching, he found the first deposit and left the new bag alongside the other two.

The moon dropped, taking its scant light with it. On his third trip to the coast, he wandered off course, coming to a stop above a crescent-shaped bay. He'd seen it exploring the island with Lorna. He was too far west.

But there was something white against the black water. A sail. On the beach, someone had even left him a rowboat. He ditched the bag under another bush and ran back to the castle for the final load. Torches burned from outside the palace gates. Walt didn't stick around to learn why. He stole up the last bag of lasers and half-walked, half-jogged north yet again, found the bags he'd stored a few hundred yards to the east, loaded them all into the rowboat, and paddled out to sea, keeping one eye on the dark sailboat anchored in the bay.

A quarter mile away from the island, he pulled in the oars, braced himself against the side of the dingy, and emptied the bags into the sea. Each laser splashed and sunk into the darkness. After a moment, the bubbles ceased. The waves slopped on as untroubled as ever.

Finished, he watched Catalina for more fireworks while he caught his breath. But the show was over. He still had no idea who had attacked or who came out of it the victor.

It didn't matter. He was done with the place. He turned his back and paddled slowly for the mainland, tossed on the swells, pulled off-course by the currents, but always moving, one stroke after another, until the miles became nothing at all.

37

Her mother smiled and lowered her pistol. "There. That's good. Let's talk."

Karslaw grinned, teeth bright in the forest of his beard. "I'm not surprised she led this little attack. She's like her mother. Smart. Bold. Willing to take the advantage."

Raina gripped her tanto. "I'm adopted."

Karslaw's grin froze. They stared, reading each other's eyes, the soul within. He lunged for the laser on the chair. Raina sprung forward, knife out. Her mother shouted. Karslaw leapt back.

"Control your daughter, woman!"

"Raina!"

Raina didn't know what black magic Karslaw was using to confuse her mother. But she knew that killing him would end it. She pulled out her second knife and jabbed at Karslaw. He jumped back again, light on his feet for such a big man. With a scowl, he grabbed a candlestick from the shelf beneath the window and brandished it.

"Raina!" To the side, her mother raised the pistol. "Please!"

"He killed my father!" Raina said. "Your husband!"

"Jim's a good man." Her eyes darted between Raina and Karslaw. "That was a mistake. He thought Will was planning to attack him."

"All I've ever wanted is peace." Karslaw lowered the candlestick a fraction of an inch. "Call off your warriors. Let us come to the table together and find a way for mine and yours to live as one people."

Raina's hand shook on the tanto. A tear squeezed from her eye. She hadn't felt so alone since the plague claimed her first family and she hid in the apartment until the world grew silent and the bodies smelled too bad to stand and she walked out into the end of all things.

"Then shoot me," Raina said to her mom. "You've already lost your husband. A daughter isn't so much more to bear."

Her mom cocked her head to the side. "Raina, I don't like what you're saying."

"You'll live, Mom. And you will be stronger for it."

She smiled, because it seemed fit to smile, and stabbed at Karslaw's guts.

He stepped back, clubbing at her blade with the candlestick. Metal clanged. His hairy forearm extended between them. One of the first things Carl had taught her was a concept known as "Defanging the Snake." You take away a snake's teeth, and it can no longer hurt you. A man's limbs were his fangs; if he tries to strike you, then you must take those fangs away.

She slashed the tanto at his forearm. He was every bit as quick as a snake and he yanked back his arm at the first flicker of movement. The tip of the knife caught his skin, parting it like a zipper. He made a face and fell back.

Her mom shook the gun. "Raina, you put down those knives!"

"Shut up."

"You are a disrespectful thing," Karslaw said, expression as dark as the night beyond the windows. "But like all things, you can be broken."

He jabbed the candlestick at her throat. She sidestepped, rolling her hands through a wheel of strikes. The knife in her right hand parried the candlestick off course. The tanto in her left flicked across the back of his hand. She struck again with her right, flaying the back of his forearm. She began a fourth attack, meaning to slash across the tendons and veins inside his elbow. His left fist hooked over her arms and slammed into her jaw.

She flew sideways, skidding into the rug. He reached for the laser. Her mother yelped and he started, glancing at her face. Raina still saw stars, but she had no time to wait for her head to clear. Like Carl taught her, she launched herself at his middle, the least-mobile part of any person's body. Karslaw bashed down her incoming knife, so she plunged it into his foot instead.

He threw back his head and roared. He staggered back, pulling the knife from her right hand. She swung the tanto into his shin. It clicked against bone. He swung the candlestick down at her head. She dodged to the side, catching it on the shoulder. The force made her sit down. Pain blared through her body. He cocked the stick for another blow.

A gun went off behind her. Karslaw glanced at his own middle, as if expecting to see blood, but the bullet had hit the wall behind him.

"Stop this!" her mother yelled.

Raina speared the tanto at Karslaw's groin. He cried out, turning his hips. The knife's point bit into his thigh. He reached for her arm. With her open hand, she chopped the blade of her hand into his wrist. Her tanto followed right behind her hand. It cleaved off three of his fingers at an angle. Blood spurted from the stumps of his knuckles. She slammed her rising palm into his elbow, knocking his arm straight up, and slashed backhand across his stomach.

He folded. A noose of intestines spilled from the cut. He said something—bargaining or begging—but Raina didn't listen. She'd once watched a ferret fight off a big yellow dog. All it had done was strike without end.

He was holding his gut, so she went for his throat. He shrugged his shoulder and the knife bit all the way to the shimmery line where the hard edge had been forged to the springy body. Karslaw kicked at her. She stumbled back, then rushed forward again, undaunted as a wave. He scooted away, warding her with his foot, so she hacked at his toes.

"Kate!" he bellowed. "For the love of God!"

"Stop it, Raina!" her mom said. "You're killing him!"

Raina smiled grimly. "And it's better than I imagined."

He had kicked the smaller knife from his foot. She snatched it up and slashed and stabbed in an unbroken chain of blows. At first he blocked with his feet and arms. She took all that was offered. When his limbs grew too useless to hold up, she cut his face instead. He yanked it to the side with a sob. The movement gave her his neck.

She took that, too.

He slumped. Blood leaked from dozens of cuts. She sat crosslegged to watch it soil the carpet. Karslaw met her eyes and Raina watched until his spirit became hers. Its power roiled over her, dazzling, a rush so potent she would have fainted if she hadn't been sitting down. He had killed so many things. Strode like a colossus across the land. It had been enough to bring him to the brink of empire. And now all of it was hers.

Her mother stood agape, face white, pistol dangling in her hand. Raina felt her father there, too. The three of them gazed upon the body, once more a family, united in the death of the man who had torn them apart.

She went to the doorway and called out. "Bryson! Carl needs help."

His head poked from the stairwell. She went back to sit beside the body. Gunshots happened downstairs. Raina knew she should care, that her friends were there and that she should help them get out, but she had made the world holy and she would not disturb its fragile perfection. She was one with all creatures and things, the center of a universe without ends or borders.

After a while, her mother sank to her knees and cried. That, too, was a piece of the order of things; Raina had cried for her first family, too. It had done her no good. She hadn't had the energy to grieve for long. Survival meant getting up. Drying your eyes. And retaking your part of the world.

She didn't stir from Karslaw's body until the men from Avalon came to the gates.

The battle had been a rout. With so little notice to organize, and the walls nullified before the fighting began, the Catalinans had offered few pockets of defense throughout the palace. There had been little sign of the lasers they'd used to dominate the Osseys in Long Beach and the rebels at the Dunemarket. After the battle for the staircase, her people had gotten into two brief firefights; following Karslaw's death, they went door to door through the palace. One of the enemy committed suicide. The rest surrendered. Bryson led a team into the basements and found a knot of women clustered in the darkness. All were taken to the main hall and held at gunpoint. One of the women informed Bryson she was a former veterinarian and he allowed her to see to the wounded of both sides, starting with Mauser and Carl, both of whom were bleeding badly.

Then came the call from the gates. Raina went to the window. Torches flapped in the distance, borne by an indistinct mob. She knelt beside Karslaw, set her tanto to his neck, took up her laser, and went downstairs, leaving her silent mother with what was left of the body. The front hall was a mess of blood, scorched carpets, bullet-splintered wood, and frightened islanders. Raina paid them no mind.

Someone bright had thought to pull up the drawbridge and tie its severed ropes back in place. Raina made a note to reward them. She climbed the stairs and stood directly over the gates. A few dozen armed men approached from outside, wary faces lit by torches and lanterns, and drew to a stop fifty yards from the castle walls.

A thin, dark-haired woman detached from the group. "What the fuck do you think you're doing?"

"I took your palace," Raina said. "And Karslaw's head."

"Bullshit. Who let you inside?"

Raina bent over, picked up Karslaw's severed head by the hair, and slung it over the parapet. It weighed seven or eight pounds and her throw barely cleared the moat. It thunked onto the road and rolled down the ruts.

The woman glanced up at her, then at the head. "What is that?"

"The end of an evil time."

The woman hesitated, then approached the dark round shape. She stopped flat a few feet a way, then sank to her knees, covering her mouth with her hand. "What have you done?"

"Freed my father from the man who murdered him." Raina gazed down from the heights. "I'm done here. Or would you rather die with your chieftain?"

The woman drew a pistol. "Fuck you!"

On the walls, Raina's troops trained their rifles and looted lasers on the woman. Her people were few in number, but they had cover and firepower. From the torch-lit mob, a man ran forward, arms raised above his head, and moved in front of the woman with the gun.

"Stop!"

"Then tell the woman to walk away."

The man turned and hissed something to the woman. Her arm quivered. She lowered the pistol. He looked back up at Raina. "What's going on in there? Did you hurt anyone else?"

"There are prisoners," she answered. "Many of the soldiers are dead."

"What do you want?"

Raina thought about opening fire. They could wipe out much of the islanders' remaining strength here and now. But that would mean the war would go on. The few they had left would become fewer.

Karslaw was dead and she had felt his will die with him. If she pressed the fight, the others would come for her. They might have someone like her. The woman with the gun, perhaps.

She didn't want this island anyway. It was a bad place, tainted by the people who had made it what it was.

"To go back to my home," Raina said. "In exchange for peace and our prisoners, you will stop the occupation and end all taxes, tributes, and claims to the mainland. What's yours is yours and what's ours is ours."

"You're rabble," the woman said from below. "You're nothing. We'll wipe you out and burn your little street mall to the ground."

The man wrapped his arms around her. "Knock it off! This war was supposed to bring us peace. Make us safe. But it's been one loss after another, hasn't it? Hannigan's mission to Mexico. Our excursion into the ship. The shelling of Avalon. Now Karslaw's dead because of it, too. We had peace before this started. You think the answer is to fight more?"

"Do you have authority to make decisions?" Raina said.

The man flung up his hands. "You just wiped out the authority. I'm doing my best. Can you give me a minute?"

"Take your time."

He spoke with the woman, who allowed herself to be led back to the group waiting down the road. The man gathered the people and talked back and forth. They were too far away for Raina to hear much.

Bryson stepped up beside her. "What happens if they come back shooting?"

"Then they earn their deaths."

He nodded. "Carl's looking like he might make it. Mauser's pretty chewed up."

"He'll die?"

"Don't know. Ate a lot of shrapnel. If he's got a chance, we need to get him out of here."

She nodded. The Catalinans continued their talk. After a minute, the man walked back to the gates alone.

"Say we accept," he said. "What happens then?"

"You go back to your town," Raina said. "Then we leave. We leave the prisoners here. In an hour, you can come back."

"How do we know you'll keep your word?"

She pointed to the head resting in the dirt. "That was all I came for."

The man bit his lip, teeth flashing in the light of the lanterns above the front gate. "You got a treaty or something to sign?"

"If you want it on paper, come to the Dunemarket in three days. Alone. You won't be harmed."

He saluted with two fingers. "See you there."

He walked back to his people. The mob retreated across the valley, disappearing behind the ridge at the other end of the bowl of grass and crops. There was a stable around back and Raina's people put together a wagon and team and loaded up the dead and the wounded. The prisoners were tied and locked in the basement.

All this had happened without Raina's approval or input. It was time to stop watching and start acting. She climbed the staircase to Karslaw's room where her mother sat vigil over the body. She had blood on her face and her hands and her dress.

"It's time to go," Raina said.

Her mother didn't move. "He was a good man, Raina. He would have made a better world."

The argument was not worth having. Raina held out her hand and her mom took it and let herself be led outside.

They opened the drawbridge and swung the wagon off the road to the north. The pale man and his crew had left sometime after the fighting and Raina didn't know if she'd see them again. It was strange to think, but they must have lives of their own.

There was no sign of pursuit from the mob of Catalinans, but the rowboat was missing from shore. Raina glanced around, spooked, but the only noise was the toss of the waves. She swam to the boat and maneuvered it closer to shore while the others broke up the wagon and lashed together a platform to float the wounded and dead to the ship.

They were halfway to the mainland when the sun rose, its yolk breaking over the hills in a flood of warm pinks and yellows that soon turned blood red. If it was an omen, Raina didn't take it for a bad one. It was a celebration.

When she told him the news, Carl smiled his private smile and turned to examine the painting on his wall. "Won't leave much time for lessons."

"I'll make time."

"So should I call you President? Generalissimo Raina?"

She shrugged. "I don't have a title. They just want me to keep the market safe."

"Sounds like it will become more than that."

"You could help me."

"I don't think so." He went to the wood stove and removed the kettle and poured them both a mug of tea. "How's your mother?"

Raina sat and touched the wood table. She liked its solidity. "She moved into the old house. She still won't see me."

Carl frowned at the steam rising from his mug. "The old people knew about a condition known as Stockholm Syndrome. In this condition, captives come to consider their kidnappers friends. Some victims even helped their captors escape police or take new victims. It defies logic, but it's real."

"I think he put a spell on her," she said. "But it should have died with him. It doesn't make sense and I don't know what to do."

He reached across the table and tapped the hilt of her blade. "Sometimes the best place for knives is in their sheathes."

"I don't like your riddles."

He rolled his eyes. "I'm just playing my part. I think you should let her be. She spent too much time too close to Karslaw. She must have had to do a lot of things she couldn't stand. Like share the same air as the man who killed your father. The only way to survive a thing like that is to lie to yourself. Convince yourself it's not as bad as you think. If anything, you should be proud of her for having the strength to make it all these months."

Something lurched in her heart. "That's going too far."

Carl shrugged and sipped his tea. "In any event, now she has space again. With time and distance to think, she'll come to see the truth."

"What if she doesn't?"

"What if?"

Raina sat back. Eventually, she nodded. She didn't like Carl's riddles, but she did like his questions. Somehow he found a way to turn them into answers.

Hers was right there. She had done all she could. If that turned out not to be enough, she would survive. She always had.

* * *

The mass of bandages groaned. "I feel like the Incredible Hulk's shirt."

"What?" Raina said.

"Ripped to pieces and tossed aside." Mauser sighed, his visible eye fluttering. The other was behind a thick pad of bandages. Some of it had been left in the grass at the Catalinans' castle, shredded by the blast.

After the vet tech at the Dunemarket had stabilized him, Raina had traveled all the way to Orange County in search of a real doctor. It had taken four days, the promise of wealth and protection, and letting slip that she had been the one who lit the spark that burned the Osseys from the land, but the man had finally agreed to come with her.

Under Raina's supervision, he asked around the Dunemarket, pricking fingers and smearing the blood on white strips of paper, scowling vaguely at the results until he found the blood he liked and propositioned the owner for a hefty donation. He had done the surgery right there in her house south of the market. The vet tech attended and Raina watched, carrying out bloody sheets and gauze. Piece by piece, the man sliced the shrapnel from Mauser's flesh and, with a series of little clinks, dropped it in a fat-mouthed jar. After, Raina took the jar. If Mauser didn't want the pieces, she did. They would be good luck.

"You're hopeless," Mauser said. "I don't know why I even bother gifting you my words."

"Then you should give them to others."

"Raina! Are you breaking up with me?"

"They put me in charge," they said.

"Of what? The market?"

"Everything."

He laughed, then winced and groaned. "Are people that easily swayed by the eagerness to be violent? Well, what's first on your agenda, Genghis?"

"Choosing my advisor," she said. "There's lots of stuff I don't understand. Sometimes when I talk to people I make them angry.

You're good at confusing people until they calm down."

"Are you asking me to your cabinet?"

"Will you say yes?"

He smiled, good eye crinkling inside the nest of bandages. "I would be honored."

But it would be a while until he could even walk. She had things to get done. If she stood still, the world would pass her by.

Inspired by the signal lights on Catalina, she established a watch in the lighthouse on the southern tip of the peninsula, placing a green lantern in its turret. If the lighthouse keeper saw any boats approach from the island, he was to light the lantern at once.

Meanwhile, Estelle lived a couple miles inland on a hill high enough to see the lighthouse. Raina gave her a lantern of her own, then found a merchant willing to relocate to the wooded ridge a few miles from Estelle. His new home was close enough to Raina's that she could see it and its signal from her front porch.

She sent a small colony to the bridges of Long Beach that the Osseys had used to ambush travelers. She armed her people with two of the lasers they'd looted from the castle and instructed them to set up a little bazaar of their own. They would send the good strangers on to the market and turn the bad strangers back. It wasn't much, but with so few of them left, even a buffer as small as that felt like a big step toward their future.

Martin's mother had died in the assault on the castle. Raina didn't like digging Martin's body from the mass grave in the Dunemarket—the corpses were so greasy and fat she could only tell which was his by his Godzilla t-shirt—but she had even less love for the idea of the son being forever separate from the mother. She donned gloves and put his body in a red wagon and bore it to the coast. At the house where he and his mother had lived for all the time Raina knew them, she dug a deep, wide grave and laid them both to rest.

After, she set down the shovel and knelt on the damp, brown dirt. Sweat dripped from her face onto the grave.

"I'm sorry," she said. "You were a better friend than I ever let you know."

Wind gusted from the shore. She turned to face it. If there were spirits in it, she couldn't tell them apart. A whip-tailed lizard skittered from the grass, saw her, and went on its way. She crouched and touched the hot sand. She supposed it was hers. Everything from the bridges of Long Beach to the bluffs bordering the path of the Pacific Coast Highway. Once upon a time, other men had ruled it, men with cars and planes and glowing computers. Men so great they sent ships to other planets. But then a plague had come and those men had died. She might have, too, but she had chosen to survive instead. Every day she faced that choice again, and every day she said yes.

She drew her knife and cut her palm and squeezed out the blood. The first drops she put on Martin's grave so some of her would always be with him. The next she shook out on the sand and surf so the ghosts of the past would know this land was hers.

EPILOGUE

He decided not to move to the green hills north of the bay after all. It was just too close. Anyway, he'd spent plenty of time in Los Angeles. It would be a shame to leave so much of the world unseen.

He meant to go further. As he headed north, he took his time to pick his way through the city for all the gear a lone person needs to enter strange lands, then followed the highway up the California coast.

He had no special regrets about the last few months. Other than the endeavor as a whole. And the possibility, however slim, that Lorna really was pregnant. He was fairly confident that was a lie meant to keep him around until Karslaw got his meaty hands on the lasers, but he had no way of knowing for sure. In the end, there was nothing to be done about it. Short of kidnapping the hypothetical little bundle of joy. Anyway, Lorna was safe on her island. She would probably make a better parent than he would. She was certainly loyal to her family.

Depending on how you looked at it, the open road was either very exciting or incredibly dull. But dull was all right. He figured he could handle several years of dull before his next attempt to die of misadventure.

The Catalinans stayed on their island. Her mom kept to the house on the shore. Raina piked Karslaw's head on the antenna on her roof. Mauser caught an infection, fought it off, and got good enough to walk around. He was missing his left eye and he had a permanent limp and he claimed the fragments the surgeon couldn't slice out of his body picked up radio signals on clear nights, but Raina was pretty sure he was joking.

Jill's house stood empty in the side of the hill. Some of the merchants suggested Raina take it, but she didn't like that it was underground. That had been Jill's problem in the first place. When you lived underground, you thought you were safely out of sight, but that was really just a way to ignore what was happening outside. The man who'd built the bunker had died, too.

Instead, she flattened the ground on the hill directly above the Dunemarket, dragged up a set of chairs, rigged up a tarp, and sat where she could see the business in the street below. She discovered she had a lot of correspondence to answer from families and small groups scattered around the city. Requests for passage and trade and alliance. Many of the merchants came to her, too, wishing to discuss the membership rates, or what projects they should pursue next. One of them had just left her on the afternoon Mauser limped up the hill to see her.

He eased himself into the chair beside her. "How goes your reign?"

"Boring," Raina said. "There's nothing to do."

"You mean you ran out of wars to fight? The horror."

"All I do is write letters and listen to people tell me what I should do."

Mauser chuckled. He shifted in his chair until he found a position acceptable to the metal embedded in his body. "Sounds like you need to relax for a while."

"Like how?"

"Specifically? Or are you unfamiliar with the very concept of taking a day off from smiting your foes?"

"What would we do? Go for a swim?"

"We could. Although I'd probably need water wings." He frowned and drummed his fingers on his thigh. He stood. "I'll get back to you on that."

He hobbled back the way he'd come. Raina watched him pick his way between the palms, then returned to her letter. She knew she was misspelling things. She should ask someone to teach her so she wouldn't embarrass the whole Dunemarket, but she didn't want to. People could understand her words well enough.

Mauser reached the road and limped over to Vince's stall of toys.

They spoke for a while, much too far away for Raina to hear. She lowered her eyes to her letter.

She didn't see Mauser for several days. The next time he returned, it was in the seat of a two-horse covered wagon. He stopped in the middle of the market and cupped his hands to his mouth.

"Hey Raina!" His voice echoed through the hills. She lifted her hand to wave. He beckoned broadly. "Get down here!"

"Busy," she called back.

"Too busy to go to Disneyland?"

She sighed and set down her pen and walked down to the street. The others were watching her, grinning. She raised her eyebrows at Mauser. "I have too much stuff to do."

"All taken care of." He swept his hand to the side, indicating a smiling Vince. "Vince will look over the administration. Bryson's agreed to assume the role of chief of security, which he should probably be doing anyway."

"What if something happens while I'm gone?"

Carl poked his head from the flaps of the wagon. "Then you'll deal with it when you get back. Now get in here."

"Go on, Raina," Vince said. "Have a good time."

She could feel the invisible pressure of the crowd willing her into the wagon. She did it anyway. She had no interest in seeing statues of a giant mouse, but the trip might be all right.

The wagon rattled along the coastline, detouring wherever wrecked cars snarled the road. Most of what she saw looked just the same as San Pedro and the peninsula: bungalows, strip malls, fancy homes on hills, sun-drenched parking lots. Two days later, the wagon rolled into a vast and largely empty lot. Mauser clopped the wagon up to the grimy turnstiles, hopped down, and offered her his hand.

"Milady," he said. "Welcome to your Magic Kingdom."

Raina rolled her eyes. She ignored his hand and hopped down on her own. Gum spots and rain-battered paper clung to the pavement. Dirt coated the closed-up shops. Most of the windows had been bashed in. Brightly painted rides climbed the sky. Sooner or later, they would rust and fall.

Mauser took her to a ferris wheel, opened its gate, then held open the door of one of the cars. "All aboard."

She snorted. "What are you doing to do, crank it by hand?"

"Shut up and get in."

She shook her head and climbed up. The car rocked front to back under her weight. Mauser lowered a bar across her waist, hopped down from the platform, and hunkered beside a large metal device at the ride's base. He flipped a switch and the generator roared to life, blatting through the silent air.

"Do you have any idea what you're doing?" Raina said.

"It's perfectly safe," he said. "Isn't it, Carl?"

Carl raised an eyebrow in mock affront. "We wouldn't risk dear leader's life in a machine we hadn't tested for ourselves."

Something fluttered in Raina's chest. She couldn't remember if she had been on a ferris wheel before. Mauser fooled with the controls and the car jolted forward, swinging back and forth as the wheel turned. The ground fell away beneath her. Raina whooped. She climbed higher and higher, soaring above the gift shops and all the rides except the looping rollercoasters. At her peak, she lifted the bar, grabbed hold of the side of the car, and stood. She could see for miles. Countless homes and stores and parks spread out before her.

Someday, it would all be hers.

He would give coastal central California that much: it was fucking gorgeous. Waves battered themselves silly on the rocks. Foam exploded with each crash of surf, lingering on the soft, luscious air. Trees grew wild from the craggy hills. They were the perfect shade of green. He wondered if the aliens had trees on their homeworld, and if so, whether they were green, too.

He took his time. Did plenty of fishing in the sapphire sea, casting right into the waves while he stood on slender little beaches pushed up against the big black cliffs. He wouldn't have argued if you'd claimed it was more beautiful than coastal Mexico. At the very least, it was close, and as an added bonus, it had several trillion less mosquitoes, ants, and jaguars.

Just outside Carmel, a stream ran down from the cliffs to the ocean. He stopped there for the day—it would be awfully handy to have fresh water so close while he caught and dried all the fish he could carry—but he had the feeling he wouldn't be going anywhere for a while.

He built a little shack on the beach. Nothing crazy. A couple of walls with a slanted roof to keep off the rain. Dug a latrine and a fire pit and set up smoke racks. He had no idea what day it was, and the pleasant weather gave him little hint, but he figured it was fall. One day he wandered into town, rooted around until he found a Tupperware of flour and a bag of bug-free sugar, then strolled back to the beach and baked himself the world's worst birthday cake. It was his 31st.

A few months later, with the winds going cold enough that he was thinking about moving to one of the houses on the cliffs, he woke to find a rifle pointed at his face. It was owned by a woman in her late twenties or early thirties.

"Come here often?" he said.

Her bent elbow stuck straight out from the gun, finger on the trigger. "Do you have any food?"

"Don't you know how to fish?"

She stuck out her left hand and beckoned her fingers. "Hand it over. No sudden moves."

"I'm handing." He turned slowly and reached for the cooler of dried fish he'd embedded in the sand by his wall. On his cake run, he'd found some wax paper which he'd been using to wrap the fish. He raised his brows at her and extended one of the bundles. "There's more. Take as much as you want."

She snatched it away, sniffed it, took a small bite, then devoured the rest, keeping her gaze on him all the while. When she finished, the look in her eyes was slightly less crazed.

"You're awful calm for a man at the wrong end of a gun," she said.

"Experience, that's all."

"Can I have another?"

"No problem." He dug into the cooler and handed her another piece. "That one came from a flounder, believe it or not. Caught it right here on the shore. Storm must have pushed it in."

She ate that, too, then sat on the sand and rested her rifle across her knees. "Sorry about this. A person gets pretty nuts when they're hungry enough."

"Not just for food," he said. Her rifle twitched. He held up his hands. "It's okay. I'm perfectly harmless for the time being."

"Well, if it's all the same, I'll keep my gun right here."

"My name's Walt." He smiled, squinting against the sun on the too-perfect sea. "What's yours?"

She smiled back, but it was a cautious thing. He doubted she'd stay. It was all right. He was in no hurry. Things moved to their own rhythm. If you could find it, move to it, you'd end up okay. All it took was a little time.

Winter came. The days were cool and the nights were cold. She opened the door one morning to go to the market and found a letter tucked under her front mat. It was as short as letters could be: "Please come."

The writing was her mother's. She ran all the way south to the coast.

ABOUT THE AUTHOR

Along with the *Breakers* series, Ed is the author of the fantasy trilogy *The Cycle of Arawn*. Born in the deserts of Eastern Washington, he's since lived in New York, Idaho, and most recently Los Angeles, all of which have been thoroughly destroyed in one of these books.

He lives with his fiancée and spends most of his time writing on the couch and overseeing the uneasy truce between two dogs and two cats.

He blogs at http://www.edwardwrobertson.com

Printed in Great Britain
by Amazon

55033963R00208